Knowing

Signy Alora, 'Ziggy,' was shocked when she was abducted by the Tokkel from her home on the human colony world of Gaia. She was appalled when experimentation was scheduled for her day, and relieved when someone attacked the ship of the invaders. Ziggy used her talent to absorb the information she needed to escape and in the process she managed to help a batch of aliens who had also been slated for torture at the hands of the troll-like Tokkel. She takes knowledge of his language, his ability to fly a starship, and a kiss that renders him senseless.

Five years later, Ziggy thought that she had made a clean getaway and hidden her involvement in the first crash of the invading ship, but when military men collect her for the anniversary of the initial attack she realises that her time of hiding what she did was at an end.

Ziggy had no idea that someone had been looking for her. The moment she spots the shifter that she kissed all those years ago, her time of hiding what she is is over and he couldn't be happier.

Accepting

Life on Gaia is predictable, boring, and just what Tiera needs to keep herself calm. When she is arrested and forced to visit her friend Ziggy and Ziggy's new shapeshifting husband, the last thing on her mind is making a new friend in an alien Fairy who looks like he works out.

Tonos has flirted his way through the universe and now that he has met this Gaian, his mind has changed from flirting to making sure that Tiera does not make a run for home. With the power of her will, he might just find his way to love.

Hiding

Daphne has spent her adult life since the Tokkel invasion fighting for jobs to support herself. With her parents dead, her family consists of one. Desperate to earn some income she takes a position as wait staff at the reception for the Gaian, Tiera MacKenzie and her husband, Tonos of the Nine.

Daphne is trained to be invisible to the members of the Nine who are attending this first cross-planetary event held on Gaia.

After the reception she is desperate for rest but a peculiar interview by the personnel coordinator of the Nine drives her into the woods and a collision with destiny.

Apolan has accepted a position as Ambassador of the Nine on Gaia. The embassy is underway and all he needs now is an assistant. He has just the Gaian in mind if she will simply stop hiding and allow him to offer her all he can.

Guiding

Teyha enjoys being a historian and educating the next generation of Gaia on how they arrived. Her weekends and time off is spent exploring the new home for humanity, bringing back information and tales of the abandoned cities of the previous civilisations.

Two Shadow Folk come to ask for her help as a guide, and with a little convincing, she agrees to head to the ancient city that their people had once thrived in.

On the way to the city, she finds that she is not taking two men on a pilgrimage, she is leading a rescue party. With one shadow keeping secrets and the other too close for comfort, she does what she was asked to do. She guides them in, and she gets them all out.

Collecting

Emharo has spent her time collecting biological samples from the world around her and giving them to her family for analysis. She can find anything you need—you just have to ask.

Rivvin is a member of the Water Folk, and from the first time he saw this woman in his element, he knew that she was far more than she appeared to be and far more vulnerable than she pretended to be. She will be a challenging mate and a feisty partner if he can only convince her that she needs to add him to her collection.

Hunting

Niika has a love for the land that goes bone deep. Even damaged by an old injury, she seeks out prey in the form of plants, animals and missing persons. Nik's life revolves around her taking groups on tours of the wild and teaching them to live off the land that offers so much. Taking a group of aliens is a definite first.

The Nine need fresh supplies if they are to remain as a defence and an assisting partner to the people of Gaia. They also wish to know where their own people used to live and how. Cavos is a historian in search of the city of the Stone Folk, and he is quite surprised to find his mind turning from the past to the future when he meets the Gaian huntress who is leading him to his heart's desire.

Designing

Ula has hidden from her own people in an effort to cease pressure from local government to create weapons against the Nine. When a man with wings comes knocking, she slams the door in his face.

Deniir has gotten as much information on the designer as he can, but seeing her taming some of the wild flying predators out back eases her rude dismissal of his presence. She is as wild as the beasts she uses to get airborne, and he sees the means to get her to follow him to the stars.

Offer her complete freedom and she will follow him wherever he leads.

Seeing

Vida has been looking for her parents since the Tokkel took them six years ago. Her sister has given up on her obsession and removed herself from the pain of her twin's hunt.

When Vida has a breakthrough and gets transported to the mother ship, she is one step closer to achieving her quest, until her own body betrays her.

S'rin is a member of the Balance, and his help enables her to recover, as well as find a way to locate those who have been lost. He needs to strike a balance between seduction and companionship; it is harder than he would imagine.

Tracking

Ianka has spent years blocking out her sister's mind and the obsession with finding their parents who had been swept into space by the Tokkel. Finally, Vida has located them and summoned Ianka to help her launch the search.

Ianka heads to the mother ship and meets those who will help her gather a group to go out and seek the star and moon base where Vida saw their parents. To her surprise, Vida has found a mate in one of the Nine and is recovering from her childhood frailty with amazing speed. Ianka is the warrior and she will track their parents.

Derion is assigned to her as her escort around the ship, but while their friendship meets all the strictures of the Nine protocols, Ianka is a temptation that he dares not give in to.

Devine Destinies
An imprint of eXtasy Books, Inc.

Return of the Nine
Viola Grace
ISBN: 978-1-4874-0423-9

First Edition published 2015
www. devinedestinies.com

eXtasy Books Incorporated
P.O. Box 2146
Garibaldi Highlands, B.C. V0N1T0
Canada

Cover Art by Martine Jardin
Cover Design by Angela Waters

EXTASYBOOKS.COM

Knowing
Return of the Nine Book One

By

Viola Grace

Chapter One

Ziggy struggled against the bonds that held her down. The Tokkel were working on another captured human and the screaming was getting to her. One of the four armed beasts was about to mark the interior of her ankle with a glyph similar to the ones on the restrained humans around her.

As the needle started to buzz, she kicked wildly, causing the creature to snarl at her and call for another to hold her down.

With two of the Tokkel working on her she tried to scream behind her gag, but only muffled whines emerged. Closing her eyes at the pain, she focussed on the hands holding her down.

The contact gave her the chance she needed. Every other alien had been wearing a glove-like membrane but the male holding her had bare hands. She used their physical connection to reach into his mind and pull out all the information she could.

He blinked and shook his head violently, trying to clear it. She held her breath, but he spoke to his companion and in seconds, she could understand what he said.

"That was weird. We must have dipped into the atmosphere for a moment."

The tattoo artist looked up. "Why?"

"Didn't you feel that? The whole ship rocked." He was holding her leg with two clawed hands.

"I didn't feel anything."

He had made a few passes with the needle when the entire ship shuddered.

Ziggy held perfectly still as a disembodied voice blared out, "Intruder alert. All hands to battle stations."

Her persecutors immediately left her and the rest of the humans for their battle stations.

Ziggy bent her arm as far as she could and caressed the switch that would release her. It took three tries and she knew that she would be bruised for weeks, but a hiss sounded and the restraints retracted to free her limbs.

She hopped to her feet and unbuckled her gag. Looking around she saw four Gaians who had been captured with her and she released them from their restraints. "Keep quiet."

They didn't need to be told twice, they kept darting frightened looks toward the door.

Ziggy's thoughts ran through the stolen knowledge and she nodded. "There are escape pods just outside the door. I can launch you."

One of the wounded was holding a flap of skin to his side. "Just show us where to go."

She shuddered at the pain in his expression but paused to slap a wide bandage from a nearby storage cabinet across his side. "That should hold you."

He looked at her with glazed eyes. "How do you know this stuff?"

She shrugged. "Just a hunch, now let's get you back to the surface. Hopefully the attack will have ceased by now."

The other subjects were looking at each other but they seemed as eager to get off the ship as she was.

Ziggy opened the door with the passcode and she slid around the corner to the station with the four emergency pods for this wing of the ship. The Gaians each took a pod and waited nervously.

They were nowhere as nervous as Ziggy was. Once she launched these pods three security officers would come running. She was going to have to get to somewhere safe awfully quickly, but given her mental situation she had a far better chance than her fellow captives.

The wounded man smiled. "We are trusting you because you are human."

She shook her head. "You are trusting me because I am offering you a way out, now hush and hang on. This is probably not going to be a smooth ride."

She closed the pods, keyed in the coordinates for Hestia, the capitol of Gaia, and punched the release.

The tubes shot the pods out of the ship and hopefully into the atmosphere.

Ziggy was basing her targeting on the experimenting officer's thoughts that they were still in orbit.

With her companions launched, Ziggy ran down the hall toward the secondary holding area.

She typed in the pass code and slipped behind the door just as the thunder of boots ran past her.

"Who are you?" The masculine voice shook her to her toes.

Carefully, she turned to see four men hanging from the wall. She looked a little more closely. They weren't men. Well they were of the masculine gender, but they weren't human.

"I am a prisoner from Gaia. Who are you?"

"Warriors of the Nine. Can you release us?"

She blinked and walked forward. The other three men were looking at her, but the one who was speaking stared into her very soul.

His skin was a dusky brown, his eyes catlike and tawny and his hair deep brown and tangled. He was huge and his ears were decidedly pointed.

"I can. Why should I?"

"Because we belong to the ships that are attacking this Tokkel vessel. If we get back to our people, this attack will end."

"May I touch you?"

He looked at her and while exhaustion rode his features, curiosity was there as well. "Yes."

She ran her hand along his chest and rummaged through his knowledge. Her talent only allowed her to access conscious thoughts of a technical bent. She could pick up languages easily, but wading through this man's knowledge base was harder than most. The language that he thought in was musical and very old.

He didn't have any connection to the Tokkel aside from being their prisoner. The men with him were under his command and they had been taken from their ship with only the battle with the Gaians keeping them from being executed or tortured for information.

Ziggy nodded and pulled her hand back. There was a tingle in her skin from where she had touched him. A pleasurable burn pulsed up her arm. "Fine. I will let you guys go. There is a set of escape pods down the hall on the left."

He stared at her in shock. "You speak the language of the Nine?"

She blinked. It suddenly occurred to her that he had been speaking in Tokkel until now. "I suppose I do, now."

Ziggy pressed the releases and all four men collapsed to the floor in heaps.

"Do you know why they attacked Gaia?"

Her conversational partner helped his men stand. "Is that what you call it? We called it Underhill."

She froze. "What do you mean?"

"We left that world eons ago. It changes those upon it." He stood and his men nodded silently to him. "We are ready to leave."

She smiled. "I hate a mystery, but you all look like you need to be somewhere else."

He inclined his head formally. "I look forward to finding you again when this is all over. You seem to be a woman with mysteries of her own."

She chortled. "You have no idea."

They didn't need to be told to be silent. She led them to the pods and the male she had been speaking to calmly keyed in the destination coordinates.

She helped one of his men into the pod.

He paused. "There are only four pods."

"I know. I have a plan." She kept her features calm. Her plan involved taking the entire ship into the Northern Ocean.

"I will not allow you to risk your life to save ours."

Ziggy sighed and leaned up to kiss him. As her lips met his she heard a low rumble and hands on her waist. Using the direct contact to his mind via the kiss, she made him sleep. He staggered and she used all her strength to put him in the pod. With a sad smile she punched the release and launched the four to safety.

Moving as quickly as she could, she hid in a storage alcove as three troopers came stampeding to the pod station.

Ziggy sat quietly and waited for her chance. Her moment would come and she would do what she could.

Her planet was at stake after all.

Chapter Two

Five years later . . .

Ziggy stood in her mother's flower shop and watched the news footage that they had been replaying for the last week.

"As you can see here, the first Tokkel ship destroyed by the Nine has been recovered. With the joint efforts of the Nine and Gaian ships, the first warship that was brought down has now been lifted from the depths of the Northern Ocean.

"The recovery efforts will bring the ship to the surface just in time for the five year anniversary of the triumph over the Tokkel. Survivors of the raids are being invited to the Nine mother ship for a gala event."

Leara smiled and worked at an arrangement. "That's nice. So many folks were affected by those raids."

Ziggy remembered the terror of being hunted and getting caught in the grav beam with a dozen other men and women. Only five of them managed to survive the exams that the Tokkel engaged in.

When Ziggy had gotten the officers of the Nine away from the ship she had waited and then cut the lines to life support with cutters she found in the storage closet.

She knocked out two troopers from behind and stole their weapons, shooting everything that moved. She wounded one of the pilots and took his grasp of the workings of the ship.

Ziggy piloted the ship in a circle, spinning it in the centre of the flight of warships, firing wildly.

Her death spiral continued until the ship started breaking up in the upper atmosphere. There was a set of emergency pods near the bridge and she programmed one to drop her near her home town before she locked in.

The ship had an auto eject for occupied pods when it was in danger. It popped her out a mile over the ocean and the pod jetted to her landing site.

The moment that she landed, she stumbled free of the pod and hid for hours, slowly making her way back home.

It had taken her two days to get back into shape to pretend that nothing had happened, and while the men and women she had released from the experiment station remembered her, the woman that they created via a sketch artist was far more attractive than Ziggy made any claim to be.

The clatter of a set of pots against the table as her mother moved things around brought Ziggy out of her memory.

"They were. They deserve a holiday in their honour. In one way, they brought the Nine back to the area. Back home."

"You are right, Signy. I know that you were upset during the invasion, but isn't it great that we survived it with minimal losses?"

Ziggy sighed. "Any lives lost were too many. Do you have the display ready for the Markaqay wedding?"

Leara nodded. "Yes. The delivery van will be here at six."

Ziggy smiled. "Excellent. Well, I am off for the night. I am just going to have coffee with some friends."

Ziggy put on her jacket but turned to see the clients who rang the bell as they entered the shop.

Two men in military uniforms walked in.

"Good evening, sirs, we were just about to close but how can we help you?"

The men looked down at data pads and then back up at her. "We are looking for Signy Alora."

Leara blinked. "That is my daughter's name, but what do you want with her?"

The men snapped into a sharp salute. "We have orders to bring her in to attend the celebration on the Nine mother ship."

"Why? She has never been involved with the Nine. Have you, Ziggy?"

Ziggy winced. Her mother hated her nickname. For her to be using it she had to be stressed.

"Not that I am aware of, Mom. Can you let Dad know that nothing is wrong, but he will need to be here for the delivery van tomorrow morning?"

Leara bit her lip. "If you are sure that you want to go with them."

She sighed. "Mom, I don't think that I have any choice."

"Ma'am, we have orders to bring her in. We also have confirming video that she is the woman we are looking for."

Ziggy smiled and patted her mother's hand. "It's fine. Everything will be fine."

Leara squeezed her hand. "If you are sure. Keep us posted on what is going on."

Ziggy laughed. "As soon as I figure it out, you will know."

The two men saluted again and escorted her out of her mother's flower shop and into a wide bodied skimmer. The flying unit was technology of the Nine. They had been very generous to the settlers on their old world.

She settled on the passenger seat and in seconds they had lifted off the street and were a hundred feet over the city. Crowds were watching them fly away, and Ziggy waved to a few familiar faces.

"Where are we going?"

"The launch area. You will travel to the mother ship via shuttle in the custody of the Nine."

She nodded. There was nothing else to do. She had chosen her options and while she had never expected to be found out, she had prepared herself for the eventuality.

She left custody of the Gaian military and walked across the tarmac to the shuttle where three officers of the Nine were waiting.

The officers she was facing were of the Giant, Dwarf, and Fairy persuasion. Three of the nine branches of the Nine.

They saluted and helped her up the stairs, settling her in her seat before lifting off. She knotted her fingers together. The light touch of the Giant's hand had given her basic information on how to fly the shuttle as well as where all of the emergency supplies were.

Since her time on the ship, she picked information out of people much more easily. It almost flowed out of them at her lightest touch.

She sat back and watched the men who had been asked to pick her up. It had come as a shock that the ship found back on Earth two hundred years ago had been a ship of the Nine. When the colonists piled aboard, it took them back to its home.

Ziggy was a third-generation Gaian. From the Nine archives, the very soil of Gaia or Underhill created a genetic potential that would soon begin to occur in the humans now living there.

She was one of those new humans. Born with the ability to gain knowledge from those around her, she found the knowing was the hardest thing to deal with when you got information you didn't want.

She waited. While the males sent her friendly glances, they didn't offer to engage her in conversation. She idly wondered what kind of trouble she was in and how bad it actually was.

The feeling of leaving the planet's surface wasn't nearly the jarring sensation of her previous capture. The giant piloting the ship moved them smoothly through the layers of atmosphere and to the mother ship beyond.

Ziggy watched the huge silvery bulk get closer and closer before she had the thought that she had been fighting since she saw the men in her mother's flower shop.

How did they find me?

CHAPTER THREE

The Fairy held his hand out to her and assisted her from her seat. Ziggy was a little wobbly but her talent surged up and did a rapid reading of the man holding her hand. He was a medic and he was studying human physiology.

He found her fascinating.

She blinked and tried not to show her nervousness. Despite the folded wings and pointed ears he looked as far from the minute flitting creatures of Earth myth as he could be. He looked more like a professional wrestler with wings.

Ziggy stood and gently withdrew her hand from his.

Instead of being offended, his lips quirked in amusement. "Please follow me, Ms. Alora."

She inclined her head and walked down the steps and followed his wings through a shuttle bay and into the ship itself.

Behind her, the dwarf from the ship followed them as they walked to an internal monorail. A pod was waiting for them, a glowing crystal banded with metal. It looked to seat around six people, but no one entered but their triad.

She took the seat that the Fairy showed her to and waited with her fingers knotted in her lap. The dwarf sat next to her and with a chime the pod on the monorail sealed shut and they started to move.

When the pod shifted around a corner, Ziggy swayed and the dwarf reached out to help her. He was a navigator and had a wife and two little ones here on the ship.

From his mind she saw star charts and calculations for travelling to planets she had never even imagined.

"Thank you. I wasn't expecting the turn." Her voice was soft but the Fairy turned to smile at her.

He frowned as he noted the dwarf's hand on her shoulder. "Makinaw, what are you doing?"

"Steadying her. It wouldn't do for her to get a concussion before she sees the council."

She swallowed. "The council?"

The dwarf nodded. "Yes. Tomorrow morning, before the ceremony you will meet with the council of the Nine."

"Why?"

"We are not aware of why you have been called to the ship, we only know that if the councillors want to speak with you, we have to bring you."

"What am I supposed to do until tomorrow?"

The pod rocked and shimmied as it passed through the ship's common areas, the vistas of the interior of the huge ship were lost on her as her stomach knotted with nerves.

The Fairy grinned. "We have been ordered to take you to VIP quarters. The other humans are simply being brought in for the event tomorrow, but the quarters have been booked for you for at least a week."

"Tonos! Need to know." The dwarf growled.

The Fairy scowled at him. "Mak, you think she doesn't need to know that?"

"Gentlemen, please. If it is a problem, I will just wait until tomorrow."

The pod slid to a halt and the door opened.

Makinaw extended his hand and helped her to her feet. They left the pod and he led her past two guards, both of the tree clan of the Nine.

"You will remain in your quarters until someone comes for you tomorrow morning. Appropriate attire has been selected and will be delivered." Makinaw patted her hand lightly.

The doors were framed with ornate carvings and as Tonos pressed the lock to open one of the rooms she noticed that the elegance continued within. She passed the Fairy with a slight nod and he gave her an appreciative leer.

Makinaw punched him in the ribs and the door closed. The pale light panel next to it went from white to red and Ziggy knew she was locked in.

The rooms were huge. An entertaining room was the first that she walked into and the bedroom was just beyond through another ornate archway.

She rifled through the dwarf's knowledge and picked out the instructions for using the entertainment unit. Seeing as how she was basically under arrest, she spent her evening watching the entertainment options offered by the mother ship of the Nine.

As she watched the images appear on the wall across from the couch she flipped through the options and though she was curious, she steered clear of the sexual programming. There were only so many traumas she was willing to endure in a day and watching members of the Nine having sex was far beyond her tolerance for weirdness.

Councillor Rothaway smiled as the request for entertainment vids came up on the screen. "Do you believe me now?"

He had tried to explain to his people that he had met a Gaian with the ability to speak the language of the Nine. While his survival and that of the rest of his team had proved that someone else had a hand in their escape from the Tokkel ship, it was only in the past week when the salvaged vessel was dredged from the ocean that he was able prove his experience was not just a hallucination born of torture.

"Yes, fine. You are right. She knows our language. I am still not sure what it means." Lyneer brought up the scans of the human and blinked rapidly.

"How long have you been out of the tanks?" Rothaway scowled.

"I have the humidity turned up in my chambers, I am just surprised at how easily she moves in our environment. What have you been able to learn?"

Rothaway sat back and stared at the images of Signy Alora on his screens. "She is third-generation Gaian. There were no reports of her being taken and none of the survivors could recall precisely what the woman looked like. They only know that she released them and sent them all home. Aside from that they were not very concerned with what she looked like."

"What about satellite scans?"

He grinned. "None of the satellites were operational in the area where the escape pod was found."

Lyneer blinked again. "How could she know where to land?"

Rothaway smiled. "That is the mystery that I want to solve. Her knowledge base is far beyond anyone from her world."

He didn't mention that her lips were soft, she smelled like roses and he wanted to feel the silky skin of her hips under his hands again. She woke every shifter instinct that he had and that alone had shaken him to his core. When he recovered, he did so with the realisation that his mate was down on the planet below and he simply needed to find her.

The issue of finding her had seemed simple until the images of the crashed ship began to stream over the Gaian news reports. His confusion had stemmed from the sense that she was alive and well.

Signy Alora would face the council tomorrow and when the footage from the Tokkel ship was displayed she would have to explain what it was that she did and how precisely she did it.

Chapter Four

Ziggy jerked awake at the knock on the bedroom wall. She rolled over and blinked sleepily, trying to bring the newcomer into focus. "Hello?"

"Please excuse the intrusion, Ms. Alara. I have your clothing for the meeting and the official reception." The male was distinctly green, even to Ziggy's exhausted gaze.

"Oh. Hello." She sat up and looked down at herself, sighing in relief when she noted that she had slept in her clothes.

The male was leaning in her doorway and he had a silky wave of blue fabric over his arm.

"I have your clothing for the event today. Your breakfast is waiting. Please prepare and join me in the outer room."

He stepped forward and put the gown on the edge of her bed. She simply watched him drop it off and as he walked out she stared after him with her eyes wide.

When he was in the outer room she shifted and grabbed the dress while easing into the lavatory. She leaned against the closed door and blinked rapidly. "Whew."

With an eye toward speed she stripped and left her clothing in a pile, entering what her mind told her was the cleansing unit.

The shower was peculiar. She stood on the depressions that were meant for feet and pressed the only button in the area while she closed her eyes.

Light and wind struck her, startling a yelp out of her. It was exactly as the memories had shown her. Her body tingled but she was squeaky clean.

Ziggy bit her lip as she held up the dress. It was long, elegant, and would not be appreciative of underwear. The fabric would cling tightly where it touched and she didn't want to destroy the line of the garment, but she was not keen on going commando.

She slithered into the gown and admired the fit in the long mirror. It certainly was flattering, and the deep blue made her midnight eyes bright and mysterious at the same time.

Her long brown hair was hanging straight, the side effect of the cleansing unit. It removed all oil and dirt but it acted as a flat iron.

The rumble of her stomach drove her out of the bathroom after she had attended to all other morning matters including a peculiar toothbrush.

She peeked around the corner of her bedroom, watching him at the dining table. "Are there shoes to go with this gown?"

The male turned slowly and smiled. "Of course. By the door. Now, come and have something to eat. Our cooks made an effort to provide you with something familiar."

She sniffed appreciatively as he lifted the lid on the tray. Eggs, toast, meat and a side of an unusual fruit were a charming way to start the day.

Eating out of reflex was the only way she could keep from staring at the man across from her. The gill slits on his neck were obvious even though she kept her head aimed at her food.

"The councillors are excited to meet you."

She almost choked on a piece of succulent fruit that crossed the line between berry and melon.

"What? How many people know about me?" She looked up and met his black gaze.

He chortled and there was a wicked gleam in his eyes. "You have been a creature of myth and legend for the last five years. The survivors spoke of you, but since you were never reported abducted there were no records to tie you to the Tokkel ship."

"What is your name?"

"I am Commander Lyneer, personal assistant and bodyguard to the shifter councillor."

She blinked. "But you are a mer. Why would you work for a shifter?"

He tilted his head. "All questions will be answered in time. But the mother ship of the Nine mixes species whenever it can to relieve racial tensions."

She swallowed and took a sip of the water on her tray. "Well, I suppose that we should get going."

He smiled. "You are correct. I should have been earlier but I was ordered to let you sleep in."

Ziggy didn't ask who had given the order. She wasn't sure that she wanted to know.

It was comforting to know that the men in the life pods had survived. Launching an escape pod during a firefight was never a good idea, but there had been little choice.

She got to her feet and checked her gown for crumbs. Coming out clean, she turned and looked for the shoes.

Satin pumps with an ankle strap were in the same shade as her gown. The heels were sturdy but she would be three inches taller. Ziggy stepped into the shoes and then bent double to buckle them into place.

When she looked back at an upside down Lyneer, he was staring at her backside in a most appreciative manner. "Take a picture because this is the only time you are going to see this view."

Standing upright she took a few careful steps and nodded. "Ready when you are."

She noticed that he was fighting a grin as he took her arm and escorted her out of the guestroom, past the guards and through the ship.

"How far are we from where you are taking me?"

"About ten minutes. May I say, your accent for the language of the Nine is quite captivating."

She blushed. "Thank you, I don't know where I picked it up."

She almost missed his muttered, "I have a fairly good idea."

She was learning from him as they walked, her knowledge of the tank and humidity system that he required for daily function was becoming extensive.

It wasn't the first time that she had wished that her talent let her learn more emotional information, but technical seemed to be her area of extraction.

She could learn how to rebuild engines, program computers and create the perfect hybrid roses, but she couldn't find out what folks had done on their summer vacations.

The block to her learning curve frustrated the hell out of her.

She tried to keep her mind calm and she accepted the information that Lyneer offered her. He may not have known that he was offering it, but she was learning about the structure and coordination of the ship as they made their way into the heart of the vessel.

The slow flow of other pedestrians indicated their path, so Ziggy was confused when Lyneer steered her into a side hallway that snaked around the main area. "Where are we going?"

"You have a meeting to attend before the ceremony."

The way he said it gave her a shiver of unease. "What kind of meeting?"

He opened the door and shoved her through. "Think of it as a reunion."

The room was circular, and a long conference table snaked around it. The only break in the circle was the small path that she took.

Lyneer whispered. "Stand on the central podium and answer what is asked."

Ziggy was nervous, there was no correlation for this procedure with any of the minds she had touched. She was in a situation that none of her knowledge donors had experienced. Shadows covered the people at the table, but she could make out nine silhouettes.

"Signy Alora, you have been brought here to answer a few questions that only you can answer."

An image hovered in front of her. She saw a human woman watching the Tokkel near her with suspicion and licking her lips lightly as one touched her skin.

A deep voice that resonated in her mind spoke from the shadows. "Do you recognise this image, Ms. Alora?"

She shook her head. "I do not."

"Can you guess where this image was captured?"

"It looks like a Tokkel experimental bay." She tried to look away, but everywhere she looked, the image remained in front of her eyes.

"How do you come to be familiar with the Tokkel experimental facilities?"

She paused. "I saw news reels after the battles."

"Do you recognise the woman in the image?" The deep voice continued.

"No, should I?" She swallowed.

"Usually, folk can recognise themselves in an image, Ms. Alora."

She paled.

"What about this image?"

Ziggy watched the image of herself speak to the people in the room and shepherd them out into the hall and to the pods.

"I have never seen that image before." It was the truth. She had been in it, not watching it.

A chuckle ran through the room around her.

The voice said, "We are aware that you have not seen those images, do you recognise yourself in that image?"

She sighed and her shoulders slumped. "I do."

"What about these events?"

Clips started and ran of her sprinting down the hall with her ankle clearly showing the black mark where they had started to tag her. They showed her entering the room where the captives of the Nine were held and emerging with them minutes later.

"Please explain the following image."

She blushed to the roots of her hair as the image of her holding her handsome alien and kissing him was played over and over until she held up her hands. "Enough. I was trying to knock him out and the only way I know to do it is to drain his current memory. So, I kissed him, stunned him, and wedged him into the pod."

The image of her closing the pod with tears in her eyes was unmistakable.

"I didn't want to keep any of them from getting home. They had a place in the fight and I didn't. They needed to be back with their troops."

She waited.

"How did you know that these were military men?"

Ziggy looked around the room, her own face superseded over the shadowed figures. "I learned it from their minds."

A murmur ran through those assembled.

"Describe the process."

She wondered at the curiosity she could feel swirling in the room. "I touch someone and I am able to copy their technical knowledge to my mind."

"This includes languages?"

She shifted from foot to foot. "It does."

A woman's voice asked. "Does the information fade over time?"

She bit her lip, unsure of how to answer the Shadows. "It goes from immediately accessible knowledge to a dim memory."

"How many of our languages do you know?" The woman tapped her fingers and there was a distinctly wooden sound.

She paused and counted, "Four racial dialects and the common language of the Nine."

The masculine voice spoke again. "Why was it a kiss, Ms. Alora?"

"Pardon?"

"When you incapacitated the officer in the pod, why was it a kiss? You could have gotten a similar reaction from contact if you had tried."

She opened and closed her mouth as she tried to think of a reason. "It seemed like the best thing to do. It was instinct."

Low murmurs filled the room and she was suddenly unsure. They were blocking her audio input somehow. She couldn't make out any of the words and it scared her.

She wove her fingers together in an effort to stop them from trembling.

Her fate was in their hands and she couldn't even see them.

Chapter Five

Just as suddenly as they had become incomprehensible, she could understand them again.

The deep voice spoke directly to her and she felt that they were the only two people in the room. "Ms. Alara, thank you for coming to this meeting of the Nine Council. We understand a little more about what happened that day. Please follow Lyneer and he will take you to the ceremonies."

The Shadows faded from the table and Ziggy was left in the centre of an empty room.

Lyneer came to her and took her hand. "This way, Signy."

"Please, call me Ziggy. Everyone does." She stepped down and let him lead her to the ceremonies.

The flow of traffic had ceased and Lyneer tightened his grip on her hand as they went through the doorway. A coliseum worth of people were already seated. Ziggy had no idea where she was going to find a seat.

The Gaian area was full, several of the military officers were wearing their uniforms and their chests were puffed with pride.

Heads turned to look as she was paraded across the VIP section until she had passed nine dignitaries representing their races and she was seated in the tenth seat on the podium.

The surprised looks from members of her own race embarrassed her, but she sat with her head high and her eyes watching the podium. Lyneer was standing behind her and a quick glance showed her that each person in her row had an attendant in the same pose.

A female from the Tree Folk stood and raised her hands for silence. "Welcome one and all to this celebration of cooperation and unity.

"The Nine races began on the world below, evolving our characteristics to match the area that we lived in. We left when our destiny took us to the stars and set up colonies on dozens of different worlds. When the humans arrived, they began the same metamorphosis that our race went through thousands of years ago. They are changing, evolving to meet the challenges that Gaia is giving them."

She smiled to the assembled folk as the translators caught up with her, repeating all of her words in Gaian.

"As we are all aware, the first attacks of the Tokkel were devastating to the Gaian people. They struck without warning and took dozens of the citizens for examination and experimentation to see how they would best use the rest of you. The ships of the Nine were fighting their way through the horde, but we could not reach the Tokkel harvesters in time. Warriors of the Nine were captured and held by our enemies on the same ships as your people."

She raised her hand and the image of the Tokkel ship diving into the North Ocean filled a glowing sphere in the centre of the event. Gaians cheered as the ship slammed into and disappeared under the waves.

"What you may not know was that less than four hours earlier, a Gaian made this happen."

Ziggy gripped the arms of her chair as her image filled the screen. The images had been cropped so that her bruised and partially exposed limbs were not shown, but one of the angles zoomed in on her ankle and its partially completed mark.

She pressed her lips together as all blood left her face leaving her clammy and cold. The Gaians watched her stuffing the warrior of the Nine into the pod after she had kissed him senseless. A few of them muttered at that, but they stared with shock as she disabled the Tokkel one by one.

Her expression in the image was so cold, she could barely recognise herself, but after she had programmed the ship and locked herself in the pod, the memories were all too clear.

From the interior cameras of the ship she saw her death grip on the interior of the pod, the violent shudders and finally the emergency eject that had taken her back home.

Silence filled the room as the reality of the situation kicked in and the Gaians and several of the Nine turned to stare at her.

"The woman who save not only her own people, but citizens of the Nine, is with us here today. Signy Alora, please come forward. There is a matter of equality to attend to."

The woman made to resemble wood and leaves smiled encouragingly.

Lyneer helped her to her feet and steadied her as she approached the podium. A slow wave of applause began and Ziggy winced when she realised that the Gaians were not participating.

The wooden woman extended her hand and reluctantly, Ziggy took it. Images of special ships, detailed birthing plans and medical procedures that made her blink all filled her mind at the woman's touch.

"I am Ravencourt of the People of the Trees. I greet you, Signy Alora, emissary of the Gaians, and welcome you to the mother ship of the Nine." The woman's green eyes were kind and her hand was smooth and surprisingly warm.

"Thank you Ravencourt. I am not an emissary, merely an average citizen." Her voice boomed and to her surprise she heard the translator working on her words. She had spoken in the wrong language.

"You are far more than you want to admit. Now for the matter of equality."

Ravencourt released her hand, gripped her shoulders and turned her toward the tall and exceptionally familiar male coming toward her.

Reflex made her try to move away, but she was held fast as the entire assembly watched the shifter stride toward her. There was an intense gleam in his eyes that sent Ziggy's heart into a stuttering beat.

He didn't stop when he got to her, but reached out and took her in his arms, sweeping her into a kiss that was shown on the image sphere and gained the vocal admiration of the crowd.

Ziggy held on to him, his lips were hot, his tongue was insistent and a pulse low in her belly pulsed with every stroke in her mouth. She was surrounded by him, he wrapped her in his arms and held her tight as his hands roamed her spine and cupped her hips in turn.

She was plastered against him from the front and the way he was groping her backside, he had a knowledge of her anatomy that her doctor would envy.

After he seemed satisfied with the length of the kiss and she was speculating at the length pressed against her belly, he leaned back and grinned down at her. "It seems that you are just as stunned as I was."

The voice was familiar and he had a wicked gleam in his eyes.

Laughter and applause filled the assembly.

She ran through the information she had caught at the tail end of the kiss and jerked back in his grip. "That was sneaky."

"I told you I would get to the bottom of your mysteries. Claiming you in front of all the races is a fairly effective way to do it." He grinned down at her and she realised that she didn't know who he was.

"What is your name?" Her voice was a low whisper, but it was translated anyway and the words caused a cascade of mirth throughout those assembled.

"Councillor Rothaway, formerly Commander Rothaway, now representative for the shifter people." He kept one hand on her arm and she could read in his body that he didn't want to let go and was afraid that she would run.

He turned and addressed the crowd. "This woman sent me home to my people knowing that she would have to make it to the bridge to achieve the final escape pod. She risked her life not only for my people, but for those of her people who had been captured and marked by the Tokkel. Her victory over the collector ship deserves the sole credit to her genes and her upbringing. She is a Gaian of the newest evolution and she will be honoured here as such."

The people of the Nine stood up and applauded. A child came forward and offered Ziggy a bouquet of exotic blooms, grinning and showing sharp teeth as she did so.

"Congratulations on your claiming, Signy Alora. Councillor Rothaway's family is honoured to have you joining them." The little girl bounced away after making that announcement.

Signy looked up at the bronze skin, hard jaw, slightly full lips still shiny from their kiss, sharp nose, high cheekbones and dark wing-like brows. "Claiming?"

She used his grip to allow her to reach into his mind and she sought regulations for claiming. Everything that she found gave her a sinking feeling.

Ziggy had just gotten engaged and she hadn't even known his name.

Chapter Six

The celebration and medals of honour were distributed, but Ziggy was being escorted down the halls by her tall, dark and handsome companion.

"Where are you taking me?"

His laugh was low and deep. "We will get to that later. For now, you need to be scanned and your talent recorded so that your species will gain protected status with the Nine."

"I don't understand."

He slowed his pace and caressed the back of her hand with his thumb. "We followed the Tokkel because they said that they were coming for a race with potential. We didn't want to stop them so much as observe what they found."

Ziggy's jaw opened in amazement. "You never meant to help?"

"It was a reaction to their attacks on our scouting ships. If they had not acted first we would not have intervened in their attack on your world."

"Why not?"

"Because our involvement brought even more attention from the Tokkel to your world. Unless we find a way to gain commitment from our citizens, we will soon leave Gaia to fend for itself."

She blinked. "Fine. What did you mean by potential?"

He slowed even more and the Nine marks for medical started to appear on the doors they passed. They entered the main medical bay and a woman in the red tunic and black trousers of a nine medical officer came to greet them.

"This is the one?" She was a giant but her voice was pleasantly feminine.

"Yes, Dr. Meevin. This is Signy Alora of Gaia. Third-generation colonist."

The giant smiled pleasantly at Ziggy. "Greetings, warrior. Councillor Rothaway has spoken very highly of you. Would you come with me please?"

She looked up at the woman and smiled. "Of course."

Councillor Rothaway followed them and Ziggy could feel him at her back while she followed the seven foot woman. She still didn't have an answer for her question and she wasn't going to leave the mother ship until she had one.

"We have a full-body scanner here and you will need to relax while we take a baseline reading. It will not hurt and you need to remain relaxed and passive while the scan is in progress."

"Fine. Can I go in like this?" She gestured to her clothing.

"Of course. This is for a biology baseline and a passive brain activity scan." Dr. Meevin smiled brightly.

Similar to a circular shower enclosure it had a gel backing and withdrawn doors. It was a fairly narrow column and Ziggy stepped into it, turning to face her observers. The door closed and the unit started to tilt, sending her back into the embrace of the gel bed.

After the surprise of the tilt, she pressed her hands flat to the bed. Ziggy tried to relax and not to think.

A whir started and then a light sparked across her body, illuminating her in a golden glow. A bright ring of paler pink lights started to hum and rotate and she closed her eyes to keep from getting dizzy.

She didn't know how long she had been in the scanner, but when it finally started to tilt upright again, she fought a yawn.

"We need to observe your abilities in action. Would you allow me to attach this monitor?" Dr. Meevin smiled hopefully.

"Of course." She stepped out of the scanner and smiled politely. "Where would you like me?"

The doctor showed her a station with the same comfort gel and after she settled, a halo of wires was carefully attached to her head.

Councillor Rothaway, the man who had announced his intentions toward her was staring at her as the contacts were pressed to her skin.

"Now, Signy, I need you to use your talent."

Ziggy focussed on Dr. Meevin and extended her hand. "Put your hand in mine and it will start."

Bemused the woman did as she asked and Ziggy let her mind do the rest.

Formal regulations for medical examination of xeno-original species ran through Ziggy's mind. Dr. Meevin wasn't just a physician, she was an alien specialist.

The Giants had a very specific hierarchy and their rituals and formalities were extensive. Ziggy would never need them all but the sheer complexity of etiquette was fascinating.

The doctor released her hand and stared at the readout. "Well, Signy Alora of Gaia, your species definitely has potential."

The giant turned to Rothaway, "I will file the reports with the councils immediately. I don't know how well the Gaians will accept the news, but they are definitely changing."

"Whoa, whoa, whoa. What does *potential* mean?" She lifted the gear off her head.

Dr. Meevin looked at her and tilted her head. "You know that our races developed on the planet beneath us, correct?"

"I do."

"We developed the way we did due to a subtle emanation of the planet that soaked into the soil and the plant life, working its way through the eco system. It changed us from our parent species into the nine separate races we have today.

"Your people have been on the surface long enough for three generations to breed and grow. Your parent species had the potential to develop extraordinary traits and if you are a good example of your people's genes, you will be eligible to join the Nine in one more generation. For now, having potential means that we will guard your world from the Tokkel."

She blinked in surprise. "It is that simple?"

Rothaway moved from his stationary position and came to help her from the exam seat. "It is not quite that simple, but it is a start, and it will keep us here."

Ziggy stood and looked at where their hands were connected. His skin was rough and smooth at the same time, sending prickles of sensation through her. The same warm pulse that she remembered from five years earlier ran up her arm.

His voice rumbled over her and through her soul. "Do you want me here?"

She parted her lips to answer when Dr. Meevin cleared her throat. "Councillor Rothaway, you are overdue for your medication."

He turned to the woman and bared his teeth. "I will take it tomorrow."

"Sir, your levels are already dangerously low."

Ziggy tugged on his hands to return his gaze to her and get him to stop glaring at the doctor. "What medication, what levels?"

He scowled at the doctor. "I had hoped for a more private setting for this conversation."

"You are exuding quite a lot of pheromones, normal for a shifter in rut. You have been militant about taking your meds for the last five years, so this is a sudden change in attitude and physiology, councillor." The doctor crossed her arms. "Your kind can be dangerous in that situation and I believe that our young miss needs to be informed before she gets any closer to you."

Rothaway tightened his hands on hers. "I have already declared my claim in front of the entire assembly. She isn't getting out of this now."

Meevin gave him a half smile. "Congratulations. How brave to be declaring on behalf of an untested species."

"I knew what she was when she first touched me. It simply took a while before I was able to find her again. My rut started with her touch, intensified with her kiss and has been idling in my bloodstream for five years. Enough is enough."

The doctor paused. "You are serious? She is the one who triggered you?"

The question was phrased toward Rothaway, but Ziggy knew it was meant for her. "I am not sure what triggering entails, but I did touch and kiss him on a Tokkel ship five years ago."

The doctor nodded sharply and checked medical reports once again. "It should work. You will have to work out the details with her at your leisure."

The words gave Ziggy a frisson of unease but the sensations that she was experiencing were starting to override her judgement.

Nothing else was said. Rothaway tugged her by her hands and led her out of medical.

He placed an arm around her waist and they returned to the assembly. He walked her to her seat and then glared at the representative next to her.

A chain reaction occurred when the shifter rep got up with a grin. He inclined his head to Rothaway and repeated the gesture toward Ziggy. The representatives all got up and moved over one until the empty seat in the centre was taken up and the seat next to Ziggy was empty.

Rothaway took the seat and while the medals were still being awarded near the podium, they were drawing more of an audience as he reached out to take her hand.

They sat side by side and watched the remainder of the ceremonies, his hand loosely clasping hers but she felt every ridge and callous on his skin. Her entire being was focussed on his hand and it was only when the rules of a Wilder bonding ceremony started to creep into her mind that she noticed that he was feeding her what he wanted her to know.

Chapter Seven

Three hours later, the ceremonies were concluded. Councillor Rothaway was given a medal of discovery and Ziggy had a heavy star dangling on a ribbon around her neck. It was a civilian medal of honour and it impressed the hell out of the audience of the Nine.

Ziggy was in a daze when the music swelled and the assembly broke up. Rothaway's hand held her in place and she waited with him and the other representatives in their row as the humans and others filed past them. The members of the nine races smiled at her, giving her friendly winks and frank looks as they passed her.

She leaned over to Rothaway, "Why are they staring?"

"You have been recorded as the first of your species to have shown potential. Our mother ship has been seeking other species for generations in hopes that one would show potential for the development of psychic or physical evolution. That the Tokkel found you first was a source of distress and embarrassment." He murmured it softly but there was an undertone to his voice that sent her nerves into sensory overdrive.

She checked the information that she had pulled out of Meevin, but the effect she was experiencing was not in the doctor's information.

She whispered again. "Why do we have to sit here?"

He nodded to a few of his own race. "So that each race is represented from beginning to end of the ceremonies."

"Your people are the Wilder?"

"We are. We are aware that your folk call us shifters, but now that you are here, you should know the proper name for those you will be surrounded by."

She swallowed as the final folk went past. "You are speaking as if I am going to be locked into the mother ship."

"Not locked in, but to keep us in defensive orbit you will need to remain as an example of why we are here."

Ziggy blinked. "But, you have been here for the last five years without anyone acting as the potential."

Rothaway caressed her hand with his thumb. "My mind was laid open and it was confirmed that not only were you gifted, you were Gaian. It was in our best interest to find the Tokkel ship to determine your identity."

Ziggy sighed and rubbed her forehead with her free hand. "So that is why the Nine participated in the salvage of the Tokkel ship."

"You did quite the job on the tracking systems and you landed it in a mineral heavy area. It was buried quite deep." There was admiration in his tone.

"My friend Tiera's brother was a sea miner. I remembered the location from his conversation."

He scowled. "You have feelings for this male?"

He had gone from being cuddly and seductive to bristling with rage in a moment. It shocked Ziggy when she realised that his hair was actually elevating and standing on edge.

"Only insomuch as he is Tiera's brother. He is like family."

Ziggy gave in to the urge to stroke his arm to calm him. "I think we can go now."

He looked up and the representatives on the other side of them were watching him cautiously.

Lyneer made himself known as he cleared his throat. "Perhaps this discussion would best be held in privacy, councillor."

Rothaway shook his head as if to clear it and nodded his head with a jerk. "I apologise I am degrading a little more rapidly than I thought."

She didn't have a chance to ask about what precisely was degrading, he gently lifted her to her feet, and they left the podium and the relieved councillors behind.

Lyneer walked in front of them, deflecting the people who tried to approach her. She tried to ask Rothaway what was going on, but his face bore a frightening intensity that told her to hold questions until later.

He seemed to have grown by a few inches and his hair was fluffed out she could swear that she saw his ears twitch as they passed other males. The Wilders that they approached took one look at him and flattened themselves to the walls to get out of his way.

She scrambled in her mind for the information as to what was going on, but there was nothing specific to Wilders in the information Meevin had surrendered. There was nothing coming from Rothaway right now either. This was an emotional matter and she couldn't hack through to the logic of it.

Silently she let Lyneer lead them through the halls until they entered a huge garden in the centre of the ship.

There was an attendant to one side and Lyneer moved to speak with her quietly. She nodded and handed him a triangle that had a slight glow.

Lyneer held the triangle out and walked down a barely visible path, the object brightened and continued to increase in luminosity as they progressed.

The green man paused next to a stone obelisk and pressed the triangle into the rock.

Rothaway tugged her past the stone and Lyneer smiled in encouragement. "It will be fine, Signy. No harm will come to you."

With that alarming statement, a barrier sprang up between them crackling with energy. Lyneer waved at her and kept his smile in place as she was hauled along.

Now that privacy was assured, she was irritated. "What the hell is going on, Rothaway?"

He looked down at her and she flinched back, the whites of his eyes were crimson and fangs were showing at the edge of his lips. "I will explain when we get there."

"Holy heck. What is that about?" She tried to dig her heels in but he gave her arm a yank and she stumbled forward.

She should have been feeling fear, but nothing that he had done was violent and it seemed that his situation was understood by those who had seen him in the halls. It was something they were familiar with so it obviously occurred enough to be recognised.

Green and lavender grass and flowers were all around them, filling the air with a heady perfume that gave her a heavy feeling in her limbs.

She stumbled as he kept forging forward and he turned swiftly to lift her in his arms. "It is the flowers. They will relax you and keep me calm."

His words were rumbling out of his chest and she bit her lip as the vibrations ran right through her to pool in her lower abdomen and between her thighs.

She breathed in deep for self-control and more of the floral scent ran into her bloodstream.

He stopped in front of a rocky altar that had the hilt of a knife sticking out of it.

He set her on her feet and stood in front of her, his teeth were shorter and he looked less wild.

"Signy, five years ago you started this when you kissed me. My people have a strict no contact policy when it comes to the opposite sex for just this reason."

"What is going on?"

He dragged in a deep breath and held her hands. "When you kissed me I was in a susceptible state and I keyed to your genetic code. Only you were able to be my match from that day forward."

"What?" Her voice came out on a husky whisper.

"I was with an all-male crew because we needed all ships in the air and I was entering a receptive phase. If I had been trapped with a female of the Nine, I may have fought for her with my crew and that would not have been a good thing. As it was, when you touched me I knew that I was doomed and despite the effect of your kiss I was elated at the same time."

She blinked up at him. "I don't understand."

"Wilders hunt their mates by scent and opportunity. If we don't find a mate before we reach a critical age, we go into the rut and seek our mate with aggressive fixation." He paused to inhale. "I was lucky enough to have a powerful female find me instead of running from me."

She blinked. "Me?"

"Indeed. Now, to end the rut we need to engage in one of two events. One, is to have sex right here."

Her mouth opened in shock.

He chuckled, his fangs flashing.

"The second option is to share blood. That will pause the effects for a few days and allow us to get to know each other."

"Option B."

He laughed. "Remove the knife from the stone. Females don't have the fangs so we have built in the assistance to make things easier."

"Seriously? I have to take a knife to you?"

He held out his hand. "Wrist to wrist."

She tugged the knife out of the stone and wondered if it would make her queen of the ancient land of England. With a giggle, she held the knife awkwardly and raised it toward him. "What now?"

He pressed the knife against his wrist and wrapped his hand around hers, pulling it sharply until his blood welled.

She gasped and jerked her hand back but his grip was tight. He raised her wrist to his lips, the blood trailing down the blade still in her fist. She winced at the flare of pain as he bit into her, but the moment he broke her skin he released her wrist and moved it to press against his own open wound.

Her mind opened wide as his blood seeped into her arm and hers moved into his. Her hand maintained the grip on the dagger as she took all of his knowledge into her including his emotions and the personal details of his life.

Ziggy's breath came out of her on a moan, and her knees buckled. She took them both to the ground and she collapsed under the burn of pain mixed with the knowledge of a lifetime that was not hers.

She leaned forward and he mimicked her, their foreheads leaning together, their breath mingling as they completed the bonding that he needed to still the fire in his veins.

In less than one day she had gone from being Ziggy, to being Signy Alora Rothaway Vaddos, and it was quite the alteration.

CHAPTER EIGHT

"Why don't you use your last names?"

He raised his head slowly and focussed on her. Rothaway's eyes were no longer crimson. "They are clan names and we only use them for formal occasions and documents. How do you know about the other name?"

She winced. *Busted.* "Your knowledge came to me in your blood."

Rothaway looked at where their wrists were still pressed together. "I did not receive that effect."

She blinked. "Do you think it could have something to do with my potential?"

"What precisely did you gain?"

She touched his knee with her free hand. "You have a scar here from when you were ten, climbed a tree and got attacked by another shifter in a feline form."

Her eyes widened as she realised that he actually could change his shape. "You can really shift your form?"

He raised one eyebrow. "You would like a demonstration now?"

She blinked. The bonding was a sacred moment on the mother ship. They were in a bonding grove and Lyneer was acting as their guardian, keeping others away while they were vulnerable. "I suppose not."

Rothaway laughed and lifted her bleeding wrist to his lips, licking the wounds closed. He did the same to his own wrist a moment later and then helped her to her feet.

She still had the dagger in her hand. "What do I do with this?"

He smiled, "Place it back in the stone."

Shrugging she walked back to the rock and slid the dagger home. It immediately sank into the edifice and disappeared. "Where did it go?"

"It is being filed for proof of our bonding. My blood and your DNA on the handle is proof of our union."

She smirked. "Or that I stabbed you and left you for dead."

"In that case it is doubtful that you would have put the dagger back into the stone." He grinned, at ease.

"Why did it come on you so suddenly? The rut is supposed to take weeks to reach its peak."

"I stopped my suppressing medications when we found the ship. I wanted to make sure that I was ready for you the moment that we met again."

She followed her impulse and hugged him. "How did you know I didn't die on that ship?"

"Because a woman who could face down an entire ship of Tokkel with nothing more than bare feet and attitude, would not die in a simple ship crash."

She blushed as his arms came around her and rubbed her back slowly but pressed her tightly against him. He was still interested in her and the ridge of his sex against her belly was both hot an insistent.

Ziggy pulled slightly away and he let her go. "What is next?"

"A kiss to finish what the first kiss started, and then we share a meal."

His eyes gleamed as he looked at her.

She held still and then went up on her toes to meet him halfway. Her mouth tingled as it made contact with his and she shivered at the static charge that flowed from his lips to hers.

Her heart started a heavy pounding in her chest that increased as the kiss intensified. Ziggy felt a cascade of heat rolling into her body and it spread throughout her limbs. She reached up and held Rothaway's mouth to hers as her reflexes took over and she sought a taste of him.

He pulled her away from him and his eyes widened in surprise when he looked at her. "Signy, does your species go into heat?"

She blinked rapidly and tried to press against him. When he thwarted her, she snarled.

He shook her lightly. "Signy, how often does your species go into heat?"

She dragged in a soothing breath of the flowers. "We don't specifically go into heat, but we ovulate every twenty-eight days."

"Then we had better get to lunch and I will explain the ritual in which we just engaged in more detail." He wrapped an arm around her waist and he escorted her back down the path that had taken them into the bonding area.

Lyneer was waiting for them and he smiled in relief as they approached. "Congratulations. I was getting worried."

"No need to worry, Lyneer. We managed it without much difficulty."

Ziggy still felt weird. Her body was hot, pulses were pounding in all the wrong places and the skin of her inner thighs was hyper sensitive.

Lyneer took one long look at her and nodded. "Do you wish to have the customary luncheon, or privacy?"

Rothaway looked down at her and frowned. "Both. No sense tempting fate."

"Can I contact my parents?" She needed to distract herself from the hormonal surge she was having and thinking about her parents was definitely effective.

"Of course. With you here as the representative of the Gaians they will be able to visit you whenever you wish." Rothaway kept his arm around her.

Lyneer lifted a small com unit to his ear and began speaking in the tradition of assistants across the universe.

Rothaway kept a supportive arm around her and they walked slowly through the garden and out into the halls. A quick pod ride later and they were in the VIP area.

"We are going to my quarters. I believe that they will afford us more privacy than the restaurant normally used for these purposes."

She didn't care, she simply wanted to be alone with him and discovering the details of his physiology. Ziggy had images of Wilder anatomy in her mind, but she wanted to learn the real thing in touch and taste.

Lyneer escorted them the entire way, speaking urgently on his com in a language that she couldn't understand. That little fact freaked her out.

"Why can't I understand what he is saying?"

"He is speaking to a member of his clan. There are sub languages of the Nine that you may not have absorbed yet."

She liked that he mentioned an oblique future where she would be picking up more knowledge. It made it feel less like a bizarre dream and more like a glowing reality.

Ziggy had gotten married to a male she had met once after she savaged his mind and took what she wanted from him. In a weird way she had made an honest man of him.

CHAPTER NINE

His private quarters were huge. There was a kitchen, a breakfast bar, dining room, living area and a huge bedroom. Ziggy assumed that the lav was off one of the hallways, but she didn't need one so she didn't ask.

Rothaway walked into the kitchen, withdrew a bottle that contained a substance that resembled wine. He gathered two glasses and set them on the table, pouring each glass half full.

He sat across from her and raised his glass. She lifted hers in reflex. "To Signy, my bond mate and companion."

She didn't drink but after he had sipped she spoke up, "My friends all call me Ziggy."

"Ziggy?"

"Yes. The consonant contrast in my name makes it hard for some people to pronounce. Ziggy is easier."

She paused and realised that she needed to return the toast. "To Rothaway, my bond mate and companion."

She sipped carefully and realised that it was indeed wine in an almost black liquid form. Crossberry wine was supposed to act as an aphrodisiac, but she didn't need one. Her blood was singing in her veins and the song was his name.

When Lyneer knocked on the door, he entered carefully as if unsure of what he would see. Relief and disappointment warred in his features as he allowed a stream of newcomers into Rothaway's chamber.

They set the table and placed nine different dishes on the surface, each covered with a dome. As silently as they arrived, they left.

Lyneer bowed low and smiled at them. "Congratulations on your bond."

Ziggy was curious and she tried to look at the dishes, but Rothaway cleared his throat. "I will describe each dish to you. There are nine dishes to honour the Nine, and all of the dishes are from the Wilder tradition."

Ziggy waited and watched as he described the four meat dishes, three vegetable dishes, one starch and one dessert.

Her arousal was increasing with every minute and she devoured the food with good appetite. The meat was almost raw but that did not bother her as it would normally.

By the time the meal was over her skin was on fire and she was done with waiting.

Ziggy lunged across the table and tackled Rothaway where he sat, the dishes went flying. She pressed her lips to his, whimpering wildly as her blood pulsed in all of her erogenous zones.

Her hands pulled at his formal tunic and when she was rewarded with warm hard skin she sighed in relief.

"Not here. Hold on." Rothaway held her tight and rolled to his feet, taking her with him as he walked to the bedroom.

She pressed kisses to his neck and chin as he walked, her skirt rucked up around her thighs.

"You are going to have to explain to me what is going on, Rothaway." She interspersed each word with a kiss to the cords of his neck and a nibble on his earlobe.

"Not now. I will tell you later."

She nipped his ear with her teeth. "Now, Rothaway. I don't normally straddle men I have just met, let alone have my hips grinding against them."

"You inherited my rut. It shouldn't have moved this fast, but your system is a little faster than that of one of the Nine." His voice was muffled against the hollow of her throat as he began a string of kisses that worked to the edge of her gown.

She blanked out conscious thought and let her body lead her actions, peeling his tunic from him completely and then working at her own gown while she kicked her shoes off.

Her back pressed against the cool silk of his sheets and with a few short tugs her dress was gone and he was removing his boots and trousers as quickly as possible.

When he joined her on the bed she lunged and threw him off balance, bringing him to his back and straddling him. She roamed her hands over him, learning the textures of him, and then she followed her hands with her mouth.

His body was taut and arched under her, giving her only a moment before he flipped her to her back and joined their bodies.

She was ready for him but it was still a snug fit as he worked into her completely. Together, they rocked and surged in unison until their bodies peaked and they clung to each other as they shook and moaned.

Ziggy's mind cleared the moment that her heartbeat returned to normal. She reached up and slapped his arm. "You couldn't have warned me about that?"

He blinked and started to laugh. She could feel him still inside her and the laughter dislodged him.

Rothaway rolled to one side and curled her against him, stroking her spine over and over. "I could barely remember how to speak earlier. Explaining that our blood bonding might send you into heat was a little beyond my comprehension."

She snorted and rubbed one of the scars on his chest. "I still can't believe that you are a shape shifter."

He gave her a long look and seconds later, a huge feline of undetermined species was lying next to her in bed. It had Rothaway's eyes and colouring, so she reached out to touch it and slowly stroked the spotted fur.

The noise he made was a low rhythmic rumble as she stroked him. She rubbed the spot between his eyes and carefully caressed his ears. The noise he was making made her drowsy and she soon snuggled against him and dozed off.

Ziggy woke with a jolt, the masculine arms holding her tight scared the crap out of her. It took her thirty seconds to remember where she was and who was with her, but once she did, it didn't relax her any.

"I want to see my parents and I need to have my friends brought up here for visits. Tiera will be wondering what the hell happened to me and I honestly can't sum it up over a com link."

He pressed a kiss to her shoulder. "You can have anyone you wish here for a visit. Do the Gaians have any particular formal wear you will need as representative of your species?"

She thought about it and decided not to lie. "Nothing formal. We wear dresses or military uniforms. I am not in the military, so nothing fancy."

He pressed a string of kisses along her shoulders. "Good. I have ideas of how to dress you and I think that the Wilder fashions will look very good on you."

She shrugged. "Well, right now I only have that gown on the floor and my work clothes up here, so whatever you decide to do, do it fast."

He laughed and rolled her over. "I think slow would be better."

She blushed as she caught his reference and then she stopped thinking as his hands woke her body once again.

They spent an intense day, coupling, parting and then coupling again. By the time they woke the next morning she knew most of Rothaway's sensitive spots and he knew all of hers.

She used the shower and came out squeaky clean if somewhat sensitive. The soothing effect of water would have been good, but it was absent.

Ziggy fastened her dress and tried to fluff out the creases with her hands. It was better than nothing but still awkward as she carried her shoes into the dining area and she saw Lyneer.

Rothaway was reading a data pad and he smiled as she entered. "Your parents have been contacted and they will be here in a few days. Your friend Tiera is on her way."

Smiling, she walked up behind him, dropped her shoes, looped her arms around his neck and pressed a kiss to his cheek. "Thank you. I will get my parents to pack some clothing for me when they visit."

Rothaway took her by the hand and got her to take a seat at the table. "The seamstress will be here in an hour. Lyneer will remain with you while she takes your measurements and after you have a day dress, you will be asked to represent your species at a children's competition."

"Where will you be?"

"Representing my species right next to you."

"Can Tiera come?"

"Of course. She can stay as long as she likes. The guest quarters you were in initially have been reserved for her."

"Who will bring her here? If Lyneer is with me who will pick her up?"

Lyneer smiled. "I have arranged for one of the Forest Folk to pick her up. He will meet her and bring her here."

With Rothaway's hand on hers she accessed everything she could on the Forest Folk.

When her shoulders started shaking both men looked at her in alarm and she explained with laughter bubbling up, "Tiera is going to have a hard time laying off the wood jokes. They practically write themselves."

As Lyneer put her breakfast in front of her she smiled and sighed in relief that at least there was no chance that Tiera would find a male in rut when she arrived. The surprises would be kept to a minimum and the fewer the better.

Ziggy looked around her. If she had known back then what she knew now, she may just have climbed into that escape pod with Rothaway back on the Tokkel ship. It would have saved her five wasted years of hiding and a lot of good sex.

It just went to show that no matter how much she knew, there was no foreseeing the future.

Accepting
Return of the Nine Book Two

By

Viola Grace

Chapter One

Tiera MacKenzie could not believe her ears. "My friend is what?"

"She is the embodiment of the potential of our race. Signy has a talent for instantly absorbing and applying knowledge, and that is something most attractive to the Nine." The military representative was impatient. "You must come with us."

Ziggy had been gone for forty-eight hours, and now Tiera was facing the Gaian military officers that Mrs. Alora had described to her when Ziggy was taken.

Tiera rubbed her forehead with two fingers. "Why must I come with you?"

"As Signy's friend, you have been invited to stay on the mother ship of the Nine. To keep her happy, her spouse has ordered that you be brought up for an extended visit. Bring what you think you will need, because we will be leaving in five minutes, and you will be with us."

Tiera arched her eyebrow. "Really?"

He crossed his arms. "Really. You can do what you will with your time, but you are coming with us. The government wants to continue good relations with the Nine, and if your presence is the price, they will pay it."

Tiera called her mother and quickly filled her in while she grabbed a duffel and filled it. "No, Mom, I don't know what they want. No, apparently, Ziggy is on the mother ship, and they want me to visit her. No, I don't know how long I will be gone. I will keep you posted. Love you."

She hung up and lifted the bag filled with underwear, comfy dresses and two pairs of shoes. Stomping back to the front door, she walked past the man in uniform and out to his vehicle. Tiera tossed the bag into the back seat and buckled into the front seat, crossing her arms over her chest.

He didn't say a word, merely got in, put the vehicle in gear and drove to the launch port. The cars in front and behind did the same, forming a secure column.

When he stopped, she got out, grabbed her bag and marched to the shuttle with its walkway down.

"Where am I supposed to be?"

37

A surprised member of the Nine with a distinctly damp appearance waved her to a chair and gently took her bag from her. He spoke carefully. "Please use the harness. It is for your safety."

She smiled. "Thank you." Tiera fastened the harness, watched as the pilot sealed the hatch and they lifted off.

"Am I your only passenger?"

He nodded. "The Potential has asked for you, and so, we will deliver you to her since she cannot come down."

That was news to Tiera. "Why can't she come down?"

"She is newly bonded. Councillor Rothaway will not let her go." There was a slight colour to the male's cheeks as he spoke, a blue flush under the pale green skin.

The phrasing was odd, but Tiera nodded and kept silent as they climbed through the atmosphere toward the huge bulk of the mother ship of the Nine.

Nine different races that had emerged from the same species were represented on that ship. That the Nine had also once lived on Gaia was not a coincidence. Something on the planet, or in the planet itself, changed the races that lived there.

Tiera had known about Ziggy's talent for knowing things simply by touching others. You could not grow up with someone without picking up on things like that.

When the marauding Tokkel had captured Ziggy, Tiera had been worried. When she reappeared with her body intact and her features grim, Tiera had let her speak at her own pace. Eventually, the whole story came out, and Tiera had sworn to keep her friend's confidence.

With the shuttle passing through the atmosphere and into the darkness, the stars grew clearer and brighter than she had ever seen them, but they soon faded again as they approached the docking area of the mother ship.

A sense of urgency started in her body. She was going where few humans had gone before, and she had been invited to stay overnight. Only dignitaries and pilots had ever had the honour before today, well, them and Ziggy.

The docking procedure was probably fascinating, but Tiera was busy looking at and cataloguing the variety of races in the docking bay.

People whose origins were in water, fire, forests, air, rock and others were all there, each in a specialized environmental suit that allowed them to work with exposure to space.

As the shuttle settled, she heard a clamping sound. The shuttle was then hauled forward by a mechanism under the landing gear. They were pulled into a compartment that sealed behind them.

The hiss of gas was audible, and when a light on the console turned blue, the pilot unclasped his harness and retrieved her bag.

"An escort has been arranged for you. He will take you to the Potential."

"You mean Ziggy."

He grinned, showing distinctly pointed teeth. "We are very big on titles."

She laughed. She couldn't help it. "Thank you for your kindness, Pilot."

"Arcolothi." He bowed low.

"I am Tiera." She tried to mimic his bow, and she must have done all right, because he grinned at her again. Tiera hoisted her bag back onto her shoulder and headed through the open hatch.

There was a small path and another doorway. She really hoped that her guide was there, because she had no idea how to find Ziggy or how many of the Nine had bothered to learn Gaian.

Her steps slowed as she exited the doorway, and when a man who had been leaning against the wall stood straight and smiled at her, she knew that he was either her guide or he was going to hit on her. Either way, she was in for some conversation.

"Tiera MacKenzie?"

"I am." She inclined her head.

"I am Tonos, your guide to the mother ship of the Nine." He bowed low and fluttered large, elegant insect-like wings. "I am of the People of the Air, so do pardon my wings."

Tiera looked at the wings and smiled. "I find them very fetching."

"Thank you, Signy Rothaway has pronounced them to be creepy."

A giggle escaped her. "That sounds like Ziggy."

"Please, let me take your bag and show you to your quarters."

He took her bag from her and slung it over one muscular arm and offered her the other. "Please allow me."

She touched his arm, and to her surprise, his skin actually rippled slightly under her touch. His wings fluttered and his eyes widened at the light contact. She pulled her hand away, but he grabbed it and placed it back on his forearm.

His eyes grew heavy lidded as he straightened his shoulders and tried to behave like nothing had happened. "So, what do you do for a living, Miss Tiera?"

She followed his lead as he walked toward a pod situated on a rail. "I am a caterer. I prepare large amounts of food for weddings and such."

"Do you find this work fulfilling?"

Tiera grinned at the memories that his words evoked, "Well, it certainly is more than I ever imagined it could be. It is a challenge and a torture at the same time."

He settled her inside the pod and stowed her bag behind her. "I thought to give you a tour of the ship and this is the best way to do it. Are you ready?"

Tiera thought about it, she was in space, waiting to see her friend who had disappeared a few days earlier and was now the living proof that humanity had potential to evolve into something else. Ziggy had also married a councillor of the Nine who could shift his shape into something else in that short span of time.

She exhaled deeply and smiled, "Yes. I think I am."

Chapter Two

"Where is she?" Ziggy was pacing back and forth in front of the VIP room that Tiera had been assigned.

Rothaway was watching her as she wrung her hands and swished her skirts. "She is getting a tour of the ship, Signy. There is no reason to worry."

Ziggy whirled on him and snarled, "Worry? The Forest representative was called elsewhere, and she ended up with that pervy little Fairy."

He got to his feet and wrapped her in his arms, purring and calming her down.

She chuckled and looked up at him, "You know, before I got your blood, there was a lot more self-control going on in my mind."

He laughed. "All this change in a few hours. I can only imagine how savage you will be if we reproduce."

She looked up at him in shock, but he quickly distracted her. "Is that not your friend?"

Ziggy whirled and faced Tiera walking on the arm of Tonos, the pervy Fairy.

Tiera smiled and ran forward, stopping just an inch from her.

Ziggy had no hesitation and wrapped her arms around her friend, initiating a hug that ended in a squeak. Her strength was increasing as the blood that she had swapped with Rothaway continued to make her into a Wilder wife.

"Sorry, about that, Tiera. I suspected that I was never going to see you again, so I kind of panicked."

Tiera's face was pale, and she gave her friend a wobbly smile.

Ziggy immediately straightened and pressed Tiera's palm to the lock. "We have to code it to you, Tier."

Taking in the shock in her best friend's face, Ziggy ushered her through the opening door and spoke to Rothaway, "Wait out here. Tier and I have a bit to discuss. Tonos, give me that bag."

Tonos seemed as bewildered as Rothaway, but he did as she asked. Her enhanced senses caused her to bristle a little at the scent he had left on her friend's duffel, but she kept her arm around Tiera's shoulders and brought her into the bedroom.

Seating her on the bed, she knelt and looked into Tiera's eyes, trying to understand what had happened to shock Tiera so deeply.

"Aw . . . hon. What is it?" Ziggy held her hands, and to her relief, Tiera began to speak.

Tiera couldn't believe it. She was on a spaceship, surrounded by aliens and even her best friend in all of Gaia was no longer hers.

"I am having a problem adapting. Tonos took me on a tour."

"If that little perv did anything to you . . ." Ziggy flexed her hands.

It was that defensive reflex that brought out a smile on Tiera's face. "No. He was perfect and polite. When I stopped responding to his comments and descriptions of the zones of the craft, he brought me right here."

"What was the problem?"

Tiera looked down into Ziggy's face, her friend's earnest query touched her heart. "What is always the problem with me, Ziggy?"

"You hate change . . . ohh." Ziggy got up and took a seat next to her.

Tiera felt the bed dip, but she was still disconnected from the world around her. It was a defence mechanism that she had always fallen back on in the past, despite its inconvenience.

"I am sorry, Ziggy. This should be a happy time for you, and I am delighted that you met someone. It will just take me time to work it into my thoughts. I should be a little un-kinked in the morning." Tiera smiled at her friend's hug.

Three days ago, Ziggy had just been the best friend a girl could have. Now she had a strength that wasn't hidden behind sarcasm anymore. Oh, the sarcasm was still bright and shining but the strength was right beside it now. The change in her best friend was more striking than anything else, and it was also the most frightening.

"I know that it is sudden, and I know that it will take time for you to get used to it. That is why Rothaway sent for you. Since I can't go to you, you are invited here for as long as you like." Ziggy took her hand.

"You are touching me a lot. I know you can't read emotions, so what are you after?" Her words came out far more blunt than she had intended.

"I am seeking to comfort you. Just two days with Rothaway has taught me the powerful effect that touch can have. You are calmer now, yes?"

Tiera laughed at the perky tone of Ziggy's voice. "Yes. I am. Now, what do you have against Tonos?"

Ziggy sighed and Tiera followed her gaze into the other room.

"Can they hear us?"

Ziggy grimaced. "Without a doubt. The Wilder have excellent hearing, and from what I know, the People of the Air do as well. It was in their base species before the Nine split. I can't believe that our folklore has them on record, and no one ever figured out that someone somewhere had seen aliens."

Tiera laughed. "It figures that you figured it out, Zig."

"It's what I do."

They sat holding hands while Tiera's world spun and finally settled inside her.

"Better?"

She laughed, "Better."

"Then, I will introduce you to my husband."

"Wait. What is your problem with Tonos?"

"He is way too flirty for one of the Nine. And those wings of his are so . . ."

"Creepy." The masculine voice from the doorway was amused.

Tiera smiled. "I don't think they are creepy."

His wings flicked in response to her words. "I thank you, Miss Tiera. I will take my leave of you now, but know that I enjoyed our time together very much."

"Thank you for the tour."

He bowed and left the room.

Ziggy's man came forward and occupied the doorway. "I am pleased to meet you, Tiera MacKenzie. Signy has been quite agitated that you come, so she would not be the only Gaian on board."

His blunt honesty made her laugh. "I am pleased to meet you, Rothaway. Ziggy has told me nothing about you, so I am dying to learn more."

She and Ziggy got to their feet. Ziggy paused her husband with one hand. "Let me just explain the workings of the lav to her, and we will join you in the outer room."

Tiera nodded. "Good call."

It took a few minutes to get everything just right, but when they left the lav, Tiera was fairly confident about her grasp of the procedure.

The next thing to learn was how to summon a hot beverage, but that lesson was taught with an interested Rothaway looking on.

Sipping at a cup of tea, Tiera asked him, "How many of the Nine have learned Gaian?"

He shrugged. "Everyone on the mother ship."

That surprised her. "But, I had an aquatic pilot, and he had a problem with speaking. He got the words right, but his mouth moved funny."

Rothaway smiled, "You caught that? His species does not speak in their home environment. Learning any spoken language is difficult for them."

Since this was her home for the interim, she took a seat at the table, and Ziggy and Rothaway soon joined her. "So, how does one go about learning an alien language in an effective manner, and how could the entire ship have done it with Gaian?"

He grinned and showed some very sharp teeth. "We do it via subliminal training. It helps to keep our minds on our duties during the day. A few of the races have representatives with a talent for language, and they were the first ones to speak with your people."

Tiera sat back and just came out with it. "How is it possible that you meet an alien woman and decide within hours that she is the one for you?"

Rothaway blinked and then grinned at Ziggy. "You didn't tell her?"

Ziggy was blushing. "There was no opportunity."

"Shall I?"

"No. That's fine. I will tell her. Tier, do you remember when I said that I met a member of the Nine and he had some men with him and they escaped from the ship I was on?"

Tiera blinked, "Yes, you said he was unwell so you stuffed him in the pod and hit the button."

Rothaway arched a brow. "Unwell?"

Ziggy's face was on fire with a blush. "Well, he wasn't sick. I needed to get him out of there, so I kissed him, mugged his mind and shoved him into the pod while he was stunned. That is what started the bond. He has been waiting for me since that day."

Tiera nodded as she absorbed the information that her friend had molested a wounded man. It was Ziggy from top to toe. She never did anything in the right order and this was proof.

Tiera grinned. "Congratulations on the end of a long wait, Rothaway. She was worth every second of it."

He lifted Ziggy's hand to his lips, and Tiera teared up at the genuine affection in his eyes. "I would have waited until the stars burned out for this woman, though I may have gone mad in the process."

Tiera sipped at her tea and felt her world settle around her with another mental click. She just needed to know a little more of the customs of the place that she found herself, and it would be like being on a holiday that someone else had booked. Fun, but out of her control.

CHAPTER THREE

"What do you mean *go mad?*" Tiera was eating some of the snacks that Ziggy had coaxed out of the dispenser in front of her eyes.

Rothaway sighed, "Tonos would be a better person to question. He is a medic."

Tiera waved her hands. "Explain please. I don't want to make any social gaffs."

He straightened, "Right. Well, our parent race mated via pheromone triggers as many do. We have evolved to determine our mate via contact. When we find a woman ninety-eight percent compatible, and we touch, our body keys itself to that female. Depending on our race, there are a variety of effects which occur after that initial contact."

Ziggy reached over and snagged a cracker, "Aggression toward other males is one of those side effects. Apparently they get horny and then they get deadly."

Rothaway looked upset for a moment, but then, he nodded in agreement. "It is an unflattering but accurate assessment."

"What stops it?"

Ziggy sipped and munched. "Well, Rothaway went to medical for several years and got suppressing shots."

Rothaway's dark skin darkened further. "I will leave you two to catch up. I will return in an hour with some more appropriate clothing for dinner. Don't fill up. There is a council dinner in three hours."

He got to his feet, kissed Ziggy in the most passionate embrace that Tiera had ever witnessed and escaped.

Tiera laughed, "He lasted longer than I expected him to."

Ziggy grinned, "I know. He has stamina. Let me just confirm that. So, what do you want to know?"

"What was your wedding like?"

Ziggy's gaze got far away. "There is a private area in the central garden, the air is filled with the scent of flowers and everything is so soothing.

"We stood in front of the altar stone, and I pulled the knife—"

"Knife?"

"I pulled the knife, and Rothaway put his wrist against it, breaking the skin. He bit my wrist, and we pressed the wounds together. This transferred his rut to me, and the first moment that we had alone, I jumped him."

Tiera laughed and then sobered. "A knife? You are serious?"

"The blood keys him to me and me to him. It is freaky at times, but I am trying to get used to it. When you finish the cutting, you put the dagger back into the altar, and your union is now official by the laws of the Nine."

"And you didn't think that was weird?"

Ziggy cackled, "I thought it was nuts. If it weren't for Rothaway being serious and focussed, I would have made a run for it. I wouldn't have gotten anywhere but I would have taken off."

Tiera grinned, "So, we don't touch the men of the Nine."

Ziggy snickered, "Not unless you want to chance being stuck up her indefinitely. I can tell you, once they find a mate, they are not eager to let them go."

Tiera tried to forget the peculiar shudder that had run through Tonos when she touched his arm, the fluttering of his wings and the flexing of the muscles in his body-builder physique.

Ziggy caught on to her change in expression. "What? What did you do?"

Tiera bit her lip.

"Wait, who did you touch and what happened?"

"It was probably nothing. I am sure it was nothing. It couldn't have been anything, I am sure that he was just cold or something."

Zig leaned forward. "He shivered? Did anything else happen?"

Tiera winced, "His wings flicked, eyes heated up and he licked his lips repeatedly. He said he was fine, but how would we know if he was affected?"

Zig closed her eyes and found the information. "The Air Folk signal that they have found a mate with a change to their wings. The delicate veins harden and the panels become as hard as steel. Basically, if he has been affected, he is now carrying four swords on his back."

Tiera winced, "What would that be for?"

"Fighting over females. It is possible for a female to be perfect for more than one male, and so they fought to get her to be theirs exclusively. If that wasn't possible, they would try and abduct the woman and keep her with them until the bonding had been enacted."

"And the women just stand for this?"

Zig smiled, "When it happens, you will know. You will do whatever it takes to get your male and nothing will stand in your way. A ninety-eight percent chance is way better than the odds of knowing that a Gaian man is meant for you."

Tiera leaned back, "So, you have embraced becoming one of the Nine completely then?"

Ziggy shook herself and sat up. "In the last few days, I have learned more about space, the races who live out here and the history of our world than I had ever imagined. The Nine came here because they wanted to know what could possibly attract the Tokkel to their old world. They stayed because we showed potential to become more than simple colonists on a tempting world."

The word *potential* suddenly snapped Tiera into understanding. "You are the reason that they are here. You are our Potential, Ziggy."

Her friend's blush was enough proof. "It wasn't my idea."

Tiera laughed. "I know it wasn't, but it is weird how things turn out. If you hadn't been going to get those crocuses for your mom, you wouldn't have been taken, wouldn't have escaped and wouldn't have met Rothaway for the first time. You have always been so very special, and you spent your time hiding it. I am glad that it is out in the light of day."

They sat in silence until Tiera couldn't stand it anymore and dragged in a deep breath. "Fine, so what do the women of the People of the Air look like? What colour are their wings?"

"Only the men have wings. It is sexist, but it is how they evolved."

Tiera leaned forward and whispered, "How sexually compatible are they with Gaians?"

"I don't know if it is because of three generations growing up on Gaia changed our bits to match but we fit together very well. Any minor shifts are being corrected by the blood exchange."

They chatted about minor matters, the rumour mill that was talking about Ziggy's sudden departure from the surface. Many folks said she was being arrested for war crimes, and in a funny way, they were right. If she hadn't assaulted Rothaway to knock him out, none of this would have happened.

"So, why is he going to get me clothing? I brought plenty of stuff."

Ziggy grinned, "They are not impressed with Gaian clothing. They like their women to look like women and not cargo operators on leave."

"Hey, I have some very nice stuff."

Ziggy patted her arm. "I am sure you do, but just wait until you get to wear some Wilder formal wear. You will feel all delicate and weird."

A suspicion filled Tiera. "Is he trying to set me up with someone?"

Zig shook her head, "No. They don't do that sort of thing. Every male is responsible for his own female. If they are compatible but there is some hesitation on her part, he kisses her in front of witnesses and that is equivalent to an engagement. Since they don't touch casually, it is a fairly serious thing."

After some less serious conversation, Ziggy showed her how to find the porn on the entertainment unit by looking at the tiny logo on the left side. A strange squiggly icon was now burned in her mind. The documentaries had an option for Gaian language, and Ziggy blinked in surprise.

"That's new. It wasn't there when I got here."

"They knew you could understand their language. Or they suspected. My guess is that whatever I eat, drink or watch in here is going to be recorded or at least observed."

Ziggy was about to say something else when there was a knock on the door. She went and opened it, allowing her mate and his parcels inside.

Apparently, it was time to dress for dinner.

Chapter Four

"Okay, I have to admit it. Rothaway has an eye for sizes. Does this look all right?" Tiera turned from side to side and took in the grey gown that set off her dark hair.

"You look lovely. The Wilder clothes suit you." Ziggy was behind her, wearing a dark rainbow version of the same gown.

"All the races have a different set of clothing?"

"Yup. Just like miners and caterers don't use the same outfits at weddings." Ziggy started to fiddle with Tiera's hair, and in three minutes, her hair was wearing a similar braided arrangement to Ziggy's.

"What is that for?"

"You are being considered a member of Rothaway's family, and as such, you have to dress the part."

"I am part of the family?" Tiera grinned. "I am pretty sure that I would have noticed a shifter at my last event."

Ziggy smiled, "You are definitely one of my family, and so now, you are his family too."

Tiera sighed and took in the complete image that she presented in the mirror. Gauzy sleeves flowed down in a grey that held a rich shimmer. Grey had always been her colour, and so, she turned from side to side once again. "Well, my brother-in-law chose well. This is a good dress."

Ziggy laughed and gave her a quick hug.

Tiera and her friend left her quarters giggling. Rothaway was waiting in the hall. He had wanted them to enjoy absolute privacy when Ziggy explained the closures of the undergarments. It was very thoughtful of him.

"So, why is there a council dinner, and why do I have to be there?" Tiera was walking to one side of Ziggy, and she asked the question out of the corner of her mouth.

Rothaway answered her. "The rest of the council is curious as to whether or not all Gaian females are as charming as Signy."

Tiera winced, "They are going to be disappointed."

Ziggy smiled, "You will be fine. I will be right there in case anything goes wrong."

Tiera took a deep breath and centred herself. "I really hope so."

Fate wasn't kind, but it did have a sense of humour. Tiera was sitting as far away from Ziggy as it was possible to be. The only bright side was that Tonos was next to her on a chair that allowed his wings to extend behind him.

"I am glad to see you again, Miss Tiera."

She smiled at the way he pronounced her name. He made it sound like *Mysteera.* It made her want to have him read the alphabet to her over and over.

"It is good to have a friendly face nearby, Tonos. This crowd looks to be a little on the hostile side." She smiled brightly at him as she spoke in low tones.

"I will protect you, no matter what happens." He reached out and touched her hand.

She watched the shiver ripple over his skin again and noted the darkening of his wings. "Should you be doing that?"

He looked up at her, his leafy green eyes innocent. "Doing what?"

"Touching me. I have heard it is not a common activity up here."

A snide voice from across the table interrupted them. "It figures that a flitter would be trying to seduce one of the new race."

Tiera snapped into a cold mode. She looked at the woman with the tree-bark-like skin. The man next to her spoke in liquid tones, and they laughed together.

Tonos was about to speak but she placed her hand on his.

"It is amazing how rude so-called evolved races can be. Speaking in the language of the Forest while everyone around you understands the language of the Nine or Gaian is exceptionally impolite. Were you raised in a field? Did no one guide you as you grew, or were you gestated on a dung heap?"

The female gasped and darkened in colour. Her male smiled slightly.

"You too, twig-man. You were the one to change language first. Know when someone is ill at ease."

The woman leaned forward and hissed. "You are only here because your friend is whoring herself with a Wilder."

That was the last straw. Tiera got to her feet, slammed her hands on the table and leaned forward. "Bring it, bitch."

Ziggy was worried, but Rothaway tried to keep her calm.

"She will be fine, Signy. No one here will harm her."

Ziggy placed her hand on the ordering pad and selected her meal. They had added several Gaian selections in the last two days, and she was relieved to see old favourites.

"It isn't the harm. It is the insults. I am well aware that my addition here is mostly due to your position."

"It is due to your skill, my heart."

"Whatever. Many folks here consider us beneath them. I have been reading the news reports, Rothaway."

He sipped at his beverage with a smile, "It is mainly the women. The fact that you can bond to one of us is shaking up a certain inbred smugness that many of the women have. They were used to having their pick of the men, and if their males can find a perfect match with a Gaian female, they will be a little upset."

Ziggy grumped. "I still can't understand while she is way down at the end of the table."

"You took too long to get ready. They had seated most of the higher ranks and only held the positions for us. She is lucky to be near Tonos, at least he will talk to her."

She was about to reply when she heard her friend's strident tone.

"Bring it, bitch."

Ziggy winced and looked down the table to where Tiera was standing and bristling with rage. The eye contact that she was engaging in meant only one thing, and when the Forest woman bowed her head and her mate followed suit, Ziggy giggled.

Tiera sighed, met Ziggy's gaze from down the table and winked before she sat down.

Rothaway was cautious, "What was that?"

"I am not the only one with a talent, my dearest." Ziggy smiled as her meal appeared from within the table.

Suddenly, she was a lot more confident of Tiera's ability to fit in.

"I beg your pardon? I have never seen Lady Thenotha bow her head to anyone, let alone a tagalong Gaian."

Ziggy held her utensils and arranged her food to her liking. "Didn't I mention that Tiera has the ability to make folks see things her way? Must have slipped my mind."

Rothaway cupped her chin and turned her head. "She has a talent for . . ."

"Making sure that her way of thinking is accepted. If she is right, the change is permanent. If she is wrong, it wears off in a few hours. Either way,

Tiera is in for a hostility-free evening." She grinned, gave him a peck on the lips and returned to her meal.

She gestured with her elbow. "Eat your dinner, it is getting cold."

He laughed and followed her instructions. The rest of the gathering was talking in low tones, but no one said anything against Tiera, and so Ziggy simply enjoyed having a meal and discussing the politics of the Nine with those around her.

After dinner, she could find out what the hell Tiera had been thinking.

Tiera bristled with rage and sent her offence, confusion and distress to the woman across from her.

There was some overspill to the woman's mate, but Tiera kept her cone of irritation aimed at the woman. When her target bowed her head, Tiera winked at Ziggy from across the room and resumed her seat.

Tonos took her hand, "Miss Tiera, what was that?"

She held up her finger against his palm as a plea for patience.

The woman across from her cleared her throat. "I apologise. I am Lady Thenotha of the Forest people, and this is my mate, Lord Arothian."

"I am Tiera of Gaia. This is Tonos, my companion for the dinner."

The males exchanged greetings, and Tonos explained to her how to order dinner.

A few heads turned their way while they were eating, but by the end of the meal, everyone seemed to have forgotten her little outburst.

As they sat back and laughed over dessert, one of the Rock Folk next to them told the dirtiest jokes in Gaian that Tiera had ever heard, but it was a good night all around.

The moment that the folks at the head of the table started to drift away, Tiera sighed. Her freaky evening had ended up being fun. Tonos had held her hand at every opportunity, and Warrock had kept them in stitches with his tall tales of sexual exploits.

When Rothaway and Ziggy came to retrieve her, she didn't want to go, and to her shock, Tonos didn't want to let her.

Chapter Five

The moment that Tiera stood, Tonos clamped a hand around her wrist. She twisted her wrist in his grip but he held on. "What are you doing?"

Rothaway spoke calmly, "Tonos, unhand her, and get yourself to medical."

Tiera blinked in shock when Tonos bent forward and his wing swung out toward Rothaway.

The Wilder seemed to be on the lookout for the motion, and Rothaway jumped back, keeping his body between Ziggy and the metallic wing.

"What the hell, Tonos? What happened to your wings? They weren't like this when we sat down." Tiera was trying to calm him down, but a red light was glowing in his green eyes.

"They are as they are meant to be, Miss Tiera. Nothing that should worry you. I will protect you. I told you that."

Rothaway said something to a nearby Wilder, and the other male nodded. "Tiera, I think we should take a tour of medical. You and Tonos can come behind us. We will lead if that is all right."

Ziggy had a worried expression on her face, and that convinced Tiera that something was beyond wrong. "That sounds wonderful. I am sure that Tonos would be happy to escort me."

It was amazing when she looked at Tonos that he had completely transformed from the good-natured winged man who had met her at the shuttle. His hair formed a wide halo, his pointed ears were exposed and literally twitching with every sound, his body was more massive and his wings held a metallic sheen that had been absent when she arrived.

Tonos shook his head. "They want to treat me, to make this go away. I won't let them."

Ziggy cleared her throat. "No, Tonos. Now that Tiera has exposed her talent to manipulate, she needs to be recorded for the archives of the Nine. It is protocol to record all new psychic evolutions, no matter the race."

He blinked, and his eyes focussed. "Of course. I will take you to medical and make sure that you are not harmed."

Ziggy and Rothaway led the way, Tonos and Tiera followed and the Wilder that Rothaway had spoken to made a call on one of the wall terminals.

Their procession was slow, and no one tried to halt them. "Is it normal for the halls to be this empty?"

Tonos growled, "They have been alerted that I am unstable. The halls have been cleared all the way to medical so no one is injured."

He seemed to be more coherent and less instinctive.

"What is going on? I know that you are exhibiting signs of finding your mate, but I am the only one here."

He paused and turned to her. "You honestly can't feel it?"

She blinked and then gasped when he surged toward her and bent her back in a kiss that stole her breath and her ability to think coherently.

When he righted her, he smiled and the pointed teeth that were endemic to the Nine were exposed. "Does that clarify things?"

She blinked. "No. But I want to try whatever you had for dessert."

He laughed and some more sanity came back to him.

As they turned to re-join their companions, Rothaway looked resigned, and Ziggy looked horrified. The councillor turned his wife, and they continued to lead the way to medical.

Tonos's grip on her hand was still warm and still sent pulses of energy up her arm, but she didn't mind. Despite what her logic said, her instincts were screaming that he was the only one for her.

"Do your people put out pheromones?"

"Yes. They help in the seduction process. Are they working?" His amusement was palpable.

She blushed to her toes and was convinced that he could gauge exactly how far the colouration went. Fortunately for her, they arrived at medical at that moment.

Standing in the gel-lined container with an audience was a little weird, but the tall woman executing the exam was encouraging. "Breathe, Tiera MacKenzie. We need regular baselines."

"I will breathe if Tonos gets whatever shot he needs. I am not going to give you a baseline until he calms down and his wings are no longer deadly."

Tonos flicked his wings out. "No. I don't want it to stop."

"Fine, don't stop it, but slow it down. I am not going anywhere for a while."

His wings shifted and made the sound of steel sliding on steel.

She crossed her arms from within the safety of the scanner. "I am not getting out of here unless you take that shot or supplement or whatever."

The giantess moved to a cabinet and prepared something that looked like a gun. "I will administer the shot now, Tonos, if you are willing."

From within the capsule, Tiera focussed her peculiar talent on Tonos, and he nodded. "I will take the shot."

When Dr. Meevin moved and gave Tonos the shot, Rothaway reached out to catch him. His wings quivered, and they began to return to normal.

Tiera nodded and leaned back to begin her scans. She made herself feel as normal as she could and relaxed into the embrace of the gel.

It took less than ten minutes for the scanners to chirp and the machine to right itself and release her.

Dr. Meevin was stunned, "We have never seen a psychic talent of this nature. You can actually force people around to your way of thinking."

Tiera grinned, "It has been very handy in dealing with weddings. I can use my thoughts to bully folks into doing what I want. It isn't subtle or graceful, but it gets the job done."

Dr. Meevin shook her head. "This changes everything about your stay here, as well as your interaction with Tonos. It was no wonder he fell for you, you radiate power, my dear."

Ziggy grinned, "I told you so."

Tiera exited the pod and walked back into the main area of medical, cautiously approaching Tonos.

Rothaway stopped her. "It would be best if you didn't touch him again, not until he is in complete control of himself."

"Um, what next?"

Ziggy took her arm. "I take you back to your quarters and get you tucked in, and then, we try and figure this out in the morning."

"The morning sounds non-threatening. Let's try that." She yawned and was only too happy to have her friend escort her to her quarters.

Tonos was sitting up, and he smiled and waved farewell as they left him with Rothaway.

"Will he be okay?"

Ziggy sighed. "He will be fine. Rothaway went through five years of the suppressing agent after all. He came through it okay."

Tiera let her friend rush her out of medical and down the hall. Rothaway would take care of Tonos.

"Are you all right?"

Tonos nodded. "That serum has a kick, but I am feeling more lucid."

"Excellent."

Tonos rubbed the back of his neck and looked up at his friend. "Did I really claim her in front of you?"

"You made your intentions plain. She's yours."

He grinned and flicked his wings. "Excellent. I can do a slow courtship, but knowing that she will be on record as officially mine will help keep the transformation at bay."

Rothaway laughed, "Good luck with that. Just smelling Signy wore on my self-control. If you want to engage in a courtship, I would speed it up, not slow it down."

He nodded as he absorbed the idea of a fast track to his woman. "Thanks for the advice. Where is she?"

"Ziggy took her back to her rooms. She is fine, safe. You don't need to worry."

Tonos shuddered as he remembered his actions, "Did I destroy any chance of an easy union with my actions?"

Rothaway clapped him on the shoulder. "If she had not been aware of what was going on, perhaps . . . but I know for a fact that your prospective lady knew what was happening every time you two touched."

"She did?"

"She did. Signy was quite firm on the fact that she had told Tiera what touching you could mean. Apparently, Tiera does not find you objectionable and initiated contact with you several times according to your dinner partners."

Hope and relief warred in Tonos's mind. "Really?"

Rothaway grinned, "Really. Now, as soon as we get you checked out and stabilized, I will get you back to your quarters and join my bride in mine."

Tonos turned to face the scowling Dr. Meevin and surrendered to his boss's ministrations. She was businesslike, thorough and by the time she was finished stabilizing him, he felt almost normal again.

"Thanks, Doc." He flexed his wings as the chemical reaction that had hardened them slowly reversed.

"You should have come to me the moment you saw the signs, Tonos. You know better."

He groaned and rubbed his face with both hands. "I didn't think that this was possible. I mean I bumped into plenty of Gaians during the ceremonies the day before yesterday and nothing happened."

Dr. Meevin shook her head. "You have also *bumped* into plenty women of the Nine. You know that the bonding isn't mandatory after contact. It is chance, happenstance, nothing more."

Tonos smiled and looked at the only physician on board who had bothered learning about Gaian physiology. "No, my dear Doctor, it is fate."

Chapter Six

After two hours of girl time, Tiera felt that she and Ziggy were finally working on the same wavelength.

"So, you saw all the signs that Tonos was attaching to you, and you didn't say anything? You are either brave or stupid, Tier." Ziggy was sitting on the couch with her feet up and her gown pooling under her.

Tiera lifted a glass of wine to her friend and smiled. "I am thinking a bit of both. I should have told you, but the odds were so remote as to be ridiculous, right?"

Ziggy grinned, "You know, he wasn't even supposed to be the one to meet you at the shuttle."

"He wasn't?"

"Nope. One of the Forest Folk was assigned, but he pulled duty on the bridge at the last minute due to a staffing shortage. Tonos is a battlefield medic, so he has most of his time off as long as he does drills and exercises."

Tiera absently licked her lower lip. "That explains why he is in such good shape."

Ziggy laughed. "No, that is all due to his being one of the People of the Air. He has to be fit to fly. If the others want to be insulting, they call them flitters."

"They are the Fairies of our folklore, aren't they?"

Ziggy nodded and held out her glass for more wine. "They are indeed, as are the Giants, Dryads, Dwarves, were-creatures, Mermen, the Balance and, of course, the Darkness."

"Balance? Darkness? I haven't heard anything about them in the news vids and certainly didn't see any at dinner." Tiera watched as Ziggy got rapidly tipsy.

"They are around, but they keep to themselves. They don't bother with the other races, but I have heard they are pretty impressive in battle."

A knock on the door brought their girl talk to a halt. With a grin, Tiera greeted Rothaway and gestured for him to take his bride back to their rooms. "She is an easy drunk. Never could hold her liquor."

He scooped Ziggy up carefully and smiled at Tiera. "Thank you for coming to the ship. She was a little adrift when she first arrived. You have given her the anchor that she needed."

Tiera grinned, "You are that anchor now, I am merely a buoy that helps her find her location. Once she sails past me into clear water, she won't need me anymore."

He frowned. "I don't understand."

"It is a nautical reference, just get Ziggy to explain it when she wakes up. She knows everything."

He inclined his head and smiled ruefully as Ziggy started to snore delicately.

Tiera covered her mouth as a belly laugh started, and she saw him out. Ziggy would call her in the morning, and the sight of that huge man looking down at her friend made Tiera smile the whole way through her evening routine right until she tucked herself into bed.

The knock woke her from a restless dream that featured fluttering wings and a kiss that tasted like berries.

She flipped back the covers and padded to the door in her t-shirt. She opened it and smiled, but her smile froze on her face. "Tonos, what are you doing here?"

He inclined his head. "I thought to continue your tour of the ship. No contact, I promise."

She looked down and blushed furiously. "I will get dressed. Give me a moment."

She beat a retreat to the bedroom and quickly dug through her clothing to find something with long sleeves and a pair of casual pants. She scooped up her underwear and headed for the lav.

The blast of energy and light cleaned her from the sleep and oils of the night, and her hair went into a braid quickly.

Why she was so eager to see him again after the debacle of last night was beyond her, but she slithered into her trousers and pulled on the loose shirt with a deliberate air of concealment.

Whether he had seen her body outlined or not, today he was seeing her buttoned down and unapproachable. It had worked for her for years, and she was willing to test it on a warrior of the Nine.

He blinked in surprise when she came out of the bedroom. "You look . . . comfortable."

She smiled. "Now that your link has been undone, I thought concealment and avoiding contact was the best option."

He nodded. "It can't hurt. Now, would you like breakfast here or near the observatory?"

She grinned. "The observatory, please." Her mind screamed at her that this was a stupid idea. She was nowhere near her comfort zone when it came to being in a new area, and yet, her hormones jumped up and down at the thought of being near him.

She was wearing running shoes, socks, loose slacks and a loose-weave, baggy, button-down shirt. The shirt cuffs were long enough to cover her palms, and that made it safe in her mind.

She smiled brightly and walked past him and into the hallway.

Everyone that they passed was wearing a uniform or gown, but she kept her head high and walked at Tonos's side.

"So, how did you find medical last night?" Tonos's question caught her by surprise.

"Um, it was fine, I suppose. I have no idea what she was measuring, but I hope she found everything she was looking for."

"What is the nature of your talent, precisely?"

Tiera laughed, "I wondered when you would ask that and not be all weird and creepy about it. My talent as far as I know is to convince people to come around to my way of thinking. It wears off if I am doing it to manipulate, but if I am insistent or believe in what I am saying, it sticks. The change becomes permanent when they accept what I have done to their train of thought. Mind you, if I am just trying to get them to shut up, it wears off when they realise I was not correct."

"Have you done it to me?"

She blinked, "No. I don't recall thinking much while you are around. I seem to fly along on instinct."

His grin made her groan. "Please tell me I didn't just say that."

He showed more of his shiny, white teeth.

"Aw geez. I hereby retract my last statement."

"Too late, it is embedded in my memory. Now, would you prefer to walk the rest of the way or take the pod?"

"How long is it?"

"That is a personal question." His smile was still in evidence.

She sighed and refrained from smacking him by an extreme effort of will. "How long a walk, Tonos?"

"Ten minutes."

"Then walk we shall." She was about to stride off but realised she didn't know where she was going. "Either catch up or I return to my quarters." He laughed, and together, they went off in search of breakfast.

Chapter Seven

It took them two hours to finish laughing and talking over an endless parade of delicacies and teas. The Nine took breakfast very seriously.

Tiera felt a little uncomfortable wearing such loose clothing when everyone around her was wearing semi-formal wear. She finally asked, "Isn't there a version of the Nine clothing that isn't elegant or formfitting?"

Tonos sat back and sipped his tea. "Not on the mother ship. We save casual clothing for when we are ground bound. Up here, we are all on duty whether there is an active battle or not. We dress accordingly."

She winced. "So, my clothing choice?"

"Is not appropriate, but you are not a member of the crew and so you can wear what you wish."

She sighed. "Is there any option for me that will keep us from touching but let me fit in a little bit more?"

He grinned, "I thought you would never ask. Come along."

He got to his feet, pressed his fingers to the pay pad, and they walked out together.

Tiera could feel the heat of his hand against her spine, but he never actually made contact. It was frustrating and intriguing all at the same time.

They were in a commercial centre—kiosks, cafes and small shops lined the walkway.

With him herding her along, they ended up in a shop that held clothing in a vast array of configurations. "Rikkait. I need a morph suit for the new Gaian representative."

A man made of shadows drifted forward and bowed. "I see. What sort of colouring do you have in mind? Her skin will take to almost anything dark and strong."

When a tendril of the darkness touched her hand, she blinked in surprise. "What the hell."

"Rikkait. Stop that, or you will infringe on my claim on her, and a challenge will be in the air."

The tendril immediately retreated. "I apologise, Tonos, but you understand that I had to try."

"Understood, but try it again, and you will be looking at the stars through a pierced veil of darkness."

Tiera had to ask, "What is going on?"

Tonos moved toward her, and the shadow receded. "Rikkait was trying to see if you were a compatible female, and when I informed him of my claim, he did the polite thing and ceased his efforts."

"I thought that after your treatment you . . ." She lifted her hands in a helpless gesture.

"That I would no longer be affected by you? You are very mistaken. In fact, proximity to you has been wearing on my self-control since I first saw you this morning."

Rikkait extended his shadowy arms, and a deep purple suit was draped across them. "This should fit the bill. It is one of my newest and is very flattering to anyone who wears it."

Tonos took it from him and handed it to Tiera. "There is a changing room in the back. You can try it on in there. Rikkait will remain out here with me."

It took all of the tricks that Ziggy had shown her last night, but she managed to do up the closures until she was in a skin-tight suit that rippled and clasped her body faithfully until it was no longer a piece of fabric but was now her second skin.

The collar was high, and all of her skin was concealed. The cuffs extended down across the back of her hand in a sort of fingerless glove. It would allow her to do everything that she needed to do without getting in her way.

With an armload of folded clothing, she returned to the front of the small shop. "I think it fits?"

Tonos had been speaking quietly when she emerged, but he fell silent and simply stared at her.

Rikkait made a small laugh. "You look lovely. Shall I have those clothes sent to your room?"

"Can you do that? I don't even know where it is."

She assumed that he smiled, but he pulled forth one of the ubiquitous hand pads. "Please press your hand in the centre, and I will have your address to have the clothing returned to you so that you may continue your tour."

She handed him the clothing and shadows wrapped it as he took it behind the counter, sealed it in a bag and entered her address into the computer before placing the parcel on it and letting it slip away.

"Is the whole ship rigged like that?"

Tonos smiled and bowed for her to precede him from the shop. "More or less. All the habitation areas are linked for deliveries of that nature. Our uniforms do not have pockets and the belts that we wear are for devices relating to our work."

She nodded and tried not to rub the surface of the fabric. "Are you sure it looks all right?"

"It looks lovely. You simply look like a crewmember on their day off." He smiled, and they left the shop. "Now, we will continue our tour."

She loosened her hair, and it flowed around her, covering her breasts and her spine to mid-back. "That is a little better. I don't feel so exposed."

Tonos looked distinctly uncomfortable, but he smiled, "Your hair is lovely. Do you wear it down often?"

They passed a number of other couples on a promenade, and she gasped when she saw the expanse of the gardens. "Oh my."

She processed his question and smiled. "I wear it down when I feel like I am running around naked."

He cleared his throat. "I see. Do you like gardens?"

She smiled and walked to the railing that looked out over what appeared to be the vegetable garden. "I love gardens. I spend every moment I can in our garden growing food for the events. I almost like gardening more than cooking."

He leaned next to her and his wings fluttered slightly. "How do you spend your evenings on Gaia?"

"We go to dances, I spend a lot of time at the library, watching vids and preparing for events. Normal stuff. What do you do on the ship?"

He leaned out to watch a person below gather a basket of tubers. "I exercise, watch the entertainment unit, go drinking with friends and I fly. The People of the Air have monthly events to gather and compete here on the ship."

She smiled. "It sounds like a summer fair."

"Here, it is summer all year round. It is quite a pleasant environment."

He was smiling in the most charming manner. His wings lazily opened and closed, and she shivered as she started to catalogue the most likely sexual positions that a man with wings would have to use.

Blinking furiously, she straightened, "Shall we continue the tour?"

Tonos nodded. "Of course. Next stop is the transport pod. We will see all of the living zones that we missed on your first day. What happened there, anyway?"

They moved at a leisurely pace toward the pod and rail. "I am a little sensitive to new environments. My emotional reactions shut down, and it takes a while to process all the new information. As soon as I catch up and orient myself, I am usually fine."

She tucked herself into the pod and smiled as he adjusted himself until his wings were settled comfortably. The pod slipped off, and in no time, they were off into the interior of the massive ship carrying thousands of warriors, their families and support staff into space.

It was a fun way to spend an afternoon, and by the end of the day, just a look from Tonos and she was wishing that the barrier against touching didn't exist.

Chapter Eight

When they entered the Wilder zone of the ship, she looked around curiously. "So this is where Ziggy lives?"

He laughed, "No, this is where the Wilder live. The Councillor Rothaway and Signy have their quarters in the VIP zone near where you are staying."

The pod cruised through on a slower track than the commuter units that whizzed past.

"Ah. But these mock forests are their environments?"

"Yes. It makes each race more comfortable to have the environment they were born in represented on the ship. It keeps us grounded, so to speak." He reached out to touch her cheek, but he pulled his hand back at the last minute.

She bit her lip. "It is difficult, isn't it?"

"It is the hardest thing that I have ever endured." His lips twisted in a rueful smile. "To think, all those years of flirting and the woman I was destined for was going to walk right up to me."

The pod continued on its little tour, stopping at the VIP zone and opening to let them out.

When they stood to leave the pod, she had to ask. "Are you sure? I mean really, really sure?"

"I have never been surer of anything in my . . . mmphff."

Tiera lunged toward him, slid her hand into his hair and pressed a kiss to his hard mouth before he could say anything else.

His body trembled and his wings flicked restlessly. He wrapped his arms around her and crushed her to him while she continued to stroke his lips with her own, occasionally flicking her tongue against the seam of his lips.

Tonos dragged a deep breath into his lungs, and the hands on her back gripped her, pulling her back to create a distance between them. His chest was rising and falling rapidly as he struggled for control.

"Step away from him, Tier." Ziggy's voice was calm, and she was standing next to her mate.

"I believe you have something to ask me, Tonos." Rothaway scowled at him.

Tonos helped her out of the pod and down the steps of the platform with one hand holding hers.

Tiera looked earnestly at Rothaway, "Please tell me that he isn't it trouble. It was all my fault. I kissed him."

Rothaway nodded. "We know. We saw. He still has to ask me something. He knows the protocol."

Tonos nodded and stepped in front of Tiera. "Lord Rothaway, may I have the hand of your charge in legal and moral bonding?"

Ziggy was grinning.

Rothaway inclined his head. "Provided that you honour her and keep her safe."

Rothaway winced as Ziggy drove her elbow into his side. "And you will have to allow my mate unlimited access to your lady."

"Of course. So, it is approved then?"

"It is."

"You will act as my second?"

"My mate and I will witness and guard you."

Tonos grinned. "Thank you for the honour."

Tiera poked him. "What is going on?"

Ziggy snorted, "Tonos just proposed to you via Rothaway, and my darling husband accepted due to your confirmation through the initialization of the kiss with Tonos in front of witnesses. You said yes, so he has the right to wed you. It is backward from the Gaian standard, but everyone gets their say."

Tiera blinked. "Just like that?"

Ziggy laughed. "Come along. We will get you dressed for your mating and by then Tonos should have finished the chemical flush at medical that will allow him a normal wedding night."

The blush that fired her cheeks made her friend laugh. "Wait. What will I tell my mom?"

"Tell her that you are getting married to one of the Nine. She will be upset and probably want to cater a reception on Gaia, but she will get over it if you are happy." Ziggy grinned. "Shall we go and make that call?"

It went surprisingly well until Tiera mentioned that she was marrying a Fairy.

"He's gay, dear?"

"No, Mom. He has huge wings like a Terran dragonfly. I have never actually seen him fly, but I have seen others of his race zipping around the mother ship."

"I don't know what the hurry is."

Tiera debated how to tell her mother and settled on, "It is a tradition of the Nine. We had dinner and a date and now we are getting married."

"Why can't you wait?"

"It isn't the way they do things, Mom." An image filled Tiera's mind of her mother meeting Tonos for the first time with his wings deadly silver and his eyes red. Oh, that would go over well.

"Can we at least meet him?"

"After the wedding, Mom. I will have him make arrangements to come for a visit. Is that okay?"

Her mother sighed heavily. "If you are happy, then I am happy. I just wish I had made his acquaintance before you decided he was the one for you."

"He is a good guy, Mom, and a medic, so he has a good job." Tiera had no idea if that was true, but it sounded plausible.

To one side where Teva could not see her, Ziggy was chortling silently. Tiera looked around for something to throw at her friend and then got an idea. "I can stay up here with Ziggy. She is so lonely, Mom. It's sad really."

A cushion flipped and landed squarely in Tiera's face. Teva grinned on the other end of the connection. "Well, if you girls are having fun up there and you are sure that this is the man for you, we will wait until you can make it down here to have a party, but we will have a reception for you, Tiera, make no mistake about that."

The threat was in the air, and looking into her mother's determined face, she knew that if she and Tonos did not make it down to Gaia in short order, Teva and Renault would make their way up to the mother ship, and they would bring the whole neighbourhood with them.

"I love you, Mom. Never doubt that. Thanks for wanting me to be happy."

Teva smiled, "And if he doesn't make you happy, Nine or not, we will come up and kick his ass."

It was Teva's standard *I love you,* and Tiera, with tears in her eyes, waved goodbye to her mother.

As the screen went blank, a chirp near the lav got her attention, and she saw the box provided by the delivery chute. The moment that she removed the parcel, the slot closed and became almost invisible against the wall.

"What is this?"

Ziggy took the box from her and put it on the bed. When she opened it, her smile ended in wobbling tears.

"It is a bonding gown for the People of the Air. You get into the shower, and I will lay out the pieces. It will go on better if we can get the layers on in the proper order the first time."

Bemused by her friend's knowledge of the clothing, Tiera went into the lav and took a quick shower of light and air.

It was her wedding day, and she wanted everything to go right.

Chapter Nine

The knock on the door froze both ladies in place.

Tiera looked up at Ziggy, and her friend since grade school smiled. "At least you know what you are getting into. I am learning more about Rothaway's ways with every day, but it is still an adjustment. It will be nice to have another Gaian to share the fun with and even better to have my best friend with me in this new world."

"I will always be there for you, Ziggy, even if we are worlds apart." Tiera reached up and squeezed Ziggy's hand the moment that her friend finished the hairstyle of the People of the Air.

"Same here, Tiera. You can come to me with any questions. You know that I can find the answers."

They laughed and hugged before walking to the door and greeting their men.

The attendant at the entrance of the bonding garden took in Tonos's wild appearance and handed Rothaway the privacy lock.

They walked quietly to the gardens, and Tiera threw cautious glances to Tonos. He seemed under control, but his wings had their blade-like appearance, and his eyes were rimmed with red once again.

As they reached the edge of the gardens, Rothaway pressed a soft kiss on her forehead, and Ziggy kissed her cheek.

Tonos led her into the gardens and following Ziggy's earlier direction when they were putting on the three silk under dresses, the heavy silk over dress and the corset, she breathed deeply of the flowers that seemed to be always in bloom on this part of the ship.

"Tonos, are you sure that you want this?" They were approaching the altar with the hilt of a knife sticking out of it.

"I am sure. While I found Signy fascinating when I met her, I believe now it was because you were imprinted on her mind, and it bled out into the air around her."

His fangs made his speech precise and slow. They had grown a quarter of an inch since she had seen him earlier in the day.

They stood in front of the altar, and he turned to face her.

She shivered as she realised that if a woman could stand in front of one of the Nine in rut and manage not to scream and run, it must be love.

"Take the dagger from the stone." His voice was a low rumble.

She followed his direction and hefted the knife that had a rough surface on the handle to catch her genetic code.

"Cut my wrist, here." He showed her the point and helped her line up the dagger for the quick slice.

When blood beaded and coursed down his wrist, he lifted her hand and the dagger it clutched, and he bit down sharply.

She inhaled, the floral scent swept through her in a wave, allowing her to calmly watch as he connected their wounds so that her blood became his and his hers.

Dizziness washed through her, and she buckled as details of his life flicked into her mind. Memories that were not hers started to work through her, and she saw the elegant home with its tall spires on an alien world, rich clothing and a formal court filled with elaborately clothed women and men with huge, fluttering wings.

"Tiera, Tiera, are you all right?" He was holding her, and the red was still in his eyes but concern was overriding his lust.

"I am fine. I was just unprepared for your memories. They overwhelmed me."

He frowned but spoke gently. "Put the dagger back in the stone and we are officially wed."

It took her two tries, but when the dagger slipped into the stone and it lowered beyond her sight, she sighed with relief. Her body was still weak and tingling from the wash of memories, and when he lifted her in his arms, she smiled as the feeling of being secure and protected surrounded her.

He walked to the edge of the shielded area, and when Rothaway saw them coming, he opened the barrier.

He tried to block Tonos's progress, but to Tiera's shock, Tonos's wings hummed, and they lifted into the air.

The feeling of security kept her calm as he flew them across the gardens that filled the centre of the ship, and they approached the zone of the People of the Air. They flew down halls and past startled occupants as they flattened themselves against the walls to allow him to pass.

Tiera was afraid of distracting him, and his intense face was far too grim for her to interrupt him while he flew.

He settled lightly in front of a door that had a strange glyph on it. "Open the lock."

She blinked and smiled as it came to her that he had put her biometrics in his rooms already.

The door slid open, and he walked inside with a long stride. The interior was a mix of soft gold, greys and blues. They were the same colours that were active in her gown.

He set her on her feet, and she looked around quickly, taking in the location and the view of the gardens from the wide balcony windows.

"You could have just flown here."

He chuckled and came up behind her, pressing his hands to her shoulders and kissing her neck. "I could have, but then you wouldn't know where we lived, and that would make your knowledge of the area incomplete."

A tear came to her eye as she realised that his courtship, the tour, it had all been part of easing her into knowledge of the mother ship.

As his lips trailed up her neck, and he turned her in his arms, she looked up into his green eyes rimmed with the red of his rut and smiled, "Now, Tonos, you can answer a question for me."

He smiled down at her, and his gaze heated as she moved close to him, rocking her hips against him and sliding her arms up his back, stroking the base of his wings lightly.

"What can I answer for you, bondmate?"

She blushed and leaned up to whisper against his neck, "How many ways can a man with wings have sex? I have to admit that it has been a pressing question for me."

His body went rigid for a moment before he lifted her up to meet his gaze eye to eye. "I will do the work, you keep count. Fair enough?"

She laughed, and he carried her into his bedroom, demonstrating that he was far more familiar with the clothing that she was wearing than she was.

When the final layer of silk was all that stood between her skin and his, he slowed down and caressed, touched and kissed each inch of her that was exposed while removing the final obstacle.

She shivered with heat by the time he moved over her and joined their bodies. They rocked, twisted and writhed together, and he held her arms over her head when her caresses on his wings became too much for him.

Her mind spun as she started to come back to herself after leaving her body and whirling through the stars. The best part had been that Tonos was with her, and when he looked into her eyes with his own clear, green ones, she leaned up, kissed him and whispered, "One."

His grin ceased before he pinned her to the bed and rolled her to her side. As he lifted her leg and entered her again, she shivered at the intensity that rolled through her.

By morning, the count was up to five, and it only stayed there because she was not willing to have him with her in the lav. Having a seat on the vanity to allow him in was tempting, but she was sore, sticky and as she told him, "There are so many more days before us."

When she tiptoed out of the lav with a sheet covering her, Tonos smiled and gestured to the delivery slot. "There is a new dress for you as well as some shoes."

With a little help from him, she managed to get herself dressed as a woman of the People of the Air, or Air Folk if she was feeling casual.

"How do I look?"

He grinned, pulled her in for a kiss and said, "You look like mine."

She laughed. "I am glad that you think so, because we are going to have to go to Gaia to prove to my family that you are mine. Ziggy may be held her as the Potential, but I am not, and my mom is a little confused as to why I would fall for a man I had just met."

His normally cocky behaviour wobbled. "You want your family to meet me?"

She started to laugh and slowly trailed her fingers down his chest. "We can live here, work here, do whatever you want to here, but they have to see us, to see us happy."

"Are you happy?" There was vulnerability in his eyes that caused an ache in her heart.

"I cannot imagine me feeling more for anyone in the universe. If that is not happy, I don't know what is."

He chuckled and spun her around in his arms, and despite the discomfort, they managed to get up to six.

"Are you happy that she is here, Signy?" Rothaway caressed his mate's creamy shoulder in the early light of the ship's dawn.

She smiled up at him, and the glow of happiness coming from her features nearly blinded him. "I am so very happy that she is here. Will there be a problem with the People of the Air for having one of their princes taking a Gaian to wife?"

"If there are, Tonos will handle it. He has always known what he wanted and that it did not reside on his home world. Perhaps coming out here was fate, destiny or just good planning on his part. All I know is that now that she is wed to him, my mate has more time for me, and so in that case, I wish them all the love in the worlds . . . that we are not using."

Signy reached up to him and pulled him to her with her rapidly increasing strength. It may be coincidence, but she had more Wilder characteristics with every passing day, and to be honest with himself, Rothaway couldn't be happier.

HIDING
RETURN OF THE NINE BOOK THREE

BY

VIOLA GRACE

CHAPTER ONE

The first time she heard of a Gaian marrying one of the Nine, she didn't believe it. Daphne Hallow still didn't believe it when it was announced that the reception for Tiera McKenzie and a huge pixie named Tonos was going to take place at the hall where Daphne worked.

Now, surrounded by alien warriors from the ship above them, Daphne was finally cluing in that it might be true.

She and the rest of the serving staff were on alert, waiting for the introduction of the couple. Her heart pounded as the gathering filled with beings that were similar to those of Gaia but different in a variety of ways.

They were predominantly male and seated separately from the Gaians. The Nine were in the shape of creatures of myth and legend, from Fairies like the groom, to shadows that clung to living flesh.

Daphne and the other servers had been selected after a rigorous security scan to make sure that the incoming Nine would be safe with them. She had never been a high-security waitress before, but she supposed that there was a first time for everything.

They had been through days of etiquette training, practice runs and disaster drills. It was the most intense thing that Daphne had been through since her parents were taken in the first of the Tokkel raids and never seen again.

The facility manager and the etiquette advisor of the Nine passed their ranks with careful attention. All the hair on the females had to be braided and fastened at the back of the skull. Sleeves needed to be long to prevent accidental contact. Trousers were to be loose and a wide sash on the long shirt fastened and flattened everything into a column. The men were dressed the same. They were all completely sexless and lacking any individuality. Perfect.

Daphne had to admit that she was happy to be lost in a crowd. Normally, she needed to exert herself into being ignored, but in this group, she blended into nothing.

The uniforms that they wore were unrelieved black. Normally, the colour would not be considered for a wedding banquet, but this was a special occasion. It was the first celebration between a Gaian and a member of the Nine.

The member of the Nine sent to prepare them was a woman of the Wilder clan. She sniffed the air carefully as she passed, shaking her head at a few of the women, sending them back for another shower to remove all traces of scent from their skin.

That the Nine were scent sensitive was an oddity that made a certain sense to the Gaians. They were picking up their own peculiarities as time went on and enhanced senses were only the tip of the iceberg.

When Daphne was authorized, she relaxed slightly. Her station in life had taken a turn when her family had died, and she had turned from a student of Gaian and Terran histories to a general labourer.

Most around the colony had something that needed doing, and she was excellent at being unobtrusive in her work, no matter what the task was.

She perked up as one of the McKenzie family stood to speak. "Ladies and gentlemen from Gaia and the Nine, welcome one and all to this celebration of the union of our two races in the embrace of this couple. Tiera and Tonos."

The crowd turned and applause rang out as Tiera McKenzie and her husband, Tonos, made their way to the head table and sat down.

With the signal given, Daphne and the others moved into action. It was time to serve.

The first hour was peaceful. A lazy dance of filling and setting of plates, but as the heat in the room increased and they began to sweat, the heads of the men of the Nine began to turn as they passed.

As she slipped between two of the seated men to refill a cup with water and another with wine, she could feel gazes on her. With a shaking breath, she pulled herself inward and disappeared to their senses.

Hours passed and several of the women were removed from service as the men of the Nine became too attentive.

Daphne's service went from three tables to ten. She forced herself to move faster, but holding the veil of perception around her became a strain by the end of the night.

She watched some of the bolder women of the bride's side haul warriors of the Nine to the dance floor, but she didn't have time to watch.

Daphne's break time came and went, with the dismissed servers working in the kitchen to clean dishes and prepare the next courses. Her feet throbbed, her back and arms ached and her head pounded.

A hand clasped her shoulder when she was on her way to retrieve another round of plates. "You have done well, Daphne Hallow. You are dismissed for the evening."

The woman of the Wilder smiled gently at her, but pointed teeth still showed.

Daphne looked around and saw that the remaining servers were almost done cleaning up, the flowers were wilted and only a few guests remained. "Thank you. But I did not get your name."

"Arvina Hekoway. My cousin is wed to another of your people, but she is restricted to the warship. I came to make sure that what happened by accident did not happen again." The woman made a gesture, and Daphne walked with her out of the warm hall and into the evening air.

A forest bordered the gardens surrounding the hall, and it was a nice, quiet night with the new star of the ship of the Nine burning above.

"It was a very nice reception." Daphne was unsure what the woman wanted to speak to her about.

"It was. Tell me, do you know of any other Gaians who have exhibited extraordinary abilities?" Arvina walked slowly down a garden path.

"What do you mean?"

"Don't be shy. Six of the men you waited on were interested, but their senses suddenly ceased to remark on you. Why was that?"

Daphne swallowed. "Um, perhaps there were women more suited to them?"

Arvina laughed. "Perhaps. The Gaian women do seem interested in the men of the Nine. Are you one of them?"

Daphne blinked, "I hadn't given it much thought. They are all of standard attractiveness, I suppose. I didn't have much time to shop around this evening."

The woman coughed another laugh. "Valid point. But if you are something unusual, would you consider the suit of one of the Nine?"

Feeling put on the spot, Daphne paused, her mind on the woods and how long it would take her mind to put her beyond Arvina's sight. "I suppose I would, however, I am nothing unusual here on Gaia. I am nothing at all."

She blinded Arvina to the sight and scent of her and ran for the woods.

Chapter Two

The woods enveloped her as they always did. Daphne called herself seventeen types of fool. Arvina knew who she was, probably knew where she lived. There would be no hiding from her, which was a pity. Hiding was all Daphne knew.

The leaves of the trees caressed her as she passed. The moment that she thought she could draw breath and relax, she stopped and leaned against a helpful trunk. Arvina had not followed, that much was certain.

In the darkness, dressed in black, she slumped to the ground and let the aches of her body unclench a little at a time. Her feet had a pulse, her arms were in agony and her back was screaming. It had been a heck of an evening.

The branches near her moved, and she froze. It was not uncommon to have predators this close to town, but they usually stayed away from the hall on nights where a party was going on.

The branches shifted again, whispering lightly to each other. With her body protesting, she got to her feet. "Who is there?"

"Arvina thought that her presence would not be welcome." The trees were speaking Gaian, so Daphne knew she had gone insane at long last.

She staggered down the path and stopped abruptly when she struck a tree that wasn't supposed to be there. To her shock, the tree was wearing the formal clothing of the Nine.

Hands cupped her elbows and held her upright. "Easy, miss."

Her impression of a tree was not far off, his body was hard, tall and the same shade as the trees next to him.

"Who are you?"

He released her and ran a hand through his hair. "Well, I messed this up. I am Apolan Leoraki. I am the new ambassador to Gaia on behalf of the Nine, and I need an assistant."

The light from the single moon illuminated him for a moment. He was indeed one of the Tree Folk of the Nine. It took her a moment to catch onto his statement. Giggles flowed through her. "You have stalked and ambushed me in the dark to offer me a job?"

She snickered, hooted and howled with laughter.

He waited patiently for her to cease.

Daphne finally straightened. "I don't think that this is a conversation for the dark of the forest. May we go into the light?"

"Of course. May I help you through the path?"

She smiled in the darkness. "Aside from the occasional alien in the path, I have never had any problem."

He made a noise that was low and similar to the rustle of leaves. She imagined it was his version of a laugh.

Daphne turned and led the way back to the hall grounds.

The pool of light was surprisingly welcome to her, considering that hiding was her normal default. She wanted to see the wall she had collided with, and there was nothing better than light to dispel the fears of the dark.

Arvina was waiting at one of the outdoor tables. Apparently, she knew what Daphne would find in the woods.

She still had an expression of relief as Daphne and the tree man exited the woods.

"I was not sure that she would be in the mood to let you find her, Apolan."

"She was gracious enough to let herself take a break under the trees. They told me exactly where she was." He spoke, and Daphne turned to look up at him.

He was indeed walnut coloured, his clothing the deepest green with slightly darker embroidery, which matched his hair. The only things that stood out were his eyes. In the light, they were a leafy green.

A tea service and three cups were in front of Arvina. They were expected.

When she dropped her exhausted body into a chair, she took a cup of tea gratefully. "All right, what do you want?"

Apolan sat next to her, fairly close. He lifted his cup as gracefully as Arvina lifted hers.

Arvina started, "We have been asked to build a presence here, but Apolan thinks that a Gaian in the administration will help the locals to accept and adjust to us. That is where you come in."

"Why me?"

"Out of all the Gaians interviewed for the reception, you were the only one who didn't ask about the guests, merely about the details of the service. You were fixated on the job and not seeing and gawking at someone new. That is an admirable trait. Also, when I began to do scent trials, you disappeared right under my nose. That is not something that happens often, I can tell you."

Daphne blushed. "I simply needed to know what was needed for the job. Nothing more."

Arvina smiled, "I know. It was the first in the more noticeable traits around you. The other was your disappearing. How do you do that?"

She shrugged. "I have no idea. I simply look at a person and disappear from their perceptions, by whatever method they use."

"Are you free to work with Apolan as his assistant?" Arvina raised her cup to her lips and arched her eyebrows.

Daphne had no jobs lined up after this one, so she nodded. "I am free. Does it pay?"

Apolan was indignant. "Of course it does."

Arvina raised a hand. "Twice the rate per hour that you were paid this evening, plus a clothing bonus as I am sure that you do not have the correct items for the position. We may have to have something that works sent down from the ship for you. I will make a note to have a seamstress visit."

Daphne wanted to be indignant about the offer of a clothing allowance, but she really didn't have anything appropriate. "When does the position start?"

Apolan smiled grimly. "Tomorrow? We have been given offices at city hall until our building is ready. It should be finished within the month."

"What time?" She could probably scrounge some proper clothing out of her mother's things if she had to.

"It is late, so noon? Ask for the temporary Embassy of the Nine, and they will direct you."

She nodded. "Fine. Yes. I agree. We will discuss duties and such in the morning. For now, I am far too tired."

Apolan asked, "Do you have a conveyance?"

It took her a moment to figure it out. "Oh. No. I walk home. It is just over that ridge there. Not too far at all." The skimmer had been the first thing sold after her parents' death and the bill collectors had come to call.

Her father's penchant for inventing had never born fruit, but debts seemed to bloom in his wake. His death just made the men more insistent on getting what was theirs.

She had sold everything worth selling, pared down her antique books and taken on any job someone would pay her for.

She shook her head. "Come to think of it, I should get home. There are things to do before I start my new job."

Apolan rose and helped her pull out her chair. "I will escort you home. This is no place for a lady alone."

She blinked up at him. "No one has called me a lady in a very long time."

"Then, it is overdue." He offered her his arm, and she took it. "Please direct me to your home. The trees were not very forthcoming."

She grinned and pointed. "That way. Straight line more or less."

They walked in the direction she pointed for a few minutes before she asked, "Why were you chosen for the position here on Gaia?"

He grinned, the white of his teeth flashing in the moonlight. "The Forest clan are the least susceptible to pheromones. It was thought that one of our kind would more easily deal with yours. I have been prepared to answer questions, to smooth the paths between our races. It has taken a bit of research, but that is why it was decided that I was to obtain an assistant of Gaian extraction."

"Extraction is a good word. Was there a reason that Arvina selected me aside from my lack of scent?"

He cocked his head as if deliberating his next words. "I believe it was also your lack of interest in the men of the Nine. Many of the others selected for the event were intrigued by the thought of meeting and mating with a man of the Nine. We do not give our affections lightly, nor do we engage in casual encounters with alien races. It seems your women were not ready to accept that."

She snickered, "Something different and new is always more attractive than the toy one already plays with. It goes for men as well, and the men of the Nine are very attractive as far as such judgements go."

"You find us attractive?"

To her amusement, he seemed to grow a little taller at that. "I do, but it is not my opinion that matters but that of your lady wife."

"I am not married, bonded or attached . . . yet." There was meaning in his tone, but she ignored it.

She nodded. "Fair enough. So, what will I be doing?"

"Your position will entail taking appointments from a variety of sources, running my calendar and accompanying me to public functions." His tone was matter of fact.

"Public functions?"

"You will have a clothing allowance and be dressed in the fashions of the Nine. The clothing of the Forest clan will suit you very well, I think. Arvina is sending for the seamstress soon, so you will be kitted out before the grand opening of our embassy."

They reached the rise that overlooked her tiny house in the centre of a ring of trees. The wildness of the area was the reason that the colonists didn't bother trying to plough through the ground. Removing the woods was far too much labour and the ground only suited to growing trees.

Apolan's voice was amused, "You live with trees."

"I do. My parents owned the house before me, and when they died, it came to me."

"I am sorry. How did they die?"

She took a deep breath and said one word. "Tokkel."

He stiffened and nodded. "I see."

She glanced up at him and really doubted that he did.

CHAPTER THREE

Daphne had never had a more restless night. Her parents' screams of shock and pain as the landing party came down and took samples of the settlers rang in her mind. With only a blind panic, she had hidden in the woods, watching the ship sweep her loved ones away from her, unable to even cry out.

Two hours after dawn, dark circles under her eyes, she poured herself a cup of tea and looked out at the protective ring of forest that enclosed her.

"This isn't doing me any good." Her cupboard was bare as it normally was these days. She had not yet been paid for her service at the reception. That event was to have set her up for a few days.

Daphne slipped into her trousers and tunic, moving into the forest to look for some berries or other edibles.

A shadow moved, and her heart pounded in her chest.

"Good morning, Ms. Hallow. I wish you a good day." Apolan moved into the brighter light and inclined his head.

"Good morning, Ambassador Leoraki. Why are you skulking in the shadows?"

He held out a basket that contained a loaf of bread, a selection of meats and cheeses and some fruit.

"When you invited me in for tea last night, I snooped. I noted that your cupboard was bare and could not have you starting your new duties on an empty stomach." He gestured with his head, and when she stood still, he passed her and went on to her small house in the green shadows.

Bemused and not a little enticed by the food he carried, she followed him back to her house.

Apolan looked her up and down. "Is that a common clothing choice here on Gaia?"

She blushed, "No. I wear this for foraging."

"And no shoes?"

"The forest doesn't demand them. There are no noxious plants here, and so, I can run around without shoes."

She watched as he removed plates, cups and cutlery as if he lived in the home with her. "You really were paying attention."

"As my assistant, your well-being is now my concern. Arvina has obtained a seamstress from the ship. She and her assistant will be here this afternoon, so we will have to start a little earlier than I intended."

He swiftly portioned the food with the ease of long practice. There was more on her plate than she would eat in three meals, but she sat across the kitchen table and ate what he offered her.

"Why don't you live closer to the settlement?" Apolan's question hit on her problem.

"Um. I can't afford to. My parents were legal archivists who wanted me to live a life of the mind. I studied for years, absorbing every bit of history and learning every skill I could. Then, the Tokkel attacked. My parents were killed in the first strike. I was left with only this house to call my own. I sold what I could while I grieved, and from there, I sought out the jobs that would take me. With no job history and everything in chaos, there were plenty of small jobs to do, but with no family left, I had no one to help me ease into a steady position. Family is everything here on Gaia, and I now have no one so I get along as best I can."

He seemed shocked by her statement, but he kept quiet. They ate together, and when she stopped, he stopped. His plate was nearly empty, so she lifted a piece of fruit to her lips and nibbled slowly.

Apolan quickly finished his meal. She stopped and put the remains in the storage unit. She could get two days of meals out of what was left on that plate.

"Excuse me a moment while I get dressed." Biting her lip, she went to her closet and selected sober wear with an elegant finish. They were leftover from her days as a reasonably well-to-do student. The shoes pinched but suited the clothing. They were going to be hell to walk in, but they matched the loose silken trousers and the buttoned tunic.

When she reappeared, Apolan got to his feet and frowned. "It will suit for today, but it is not appropriate for much more than this week."

Daphne was embarrassed. "I apologise. I have not needed clothing with any formality for years."

He immediately came to her and gripped her arms. His skin was deep brown with a green tinge, and his touch was tight but not confining. "I do not take you to task for your clothing, but I think that the fashions of the Nine will suit you well. The sooner we can get you looking the part of my assistant, the better."

She sighed in relief. "I didn't want to be inappropriate on my first day of a job that no one has seen before."

He chuckled. "You cannot be inappropriate. You were the only candidate considered for the position. You are the only appropriate selection."

A smile crept over her face, her grin taking over. "Then, let's get walking. It will take close to an hour to walk to the settlement."

"I have a better idea." He took a small item off his belt and pressed it.

She heard a whirring sound, and the feeling in the air changed.

"I have a transport."

He took her hand, and together, they watched a small platform ringed with a guardrail land in her front yard.

"Is that safe?" Daphne eyed it with nervousness.

"It is. I would not risk you." His voice was deep and sincere.

The weird intensity she had noted tinged his tone again. Again, she pushed it back, and instead, got a grip on the railing of the platform.

Apolan used his remote and directed the platform to take them up and away. They skimmed across fields at a height of ten feet or less. When they moved over the forested areas, they caressed the treetops.

In ten minutes, they were landing on the roof of city hall. Daphne breathed deeply and exhaled quietly in an effort to control her racing heart. The settlement's mayor greeted them, and he was definitely surprised to see her standing next to the new ambassador for the Nine.

"Ms. Hallow, what are you doing here?" Mayor Tetra smiled brightly, but his mouth was tight.

"Ms. Hallow has been retained as my assistant." Apolan was polite but firm.

"As Ambassador Leoraki has said, I have been retained as his assistant to be his liaison to the settlers." Daphne tried to behave in a reserved fashion, but the look of disdain on Mayor Tetra's face was unmistakable.

"We will find you a more suitable assistant, Ambassador." Mayor Tetra extended his hand to Ambassador Leoraki.

Daphne raised her hand to forestall him, but Apolan walked past the hand to the stairwell. She told the mayor, "The Nine do not shake hands. They can have biochemical reactions that are not predictable."

She followed Apolan, and he waited until she caught up with him before starting down to the next level. Her hard-soled shoes skittered on the stone steps, causing her to clutch at the railing.

"Are you all right?" Apolan gripped her arm.

"I am fine. There is a lift on the next floor. I forgot how slippery these steps were." She smiled and moved more carefully.

They exited the stairs at the next door, and he continued to hold her arm all the way to the lift.

"We are on the third floor."

She struck the third-floor button, and this time, he clung to her for support. When the doors opened, they passed a security team of personnel of the Nine. They snapped to attention as Apolan passed, and one tried to bar her from entering the offices.

"She is my assistant, Drakil. She has full authorization to come and go as she pleases. You can call her Ms. Hallow."

The Wilder that had his gloved and fully covered arm extended retracted it with a smile. "Pleased to meet you, Ms. Hallow."

"Pleased to meet you, Drakil." She shut down her scent, or at least his perception of it, as quickly as she could.

His smile went from beyond friendly to confused in an instant. The other three guards did the same.

Apolan smiled and held out his hand. She took it, and he tugged her into the offices that he had been allocated.

"Oh, my." The offices were decorated in what seemed to be Nine fashion. Rich colours, white marble floors and lovely vases full of alien flora made the room a definite representation of a foreign world.

"My office is back here, your desk and com unit are there." He took her on a tour of the floor. There was a kitchen with rations suitable to the differing species of the Nine, three sets of lavs, an entertainment area, a dining room, boardroom and sitting room.

After the tour and meeting the rest of the guards who prevented them from being inundated with folks who were not invited, she was seated at her desk.

Daphne's duties would be to take calls, arrange meetings for those who had a genuine concern and prepare lunches for the persons of the Nine who were on duty or visiting.

She settled at her desk and practiced with the com a second before it chirped at her. "Embassy of the Nine, how may I direct your call?"

A stream of words came through the line. Unfortunately, Daphne couldn't translate any of them. Fortunately for her, her com system translated and displayed the information on the screen. "Madam, I am calling for Ambassador Leoraki. He has requested a seamstress at the embassy, and I wished to know if I was welcome to come now?"

Daphne sighed, "Yes, please. We are expecting you. You will be welcomed."

There was a pause on the other end as the other party was reading her words in the language of the Nine. "Thank you. We look forward to the meeting."

"Where will you be landing?"

"Designated spaceport."

"I will have someone pick you up."

"That will be most welcome."

The call disconnected, and Daphne looked up to see Apolan leaning against the side of her desk with a small box in his hand. "I forgot to give you a portable translator. It will help you until you learn Nine Common and Forest select. While most of those travelling here have learned Gaian, not all of them have. I do not want you at a disadvantage."

She nodded. "Thank you. Am I allowed to send some of your guard to escort the seamstress to this office?"

He blinked. "Of course. Did they call?"

"They did. The computer translated for me. The earpiece will be faster, I think." She extended her hand, and he gave her the box with great formality.

As Daphne opened the box, she gasped in surprise. It wasn't just an earpiece, it was a finely crafted piece of jewellery that had a piercing for the lobe as well as a cuff for the curve of her ear, all draped with tiny jewels and chains.

A little nervous, she placed the item on her ear and settled it until it was comfortable. She looked up at Apolan, "Is this right?"

He smiled. "Lovely. You look as if you were born to it."

She blushed, and then, her eyes widened when she realised that he was not speaking Gaian. "Oh, that is strange."

"It combines audible with mental impulses. If you are thinking about speaking to me, I will hear the words you intend, even if they are not the ones you speak. I also have a subliminal learning unit that you can link to at night. You should have a grasp of the common language of the Nine in a week or less."

He grinned, patted her hand and returned to his new office.

Shaking her head in amazement and the strange feeling of the ear unit, she got to her feet and walked out of the embassy to speak to the guards. Her first day already held so much more than she had ever anticipated, and she had the feeling that the new experiences were not nearly over.

Chapter Four

"Hold still, Ms. Hallow. The formal clothing of the Forest Folk is delicate. You don't want it hanging improperly." Xeero, a charming man of the Stone Folk, had the lightest touch with a needle that she had ever seen.

Daphne held her breath as he carefully adjusted the fabric until the drawn tangle flowed gracefully to her ankles. She had already been measured for daywear, office wear, footwear and underwear. The formal gown was an issue, because the embassy gala was scheduled for the day that the building was completed and outfitted.

They had taken over the conference room for the fittings, and Xeero and his assistant spoke in low tones while they fussed, fitted and pinned her into each item.

While Xeero did the final fitting on the formal gown, his assistant, Xalik, was working with blurring fingers to finish some office clothing for her. The speed with which he assembled each article of clothing was astonishing.

He had already completed a set of flowing trousers for her. Now, he was working on the matching tunic.

Xeero stepped back, and a smile crossed over his grey features. "Lovely. I do good work, and it doesn't hurt that the framework was such a pleasure to dress."

She blushed and looked down at the leaf green silk of the simple gown. It hugged curves that she didn't know she had.

Xalik looked up from his work and smiled. "Perfect. The colour suits you, Ms. Hallow."

She waited while Xeero made minute adjustments.

Xalik held up the tunic with a grin. "Done."

Daphne was amazed. In less than two hours, she had put on twenty changes of clothing with matching undies and had been analysed by two complete strangers in every detail of her physicality. Against all logic, her day had gotten stranger.

Apolan was answering his own calls while she had her fitting. It was a peculiar turn of events when her boss was doing her job while she shopped, but it sort of fit the day.

Xeero smiled, "Time for a change of clothing."

He selected the proper undergarments, which should have made her nervous, but the fifth time she had been standing naked in the middle of the boardroom, her mind had simply shut down embarrassment and mimicked a doll.

With the ease of repetition, she slipped off the panties she was currently wearing and exchanged them for the pair that Xeero was holding. The swift shimmy put the delicate things exactly where they should go.

"Hold still now, Ms. Hallow. We don't want you bleeding on the gown."

With Xeero on one side and Xalik on the other, she held still and moved with them as the wisp of gown was pulled over her head and the matching slip followed. Xalik folded the items away while Xeero brought her the new clothing.

In five minutes, she was dressed, had a bodice wrapping her from breast to waist and a sash around her hips. Every bit of clothing was in a variety of shades of gold and green.

The sleeves of the tunic made her smile. They were wide and had a graceful sweep that made every move seem like a dance. Soft calf-high boots were far more practical than the hard-soled shoes she had worn for her first day.

Her flowing trousers covered her boots to the ankle, and she had to admit, as she ran her hands down the new silhouette that she sported, she looked good. With absent hands, Daphne moved her hair to one side, framing the earpiece that was her only jewellery.

"Perfect. Just lovely." Xeero smiled and clapped his hands. "You can return to your duties now. We will finish our day here and send a courier with the rest of your clothing when we have completed them."

She nodded and smiled. "Welcome to the embassy. May I get you a beverage or something to eat?"

They looked at each other and burst out laughing. "You may indeed. Thank you, Ms. Hallow."

She inclined her head and stepped out of the conference room in her new finery. She walked silently down the hall to the small kitchenette and sought the icon for the Stone Folk. Apolan's morning briefing had explained how to select foods for the variety of the Nine. Each pack and item had a small icon on the bottom of it as well as a code that would be read by the preparer.

With her mind sorting through everything she needed for afternoon tea, she set the kettle on, prepared the tea set and slid sandwiches for the Stone Folk into the preparer.

It was her first act as hostess to the ambassador, and she wanted to get it right.

Daphne grinned as she walked away from the conference room where the dressmakers were having tea. In an hour, she would return and retrieve the tray, but in the meantime, they had fallen on it with good appetite.

It was the right food for the right species in the correct quantity. Her first act as assistant to the ambassador was complete.

He seemed so surprised to see her when she stood in his doorway that she fought a smile.

"The clothing suits you, Daphne." His gaze, however, strayed to her earpiece.

"May I get you anything, Ambassador? Tea or food?"

He smiled. "Water please and a light snack."

"I will return in a moment." She gave him the serving bow that she had been taught for the reception and backed out of his doorway.

Mentally, she was whistling happily when she retrieved his requests and brought him a tray. It was nice to be efficient at something.

She checked on the dressmakers and refreshed their tea. Xeero and Xalik were only too happy to show her their progress. She had a change of clothing for every day that week, an afternoon dress that was both graceful and sturdy, and enough underwear to see her through.

"Xalik enjoys making undergarments. It is his personal fetish." Xeero smiled grimly.

She chuckled. "Everyone has their hobbies. Mine is learning. Any day I can learn something new is a good one."

"It's a good goal. We have been enjoying seeing the two Gaian ladies who are living on the ship. They each have peculiar talents. Is this true for the rest of your species?"

She looked at him in surprise. "It isn't something that any of us discuss. I heard something about one of ours being declared someone of import to the Nine, but I never got the details."

They looked to each other and then inclined their heads. Xeero spoke, "It is good to see you, Ambassador Leoraki."

She got to her feet and turned to her employer. She blushed. "I apologise for my dereliction of duty. I will return to my desk."

She tried to pass him, but he caught her arm. He whispered in Gaian. "You have done nothing wrong. You are hostess here, and that is what comes first at all times."

Daphne paused and nodded with a slight smile. "Then, I will return to work and leave you to greet these hard-working contractors."

He released her arm with a slow slide of his fingers. "They are quite the artists. I will indeed compliment their work."

A knock at the front hall got her attention. With a small nod, she said, "Time to earn my keep."

Chapter Five

"Mayor Tetra, while I appreciate the horrible imposition of you coming up two floors, the ambassador is otherwise occupied this afternoon." It was day three of Daphne's odyssey as the assistant to the ambassador and this was, by far, the most satisfying moment to date.

The mayor scowled at her. "I wish to speak with him."

"I can schedule an appointment for tomorrow afternoon, but today is out of the question." It was the truth. Ambassador Leoraki was in meetings with some of the Shadow Folk who were asking him about the likelihood of finding matches with some of the Gaian women from the reception.

As she was about to get verbally blasted by the mayor, the ambassador in question poked his head around the corner. "Daphne, come in here please."

The mayor fluffed himself up. "Ambassador Leoraki, I am happy to see you are adjusting to your surroundings. I was wondering if you would have time—"

Leoraki cut him off. "Not today, Mayor Tetra. I will be happy to meet with you tomorrow afternoon. Today, I am involved in a matter of urgency. Daphne, now please."

The guards on the interior of the door stepped inward, blocking the mayor from following and herding him out.

Daphne got to her feet and followed the ambassador into his office. As he had instructed her, she stood at his right hand and looked from one Shadow to the next.

"Gentlemen, please explain to my assistant what you require."

The Shadows shifted in their seats. One spoke, "I saw a woman at the reception, and I wish to court her, but I am unsure where to start."

Smiling, Daphne ran through all of the protocols that Gaian's enjoyed clinging to. She started with the first meeting, then getting the name and address of the lady or gentlemen of their choice and arranging the second meeting. After that, it was a series of progressively intimate meetings the culminated in one of two ways. Proposing a permanent connection or physical intimacy. Either one was acceptable.

The Shadows shifted violently while she explained the methods standard to

Gaians. "That said, there is nothing wrong with carrying out the rituals of the Nine and seeing if the woman is willing. If she is, proceed as you would with a woman of your own kind."

Apolan reached out and took her hand, rubbing his thumb along her knuckles. It was an intimate gesture in front of the strangers, but the Shadow Folk seemed pleased by her acceptance of the touch.

"Daphne."

Something in his voice made her turn her head to look down at him, and his deep green eyes held a wealth of emotion. The motion exposed her earpiece to the Shadow Folk, and she heard a small gasp.

"Thank you for your help, Ms. Harrow. You may resume your duties." He stroked her hand again and smiled.

Dismissed, she returned to her desk and continued her research on the eating habits of the Nine. The earpiece was so comfortable, she didn't even need to remove it in the shower. It held to her ear as if designed to be there.

She wouldn't need it in a few days. Her subliminal lessons in the common language of the Nine were coming along. Each night, she put the unit in her ears, and she was slowly taught how to speak the words that her earpiece simply translated for her.

It would be handy if she was every caught without her jewellery, but she couldn't imagine a day when she didn't want to wear it. Aside from the curious glances she got when she went into town, she truly enjoyed the piece and the workmanship on it.

Her account was full. She had been paid for her first quarter of service up front, and it enabled her to get her pantry back to standard levels. The shopkeepers eyed her speculatively when she was able to pay without checking her balance first, but she was able to get what she needed.

It felt so strange to finally have the funds when she needed them that she wasn't sure what to do first.

She spent her time as his assistant answering the com, checking his schedule and making sure that requests for specialty items were filed with the warship. It wasn't a hard job, but she wasn't sure how long she was going to be able to do it.

Her attraction for Apolan grew with every passing day. He picked her up in the morning and brought her home every evening. Each day, he made excuses to touch her hand or arm, and she felt an ache for him when more than three hours passed and she hadn't seen him.

Falling head over heels for the alien ambassador wasn't precisely a good career move.

Her com unit chirped, and she smiled as images of the new embassy came in. The Nine were sending the building down in complete chunks. The sole delay of the opening of the embassy was the landscaping necessary to create suitable environments for the members of the Nine who decided to visit.

She got to her feet and knocked on the doorframe of Ambassador Leoraki's office. "Ambassador, the construction update is in."

He inclined his head and smiled. "Thank you, Ms. Harrow."

There were intercoms in the office, but he preferred to have her announce the markers of the day. She was beginning to suspect that he enjoyed seeing her and that was the sole reason for the announcements.

With a short nod of her head, she returned to her desk and continued her education in the ways of the Nine. There was a ton of information to absorb, and she did love to learn.

Apolan watched Daphne disappear around the corner once again. Moryk and Devokian watched her as well. He cleared his throat.

"Now, you were saying that you have both chosen Gaians to pursue?" He brought their attention back to him.

Moryk nodded, the shadows that cloaked his body shifted. "I have seen her, but I am unsure how to proceed. I am not fond of the idea of seducing her first and wedding her second. It is not our way, as you know."

Apolan grimaced. "Try to think of it as an extended courtship but draw the line at physical intimacy. From what I have been able to ascertain, the Gaians take to the courtship easily, and you do not need to tell them what your intent is."

"Your courtship seems to be coming along."

"I plan to take her as my bride the night of the embassy opening."

Moryk whistled quietly. "That is a week away. Can you hold out that long?"

Apolan looked to the wall that hid his view of Daphne. "I will have to. She does not know where the new embassy is to be located, and I am sure that she will be a little upset when she finds out."

Devokian cocked his head, "How can she not have seen it? It is right in her back yard."

Apolan smiled, "I keep myself between her and the construction site at all times. There is a reason that she does not know where I sleep, but I have to admit that the proximity is tempting."

The men laughed at the shared amusement, and Devokian asked, "Will there be a bonding garden?"

"That is the delay. The construction is almost complete. It is the gardening that is taking the time." Apolan kept his gaze on the wall. "It is almost complete."

Moryk chuckled. "I hope so, for your sake."

"Invite your Gaian to the opening gala. It will let you get close enough to mark her."

"Our marks are not as obvious as yours, Apolan. I am not sure that I can convince a Gaian to take a piece of me inside her on a dance floor."

Apolan laughed, "Don't put it to her like that. They will think it is something sexual, and she might balk. Suggest that she absorb a piece of the shadow. It might sound better."

"We can't all simply give our beloved jewellery that links her mind to ours."

"You know it only works if we are compatible. I have to tell you, it is exhausting to keep up with her mind. She has gone through all of our food requirements, clothing, planets of settlement and, tomorrow, she is going to work on courtship. It will be difficult to concentrate."

"Isn't tomorrow a rest day for the colonists?" Devokian asked.

Apolan smiled, "I believe you are correct. I think I will ask my assistant to show me the sights."

The men chuckled, and Apolan leaned back. A day off was just what Daphne needed. She was way too tense. A day of picnics and walks in the green might just help her breathe again.

Chapter Six

Spending her first worry-free day off with her boss was peculiar to say the least.

"Are you sure that you want to spend a whole day with me?" Daphne bit her lip.

"There is no one else I would rather spend the day with. Besides, you are here to help me integrate into the Gaian culture. The best way to do it is to immerse myself with your assistance. Lead the way, Daphne. I am yours for the day."

She looked at his casual clothing, the brown leather and woven vest. His skin's greenish brown colour glowed in the morning light, and he held another basket of food.

"Well, if you are mine, I have just the spot to show you. I think the Stone Folk would like it, but I am not sure about your people."

"Show me, and I will let you know." He gestured for her to join him on the platform.

She snickered as he carefully positioned himself the same way he had for the last three days. "I will have to see the embassy sooner or later. Despite your efforts, I am well aware that my skyline has changed."

He drew upright in shock. "You know?"

"Since the first disk thudded down onto Gaian soil. I am in tune with my environment. It is key to my survival." Daphne smiled.

"Well, since you are aware of it. Are you up for a tour? They are working on the bonding garden today. We can see any area except that one."

"It sounds like you are taking control of this outing. Good. I didn't have anything planned."

He smiled, "We can see your spot later."

She grinned. "Good. It really is beautiful. A natural garden underground."

Daphne could tell that she had gotten his curiosity up, but he controlled the platform and took them to the build site half a mile from her home.

She laughed as they approached. She would have had to be blind to miss the five stories of building that spiked into the sky. The building had a surprisingly organic look, as if it had grown from the stone beneath it.

"That is quite something. It matches the surroundings quite well."

Apolan inclined his head. "We try not to stand out on any world we put an embassy on. Our worlds are far away, but we bring pieces of them with us."

She blinked. "Thathonic?"

He nodded. "That is the home of my parents, yes. You really have studied the Nine."

She blushed. "I can't help it. I have to learn. It is a compulsion."

"I don't mind. At least you are taking an interest. It is better for both of us if you understand my society and I yours." He smiled and brought the platform down in the centre of a manicured courtyard.

The tour was extensive, and she was ravenous by the time they entered the gardens at the rear of the new facility.

The grass had the standard purplish tinge of Gaia, but the rest of the flowers and trees were carefully potted and contained. Apolan took a small square out of the basket he had been carrying and flicked it out to provide them with a charming picnic area of layered silk.

They ate, chatted and simply enjoyed the bright newness of the area around them.

"How many of these buildings do the Nine have waiting?"

"None. They have a fabrication department that crafted the layers over the last few weeks." He packed away the remnants of their meal.

"I have something to show you that was crafted way before last week. Can I pilot the platform?" Daphne's tone was bright and eager. For years she had wanted to show someone her find, but since she had no social circle, there was no one to call.

Apolan's hands covered hers on the controls, his body was pressed against her back, and she was having a hard time focussing on their destination.

"We are approaching your home." With his chest pressed against her back, she could feel his speech more than hear it.

"Sort of. A little further north and we are there." She shivered against him before she stiffened her back and reduced the contact.

With his help, she set them down neatly in a tiny glade within the ring of trees that surrounded her home. It was at the far north of the forest, a small green glade filled with some of the flowers native to Gaia. Daphne always felt calm when she was here. Serene, clean and right were the feelings that came over her in this place.

"Daphne, where are we?"

She could hear the wonder in his tone.

"The expanse north of my home. This is my place to run and hide when the world grows dark. It relaxes me from the inside out." She smiled and grabbed his hand, pulling him along.

"Where are we going?"

She laughed. Joy was spilling through her as it always did when she was here. "You can't see it from here. You have to walk to it straight on or the trees won't let you see it."

The grasses were soft, the flowers bright sparkling white, stars against their deeply coloured bases. She tugged her bemused employer through the glade as he tried to look at everything.

"This looks just like our . . ."

She stopped and raised her brows, "Just like what?"

"Never mind. What were you going to show me?"

Daphne laughed. "This way."

She used the small stones in the ground to line herself up, and she hauled him toward the woods one step at a time.

They moved together and the moment that the optical illusion faded, she heard Apolan gasp.

He kept moving forward with her, his footfalls eager.

The crevice in the rock was invisible to anyone who didn't know how to approach it. Daphne had been to the glade dozens of times before the hidden cavern had called to her.

The crystals that lined the cavern walls lit as they walked between the trees and into what Daphne privately called the heart of Gaia.

"I am guessing that the walls sense the electromagnetic field of living things. They wake when we enter, and they darken when we leave." She kept her words quiet. He was too busy exploring the interior of the cave.

The white flowers that marked the clearing above also grew in the darkness of the cavern. The scent here was heady. It woke parts of her that she didn't know she had.

With Apolan exploring the walls, she walked to the stone that took centre stage and watched him as he caressed the walls, stroked the crystals and murmured to himself.

The large crystal in the middle of the stone tablet drew her attention. Idly, she stroked the flat panel before she delicately drew her fingers down one sharp side.

"Daphne, what do you think this is?"

His loud words in the silence startled her. She drew her fingers back, and the edge of the crystal drew blood. "Ow." She put her bleeding fingers to her lips and sighed. "That has never happened before."

Apolan looked at the stone, and his eyes widened. "Oh, goddess."

The crystal that had tasted her blood was bright blue with light and power. It hummed.

"Daphne, I believe that you have stumbled upon the original bonding chamber of the Nine." Apolan looked at her fingers and the blood that still welled there.

She looked around her in wonder as she realised where she was standing. Generations of the Nine had come to this place and joined together as one.

The joy and warmth spilled through her over and over, and as she turned to imagine the couples that had stood in that place, searing pain ran through her hand.

Apolan looked from her to the stone and back again. "This is coming on much faster than I anticipated, but since you started the ritual, I must complete it or you will suffer."

Her knees buckled as the pain coursed through her, and it radiated from her fingertips down her arm.

"What do you have to do?"

He smiled and kissed the back of her hand, helping her to her feet. "I have to marry you."

CHAPTER SEVEN

"What?" She wasn't sure she had heard what she thought she heard. "You started the bonding ritual. We exchange blood, and it bonds us on a cellular level."

She blinked and clung to him with the unwounded hand. "Can't I just get some medical treatment?"

He sighed. "Does it feel like it is getting better?"

Fire was spreading through her in waves. "I am sure I will be fine." She gasped and held onto him, her nails gripping his shirt.

"I have intended this all along. I was hoping that things could move at your pace, but it seems that you have taken matters out of my hands." He supported her with one arm and focussed his attention on the crystal.

He grazed his fingertips along the edge of the crystal, and it parted his skin as easily as it had hers. He turned his hand to hers, and his wounds matched against her fingers.

She felt heat, but not the burning of earlier. They held their fingers together palm to palm, the wounds lining up on their hands.

"Daphne Harrow of Gaia, I take you."

She blinked and remembered her late-night reading. "Apolan Leoraki of the Forest Folk of the Nine, I take you."

The crystal sent streamers of light into the room, bringing Apolan's face into bright relief. He was grinning a foolish, happy grin.

She didn't have much time to admire his smile. His kiss met her lips with a passion and conviction that stunned her.

Being held against him sent her mind reeling. He wrapped one arm around her while his other hand slipped his fingers between hers. Her hand felt complete, no open wounds, no crystal cuts, nothing but his fingers with hers and the pulse of his palm against hers.

The light took on a softer ambiance. A romantic ambiance.

When Apolan raised his head, she gasped and leaned her head against his chest. Her heart was pounding, her skin was hot and her body was rapidly coming alive. She licked her lips. He tasted like wild berries and male.

Apolan released her hand and wrapped both his arms around her waist. He pressed a kiss on top of her head. "Hello, wife."

She looked up and smiled. "Hello, husband. Does this mean I get a raise?"

He laughed, "You can get anything out of me you wish, but we will need to consummate our union within the week, or the pain you felt will begin to wrack us both. We are now two halves of a joined power, but until we actually join our bodies, the link is incomplete. It will begin to degrade without completion."

"I suppose it is time to leave then." Daphne looked toward the exit, but it was gone. "What the hell?"

Apolan looked around and examined their environment. "Fascinating. It was said that the chamber confirmed all matches, but I was not aware that it was this determined."

She looked around frantically. "That room wasn't there earlier."

He smiled, "Then the chamber must want us to enter it."

Apolan kept hold of her hand, leading her into the new chamber. There was light, there was water and there was a bed made of thick moss, the white flowers interspersed throughout.

She got nervous at the sight of the bed. As much as she wanted to seal the deal with Apolan, it was still too soon.

Fully clothed, he tugged her onto the bed and wrapped his arms around her. "Rest for a bit, Daphne. The blood exchange will continue to move through our systems. When the chamber lets us out, I will wake you."

Unsure of what to say, she turned her back to him and snuggled in his arms. The flowers crushed under their bodies gave off a scent that relaxed Daphne until she rested in the arms of her new husband.

Apolan watched Daphne succumb to the effects of the bride flowers. Her body was being rewritten on a cellular level, and it was bound to cause her some trouble.

With her eyes closed, he could finally free his delighted grin. He had thought it would take weeks to win her to his side, but he hadn't counted on her link to her world.

Not only had his bride brought him to the one place that the Nine had been looking for for five years, but also she had done it innocent of its true purpose.

The power that the crystal had used bound them together. No matter where Daphne went, she would be able to track him and he her. Once they consummated their connection, their minds would join the linkage that their bodies were now working on.

The Forest Folk or People of the Trees were linked to the green and growing spaces in the universe, and it seemed to him that Daphne had already been headed down that path.

He sighed and tucked her close against him, the press of her curves delighting him. His third-generation Gaian trusted him enough to sleep in his arms. From the moment he had authorized Daphne as a server for the reception, he had been obsessed with her. The talent for hiding in plain sight that she exhibited was as much a part of her personality as it was a true psychic demonstration. She could not only shut her own body's outward signals down, but she could reach into the minds of those she was avoiding and force them not to see her.

Perhaps one day, she would trust him enough to tell him about the day that the Tokkel took her family, but he could wait. It was traumatic enough for a warrior of the Nine to face the hideous beasts in battle. He could only have imagined the trauma of a woman who had never expected to see creatures of that nature landing in ships.

Her files showed no family to claim her or help her through it. The Gaian settlement had been in such disarray after the initial attacks that they had been unable and unwilling to help the survivor left on her own.

Apolan was going to give Daphne whatever she needed, whether it was psychological, physical or financial. His family own five harvest worlds where they kept the plants happy and the animals healthy. It was peculiar for him to have been born a farmer and ended up an ambassador, but the Nine council wanted a presence on Gaia that was in tune with the planet. No one had any idea that a simple Gaian had beat them to it.

He stroked her rich brown hair away from her face and admired the jewellery that she wore each and every day. His great grandmother had worn that same earpiece when she met his great grandfather. Dilora had not been too fond of Jenyak when she met him, but she adapted quickly. Their love had eventually become a Leoraki legend—two contrasting souls that had managed to find common ground.

Apolan closed his eyes and embraced the feeling of his body synching to Daphne's. He was hoping that he and his Gaian would repeat that very admirable tradition.

CHAPTER EIGHT

"**D**aphne, the cavern has let us out."

The low voice in her ear sent shivers down her spine. "Hmm?"

"Come along, my bonded mate, before it changes its mind."

Hands pulled at her, helping her to sit up. She opened her eyes to see Apolan's concerned face near her own. With a sense of wonder, she lifted her hand and saw the thin pink line crossing three fingers. "It wasn't a dream."

He sighed and lifted her in his arms. "No, it wasn't. Come along. I don't know how long we have been here, but we need to get back to the surface."

She leaned against him, her head spinning and senses overloaded. "Sounds like a good idea."

With her eyes closed, she could still feel the exact moment that he entered the glade once again. Her smile was genuine, and her breathing came easier. "That's better."

"You feel it too?"

She chuckled. "Oh yes. There is a reason that I never moved to the settlement. Nothing feels as good as this." Daphne opened her eyes and looked up at the starlight streaming into their one small part of the forest.

He set her on the floor of the flying platform and checked the chronometer. "Oh, thank goodness. It is the same night. We were only underground for a few hours."

She smiled and slowly got to her feet. "Is that all? It felt like the beginning of forever."

He turned to her in surprise. "Daphne, are you all right?"

She took a step off the platform and walked a few feet away before she turned to him. "You hear them all the time, don't you?"

Understanding lit his eyes. "I do. You can hear them now?"

Daphne looked into the dark of the forest all around her. Thousands of trees whispered to her in greeting. Congratulations were offered in low murmurs. Not congratulations for the bonding, but for the small bit of evolution she had just undergone. They considered it the height of sophistication for one of her race to understand them.

She giggled, euphoric at the thought that she could understand the forest in which she lived.

"You can commune with them tomorrow. I regret to disturb your first moment with the forest, but we need to report both of our discoveries to the Nine." He gently wrapped an arm around her waist and steered her back to the platform.

The forest's consciousness thrummed through her, and she swayed gently, humming to herself as the song became part of her.

Apolan watched her with a smile on his lips. "You were almost there on your own, you know. There was only a slight nudge needed to push you over the edge."

She grinned at him, "Thank you for nudging me."

He sighed, "You have no idea how I want to answer that."

She snickered, a happy giggle that continued until they landed at the new embassy building.

Daphne sighed. "Why are we here?"

"We have to register our union with the Nine. It is important that we lock it in with the registry office as quickly as we can." He held his hand out and escorted her through the guards watching the front doors.

The Wilders lifted their heads and sniffed at the couple. "Ambassador. Congratulations on finding of your bride."

Apolan smiled, "Thank you. Daphne Harrow Leoraki is about to be registered."

She clung to his hand as the Wilders very obviously scented her.

"You may want to complete the union. It could become awkward if her people object and bad for her if you wait too long."

Apolan nodded his head and continued to pull her further into the new building.

Daphne asked quietly, "What did he mean?"

"Each race of the Nine has its courtship rituals. The Wilders and the People of the Air trigger a heat in their mates. The Shadows put a piece of their darkness into their prospective mate that grows to fill her. The Forest people are more subtle. We match our minds to that of our chosen companion using a mechanical means. It is a little bit sneaky, but we get by."

She paused as they entered his private quarters. "What do you mean *mechanical?*"

"A small bit of resonance technology that routes conscious thought through our minds until our mind shifts to match that of our mate. It's complicated, and I am not sure about why it works, but my family has one of the best

104

acquisition records for perfect matches. I suppose part of it is luck, but most of it is instinct. The moment I met you, I knew that you were the one for me, and I brought out a family heirloom."

She blinked, wide-eyed as she touched the earpiece. "This is a machine?"

"It translates for you by running what you hear through my mind."

She wanted to take it off, but her hand didn't move. "It's an heirloom? Your family always hijacks brains?"

He took her hands and stared into her eyes. "I did not hijack, I simply learned the patterns of your mind and helped you to learn the common language of the Nine as well as anything you thought about learning. We also only use the mechanical means with women not born of the Nine. My great grandmother was from outside the Nine, and while she challenged my great grandfather, they lived happily for a very long time. The earpiece that you are using was designed for her."

She blinked in surprise. "Your great grandmother?"

He smiled, "I will tell you all about her, but first, we have to register our union. Come with me."

At a loss for words, she walked with him into his private study. He sat in the chair and to her shock, the moment he had made the call to the ship, he yanked her into his lap.

A com officer was on the other end of the visual, and he looked at them in surprise. "Ambassador Leoraki, how may I direct your call?"

"I need a conference call between the historical archive and the registry office."

The com officer looked a little confused, and his wings fluttered. "That is an interesting combination."

Apolan's voice was wry. "I am aware of it."

The officer's cheeks darkened, and his fingers moved across the keyboard. "Connections are being processed."

A moment later, the screen was split, and they were looking at two people. One of the Stone Folk was staring at them from the left and Forest person was on the right.

The Stone representative cocked his head. "Ambassador, what can I do for you?"

"Registrar Yessik, I would like to register the bonding between myself and the Gaian, Daphne Harrow."

The grey man frowned, "I thought you were going to wait until our garden was operational."

"That brings me to the reason that I am also speaking to Archivist Utasi. My mate found the original bonding cavern, and the crystal has bound us together already."

The woman with the nut brown skin, hair and eyes looked excited. "You know where it is?"

"I have been there, and I will give you the coordinates when you come down for the celebration next week. I will expect that you bring what you need and that you take care not to disturb the area. It is a sacred space, and we must treat it as such."

Archivist Utasi nodded and smiled. "It will be an honour just to scan the place where so many of our people began."

"It has missed your people." The words came out of Daphne's mouth before she could stop them.

Everyone involved in the conversation paused and stared at her.

Apolan caressed her arm. "Has it, Daphne?"

"It has. All those lives bound together in its presence, and then, you went away and my folk have not seen it, nor are we ready to use it. Well, most of us cannot use it. There are a growing number who can and will, but they are not here yet." Daphne felt a pressure on her mind, and Apolan caressed her arm in a slow pattern.

"Are you speaking for the forest, Daphne?"

She frowned, "No, for the cavern. It is the heart of Gaia after all."

The archivist was rapt, as was the registrar. The attention that she was getting made her uncomfortable, so she did what she did best—she hid.

Snuggled against Apolan's chest, she held tight to him and pulled herself in. She heard comments and felt Apolan's body vibrate as he spoke.

The room went silent, and he pressed a kiss to her forehead. "We are alone again. You can come back."

She looked up at him and smiled. "Sorry. I wasn't expecting that."

"The conversation or being used to speak for a five-thousand-year-old consciousness?"

With nothing in her field of vision but him, she cupped her hand around the back of his neck and drew his mouth down to hers. "Yes."

Chapter Nine

"Daphne, are you sure?" His hands were stroking her back as she pressed kisses across his face and down his neck.

"As sure as I can be. I *need* to be with you, Apolan." Her hands stroked the heat of his body, the rigidity of his muscles and the smooth texture of his skin.

Apolan didn't need to be told twice and swiftly took her to his bedroom, setting her on the edge of the bed while he removed her clothing with feverish intensity. His clothing followed hers into a heap on the floor.

As he moved over her, stroking, waking, caressing, she shivered and returned each touch with one of her own. While the Forest Folk looked to be made of bark and moss, they felt wonderful.

Apolan took care with her, bringing her to the edge of sanity before he moved over her and joined them. Their connection went from tenuous to flaring life as he surged into her, and her body surrendered to the sensations he woke inside her.

Her mind chanted to her as her heartbeat slowed in the aftermath, *for better or for worse.*

Dawn was streaming through the skylight when fingers caressed her shoulder. "Good morning, dearest wife."

She smiled and blushed, turning into his arms. "Good morning, husband. What is on your agenda today?"

"You are the only item on my agenda, though I believe I have something for you." He rolled to his knees, and he had a box in his hand.

"The crystal chamber forced my hand, but we would have ended up here eventually. While my folk are known for their patience, none of us have had to deal with a Gaian before, and so my self-control was waning quickly. This is the earpiece that my great grandmother wore every day of her mated life. While the one creates a link, this one shows any and all members of the Nine that you are taken."

She smiled and opened the box. It was indeed the matching earpiece, set with the same tiny stones. Apolan helped her set it in place, and once it was, he pressed a kiss to her earlobe and then worked his way down her neck.

Daphne sighed happily and relaxed into his arms. She was naked next to a stranger, but right now, the last thing she wanted was to hide. It might not be self-confidence, but it was a good first step.

One week later . . .

She was standing next to Apolan in the receiving line and accepting the congratulations of every dignitary of the Nine that was willing to walk on Gaia.

When Mayor Tetra paused to shake her hand, he surprised her. "Daphne, I knew that you didn't fit in with Gaian society, but I didn't know why. This has explained much, and I can only wish you and your husband the best of luck in your role as representatives."

"Thank you, Mayor Tetra. I have been lucky as well. My parents gave me what few children ever have, a chance to find out what I was. I know what I am now, and it is a relief to find a man who accepts it. Narrow-minded societies can be so restricting."

Apolan's hand ran over her back, and the emerald silk was no barrier to the heat of his skin.

The mayor gave her a look, "You don't mind that he is an alien?"

Daphne drew a deep breath that brought many masculine gazes to the cleavage exposed by the dress. "The Nine evolved here. They are of Underhill, just as we are of Gaia. This soil shaped us all. They have merely come home after a long trip."

Slow applause began just at the edge of those who could hear her voice. It was the Wilder representative that began it, and it spread in a wave through the party.

The mayor faded away as Daphne was introduced to members of the Nine who were interested in seeking out Gaian mates. They had been drawn to the warship not knowing where the battle with the Tokkel would take them, and now, they were in orbit around their ancient home.

If fate had brought them this far, they were not going to disappoint her.

Apolan held her close as they danced. Each step brought them closer to the exterior, and in a rush, he grabbed her hand, and they rushed out into the night.

She laughed as they rushed into the newly completed gardens. "We are missing our own party."

"They will go on without us. I need to show you this."

The privacy-garden attendant let them pass.

He lifted her in his arms, and she shrieked and kicked at the lack of balance.

He swept through the gardens until they faced a huge tree with great, sweeping branches.

"Apolan, it's beautiful. Who is it?" she knew just looking at it that it was not simply a tree. "For that matter, how did it get here?"

He laughed and carried her to the tree and set her down, inches from its trunk. "When the Forest Folk wed, we do it for life. It does not matter when we pass into the next world, we will go together."

She clung to his hand, sensing that he was doing more than dropping a passing reference to mortality.

"When we die, if we are lucky enough to be blessed by children, they will take our bodies and bury them beneath a tree, and ten years from the date of our burial, they will take seeds from that tree and spread them through the family.

"When those children find mates, they will choose a home and select a young tree, planting it near their home. The seed that they hold will be buried in the roots of the tree and it will begin to grow. This tree is the seed of my great grandparents.

"The ancestor's tree will offer council, guidance and shelter to any nearby. You can come here and speak with them whenever you wish."

She reached out and touched the bark of the tree, swaying as the wave of love came over her. "The rest of your relatives are alive, aren't they?"

He smiled and pressed his hands over hers, "They are. We burn for a very, very long time. The Nine were not the only off-shoots given to the universe by Underhill, but we are the longest lived."

Daphne pressed her forehead against the tree before leaning back against her husband. "A love like that can grow from a seed?"

"No, but a seed can carry it. I have carried the seed of my ancestors my entire life, holding it when I was unsure about what I was feeling and waiting until I knew that I had found love. To know what it is supposed to feel like is a great boon to my kind, but it helped me know what I felt the moment that you ploughed into me in the forest that night."

"I felt rather flat after the impact, but there was a connection. My heart kicked in a few days later, and my soul was yours by the time we finished our picnic." She smiled up at him under the shade of his great grandparents' tree.

He stroked her hair back from her face and pressed soft kisses across her cheeks.

She asked softly, "How did the tree grow so fast?"

Apolan held her gently but firmly, and he grinned, his teeth white in the darkness, "You know as well as I do that love takes no time to grow. It just needs to have the opportunity to find the light."

Her laughter was stifled as his kisses found her lips and under the cover of the ancestor tree. They enjoyed a moment of simply being together before the stresses of being representatives of their worlds took over.

He was the ambassador and she was done hiding.

Guiding
Return of the Nine Book Four

By

Viola Grace

Chapter One

"... looking up at the sky, Henrietta Barrows knew that she had to leave the Earth. The tiny sliver of sky was so small, she could barely make out a single star. The moment that she made up her mind, she signed the paperwork and prepared for her journey. For better or worse, she was going to Gaia." Teyha smiled. "And that is all for today."

The two-dozen children groaned. They were seated in a semicircle around her chair with their faces turned up, eager to catch every detail of their ancestors' voyage.

Teyha closed the book. "Same time next week, and we will find out how Henrietta fared on the journey here."

The teachers thanked her and herded the children out of the Archive of Gaia. The plan had been to introduce a bit of Gaian colonist history into the classroom, but Teyha found that the children became part of the story if they were surrounded by it.

She tidied up the Hall of the Colony, smiling at the shift in shadows near the doorway. When she was finished, she turned her head, "Was there something you wanted?"

The shadows parted and Daphne Leoraki came bustling up. "Teyha. Am I glad to see you."

Teyha had gone to school with Daphne and came forward to speak to her as the shadows continued to shift. The children had probably run right past them, but they stood out like bright candles to Teyha's senses.

"Nice to see you too, Daphne. Who are your friends?"

Daphne smiled. "Shadow Folk. They need you to take them to the Temple of Shadows. Does that ring a bell?"

Teyha blinked and laughed. "Yeah, I know the spot."

She walked out of the hall and shooed her guests out in front of her, putting them in the light of the atrium. They were either male or the Shadow Folk had some enormous women. Each man was over a head taller than she was and wreathed in ever-shifting shadow. It was easy to see where they earned their name.

"What do you want there?"

The shadows shifted and one said, "You do not need to know."

She crossed her arms and scowled up at where she imagined his face was. "I do need to know. I take folks into the forests and hills so that they stay safe. Once we hit the foothills near the temple, no electronics work. We will be in a silent zone and unable to call for help by standard means. It is not a place for sightseeing."

His head shifted, and he looked at his friend before directing the shadows back to her. "It is a religious pilgrimage. We have not been able to walk to the temple on Naccru due to our placement on the mother ship of the Nine. It is important to us, and you will be paid well."

Teyha listened to what he wasn't saying. The tone of his voice was urgent and not with religious fervour. There was no greed or manipulation aside from the obvious. He was lying to her.

"Fine. I am guessing that this is an urgent pilgrimage?"

"Yes." He paused and said, "Please."

His friend spoke, "Please."

Teyha looked to Daphne. "Introductions?"

Daphne smiled, with relief on her face. "Ekinar Rossing, Representative of the Shadow Folk of the Nine."

The shadow that had spoken to her bowed low.

"Nosku Sheval, biologist on the mother ship."

The other man bowed as well but said, "Can we leave now?"

His urgency was palpable, and more than that, he was worried.

Teyha nodded. "I need to stop for a change of clothing and supplies. Do you have rations that are suited to your biology?"

Daphne nodded, "I will get them."

"Do you have a transport to the foothills?" She started calculating the supplies she would need for the one day in and one day out journey, with some extra for unforeseen circumstances.

"We do." Ekinar replied.

"Good. Meet me in the field nearest the embassy in one hour. I will be waiting. You will need food, water and boots. It is a two-day round trip."

She turned and left the men staring at her with Daphne snickering between them and trying to get them moving.

Teyha checked in at the office and informed the facility manager that she would be out on a guiding tour for a few days.

Reesha smiled and nodded. "Take pictures. That area is amazing."

"Can I use the manual cam? I am going into the foothills." Teyha raised her eyebrows.

Reesha sighed. "Take good care of it, or you will have to make another one."

Teyha crossed the room and opened the safe, getting the camera bag and several spare rolls of film. Since she was heading into an ancient settlement, there was no reason not to use the opportunity to take more images of the Temple of Shadows and the glyphs and markings that it contained.

The first time that she had gone to the temple area, it had been curiosity, and she had been rushed. Now, she had another chance, and she wanted to go in prepared.

With the bag over her shoulder, she waved cheerfully to Reesha and headed out to her small apartment.

As Teyha entered, she began to shed her clothing on the way to her bedroom. The wardrobe that held her expedition gear was code locked, but a few well-placed digits and it opened to her touch. Humming to herself, she tugged on her wilderness suit, stomped into her hiking boots and wrapped her wrists.

Her hair was swiftly wrapped up in a tight braid that restrained the fine tendrils from floating loose.

Whistling softly, she strapped on her knives, checked her compact bow and bolt supply, grabbed two weeks' worth of compressed rations, placing them and water packs in her backpack on top of the flare gun and flares. She could only carry enough water for two days, but she knew where the streams were in the area, and tests had proved them potable.

Her first trip into the foothills had been to discover why the area repelled technology. Between the mineral samples that she had obtained, the water samples, and the first-hand viewing of an ancient city of the Nine, it had been a surprising and bittersweet success.

Teyha's exploration had been her attempt at grieving. Her parents had been a geologist and a historian respectively, and looking for proof of the previous occupation of Gaia by the Nine had been her way of honouring their memory. They had died in a landslide in the foothills six months before the Tokkel attacks, and when the planet had been at risk, Teyha had found other things to occupy her time.

After her discovery, she had been called to confirm the ancient settlement and swore to her observations in front of the Gaian council. It had been a testimony that cemented their agreement to working with the new aliens in orbit above them. With Teyha's confirmation that there was indeed an ancient ruin of the Nine, it was confirmed that they were what they claimed, kindred spirits with a common enemy.

Carefully, she tucked the camera into her pack and sealed it. With a grunt and a move that she had practiced for years, she hoisted the pack onto her back. A sharp jerk tightened the shoulder straps. A buckle fastened it to her waist.

She looked in the mirror and made a face. Her ice grey eyes stared back at her as her lips twisted. Sighing, she smoothed her features, checked her gear and her ability to reach the weapons one more time and left her apartment, locking the door.

It was time to catch her ride.

Chapter Two

Teyha followed Ekinar's instruction and keyed in the details of their proposed landing site. The transport lifted and began its rapid cruise over the landscape.

She took one last look at the watchtower where her friend Lazkiy was on duty. Two days from now at sunset, Lazkiy would be waiting for a signal.

Teyha had not told the Shadow Folk about the planned safety check. They kept things from her, and she kept things from them.

"How are you qualified for this mission?" Nosku's voice was far more grating than that of his companion.

"I am a guide, and I have never gotten lost. How is that?" She watched the landscape spin by, and her mind automatically reset her orientation. She didn't discuss her radar with strangers, so they weren't going to learn that either.

Ekinar shifted, his shadows flowing around him. "Have you truly been to the Temple of Shadows?"

"I have been to the site. I did not go inside."

Nosku muttered, "We should have found someone else."

Ekinar shifted and leaned toward his friend.

Teyha held up her hand to interrupt what he was about to say. "Let me be clear here. There is no one else. No other Gaian has explored that range. If you could have found your way there on your own, you would have. I have actually been there before. I am prepared for the local predators and aware of the landslide dangers. I will get you in for whatever you really want, and I will lead you out again. We will do it safely and securely and in an organized manner. Are we clear?"

Ekinar leaned forward, "What do you mean, what we really want?"

She looked at him with calm eyes, something that most folks found unnerving. The paleness of her eyes gave her the appearance of someone who had been blinded. "I am not a fool, nor am I ignorant of body language. You two lied about your reasons for being out here, and I don't care. Daphne asked me to take you, so you are above board, but aside from that, I know you lied to me about your true reason for the visit."

Silence fell. No one said a word. The transport continued to approach the foothills, and an hour later, the systems started to malfunction.

"Please land the transport, and prepare to start your hike." Teyha settle back into her pack and kept her voice chipper and cheerful, in true guide fashion.

Ekinar brought the transport down near a copse of trees. "Will the vehicle be alright here?"

"Yes. The keedu can't get over the edge, and the electronics will be fine as long as they don't reach further into the disruption field generated by the minerals." She huffed as she repositioned her pack before strapping it into place.

Nosku got to his feet, and he picked up two flat packs from under a seat in the transport, handing one to Ekinar.

Teyha looked at the swirling shadows and shrugged before starting to walk. This was going to be so much fun, she could barely stand it.

The foothills rapidly gave way to narrow canyons and eerie echoes.

The shadowed figures stayed behind her, but she could hear the huffing and puffing that accompanied their efforts.

Two hours in, the light was beginning to dim. Her other senses were compensating, but she had no idea what the capabilities of the Shadow Folk were. "We are going to stop for a rest."

Nosku said, "No, we have to continue."

She shook her head. "I am in charge. You will do no one any good if you drop from exhaustion. Sit, drink, have something to eat, and we will continue our discussion."

Nosku shook his head. "We have to move as quickly as we can."

"Ekinar, please get your friend to sit and eat. We won't make it to the temple before dark, and I have some questions to ask you." Teyha sat and fished out a ration pack, sipping at water slowly, washing down the compressed food.

Ekinar sat and took out his own meal, leaving Nosku fidgeting, his shadows flickering and flaring.

"Well, I suppose we are free to tell you what we are actually looking for."

Teyha looked at him as her night vision began to take hold. "Please. I can be of better use if I know what I am seeking."

Nosku was seated away from her, and he was vibrating with tension. "My nephew and two of his friends stole a shuttle to seek out the Temple of Shadows. We tracked them here, but we lost the signal. If we reported the stolen vehicle to the Nine, they would put it on my nephew's record, and it would damage his chances for advancement when he enters the service."

Teyha nodded. "And if you had told the Gaians, they would have had to report it to the mother ship before authorizing you to run around the surface."

Ekinar nodded. "Correct. Any way we look at it, the children would suffer for being children."

Teyha groaned and rubbed the back of her neck. "Okay, that is something completely different. How is your night vision?"

Nosku sat up, and his body language changed. "We can see easily in the dark."

"Lucky you, so can I. I can get us to the site tonight, but we can't try anything until the morning. The area is covered with glyphs and ancient language markings, and I have only managed to translate a few. Now, tell me about your myths and legends about the Temple of Shadows."

Nosku nodded. "Thank you. Well, the Shadow Folk have always believed that the Temple of Shadows was the centre of our ancestors' lives here on Underhill. It is an opening in the side of a mountain and only accessible by our kind."

Teyha frowned. "That doesn't sound right, but we will see when we get there."

Ekinar finally stated the question that she had been waiting for. "Gaians can't see in the dark."

She blinked at him, her vision finally giving her an idea of the man behind the shadows. It was too early yet, too much light getting in the way, but she could make out sharply chiselled features and a quizzical expression. "Who said I could see in the dark? I have night vision. It is a very different thing."

She had them wait while she attended to nature and returned to rifle through her pack, bringing out her bow and bolts.

"Why are you arming yourself?" Ekinar was close to her, and she found she didn't mind.

"There are quite a few deadly beasts here in the area. Most are nocturnal, so our journey is taking us through their hunting grounds. Better safe than stupid."

She put her pack back on and continued to sip on her water as she began to move again. They would follow her. She was their only chance.

Her senses were fully attuned to the night around her. A slow, rhythmic thudding was horribly familiar. Teyha whispered, "Get to the canyon walls and hold tight. We don't have time to get out of here."

Ekinar was moving as she ordered, but he asked, "What is it?"

"Stampede of Risshin deer followed by a Caplan." She settled her back against the wall, and when Nosku stumbled to join them, she raised her bow and waited.

It took two minutes for the stampede to become audible to the others, and a minute after that, the deer rushed past them with the Caplan right behind them.

It was silly, but the initial settlers named animals on Gaia after themselves. The large feline known as a Caplan had six legs, teeth over a hand span long and a wicked temper.

The animal paused as it scented them, shaking its head in confusion. Teyha took aim, but she didn't want to strike the Caplan if it wasn't necessary.

Ekinar put his hand on her arm, and she watched him extend his other arm, snapping at the Caplan with the shadow that normally covered his body.

The Caplan whipped around in confusion, and Ekinar struck it again. Within fifteen seconds, the Caplan continued to chase the deer through the canyon, leaving the hikers alone.

"Nice trick." Teyha released the tension on her bow.

"You didn't want to kill it, and it didn't need to die. It just had to be reminded of its food source."

She chuckled. "Thank you. I thought those shadows had to be useful, though you do have striking features beyond it."

Nosku gasped. "Ekinar, you showed her?"

She looked over at his face, and based on the Earth histories she had read, his face wore the stamp of the privileged classes. "He didn't show me anything, and get that sneer off your face. It isn't pretty."

Nosku looked ill.

"If you are going to puke, do it over there." She pointed across the way.

Teyha looked into Ekinar's surprised face. "Well, shall we continue?"

He nodded, bemused. "Of course. They are depending on us."

She hoisted her pack once again. "Damned straight."

He clapped Nosku on the shoulder, and they resumed their walk.

Teyha took point once again and extended her senses into the dark. A few predators took a close look at them but decided better of attacking.

The hike took on a numb, exhausted mindlessness for her, but if there were lost teens, she wasn't going to let her body pull her down.

She kept her thoughts focussed on the children, and when they finally stumbled out of the last rock canyon, it was with no small relief that she was able to say, "We have entered the Valley of Shadows. The temple is to the left."

The huge valley was dotted with stalagmites, which gave it the daytime appearance of having thousands of shadows throughout.

"Do you see them?" Ekinar was at her shoulder.

"No, but their shuttle is right over there. Do you want to start there?" She pointed, but Nosku was already stumbling his way across the valley floor. "I will take that as a yes."

She followed while she widened her personal sensory net. Three heartbeats were muffled but alive. There was only one problem. They weren't in the temple. They were in the prison. .

CHAPTER THREE

"Ekinar, what was the description of the temple again?"

They were inside the shuttle, and Nosku was looking for any traces of his nephew.

"The fissure in a cavern wall, a place only the Shadow Folk can enter. Why?" Ekinar was watching Nosku's attempt to start the shuttle, so he could check the records.

"This ship is dead. Unless you chop it into pieces and haul it out manually, this isn't going anywhere." Teyha was barely able to stay upright. Using her talent for an extended time was more exhausting than hiking in the dark.

"There has to be some trace of them here." Nosku's voice broke.

"There is. They are exactly where you said they would be. In the fissure, in the cliff, in a place only the Shadow Folk can go." Teyha sighed, "But based on my early translations, it isn't the temple, it is the prison."

Nosku froze. "The pit?"

"Not so much a pit as a crevice with a warning around the door. Your folk were not here the last time I came, so I had to guess at the meaning."

Ekinar put his hand on Nosku's arm to calm him. "Where is it?"

"Come with me."

She left the shuttle and made her way carefully to the doorway in the cliff face. In the dark, the glyphs were surprisingly clear to her. They were bright and seemed to glow from within.

"Where are you looking, Teyha?"

It was the first time that Ekinar had called her by name, and she had to throttle down the pleased surge of emotion that occurred when he wrapped his lips around her syllables.

"The glyphs around the doorway. Don't you see them?" She pointed, and when he still frowned and squinted in the direction she was pointing, she took his hand and pressed it to the stone.

Nosku grabbed her shoulder. "Where are they?"

"They are in the cave. Three heartbeats, all stable." Teyha compared the beats to the men in front of her. "Maybe the heartbeats are a little fast."

Nosku pushed past her and into the cave.

"No, don't go in there." She spoke to his back, and when he passed the threshold that lined the chasm, he was trapped. "Damn it."

"I can't see him. Where is he?" Ekinar was frowning. His hands were still on the wall, tracing the carvings one by one.

"He is in the Prison of Shadows if these glyphs are any indication. Can you read them?"

He jerked toward the opening. "We have to get them out."

"We will, but we need to know what we are going into. I can't read the glyphs properly until it is light out, so we either get you to translate by touch or you blunder into the cave and get stuck like the others." Teyha leaned against the wall and gave into the urge to use it for support.

"You do not look well."

"I don't usually use my talent for stretches that are this long."

He took her arm and helped her sit. "Relax. If you need light, we will wait for light."

She nodded and got out some water. Sighing as she sipped and let the rehydration sooth her body. "Well, Nosku has rations and water, so the kids should be fine for a night."

"You are right. How is it that you can see us as we are?"

Teyha chuckled. "I see a version of you. My talent is primarily a version of echolocation. I can feel heartbeats and sense shifts in topography. It does no good in the city, but thanks to my parents, I got plenty of practice out in the canyons and abandoned settlements."

"You have been to other cities?"

She chuckled. "Until the Nine locked into position above us, a few of us were still busy learning everything we could about Gaia. Once the Tokkel attacked, we all concentrated on recovering from those first devastating days. It is amazing that so few deaths could make such a huge impact."

Teyha knew she was rambling, but she was just so tired. She used her pack as a cushion and relaxed against it, breathing evenly until she was able to slip into a light sleep.

Ekinar sensed her shift into sleep. He couldn't feel any of his folk around him, and if he hadn't known about the barrier she had mentioned, he would have followed Nosku into the chasm.

The small Gaian was a curious creature, but she was making every effort to allow him his privacy. It was something that he appreciated, but once he had touched her, he knew something she didn't. Teyha was going to be his.

Ekinar Rossing had searched for a suitable female for ten years. In a few hours, this woman had not only seen through the mask that he and the rest of his folk wore, but she had been unmoved by it.

It was a slight prick to his ego that she had not fallen under the spell of his physical perfection, but since she was on the clock, he supposed that he could put his ego aside and simply enjoy her nearness.

There were formalities to go through. He needed to give her a piece of his shadow to sync her body to his and let him know her moods, but that would wait. He didn't want to chance the dark energy disrupting what he had just read.

And so, when they have displeased their folk, the Shadows shall be pressed into the cavern until such time as their sentence has been accrued. Once that time has gone, they will only leave with the touch of the light and drawn through the barrier that marked their imprisonment.

It was formally worded, but Ekinar was hopeful that Teyha qualified as the light and that she could bring the children and Nosku back through.

Teyha woke with a jolt as light started to caress her. She sat up, groaned and looked to Ekinar.

He was seated in the same position she had just been in, and he stirred when she dropped her pack and stood up.

"Nature calls. I will be right back." Teyha moved and stretched her stiff limbs as she located a suitably hidden outcropping.

After she was suited back up, she returned to the chasm, staring at the now-visible glyphs while she washed her hands in some of her drinking water before grabbing a ration pack out of her bag.

"What did you learn from the archway?" Teyha munched quietly.

Ekinar stretched, and she watched his shadows flex and twist around him. He was back to being hidden, and she couldn't stifle a sigh. He was so pretty when her senses were on high alert.

"You may be able to bring them out. It says that the touch of the light will bring them out. You are definitely not shadow, so you might qualify."

She grimaced. "If I can't get out, there is a flare gun in my pack. Just after dusk tonight, fire the blue flare. Help will come and to hell with the kids' job future, we will get them out alive."

"I hope it does not come to that. Try and see if you can get in and out." Ekinar's tone was encouraging.

Teyha looked into the darkness of the prison and sighed. "Fine. Don't forget. Blue flare, straight up."

"Blue flare, straight up. Good luck."

He touched her arm, and she felt part of his shadow touch her cheek. When she looked at him, it was gone, but there was no doubt that something had just happened.

Teyha breathed in deep, striding forward. For better or worse, she was walking right into the mouth of hell.

Chapter Four

The texture of the air changed, growing thick and heavy. Teyha exhaled and inhaled again sharply. The air was fine. The sensation was on her skin, clawing at her senses.

As suddenly as it started, it stopped, and she stumbled into an antechamber.

Four pale faces stared at her. Nosku seemed uncomfortable. "Why are you here?"

"The translation indicates that I may be able to take you out of here, one by one. Who is first?"

The young men frowned at her, and it was easy to see which one was Nosku's nephew. The young woman looked exhausted, so Teyha extended her hand. "What is your name?"

"Hiska. Hiska Kandor. This is my brother, Ritgar."

Teyha smiled at the manners that were in evidence in this young woman. "I am Teyha Wynn. Pleased to meet you."

Nosku cleared his throat. "This is my nephew, Darku Sheval."

Teyha nodded toward the young man. "Pleased to meet you as well. Now, someone is going to have to go first, and I would rather it be one of the folk who have been here for a while."

Hiska stepped forward. "I will try. It was painful to attempt it the first few times, so I am really hoping this works."

Teyha smiled. "You and me both. Boys, I will be back as soon as I can if this works and sooner if it doesn't."

She held out her hand, and Hiska took it. The teen was taller than Teyha already and her skin was cooler than it should be.

They walked back to the barrier, and Teyha tightened her grip as she stepped into the column of air that seemed to stop the Shadow Folk. Hiska slowed but forged forward, and in fifteen seconds, they were out in the open with Ekinar waiting for them.

"You did it!"

Teyha laughed as she bent forward, resting her hands on her knees. "I did one, now for the other three. This is not going to be fun."

He was at her side with his hand on her shoulder.

Hiska was sobbing softly, her shadowed face tilted to the sun. Now that she was in daylight, her shadows were wrapped around her once again.

Teyha drank some water, took in a few mouthfuls of rations and turned back to the chasm. "Okay, calm controlled. I can do this."

She forged into the prison once again and smiled brightly as she caught her breath. "Hiska is safe. Who is next?"

Ritgar took her hand and went to join his sister. He whispered as they paused before crossing the barrier. "Thank you for doing this. Thank you for finding us."

"Thank me when we make it out to the other side." She breathed deeply, watched him do the same and charged through the barrier without looking back.

She stumbled and fell when they made it out the other side.

Ritgar went forward and embraced Hiska. The siblings sat together, whispering their relief.

Teyha knelt and struggled for her body to calm down. Her pulse was racing, her vision was blurry and her knees were weak.

"Take a rest. You can't do this twice more and stay conscious." Ekinar was at her side, stroking tendrils of hair from her face.

"I will have to do it once and make it count then." Teyha nodded. She drank more water and turned to plunge back into the barrier for the final time.

Nosku and Darku were waiting nervously.

She gasped, coughed and straightened. "I don't have the strength to do this twice more today, so if I am going to pass out, I would rather it be in daylight with everyone safe."

Nosku scowled. "What do you mean?"

"I mean, you are each going to take one of my hands and cling to my arm if you have to, but I am getting you both out of here right now." She tried to make it look like she knew what she was doing, but she really had no clue.

She moved to the edge of the barrier and extended her arms. Darku took her left, Nosku her right and each grabbed a bicep. As one, they moved forward, and it took thirty seconds to walk ten feet, but on the other side, sweet air greeted them.

Teyha fell into Ekinar's arms, and he lifted her, seating her next to her pack.

Spots were flickering in her vision, and they grew closer and closer together until the shadow casing Ekinar was the last thing she saw.

"What is wrong with her?" Nosku's strident demand grated on Ekinar's nerves.

"She used up her energy hauling you through the barrier. Her power wrapped around you and burned off as you passed through the gateway. You owe her your life."

Nosku frowned. "This was her duty."

Ekinar rounded on him, lashing out at the other male with his shadows and lifting Nosku off the ground. "Her duty? She is a historian. This is her hobby, what she does for fun and personal education."

Darku put his hand on his uncle's arm. "We owe her our lives. You would not have found us without her. No electronics work here. We dropped out of the sky and nothing we could do would stop our descent. It was Hiska's piloting that got us in alive."

Ritgar stood up with his arm around his sister. "It seems that women have saved us at all critical points in this adventure. Can we be going now?"

Ekinar shook his head. "No. We can't find our way back without her. Let her rest."

As if his words were prophetic, Teyha heaved in a deep breath and struggled upright. His heart lurched as her bloodshot eyes focussed on him. She smiled weakly. "I am okay, but I have one question, does anyone here actually want to see the Temple of Shadows?"

The expressions on their faces were enough to lift Teyha's spirit. "If someone can carry my pack, I can take you there now. It isn't far."

Ekinar helped her to her feet and slung her pack over one shoulder, surprised at its weight. "You carried this all this way?"

"Well, it was heavier when I started. There are a lot of emergency kits in there as well as the flares." She tottered but stabilized when Ekinar offered her his arm.

Holding to his arm, she smiled at the amassed Shadow Folk, "Well, do you want to see the temple?"

Nosku cleared his throat. "If we are able to, please. We appreciate your assistance in this matter."

Teyha blinked. "Um, my pleasure. It is always good to share knowledge when one can. Who knows, you are probably the only folk of the Nine who have been to this area since your ancestors left."

Ritgar and Hiska took on an anticipatory posture. Hiska asked quietly. "Can we go? Please?"

Teyha laughed, "If you want to head for that third pillar, turn north, go around the rocky outcropping and then see if you can find your temple. It's wiley."

The teens and Nosku took off.

Teyha smiled up at Ekinar and walked slowly with him.

"You did an excellent thing getting them all out."

"I know. I just wish I wasn't so tired. I have a lecture in two days." She smiled. "I will need to get some sleep before then, and I don't know when I will fit it in."

They walked slowly toward the outcropping that Teyha had identified, and as they reached the first turn, shouts of astonishment echoed along the rocks.

"I believe they have found it." She chuckled as the excited chatter reached them.

Ekinar held her steady as they rounded the curves of the path, and when he saw the Temple of Shadows, he let out the same amazed sound as the others.

Chapter Five

A pyramid of buff stone with a polarized cap sat in the centre of the valley floor. It was beautiful, and Teyha smiled the same way she had when her parents had been at her side.

Ahead of them, Nosku and the teens were running toward the temple entrance. Teyha smiled at Ekinar, "If you want to run down there, I can manage on my own. I will get there eventually."

"It has lasted thousands of years. It will manage to survive for the ten minutes it will take to walk there."

"Very practical." She was relieved. Her body was not up to supporting itself. "Once we get there, if you want to run around and be all Shadow Folky, I will understand. Just park me in a corner and let me flip out my bedroll, and you can cease to babysit me."

He turned the dark flickering shadows surrounding his face. "You wouldn't mind?"

"I wouldn't mind sleeping here under full sun."

He chuckled. "Fair enough. I will wake you at sundown."

She gave him a thumbs up but wasn't sure if it translated. "It means everything is good."

He nodded. "I have taken the Gaian euphemism classes. They also included some colourful language that I will need help with one day."

Teyha laughed, "Call Daphne. She is an expert on language not fit for mixed company, though she rarely uses it herself."

"I thought I might come to one of your lectures and meet you after for tea or dinner." His words—though casual—dropped heavily between them.

She blinked. "I don't know what kind of company I would be. My brain tends to be locked onto the ancient sites on Gaia and the diaries of the first colonists."

"It sounds fascinating. I was interested in the history of Underhill before I entered the service and ended up as the Council Representative for the Shadow Folk." He continued to walk at her pace, but the ball was now in her court.

Teyha bit her lip. "Sure. Dinner would be nice, I mean, whenever you get back down here."

She paused, not sure if she was overstepping her bounds. "I have come up with a reasonable excuse for why the teens ended up on the surface. Something close to the truth, but it does lay a bit of blame on Nosku. Nothing major, just a little bit of negligence on the part of an uncle. I will need to find out how they knew to come here though, in order to make the story more plausible."

Ekinar was grim. "Nosku will cooperate. He will do what you ask and say what you tell him to."

She smirked, "He doesn't seem very cooperative to me."

"He will be when I get through with him, but you have brought the matter up that I did not think of, how did the children learn the coordinates?"

They reached the great doors to the temple and passed through and into the past of the Shadow Folk. Teyha tugged at Ekinar to take her to the side of the huge entry hall so that she could get some sleep.

When he put the pack down, she grabbed the roll tucked under the carrying portion of the pack, flipped it flat and struck the corner to inflate it into a comfortable bed. A foil blanket would keep her body stable, and the water that she put next to her head would help her out when she woke.

All tucked in and exhausted beyond bearing, Teyha relaxed and left the Shadow Folk to their own devices.

Ekinar was torn between watching his soon-to-be mate and exploring something his folks knew of only through myth and legend.

Nosku skidded back into the anteroom and waved his arms with urgency. Unable to resist the normally taciturn Nosku's sudden enthusiasm, Ekinar followed the man into the other room, promising to come back and check on the lightly snoring Gaian.

Teyha's breathing was deep and even, so he felt better about walking into the huge audience hall with its five seats.

"It is actually here." All his life he had been told about the Temple of Shadows and its importance to his people. The councils that they now used instead were pale imitations of the five grand seats spaced evenly around the room.

"Try one. They are inactive so it won't harm anything." Nosku walked across the room and took one of the two unoccupied seats.

The children were in the other three.

Shrugging, Ekinar took the final empty seat and sat back, rubbing his hands along the grooves in the throne that had been worn by generations of hands over time.

He relaxed into it, breathing deeply, imagining his ancestors sitting in this very chair.

He was caught by surprise when energy coursed through the chair, locking him and the other four in place, unable to even call for help. Their shadows burned off and they stared at each other in shock as the chairs cast judgement and found them wanting.

It was not enough sleep, but Teyha's reflexes woke her anyway. She stumbled to her feet and followed her instincts through the entry hall and into the room beyond.

Teyha wanted to be surprised, but she couldn't manage it. She looked from one lovely, pain-filled face to another and shook her head. "Why am I not surprised?"

She read the glyphs on the floor as best she could, and while Ekinar's face begged her to run, she wandered right to the centre of the room and then shifted a few inches to the left.

Power surged through her, perking her up considerably. "I would get out of those chairs now if I were you. I don't have much more patience for this sort of thing. Once was an accident, twice is really bad judgement."

They scrambled free of the large thrones, and as they left, the field she was disrupting dissipated.

Unable to do anything else, she sat where she was. "Okay, who wants to tell me what just happened? Why were you fiddling around in the Hall of Judgement?"

Ekinar was shaking, but his shadow was wrapped around him again. "We thought we were in the council hall."

She scowled up at him. "Don't any of you read the signs over the doors? This says Hall of Judgement. I am guessing that the chairs were making sure that the accused could see their judges. Was it painful?"

He frowned. "More uncomfortable than anything else, I am also intensely embarrassed."

She held her hands up in a mute request. When he complied and helped her back to her feet, he stood next to her, rubbing the back of her knuckles with small motions.

"Perhaps you should wait until you know what you are doing or there is an expedition down here to explore this city of your past."

The teens were huddling close to each other, and Nosku had the arrogant stamp on his features.

Sighing, she yawned. "Do you want a quick tour?"

The teens nodded and Ekinar grinned. "Please. We may not be on the expedition who gets to come here, so this could be our one chance."

She laughed, "Okay, first the fountain. I really need to soak my head."

Chapter Six

Water ran under her hiking suit, but she felt much better. The clear fountain with drinkable water was received well by all.

Hiska looked at it wistfully when it was time to leave, and Teyha silently promised her a bath before they left.

They investigated private homes, market areas, small abandoned cafés and a number of other vital areas before the sun tinged on its way down.

"I have to get back to my pack, and we need to be on our way." She smiled regretfully.

No one protested. It had been educational, but they had blundered into two traps left by the ancients and that had a sobering effect on their urge to stick around.

Back in the entry hall, she rolled up her bed, fastened it tightly to her back and then folded up her blanket until it was a palm-sized packet.

She fixed the pink *out in 12 hours* flare in her gun and started the walk back through the jungle of rock without another word. She needed way more sleep than she had gotten, but if she got them out in five large pieces, she would be pleased with herself.

"I will carry your pack. It is heavy."

She snorted at Ekinar. "I carried it in, I will carry it out."

He didn't argue, but as the darkness covered their trail and she saw the Shadow Folk sans shadow, his face was concerned.

She set a brutal pace for their trip out. Everyone was tired, but if they waited too long, they would lose momentum. The ground around them didn't only work on electronics. It had a strange effect on the mental patterns of anyone who stayed too long.

The teens stumbled but helped each other around obstacles, and Nosku huffed along without speaking. If Teyha was being honest, she was keeping up the paces so she wouldn't have to listen to his whining.

With the night firmly in place around them, she stopped. "Take a short break. I have to check in."

Nosku wasn't sure what she was going to do, but as the flare exploded and arched skyward, he looked at her with horror. "What did you do?"

"What I always do. I sent a signal to our watchtower that I would be out of danger in twelve hours. If I don't show at the tower by then, they will send a search party for me."

"You?"

She looked at him with a frown. "For such pretty faces, you have such a penchant for scowls. Yes, me. As far as anyone knows, I simply took the ambassador and his wife on an expedition to see one of the ancient cities of Gaia, or Underhill in your case."

He relaxed, and she could see embarrassment.

Darku cleared his throat. "Thank you for your discretion. Hiska and Ritgar don't deserve the stigma of stealing a ship."

Teyha laughed, "Especially since you were the one who stole it and convinced them to come along."

He looked shocked. "How did you . . ."

She held up her hand. "Hiska and Ritgar are followers. You are a bully. My guess is that you wanted to impress Hiska with your daring, and it backfired in the prison. Fortunately, as a good girl of the Shadow Folk, she refused to go without her brother and that alone saved her from whatever you had planned."

Nosku scowled. "How could you know that?"

"Hiska and Ritgar have not spoken to your nephew unless it was necessary since they got out of the prison, even you have avoided him. So, either he has worse body odour than the other two, or he did something that lost him trust."

The men were opening and closing their mouths.

"There are also recent bruises on Hiska's arms, and based on position, I am guessing that her piloting in was done under duress, because Darku didn't want to take responsibility for the crash. Her hands on the controls would shift blame if scans were done. Funny thing. No scanners work here."

Teyha loaded the next flare and kept it at her side. "We have twelve hours to get me home or alarms will sound all over the planet. The last thing you want is to try anything out here Nosku. You are not the only adult Shadow Folk here, and Ekinar is looking none too impressed."

She grabbed a ration pack and bottle of water. "Okay, I am moving, so come with me if you want to get out of here."

Hiska moved up just behind her and spoke quietly. "How did you know?"

"The bruises? You tried to cover them up in the cave, but they were already blue-black. They had been there a while."

"No, about Darku."

Teyha kept hiking. "Gaians have teenage boys too. They press every advantage they can and have even been known to pull some ridiculous moves to win the attention of their chosen girl."

Hiska nodded. "How can you see us? I mean our faces. We have always been told that if one not of our folk saw our face, they would fall in love with us and pine until they died."

"Really? From what I see, you folk are like statues. Pale and perfect but with little exposure to a reality outside your folk. You don't even interact with the others of the Nine, do you?"

Hiska shook her head. "No. Same reason though. We don't want to dazzle them."

"You may want to test that in controlled environments. Can you drop the shadows at will?"

The young woman frowned. "I don't know. I know it fades when we sleep, so it could be a learned behaviour."

"We accept the reality with which we are presented. Make sure you are safe but experiment at will. Don't tell Ekinar or your brother that I told you to though. That is a conversation I am not interested in having."

Hiska giggled, and for a moment, she was relaxed and her face did have an unearthly beauty.

Two more hours and a short break. Everyone was exhausted, but they were only two hours from seeing the plains ahead of them.

When they all staggered to their feet, Teyha led the numb march through the hills, pausing to let a shale slide run its course before slowly and carefully making her way over the small shards of rock. "Be careful. This stuff is sharp."

She heard one of her party cry out, but it was only one, and as Nosku helped his nephew over the slide, she saw the telltale blood on Darku's hand.

She set her pack down and retrieved a medical kit. With even motions, she took his hand, rinsed it, applied a standard antiseptic and wrapped the palm carefully to keep pressure on the wound.

"Why did you do that if I am such a monster?"

She sighed. "You are a teenager. Your hormones dictate most of your actions, but you have to take responsibility for those actions. Shoving responsibility off is the act of a child. If you want to be seen as an adult, act as an adult."

He looked at the bandage on his hand and back to her. "What if it changes my life?"

"Then, it makes the change and alters the man you will become. A future built on a lie and the act of a coward will definitely have an effect on your reality. You made a mistake, own up to it. You took a chance, bear it proudly."

He nodded and there was a shy smile. "Thank you for your repeated rescue. It seems that there are some Gaians who are not simply pathetic sheep waiting for the Nine to save them."

Shaking her head, she snapped the kit together and put it back in her pack. "It just goes to show you, anyone anywhere can be exceptional. They only need a chance."

She shifted her pack back into position and kept going. When she put the pack in, she had pulled the bolt gun out, and she led her small party through the stone, keeping her senses honed for any sign of predators attracted to blood.

The moment that the rock face ceased and the plains opened before them was so sudden that even Teyha gasped, and she had known where they were.

With wobbling knees, she made it down the graded slope. The transport was right where they had left it, and a chunk of metal had never looked so welcome.

She climbed into the back, sat with a thud and waited for the rest of her party. Hiska sat next to her, holding onto her arm tightly. Ritgar sat next to his sister, exhaustion and relief on his features. Darku sat with his uncle, and Ekinar took the controls.

With no other words between them, the transport lifted, turned and raced back across the plains.

Teyha nodded off, but when Hiska shook her arm, she woke. "Damn. I need to get back to town."

Hiska smiled, "I am sure they will take you there in the morning. For now, baths, clean clothing and hot food."

The ambassador and his wife were standing in the courtyard, wearing long robes in silky green fabric.

Daphne smiled at Teyha and Hiska. "Come this way, ladies. We will get you sorted and comfortable in no time."

Teyha smirked. "Were you expecting us?"

"Something like that. We always keep guest quarters ready for whatever representatives from the Nine decide to show up. The servants are arranging a meal for the men, but I will take care of you, and I think a bath, clean clothing and a good meal is right in line. Come this way."

CHAPTER SEVEN

Following Daphne's silk-clad back was difficult when Teyha's system was trying to flick between her enhanced vision and normal sight due to light.

"This is Hiska's chamber. There is clothing in the wardrobe, and when you are ready, join us for dinner in the common room."

"This is your chamber, Teyha. Shower, get dressed and come on out. I have caf for you and three types of tea."

"Tease." Laughing, Teyha hauled her kit into the room and smiled at its lush comfort. An inviting bed, a large bath and wide shower all called her with equal voices, but if she was to debrief Daphne, she had better turn to the shower.

She unravelled her braid before she stepped under the hot spray and groaned as the shower pulsed and relaxed all tight muscles, one by one.

The grey puddle of rock dust and grime proved her need for a shower.

Finally clean, she towelled off and checked out the options for clothing. She selected a long black silk shift and a red robe so everything was covered.

The soft carpet under her feet made her toes crinkle in happiness. She joined the ambassador's wife in the common area and clapped her hands happily at the spread of food before her.

Hiska came in behind her, wearing a deep purple robe. They took their seats, and Daphne smiled, "Eat. You look like you are starving."

Teyha didn't need to be told twice. While she was eating, Daphne announced, "We called the watchtower and told them you were safe."

Clearing her mouth by swallowing, Teyha said, "Thank you."

She had no desire to be hunted by her friend, but if she had been lost, she trusted no one other than Ioy Lazkiy to find her.

When she had eaten her fill and had three cups of caf, her body announced that she needed sleep.

Her yawn was uncontrollable. "Excuse me."

"The Shadow Folk Representative would like to speak with you before you retire."

She blinked at Daphne, "Huh?"

136

Hiska said softly, "Ekinar Rossing. He is our species representative when we deal with aliens. You qualify."

She nodded, "Okay. Where?"

Daphne gracefully got to her feet and walked around to Teyha's chair. "Come this way. There is a study where you can have some privacy."

Teyha was feeling like a sheep. She would go wherever she was herded.

Daphne opened the door, and within, Ekinar ceased pacing. He looked into Teyha's eyes and asked. "How much time do I have?"

She smiled blissfully. "I plan to be unconscious in five minutes."

"Right." He walked up to her and pressed his hands to her shoulders. "Teyha, in you, I have felt something that my life has been missing. I want to be with you always and have you at my side, but that will take some major manoeuvring, so until then, I will leave you with this."

The shadows of his body faded away, and she watched, bemused, as he got closer. When his lips caressed hers, her eyes widened as she finally caught on to what was going on. His lips were silky and cool, so she leaned up into his kiss, and he parted his lips against hers, spurring her mimicry. With their mouths connected and slightly open, he exhaled into her mouth, and the power and cool slip of a piece of his shadow into her was unmistakable.

He deepened the kiss again, stroking her lips with his tongue and warming her skin. She shivered and moaned, pressing against him, the robe and slip no barrier to his own dark robe.

A throat clearing in the doorway broke their kiss, but Ekinar kept his arms around her, holding her hips to his.

Apolan Leoraki was standing there, scowling at them in all his forest-shaded authority. "That will be enough for now. There is time for everything else later, and my lady wife has informed me that Teyha is exhausted beyond reason. Anything you do now is with an impaired woman."

Ekinar growled low, but he released Teyha from his embrace. "We will speak of this soon."

She blinked as she tried to remember what they had been talking about, but it was lost in a haze of pleasure and the slow expanse of something within her. "Good evening, Ekinar. It was nice meeting you."

She drifted past Apolan and returned to her room. The bed beckoned, and she was not one to ignore such a direct summons. Before she could wonder at the shadows flicking at her mind, she was out in a deep and healing sleep.

When Teyha sat up, she felt that something was different. She yawned and stumbled out of bed and into the lav.

Her face was the same, but there was something in her mind behind her eyes. The cool crystal gaze stared back at her, but something was awry. She didn't feel quite like herself, and it confused the heck out of her.

She combed her hair, washed her face and found some clothing in the wardrobe. Loose trousers and a long tunic with a sash fit well enough, so she put on the sandals that matched the clothing and went in search of the ambassador or his wife.

Daphne was sitting with her feet up in the area where Teyha vaguely remembered eating a meal the night before. A breakfast plate was waiting for her.

"Morning, Teyha. Or should I say afternoon. You have been out for sixteen hours." Daphne smiled brightly.

"Yech. No wonder my mouth tasted like the bottom of a sand dune." She took the open seat and looked around. "Where are the Shadow Folk?"

"Gone. They are back on the mother ship by now, and those younglings are getting swatted and hugged in equal measure. How was your trip?"

Teyha felt unaccountably disappointed that Ekinar had not come by to say farewell.

"Thinking about Representative Rossing?"

Daphne's voice cut right through her mopey thoughts.

"Yes. How did you know?"

"Because I look that way every time Apolan has to take a trip to the mother ship for status reports. I have seen it in the mirror." Daphne's lips were twisted in amusement.

"I don't event really know . . . I mean, I thought there might be . . . I mean he kissed me." The last came out on a rush.

Daphne's brows lifted as she smiled. "A very good sign, that. The Nine only come into contact with us under duress or attraction. I am guessing it was both in your case."

Teyha thought about it. "No. He touched me first. I mean, I had to take the hands of the others to get them out of the oubliette but that was duress, but he wasn't dumb enough to walk into it."

Daphne blinked in surprise. "You have a lot to tell me, but eat first, you are so pale, I can almost see through you."

Before stuffing her face, she had to ask, "Did I miss my lecture?"

"We postponed it. You looked a little rough when you arrived. The university understood."

Teyha found that hard to believe. "Are you serious?"

Daphne laughed, "No, but Apolan agreed to do a speaking engagement, and they jumped at the chance to have one of the Nine speaking."

Snickering, Teyha finished her breakfast. "So, what did I miss?"

Her friend smiled slowly. "Well, you have not seen the last of Ekinar . . ."

CHAPTER EIGHT

Ekinar paced restlessly. The children had told their stories to the governing body, Nosku had tried to cover up for his nephew, and Ekinar had contradicted his version. They had to wait for the verdict of the council.

It was peculiar to have part of him so far away, but the emotions that he was picking up from his mate soothed him when his impulses started to rise. In the two days since he had returned to the mother ship, his every waking moment had been spent thinking about Teyha.

He felt her confusion the first time she woke and every emotion she had had since. There was nothing that Ekinar wanted more than to get down to Gaia and claim his mate, but until this inquiry ended, there was no chance of that happening.

His shadow was barely under his control today. It lashed out at anyone who got too close and that alone had him worried. If he didn't get to Teyha soon, he was going to go mad.

"Representative Rossing? They will see you now." The voice was calm and low as if trying not to enrage him.

Ekinar jerked his head in affirmative and followed the messenger back into the council hall. The chairs were arranged in a semicircle, and he walked to the central point to wait.

They did not leave him waiting long.

Councillor Rothaway leaned forward, "There is some conflict in your stories, Ekinar Rossing."

"I suspected as much." He was resigned to whatever disciplinary actions the council chose to enact as long as he could return to Gaia and claim his mate. After that, he didn't care as long as she was next to him and safe.

"We have had to engage in a last-resort effort and made arrangements to contact your guide. Do you have any objections to this?" Rothaway had a smile at the corner of his mouth.

Ekinar was glad that they couldn't see his grin, but then, Rothaway could probably smell the change in his biology at this distance. "I have no objection."

"Good." He pressed a few controls, and an orb rose in the centre of the room, mere feet from where Ekinar stood.

Ekinar could feel the curiosity in his mate even before her face appeared in the orb.

She grinned down at him. "You called?"

His heartbeat sped up, and the tendrils of his shadow reached out for her before he could call them back. He was sure that the council had noticed.

Rothaway cleared his throat. "The council of the Nine needs you to fill in the details of what occurred during your trek through the Shadow Lands."

Teyha sobered, her mood chilling through their link. "Shall I begin at the beginning?"

"Please, and leave nothing out. Careers are at stake."

Teyha shrugged and left nothing out.

Ekinar winced at her initial opinion of him and his shadow as *creepy.*

The rest of her story was plain and direct, including things she had noted that he had not.

The chair in the shuttle had been set for a far larger male, so Darku's claim that Hiska had landed the ship was ridiculous. Hiska had bruising consistent with someone gripping her forearms and forcing them onto the controls.

When she finished her statement, she appeared outwardly patient, but Ekinar could feel the curiosity in her from orbit.

He grinned at the way she was able to hide what she was truly feeling with a calm demeanour. Inside, she was hopping up and down to find out what was going on.

The council nodded and Rothaway spoke. "Ekinar, no charges will be filed, but we have decided to sentence you to a minimum of six months on Gaia, after which, we will assess your situation and consider allowing your return to the mother ship."

Ekinar was stunned.

Rothaway smiled, "While you are on Gaia, we will outfit you with equipment and recording devices to investigate all of the available ruined cities. I trust that you can find a reliable guide, Emissary Rossing?"

He fought his howl of relief. "It is an acceptable compromise for my participation in this covert activity. May I reside at the embassy?"

"Ambassador Leoraki has the Shadow Folk floor ready for you. You may take one of the two-seater shuttles and leave whenever you are ready."

He nodded and bowed shortly. "Thank you, Councillors."

The bubble with Teyha remained.

Rothaway waved for him to leave. "You are dismissed, Emissary. Enjoy your new posting."

Confused, he exited the hall and took the rail to his quarters. He could feel Teyha's emotions go from shocked to confused, then finally pleased, and he was damned if he didn't want to know what the hell they were talking about.

Facing the representatives of the Nine felt peculiar, but since Teyha was sitting in the embassy back on Gaia, she felt comfortable telling the absolute truth.

When Ekinar was dismissed, she wondered why they still wanted to talk to her, but before she could ask, the Shadow Folk contingent stood up.

"What is your name, miss?"

"Teyha Wynn. What may I call you?" She raised her brows and waited.

A low chuckle came from within the shifting shadows. "Representative Naluriak Rossing-Deenar. I believe you are about to become my sister-in-law."

Shock rippled through Teyha. "What? I am sorry, but Ekinar never mentioned anything of the kind." She snorted. "Mind you, I didn't know he had sister either."

Naluriak laughed. "We are not a forthcoming folk. You will eventually draw him out, but he is already within you, learning your moods."

Blinking rapidly, she asked again, "What?"

"He kissed you, yes?"

"Yes."

"And in doing so, he placed a tiny bit of his shadow, or his soul, within you. He has been using it to monitor your moods."

"I beg your pardon?"

"In public, even amongst the Nine, we always wear our shadows around us. For our males to keep out of trouble, as the third step in courtship, they place a piece of their shadow inside their female. That tiny piece of him allows him to know your moods and your location. It is a handy thing on wilder planets, and I believe that Gaia counts."

"Naluriak, I am not sure that that is the case with me." Teyha bit her lip, though she knew she was lying. Whatever had changed inside her was enhancing her normally impressive echolocation, and she could feel that she was being monitored during her waking hours.

"I am sure that it is. I can see it. My family's shadow has a distinct pattern. It is flickering behind your eyes every time you look around. I formally greet you, sister, and I welcome you most heartily." The woman inclined her head.

"How is it that you were allowed in here as councillor to your people with your brother facing charges?" Teyha had to ask.

"I could always be outvoted by the other eight. It is really that simple. I was here as a character witness."

Teyha nodded her head and sat up straight before she inclined her head in a mimicry of Naluriak's. "Thank you for your greeting, sister. I look forward to one day meeting you in person."

There was a concentrated sigh from the eight chairs, and Teyha knew she had done something significant.

"I just sealed my fate, didn't I?" Her tone was wry.

The shadow laughed. A bright, cheerful sound. "Public acknowledgement of my brother's claim. In the eyes of the Nine, you are now declared to him and he to you."

Rothaway wished her luck with Ekinar, and he closed communication, leaving her sitting and facing the Forest Folk ambassador and his Gaian bride.

"I am completely hooped, aren't I?" She sighed.

Daphne got to her feet. "It isn't that bad. Living on a spaceship, they mostly clean up after themselves."

Apolan snorted and he grimaced. "For a woman who can turn invisible, you are around an awful lot lately."

She smacked her husband in the arm and leaned down to whisper in his ear.

Apolan's cheeks darkened, and he got to his feet.

He stood in front of Teyha and took her hands in his. "Congratulations, new daughter of shadow. May your souls twine brightly."

Looking at Daphne, she shrugged, "Um, thank you?"

He snorted and patted her on the shoulder, his face in a wicked grin. "Close enough."

Chapter Nine

Teyha was nervous as she went through her daily tasks of cataloguing the few photographs from her first visit to the Temple of Shadows. She hadn't put them into the archive, because they were her last link with her parents and their last trip together.

It was that emergency that necessitated the flare system at least once per day or at scheduled times.

She tried to remember them in everything that she did, and her job of archivist and guide crossed both of their disciplines. She hoped that she made them proud.

The access to the Shadow Land had been an alternate from the one she had first taken with her parents. The first route was faster but far less stable as her parents had found out after she had left them to engage in a meeting with the faculty of the Gaian University. Speaking engagements had been arranged, and she had returned to her parents as quickly as she could. She was too late by twelve hours.

It was something she lived with every day that she walked into the archive and saw the discoveries of her family posted on the walls.

A shadow caressed her arm, and she turned to see Ekinar in the doorway. She wanted to tell him that he startled her, that she was surprised, but she had felt him coming, and he had known she was expecting him.

Teyha tried to keep her mind blank as she walked up to him. "So, I hear that we are a pair now."

He didn't say a word but lifted her off her feet and pressed her against the wall, his lips found hers and shadows covered her completely, wrapping her in a cocoon that felt like being surrounded completely by the man holding her.

His lips teased at hers, and she gave into him without a second thought. She wrapped her thighs around his hips and hung on as her body soared under the all-consuming touch that was not barred by clothing.

Ekinar's kiss lit a fire in her that burned along her limbs until she bucked and shivered in his arms from no more than his lips on hers and his shadows around her.

144

She gasped and waited for the trembling to subside. He slowly, deliciously, let her body slide down his until her feet were on the floor.

"I believe that Apolan has some information for us so that we may complete this bonding with a bit more dignity than a wall in an office." He trailed her lips with a tendril of shadows.

When Teyha turned her head, Reesha was staring from the hallway. "I was coming to tell you that you had a visitor, but I am guessing that you know that."

Reesha's unacknowledged talent was to share vision. She could touch your head and project what you saw through your own eyes. It was one of the spookier talents that Teyha had met in her life and not one that you wanted enacted on you.

It took a few tries, but Teyha said, "I figured it out. Reesha, this is Ekinar Rossing, Emissary of the Shadow Folk, and he will be requesting that I help with explorations of the ancient cities."

Reesha nodded. "Of course. There is no one better. Do you want me to cancel the readings to the children?"

Teyha frowned. "I have not thought that far ahead."

Ekinar put an arm around her. "I have an idea for that, and I am sure that Apolan will be amenable if you can take the journal you were reading from along with us."

Teyha shook her head. "No, but I can make a copy."

"Good. I would hate to disappoint those little faces. They were hypnotized by your voice." He squeezed her waist.

"Okay. Can you suspend my speaking engagements at the Uni? I get the feeling that I will be a little distracted for the next few weeks."

Ekinar didn't give Reesha a chance to continue the conversation. He used his grip on Teyha's waist to lift her up and out of the archive to a waiting transport.

She didn't make a noise, her body was completely supported by the shadows, and they had chosen interesting areas to support her.

"How much can you lift with the shadows?"

He smiled as they sat in the transport and the driver aimed for the Embassy of the Nine. "Up to five hundred pounds. Your weight barely registers."

She snickered and let second thoughts creep in.

"What are you thinking?"

"Is this correct for you? I mean, I met your sister, and she is obviously wed to another of the Shadow Folk. Isn't there a dark, mysterious woman out there for you somewhere?"

He held her close. "I have been actively seeking a mate for ten years. You are the only woman who has woken my senses and made me want to be at your side all times, day or night."

Instead of going inside the embassy, Daphne met them at the cul-de-sac and spirited Teyha away to get her dressed in a lovely tissue-thin gown that wrapped her in all the right places.

"The ceremony is finalised with an exchange of blood in complete privacy. You don't drink it, he bites you and you cut him. Then, you slip the dagger into the stone it came out of, and it registers you as a bound couple. It is a lovely ceremony and very above ground."

"That is a strange non-sequitur."

"I will tell you about it one day, but it caught me by surprise." She winked.

With the bride ready, they walked to a huge garden at the back of the property. White flowers gave off the most calming scent, and when Ekinar took her hand, Teyha smiled.

They entered the garden with a shield snapping into place behind them.

It all went as Daphne had said, Ekinar bit her, she used the knife in the stone to slice his wrist, and when it was over, she slid the blade back into the stone. The kiss took her by surprise, but she leaned into it, her body pressed to his in an intense need that swept through her.

"I think we need some privacy." Her voice was low and husky to her own ears.

"Excellent thought."

He lifted her in his arms, her skirts foaming around her legs as he carried her into the embassy.

The floor of the Shadow Folk was surprisingly bright. She didn't have a chance to admire the décor though. He carried her into one of the guestrooms and set her on her feet.

"My bride, I have waited for you, hoped for you and dreamed for you. To have you here within my touch is enough."

From inside her, the words came. "My husband, I have hoped for you, waited for you and now that you are here, I wish for nothing more than your embrace."

To her shock, his shadows moved away from his face and body, answering a question that she had never dared ask before. "Oh, so you do wear pants under the shadows."

146

He laughed and took her in his arms, bearing her to the bed and using the remaining tendrils of his shadows to peel her gown from her and wake her body using delicate touches.

Ekinar removed the impediments to her seeing every inch of him, and while he was chalk white, his muscles were well defined, and there was nothing untoward about the erection that called to her with silent desperation.

Smiling, she rolled him to his back and woke his body the same way he had woken hers, but she had to use her fingers, and his shock and arousal finally necessitated her joining their bodies and beginning a slow dance that ended with their room covered in darkness and their bodies glowing within.

Epilogue

After they had gone through every inch of the Valley of Shadows, they had moved onto the Wilder Lair. It was a larger site, and it proved that the Wilders were highly territorial.

Teyha loved exploring with Ekinar at her side, and he gave her surprising insight into the purposes of most of the buildings.

"When are we getting the new interns?" Ekinar returned to base camp, his shadows flickering as he bent to kiss his mate.

Teyha smiled for a moment before she remembered what he had asked. "Oh. This afternoon. The mother ship has sent them down, and they are at the archive getting basic orientation with the Gaian volunteers."

It had rapidly become apparent to her that once they identified the traps at a site, it was the perfect educational tool for bored teens. Hiska and Ritgar were going to be seeing the Wilder site along with three Gaian teens who had an aptitude for history.

"Then, we should probably take this time to enjoy our fleeting privacy, my love." Ekinar lifted her from her desk and swept her to their large bunk at the back of the tent. Life of exploration was not for everyone, but he had taken to it with ease and grace, and when she woke in the dark of night and his beautiful features glowed pure and bright, she knew that her adaptation had come full circle as well.

Life and love with a strange warrior, not knowing when or if they would have to re-join the mother ship gave their time together a sweetness that it wouldn't have had otherwise. They had been forced together rapidly and that forging had made them strong.

COLLECTING
RETURN OF THE NINE BOOK FIVE

BY

VIOLA GRACE

Chapter One

With the seaweed gathered into her sample bag, Emharo looked at the tempting waves and debated continuing her search for vegetation with antiseptic properties versus taking a nice dip in the waves.

Emharo looked up at the bright ball of the sun and smiled. It made her mind up for her. She carefully put her sample bag up where the shifting surf could not reach it and was slipping out of her shirt when a transport skimmed around the headland and came toward her.

It must be the specialists from the mother ship of the Nine.

The transport flew past her and up the beach. Its air cushion spewed sand left and right until it moved up to the ridge and approached the lab.

"Well, if everyone is over there, I think it is time for me to cool down." Her parents wouldn't begrudge her a short swim, and she might find another sample to take back to them.

She wore undergarments made of cured fish skin, and the leather made supportive and waterproof underwear. Em removed her outerwear and folded it neatly, tucking it up where it would remain dry. With a knife strapped to her thigh and a fishing spear in one hand, she went into the water to do some collecting.

"Doctor Harold Baker, Doctor Emaline Baker, please allow me to introduce Morro Nefurik, biologist and Weelar Tish, chef. They have been invited by our government to run their own tests on native species in an effort to replenish some stores on their ship." Daphne Leoraki smiled as she made the introductions.

Morro cleared his throat. "Rivvin Sequelar is also with us, but he required some time in the sea before joining us here. We dropped him just past the headland, and he is swimming in."

"Swimming?" Emaline Baker blinked and frowned toward the headland with a worried expression.

"Yes, Dr. Baker. He is of the Water Folk, and he has been craving open water for years. The temptation was too much to resist."

Emaline Baker looked to her husband. "Call her. See if she answers."

Harold Baker went to a primitive com unit and tried to make a connection. "Em. Em, are you there?"

Dr. Emaline Baker covered her eyes. "Something tells me that your associate is about to get an eyeful."

Morro looked interested, Weelar was busy nibbling on a piece of seaweed and Daphne was left to figure out what was going on. "What does she wear when she swims?"

Emaline sighed, "As little as possible."

With the penchant of the other races of the Nine to recognise their mates on sight, this would give Rivvin the ideal option to see if the Gaian Emharo Baker was the one for him. Daphne groaned and hoped that her friend was not as heavily armed as she normally was when she went into the sea.

It was Daphne's first time escorting men of the Nine around on her own, and she wanted to bring them all back alive.

Em was on her ninth dive, looking for shellfish, large fish that got close enough to spear and anything that qualified as the object she had been sent out to collect.

A pale silhouette approaching her got her attention.

Em kept neutral buoyancy and moved carefully as she kept the incoming predator in her sights.

It swam slowly toward her and paused, facing her.

The tension in her chest reminded her that she needed to breathe, so she kicked up and away from the pale man with huge black eyes who was staring at her from a few metres away.

She broke the surface and exchanged her air before looking down once again. The man was remarkably close, and he showed no signs of needing to breathe.

He swam underneath her and up behind her as he examined her from all angles.

She watched him as long as she could before she needed to breathe again. She slowly began to move toward the shoreline. He didn't impede her in any way. Em staggered up the pebbled beach and whirled to look behind her.

The man walked calmly out of the surf, and a small spray of water jetted from his neck. He was wearing a short hip wrap, pale skin, dark blue hair and nothing else.

"Hello." Em walked over to her clothing and put her spear down.

"Greetings, miss. Am I near the research lab?"

She nodded and turned to see that he was within inches of her and she hadn't heard him move. "Oh. And here you are. Um, yes. It is right on top of that ridge over there. I am on my way back if you would like to come with me." She mentally kicked herself the moment that the invitation came out of her mouth.

He extended his hand to her. "Rivvin Sequelar, pleased to meet you. You work at the lab?"

Em took his hand and felt a peculiar slickness leave his palm and wrap around hers. "Emharo Baker. My parents run the research lab. Is there something on your hand?"

He looked down and a hot lavender colour ran under his cheeks and across the muscular expanse of his chest. "I apologise. My body is attempting to chemically analyse yours."

"You are a member of the Nine?"

He inclined his head. "I am. I am of the Water Folk."

She smiled at the obviousness and gradually eased her hand from his. The slickness absorbed into her skin without a trace. "I gathered as much. Well, I suppose I should get dressed and escort you to the lab."

"If you insist. I have no problem with your current attire. Is it fish leather?"

She nodded. "It seemed the most practical swimwear. It dries quickly and identifies me to other predators."

She slipped on her shirt and shimmied into her trousers before sitting, dusting her feet off and tugging on her boots. "Just a moment while I grab my line and my samples and we will be on our way."

Em kept her gaze on Rivvin as she flipped her collection bag over her shoulder and hauled her line of fish in and flipped it over her other shoulder.

Rivvin was watching her with surprise. "You eat from the sea?"

She paused. "Oh, are you vegetarian?"

He shook his head. "No. We eat whatever swims past. I am simply surprised that you hunt in the sea."

"It's a thing I do. My parents send me out with a list, and I bring it home. Doesn't matter if it is fish or topical anaesthetic, I will bring it home." She chuckled. "Shall we?"

He blinked, and she noticed the secondary membrane that flicked over his eyes. "You are walking?"

She shrugged. "Yes. I walk everywhere. You are welcome to swim up to the lab. There is a set of stone stairs that leads out of the water so you will know it when you see it."

Rivvin looked down at her, and his hands flexed.

She noted the webbing between his fingers and quickly looked up when she saw that his wrap was slightly distorted.

Em cleared her throat. "Well, I will get moving, and you can make up your mind."

She turned and made her escape, shifting the thirty pounds of fish on her shoulder. The fish was taken from her as Rivvin came up on her left. He inclined his head, and she let him carry it. It was only fifteen minutes of walking anyway, so why did she feel like he had given her an armload of flowers with that small gesture of taking her burden?

CHAPTER TWO

The lab was full of people, so Em walked straight in. Her parents were speaking with the representatives of the Nine, and it was too hard to resist. "Mom, it followed me home, can I keep it?"

The shock on the faces of the representatives was hilarious, but Daphne's bark of laughter broke the tension.

"Em, I don't think they get the joke." Daphne came up and gave her a hug.

"That's okay. They will get the hang of my sense of humour if they are here for more than a few hours." Em muttered it in Daphne's ear.

Rivvin spoke from behind her. "Weelar, see what you can do with the lady's catch."

The other pale man rushed forward and took the fish with the reverence of someone taking a holy object. "Where can I prepare them?"

Emaline Baker stepped forward. "I will show you to the kitchen and make sure you get settled. We laid in plenty of supplies for this week. Em will make sure that the fresh fish keep coming."

The male almost passed out with joy at the mention of more fresh fish.

Rivvin smiled, "Emharo, that is Weelar Tish. He is a chef for the Water Folk. We ran out of living food a few months ago, and this is our first opportunity to scope out fresh supplies."

Em looked up at him. "Oh, so that is the nature of this visit?"

The Wilder was on the other side of the room, "That and we are looking for biological samples to restock our genetic banks for replication."

Harold Baker blinked rapidly. "Oh, I am sorry. Morro Nefurik of the Wilder, this is my daughter, Emharo Baker, our collector. If you need something, she can find it."

Emharo nodded. "Pleased to meet you. Oh, Dad, I got you that topical anaesthetic you were after." She opened her bag and hauled out the seaweed. "It emits a gel that is highly effective."

Morro inclined his head and turned to Rivvin. "They have arranged the guest quarters for us, your bag is there."

Daphne was standing by. "Well, if you are all situated comfortably, I will be

153

off. Call for anything you need and I will have it brought out, otherwise I will see you in a week."

She nodded to Rivvin and Morro, gave Em another hug and was out the door before Em could do more than raise her hand in goodbye.

Rivvin blinked both lids again. "She was certainly in a hurry."

"Daphne worked here one summer and one of the biological samples bit her. She isn't fond of this place." Em shrugged. "Dad, do you have a list of what you need for their visit?"

Harold grinned, "Here. Weelar filled me in on how much protein and vegetation they consume, so we will need a little more than initially anticipated."

She lifted her spear. "Done. That's it?"

Harold nodded. "Unless any of our esteemed guests have any specific requests?"

Rivvin blinked, "Are you going back in the water?"

"I am."

"May I accompany you? It has been a long time since I hunted in open waters."

She looked from Rivvin's intense features to Morro's shocked face and shrugged. "Sure. Do you hunt with a weapon?"

He frowned. "I think I might use a spear similar to yours. Do you have a spare?"

She grinned. "Of course. Come with me, and you can choose your weapon. I will show you the guest quarters while we are on our way."

He smiled and placed a hand on her shoulder.

She heard Morro gasp but ignored him for the feeling of warmth that spread from that slight contact.

"Thank you, Emharo."

She shook her head and walked out of the lab, down the hall and out into the warm afternoon air. Em used her fishing spear to point down the yard. "There is the guesthouse. My mom had me clear all my stuff this morning. You will be nicely segregated from the Gaians."

"That is not necessarily something we require." He was close to her again, very close.

"We were told that the Nine didn't like contact with Gaians, well not casual contact anyway." She shrugged. "The doors don't lock anyway, so you can come and go as you please. Will you be here all week?"

Rivvin made a rumbling noise of assent. "That is the plan. I need to put a locator tag in a few shoals of fish and our mother ship can send a transporter down to bring them up to replenish our stocks."

"So, you exclusively eat fish?"

"It is our preferred food, though we can and do eat other proteins while on the mother ship." He shrugged. "It has been a rather unappealing few months since we consumed the last of the live stores. They tend not to breed in space, so we only have what we can bring with us from likely planets."

"And since Gaia is the planet you evolved on, you can tolerate the foods here."

She walked to the shed near the dock. "Here is the weapons shed, it also contains fins, masks and other equipment for diving. Take what you need."

She grabbed a mask, snorkel and set of fins before setting out down the smooth wood of the dock. Her holding line was coiled neatly on the last support. She tied it to the edge of the support, removed her outer clothing again and walked down the steps to affix the fins on her feet.

She prepped the mask, and Rivvin sat next to her. "What are you doing?"

"The mask helps me when I am actively fishing. It increases my ability to see what the heck I am aiming at, and since you are going to be in the water with me, you really want me to see what I am doing." Em slid the mask on her head and grinned in the peculiar way that folks in masks always grinned. "Ready when you are."

He blinked at her, and with a smile that showed sharply pointed teeth, he dove into the water, leaving no trace of him on the surface.

Shrugging, she tested her snorkel before she followed him into the waves, her spear at the ready.

Emharo used her fins to slowly make her way into deeper water. Her breathing was loud in her ears as she used the tube to keep her head aware of the predators around her.

Rivvin was slipping through the water at the edge of her vision. Her senses told her that he was fishing successfully, the talent that drove her out into the wild to collect samples told her when there was something nearby that she wanted.

Despite the fact that Rivvin was not on her shopping list, Rivvin lit up with a hot blue pulse. It was not the colour that her mind associated with prey. Edible fish were bright gold, toxic fish were red-black and vegetation that could be eaten by Gaians was an electric purple to her senses. Medicinal items were a variety of colours across the rainbow.

Hot blue was not a colour that she had ever run into before.

A fish darted past her, but it was too small to pursue. She continued her slow exploration while keeping an eye out for both Rivvin and other predators.

A sudden rush of gold caught her attention. Huge, fat fish swam toward her, and she struck out with her spear, catching two of the fish before quickly backpedalling to get away from the large predator that had driven the fish toward her.

Stubby legs, a huge jaw and flat black eyes, the beast came toward her, following the flapping of the fish on her spear. It was three times her length, and its jaws could snap her in two.

She sighed, preparing to give up her catch.

A flash of light skin moved between her and the beast, and Rivvin took a defensive posture between her and the animal that wanted her kills.

He stabbed at it a few times, and the beast turned on its tail with blood streaming from small punctures around its head.

Rivvin turned, grabbed her around the waist and swam back to the steps. He took her spear from her and chucked the fish onto the dock, striding out onto the steps with her tucked under his arm.

Irritated, she blasted water out her snorkel. She spit it out and said, "Put me down."

"Not until you are safe."

He set her down on the dock, and she took her flippers off with disgusted movements. "You didn't need to do that. I would have lost my spear but that would have been it."

She ripped her mask off and scowled up at him. His hair curled on his cheeks and clung to his chest.

He growled. "You are not fast enough to hunt in the water."

"I have done it so far, and I will continue to do it long after you are gone, so get used to the idea."

Rivvin's mouth opened and closed with a snap reminiscent of the predator she had just faced. "We have enough for today. Come on, back to the lab so I can discuss a few things with your parents."

She got to her feet, gathered her clothing and grumped, "Since you are so keen to do the heavy lifting, bring in the fish."

He reached down, and his arm flexed as he pulled up a truly spectacular haul. He lifted her two fish and added them to the stringer, carrying the whole works over one shoulder.

She didn't bother getting dressed, merely stowed her gear and stomped into the habitat wearing her swim gear. Em paused and pointed. "The kitchen is down there."

Rivvin opened his mouth to speak, but she slipped through the habitat doors and closed them behind her. Emharo sighed and clenched her hands into fists. "Damn it."

"Em, precious? Why are you here in your swimsuit?" Her mother was coming toward her with a stack of journals.

"My collecting was interrupted by Rivvin getting between me and a predator. I didn't want to stop to change." She stalked to the steps that led to her temporary quarters.

Her mother was looking up at her in surprise. "I have never seen you this rattled."

Em frowned. "He can do all the fishing. I will look for medicinals in the tide pools as far from him as I can be."

There was a smile on her mother's lips as Em stared down at her from the balcony. "Why are you smiling, Mom?"

Emaline Baker made her way to the door to the lab hall. "Oh, nothing. Take a shower and get changed. You may want to keep your distance, but you will be joining us for dinner."

Chapter Three

The greenhouse had been arranged to accommodate the guests and the doctors working at the research lab.

Emharo was dressed for dinner, her hair was up and she was politely serving the guests the food that Weelar had prepared. It smelled great.

Rivvin was dressed formally, as well, wearing a deep blue shirt the same colour as his hair and dark trousers tucked into military-style boots. His hair was braided away from his temples, and the rest of it flowed loose down his back.

Morro and Weelar were dressed for dinner, as well, but they were barely noticeable to Em, who kept her gaze as averted from Rivvin as possible. She wanted to stare at him, but it would have been glaringly obvious during their little dinner party. Instead, she did rounds with water, wine and trays of food kept warm on the sideboard.

Morro commented, "This is an amazing range of foods, Harold."

Em's father smiled, "We are fortunate in our child and our niece. Our niece Neeka is away from the lab for now, but she is as skilled at hunting as Emharo is at collecting what we need for any given project."

Emharo paused when everyone at the table turned to look at her. "What?"

Rivvin cocked his head. "Have you always had this skill?"

Em looked to her parents and nodded. "It is one of my mother's favourite stories."

Emaline lifted her wine glass and smiled. "The first time we noticed it, Em was five. She and Neeka were playing on the beach, and Neeka cut herself. Instead of running for help, Em ran to the shoreline and picked up a fish, opened it up with her fingers and took out a nasty-smelling gland. She pressed it to Neeka's cut, and then, they walked back to the lab together. When we wiped the residue away from the cut, it was gone, only a wide line remained. The gland she had found had the ability to knit tissue. The only perplexing thing was how she had found it to begin with."

Harold smiled, "She explained how she found the fish and it glowed and the inside glowed brighter than the outside, so that is what she used. We tested the fish and have now crafted a coagulant for use after surgeries."

Em continued to eat her meal while keeping an eye on everyone at the table to make sure they were not missing anything she could provide.

Morro asked her parents, "Do you harvest the fish for the product?"

Her mother smiled. "No, we have protein synthesizers that are used to provide basic ingredients. Once she brings something to us, it is our job to copy it for use in the city."

Em finished her meal and got to her feet, picking up the water and wine pitchers and making a swift round of the table.

Rivvin looked up at her while she refilled his cup. "Does your cousin share this skill?"

Emharo frowned, "Not precisely. She is a hunter. Her skill lies in tracking and dispatching her prey. I like the sea, she prefers the land."

Morro cleared his throat. "Is she nearby?"

Em smiled, "No, she will be gone for a few weeks. She is taking some of the city folk on a trip through the wilds. Ever since the Tokkel raids, more people have been interested in learning how to live away from the city. Neeka teaches a crash course in survival."

She poured Morro a glass of water and finished her rounds before resuming her seat next to her parents.

Rivvin looked at her directly, without any subterfuge. "Emharo, are you engaged or have a gentleman caller of any species?"

She blushed and squirmed in her chair. "Um. No. Aside from the Gaians, the only compatible species here are those of the Nine, and you are the first that I have met."

Her mother piped up. "She isn't seeing anyone. The last eligible male in the area left after the summer training session here at the lab, and she managed to ignore him the entire time he was here."

"Emaline, what are you doing?" Harold Baker was curious.

Emharo buried her face in her hand and leaned on the table. "Well, Rivvin, as you have heard, the answer is no. I am not socially seeing anyone."

He had his shark-like grin in place once again. "Good."

Morro looked at him with concern. "Rivvin?"

"Be quiet, Morro. If you have an objection, raise it privately." Rivvin's voice was flat.

Morro shrugged and continued to eat.

Emharo turned to Weelar, "Thank you for your excellent managing of the ingredients. The food was wonderful."

Everyone immediately followed that train of conversation, and soon, Weelar's pale skin was turning lavender from the praise.

Em exhaled and took a gulp of the wine.

Conversation turned to the research, into the uses of renewable products and the exclusive discoveries that were unable to be synthesized. Em didn't bother chipping into the conversation, she simply sat and nursed her wine while the biologists, chef and her parents spoke.

The urge to do something took over, so she whispered to her mother, "May I be excused? The nocturnal plankton is blooming."

"Yes, dear. Please be careful." Her mother leaned over and gave her a peck on the cheek.

Em got to her feet with relief. "Please excuse me."

The three men of the Nine rose to their feet as she exited, and she could feel Rivvin's gaze on her back. Fortunately, she would soon be underwater and he was stuck being a guest.

Rivvin watched the relieved set to Emharo's shoulders and smiled inwardly. He looked to her mother, "May I ask where she is off to?"

"There is a phosphorescent plankton bloom out in the bay, and she wants to gather samples. She is taking the boat, I hope." Dr. Emaline Baker smiled hopefully.

"You can't keep her in, can you?" He was beginning to realise that whatever Emharo's talent was it was part compulsion.

Emaline shook her head. "No. She would always leave in the middle of the night and come back with what she felt was needed for the next day. It got to the point where we would simply give her a list to collect before she went to bed so that we could generally control where she went."

"Would you excuse me to accompany her?"

Emaline looked at him with hope. "Would you? That would relieve my mind."

Morro frowned at him. "Rivvin, what are you up to?"

Rivvin sighed, "What nature intended. You will understand when it strikes you, Morro. I will see you after I return."

Rivvin got to his feet, bowed to those sitting at the table and quickly moved to follow his lady down to the dock. If he gave her the chance, she would be free of him, and with their bond so tenuous, he needed to strengthen it as quickly as he could. The chemical bond he had formed with her would only last another two days. If he didn't press his suit, she would be lost to him.

He jumped in the boat next to her, and she shrieked in surprise. "What are you doing here?"

"Accompanying you on what I am sure will be a matter of biological interest." He meant his biology, but it was not necessary for him to inform her. Rivvin was sure she would figure it out soon enough.

CHAPTER FOUR

Em paused. "I will have to go back to the habitat."

Rivvin cocked his head, his dark eyes unreadable. "Why?"

"I don't usually bring a suit for night dives, and today was no different."

His teeth flashed in the darkness, "I don't mind if you don't. My swim wrap is in the guest quarters."

She snorted. "I don't mind. Skinny dipping for science, why not?"

She freed the mooring rope and turned back to the engine.

He sat as she activated the small propeller and the boat eased into the dark water. "Do you often go out at night?"

She shrugged. "Many of the samples my parents want are night blooming. We are trying to grow planktons and lichen to light pathways and give passive evening light for larger buildings in the city."

"You have an affinity for the sea?"

She smiled as she listened to the waves against the hull. "I suppose I do. I know the habits of the animals, the signs if they are going to flee or attack."

"Have you been damaged?"

"Of course. One can't go into a living ocean and not face danger every time. I have had my share of bites and scars, but I also have access to the very compounds that will mitigate the damage."

They glided out into the centre of the bay, the large glow under the surface indication that they were in the right place. "Can you drop that rock?"

Rivvin followed her gesture and lifted the rock easily, dropping the makeshift anchor into the softly lapping waves.

Em took a deep breath and stripped out of her shoes, trousers and, finally, she untied the sash that held her shirt closed. She unpinned her hair and let it cascade down as a partial covering before tying her knife to her leg.

Rivvin was completely nude, and unless the Nine had a completely different physiology, he was interested in her lack of clothing. Hopefully, the cool water would chill his interest.

Before she could change her mind, she slipped the shirt from her shoulders and dove into the water. The light of the plankton attracted her, confirmed by whatever it was that showed her what she needed. Talent, instinct, intuition, whatever it was, she knew what she needed when she saw it.

She assessed her surroundings for a moment before turning toward the surface.

Rivvin stopped her from returning to the air, and instead, he pressed his lips to hers.

She clutched his shoulders for balance and felt his chest swell as he exhaled into her. Oxygen came to her through his mouth, and she quickly plugged her nose shut as he breathed into her.

Able to continue, she broke free of him and noted his smug smile. It may have been a sneaky way to get a kiss in, but it was effective.

He held her hand and pulled her down toward the base of the vegetation. She quickly worked and cut a dozen strands of the stuff, hauling it toward the surface.

Rivvin took it from her and moved swiftly through the water.

She kicked gently back to the surface, exhaling as she went.

Inches from the surface, Rivvin caught her again and breathed for her. This time, she relaxed into it and held tightly to him as he gave her the air she craved.

He held her with barely an inch between their bodies as they tumbled along with the current. When he began to swim them back toward the boat, she lifted her head, a stream of bubbles coming out of her mouth. She saw the predator a moment before Rivvin did.

Em went limp and immobile while Rivvin went on the offensive. He swam toward the beast, and to her astonishment, in the dim light of the plankton, she could see spikes emerge from his forearms.

He slashed at the predator, and the predator's head flipped around, sending a tendril of blood through the water. Whatever was in Rivvin's spikes, the predator slowed and fluttered slowly toward the sea floor.

Em went into action. She swam to Rivvin and grabbed his uninjured arm, swimming with him back to the boat. More predators were only a minute away and getting out of the water was the best idea for both of them.

She climbed the ladder into the boat and held her arm out for him. He waved her off and made his way out of the water just as the huge bulk of an even larger beast cruised below them.

Rivvin sat and looked at the wound on his arm. "It isn't bad."

Em was already looking through her very personal med kit. "It isn't bad, but if you want to hit the water tomorrow, it needs to be tended to. Hold still and stop poking it."

He prodded gently at it one more time. "I heal quickly."

She took out a powder and sprinkled it on the wound. "This will speed the healing even more then."

He wrinkled his nose. "It stinks."

She laughed. "I am aware of that. The smell belongs to the protein, so when you can no longer smell it, it has fully absorbed."

She set the powder aside and looked at the wound. "Do you mind if I wrap it?"

"If you stay unclothed, you can carve me off piece by piece and I will sit here quietly." His tone was low.

A blush scorched her cheeks. "You just had to mention that, didn't you?"

She quickly went and slipped into her shirt, tying the sash in place.

"You were really so worried that you tended me before your modesty?" He reached out and touched her cheek.

"Bleeding in this water is rarely a good idea."

"I can see that. The water under us is teeming with predators. How do you normally manage?"

She shrugged, "I normally hide in the plankton for as long as I can then swim to the surface with as controlled a motion as I can manage."

"How did you see it before it was there?"

She knew what he meant. "Everything down there has its own colour, even you. The colours tell me if something is friendly or not, toxic or not."

Em put a wrap on his cut and a light sniff told her that it was almost complete.

He pulled his trousers on, to her relief, and she did the same. She left off her shoes as the boat was covered with plankton and the shoes would get in the way.

Rivvin sat next to her and asked, "What colour am I?"

"Electric blue."

"What does that mean?"

Em bit her lip. "I don't know. I have never seen anything that colour before. Will you be taking a boat out tomorrow?"

Rivvin nodded. "Yes, it is being delivered by shuttle tomorrow morning. If you would care to assist, we are looking for shoals of fish suitable for consumption but not rare."

She thought about it. "Does the size of the fish matter?"

"They should be no more than four metres long. We are looking for larger meat fish with the option to eat them raw."

Em nodded. "I know a few places where there are likely gatherings of suitable fish. You plan to tag them and then take the whole shoal?"

He nodded. "That is the plan."

She grinned and took the helm once again. "Well, we have our target vegetation for this evening. Back to the lab with it."

His skin seemed to slough off the saltwater, but hers was itching. "And a shower."

He blinked. "You bathe after swimming in the sea?"

"My skin doesn't do what yours does. It gets dry and flaky if I don't wash the salt off, but I have a place for that when I don't want to wake my parents."

"Is it nearby?"

She chuckled. "Well, since you don't need it, allow me to have this one little secret."

He didn't look happy about that while he slipped his shirt on over the bandage. "You didn't ask about my spikes."

"I thought you would mention them as you felt it appropriate. They are normal for your folk?"

He cocked his head. "Not really, they come out when our mate is in danger and at no other time."

She blinked. "Are you saying . . ."

"That I would like to begin a courtship with a union with you as the goal, but I will need clues as to how to do it within your traditions."

Em was stunned. "A mate? You want me as your mate?"

He smiled at her, a slow and wicked smile. "I believe that you will exhaust me, run me a merry chase, run out and do whatever you feel to be right at any given time, and still, my body is called to yours."

CHAPTER FIVE

Emharo tied off the boat while Rivvin collected their harvest. "Have you not experimented on samples of this before?"

She was relieved to have another topic to discuss. "Of course, but we only take what we need for any round of work. Fresh plants have different properties to the dry ones, and so, I hack off only what my parents require."

"You swim there alone, at night?"

She could feel his disapproval. "Of course I do. You already knew the answer to that."

"Why?"

Em rubbed her forehead as they walked up to the lab. "It is in me to be busy. I crave occupation. It is more of a compulsion than anything else."

Rivvin hefted the plants as they moved through the doors into the greenhouse area of the lab. Em opened the storage tank, and he dropped the plankton into the cool seawater.

She yawned but knew that she needed to get cleaned up before sleep would be possible. "Thank you for an intriguing evening, Rivvin."

"I will escort you to the habitat." He inclined his head and offered his arm.

Em paused. "I am not going to the habitat quite yet. I need to wash the salt off, and there is a place nearby that will serve that function."

"I will escort you there, then, wait for you and return you home."

She wrinkled her nose. "Fine. I hope you are comfortable in the wild."

She stomped into her boots and pointed in the direction that her private grotto was located. They walked together in silence, she directed him with gentle nudges on his arm and they passed through the tumbled rocks of the landscape until they reached the imperceptible crack in the large rock. "This way."

He frowned down at her with a sceptical look in his eyes. "How can you fit?"

"The narrow entrance is an illusion cast by shadow. Come with me."

She took the lead, pulling him into the damp darkness that suddenly came alive with phosphorescent light.

"Rivvin, welcome to my private office." She smiled and relaxed as she always did when she saw the wide pool with gentle ripples caused by the waterfall.

"This is amazing. It is like one of the ancient retreats in our histories."

Emharo smiled and walked to the edge of the pool. She took down one of her towels and set it on the smooth stone worn by time.

She turned her back to Rivvin and quickly undressed, slipping into the water before she could lose her nerve. The water was cool and sweet, refreshing and calming her.

When a pale figure circled her under the water, her calm turned into embarrassed heat.

Rivvin emerged from the water with a smile. "This place is amazing. How did you find it?"

She gave him a sarcastic glance. "I found it because I was looking for it. I didn't know you liked fresh water."

He shrugged. "It is just water. That is the bonus to being one of the Nine and not an actual fish. My body is far more adaptable."

She treaded water and then exhaled to let the water close in over her head. She rinsed her scalp and reappeared on the surface, looking for traces of her visitor. When she didn't see him, she began to slowly make her way over to the waterfall.

Her shoulders ached and the pounding of the water untied her muscles. When she felt clean and relaxed, she slipped back into the water and right into Rivvin's arms.

"Oh, excuse me. I didn't see you there."

He grinned, "I was merely getting some nice exercise when I saw your toes re-entering the water, and I thought to ease your entry. You seem tired."

"I am. If you are in the mood, please haul me back to where I have that towel, and I will feel markedly better about being naked in front of a stranger."

He chuckled. "Amongst the Water Folk, there is nothing unusual in nudity. It is preferable to be circumspect with strangers, but no one comments on it."

She blinked. "Oh. That makes me feel a little better."

"Good." He didn't appear to move, but they floated toward the spot where she had entered the water.

"I think I might need swimming lessons. You move so easily that I have to confess I am jealous."

"It is something that comes with practice." He stood and helped her to her feet.

She quickly bent and wrapped a towel around her. The warm, fluffy fabric felt good against her skin.

She asked, "Do you want a towel? I keep several stocked."

Rivvin smiled. "No. My skin does not need it. I exude a non-permeable layer while in the water."

Em nodded and pattered up the stone slope to the desk. She flicked her heater on and the temperature in the room rose in a few seconds.

She yawned and took a seat on the small couch.

Rivvin joined her. "You seem tired."

"I have been awake for a while, and it has been a trying day." She smiled and propped her head on her fist. "Why are you on the mother ship?"

He sighed and leaned back, his thigh touching hers. "I was on the planetary council of Vmesh when the call went out for representatives of the Water Folk to join the mother ship. I had no family to worry about, and I craved adventure. I signed up, got the basic training offered to all members on the ship and majored my studies in the biology of Underhill. It never occurred to me that we would actually make it here or that another species had taken up residence."

"It surprised us, too, to find out that the owners of the ancient cities were still out there somewhere." Em chuckled.

"I believe we should return to the lab before you fall asleep." Rivvin touched her arm.

She smiled. "You are probably right." Em got to her feet and dropped the towel, walking calmly to her spare clothing. The dress dropped over her head and the sandals were snug on her feet as she picked up the towel and dried her hair.

"Okay, I will be alert for about ten minutes. Let's get going." She yawned. She walked to the desk and flicked off the heater, double-checking that it was off.

He was dressed and at her side in seconds.

"I will walk you back to the habitat and then join my companions in the guest quarters."

She walked with him and paused while her eyes adapted to nothing but starlight.

Her path lit up in her mind, and she took his arm to lead him through the stone forest and back to the coastline.

Chapter Six

Em woke, and there was a smile on her lips. He had kissed her good night. She touched her mouth in remembrance as her parents started to move around in the main living area.

"Em, are you awake?"

She cleared her throat. "Yes. I will be down in a minute."

Em grabbed one of her swimsuits and tugged it on before slipping into a shapeless jumpsuit. If she was going to be in and out of the water all day, she wanted to make it easier.

She joined everyone in the kitchen and was unsurprised to see Weelar there, working on breakfast. He flipped, cracked and whisked his way through the morning supplies until the moment when he said, "Morro has set the table. We can join him in the dining room."

That was the hint to each to grab a platter and carry it in to the dining room where the table had, indeed, been set.

Morro was standing next to Rivvin, and they were in deep discussion about something when everyone trooped in on them. They parted, but Morro was scowling intently at the member of the Water Folk.

Em set the platter of scrambled something or other on the table and took her seat. Rivvin sat across the table from her and her mother sat on her right.

Weelar proudly went through a description of the breakfast foods, and with her determination screwed into place, Emharo took some and passed the first platter to Rivvin.

Their move started everyone reaching for the platters, passing them around and starting the meal.

Em shrugged as she ate her way through the fish and all the other options. "Weelar, I am guessing that you like fish."

He grinned. "It has been a few months since the last one was consumed on the ship. I have been looking forward to this trip more than you can imagine."

"No, I can imagine the excitement of the familiar being all around you again, even if it is a food ingredient. Not having it makes it the entire focus of your consciousness." She smiled and took a huge sip of tea to wash down the scrambled eggs and squid.

Morro and Rivvin were eating with enthusiasm, and between the three men of the Nine, the meal gradually ended in empty platters and full bellies.

Harold asked the other men, "So, what are your plans for today?"

Morro inclined his head. "I would like to look into your laboratory procedures and findings to see if I can assist in any way."

Rivvin said, "I will need to take a boat into deeper water to tag some shoals of fish. Do you have a vessel or will I need to request a shuttle from the embassy?"

Emaline looked at Em and smiled, "You can take the Nitka out."

Em nodded to Rivvin. "We have a vessel. I will take you out."

Morro frowned, "Out where?"

"Deep sea over a warm current that hosts hundreds of species. I can show you the maps after we tidy up." She turned to Weelar, "If you have a shopping list, we can pick up just about any aquatic species on our way back."

Rivvin shook his head. "Weelar will just have to deal with any samples we bring back. I promise to bring back enough for dinner, aside from that, you are on your own."

Weelar frowned, "I could come with you."

Em smiled. "Sure. There is plenty of room."

Rivvin grimaced. "That will be appropriate. When do we leave?"

Em lifted her plate. "As soon as all the dishes are in the washer."

The men got to their feet, and Em and her mother watched the miracle of four men doing all the dishes. Even Harold held his own with the scarier men of the Nine around.

Em quickly loaded her dishes into the washer and went to the tech room of the lab to get the remote for the Nitka as well as some tanks for her own use.

Her arms were full as she left the lab, and she waddled to the weapons shed at the base of the dock.

Weelar was squirming like a small mammal and rubbing his hands together in delight. Rivvin looked a little irritated.

"Are you ready?" Emharo kept her voice pleasant.

Rivvin nodded. "Where is the vessel?"

"I have to call it."

"It's alive?"

"No, but we don't like to keep it too close to the lab, just in case." She raised her arm and pointed the remote at the headland.

A dark shape rose out of the water and sped toward them, riding high on

170

the water.

"That is a Tokkel ship." Weelar's voice was nervous.

"Not anymore. It has been rewired to my genetic key. The Nitka crashed in the ocean, and my cousin Neeka and I worked to reprogram it and make it suitable for our work."

Rivvin watched the huge, open-topped vessel approach. "How did you know how to reprogram it?"

"Um, we had a friend who helped us figure it out. Techs are not thick on the ground here, but she managed to give us a schematic after she worked things out."

"What is her name?"

"Ularica. She's on a retreat right now. She is trying to still her mind."

"Ah, I thought it might have been the Potential." Rivvin smiled.

"Nope. Signy isn't mechanically inclined. She can understand stuff but not repurpose it. Ula agreed that if we had the vessel, it would be more useful than leaving it in the water, so she helped us design the changes. It took us the better part of the year, but we got the Nitka up and running."

Emharo watched the beast of a ship come to the dock and settle in the water, the gangplank descending with a smooth move.

"So, you and your cousin rebuilt the brain of this ship?" Weelar swallowed nervously.

"No, we built a brain for this ship. There wasn't one. The whole front compartment was ripped wide open by your ships. We used the engines and the framework. The rest was shaped one panel at a time."

She heaved the tanks onto her shoulder, lifted the bag of items she had collected and walked toward her pride and joy.

Rivvin had a bag of his own with him, but he grabbed her tanks from her without a word. Weelar was hanging back as if afraid to get too close to the Tokkel construction.

Her boots thudded on the plank as she headed onto the deck of the Nitka. She caressed the side of the ship, "Hello, sweetie."

Rivvin looked at her with an amused expression, and Weelar rushed onto the deck, relaxing by inches.

"Are we ready? Do we need anything?"

Rivvin gave her a challenging look. "Do we have water and food aboard?"

Em lifted her bag. "Dry rations and well water, but it will do."

Weelar swallowed, "If we find likely species, we can have something for lunch."

She chuckled and went to the controls, withdrawing the plank and placing her hands on the flat screen for identification. A halo emerged from the ship, and with a smooth move, she settled it on her head.

"What is that, Emharo?"

"The controls. Take a seat, we are on our way."

With no other warning, the ship lifted in the water and headed out to sea.

Chapter Seven

The Nitka was stable in the water. It rode high on a cushion of air and water for balance. Ula's engine design was amazing, and it always struck Em that her friend was truly one of the most brilliant and tortured people that Em had ever met.

She came to the seating area and smiled at her guests. "So, do you have a plan once we arrive?"

Rivvin smiled, "Of course. I have a series of tags that I will use to mark the species that were identified in our histories as being suitable for tank raising. Once the markers are in place, I will summon a collecting ship, and it will come and scoop up the entire shoal of fish."

"Good. Weelar, will you be entering the water? We have a wet hatch in the bottom of the ship." She offered it to him, sensing that he would prefer to enter the water from a secure are.

"I will. It has been a while, and I don't think I have ever been in open water before."

Em was confused, "I thought you were one of the Water Folk?"

Weelar sighed, "I am. I have spent my life on star ships, so open water is actually a foreign thing to me."

Rivvin explained, "Just as most of the city dwellers here would not be able to forage in the woods or sea, not all Water Folk have experience in wild water."

Em blushed. "I am sorry. I should not have assumed."

Weelar waved his hand to dismiss her words. "It is fine. It happens a lot."

"I can swim with you if you like?"

He looked at her in confusion. "How?"

"I brought a dive suit and swim tanks. I can't breathe water, but I can swim with fair dexterity, and more importantly, I know what the sea creatures around here consider to be normal behaviour." She smiled in a helpful manner.

Rivvin frowned. "I don't want you in open water."

She smiled brightly. "Tough. This is my job, and I will do it. You do yours and keep yourself safe. I will take care of me."

"That is not going to happen."

Em crossed her arms and frowned at him. "If you cut my lines, I will free dive."

Weelar was looking frantically between the two of them. "You two are pairing off?"

Em scowled at him. "Not if Rivvin doesn't pull his head out of his ass."

She stalked back to the front of the vessel and looked out over the waves. She leaned her head back, closed her eyes and focussed on finding the current. In the distance, a low lavender gleam began, and as the Nitka got closer to it, it shifted into her gold identifier for a desired object.

Rivvin came up next to her. "I apologise. I am dealing with some changes within me that I am not completely at ease with."

She turned and went up on her toes, kissing him softly. "I am dealing with this as well. I don't know what being with you will entail, and it scares the hell out of me."

He brushed his hand along her cheek. "There will be change, on both our parts. I am afraid that the bulk will fall on you after we formalize our bond."

"You are that sure of yourself?"

"I am that sure of you. You knew that I was yours the moment that you saw me. Your heartbeat changed and your blood warmed."

She swallowed nervously. "You can see all that?"

"My people developed as ocean predators. It is what we are designed to see." He pressed a kiss to her cheek.

"We are almost to the current."

"I will prepare the tags." He nipped gently at her lower lip before he turned and joined Weelar in the rear of the vessel.

Emharo tugged her duffel open and withdrew her dive suit and gear. She tested her tanks and waited until they were coasting into the dive spot before putting the portable remote on her wrist.

A jump, wiggle and jerk and she had her dive suit on to the waist over her swimsuit.

Weelar saw her, and his eyes widened in shock. "You are wearing that?"

"The suit has insulating properties. I don't repel water like you do, so I have to wear the suit on dives like this." She wedged her arms into the sleeves and jerked the suit up into position. With smooth moves, she sealed the suit. "The wet entry is this way. Nitka will remain here, in position, unless I call for her."

She grabbed her tanks, mask and fins and smiled as she led the way down a ramp that opened at her approach. The Nitka settled in place.

Rivvin had his own bag with him, and Weelar looked like he was about to be sick.

Inside the underbelly of her ship, the wet entry opened at her touch. It was an octagon fifteen feet wide and a bright UV light was aimed at the opening.

"The Nitka puts out a repulsion field that keeps the entrance clear. No predator will follow anyone who is not us under the ship. Weelar, is that understood? If you just want to look around, stay under the ship."

Weelar nodded.

"With the mask in my mouth, I won't be able to speak and I don't have time to teach you the hand signals that I have worked out, so go out, do what you have to and come back to the ship."

Rivvin knelt and assembled the gun that would fire the trackers, putting the spares in a net bag tied to his thigh. He nodded. "Understood. Weelar will be able to find me if I end up getting lost."

Emharo smiled, "As will I. Don't make me come looking for you."

He grinned and jumped into the water, circled and then swam away.

She put her tanks on her back and sat at the edge of the entry. "Coming?"

Weelar nodded. "If you can do it, I can do it."

With her mask and respirator in place, she tipped backward into the cool embrace of the ocean.

A splash next to her brought Weelar into sight.

Smiling around her respirator, she pointed and led him through the water and toward the reef teeming with life.

The bright colours of the fish were a delight to Weelar. His face was expressive and his hands were curious. She stopped him several times when he reached out for something poisonous, and he hopefully read her warning in what was visible of her face.

Out in the column of the current, Rivvin flashed and flickered as he moved around and found his target species.

She pointed out several edible species to him, including her personal favourite, sugar fish. What the Nine called them, she had no idea, but the meat was sweet and had a hint of citrus. She loved them.

When the first predator swam past, Weelar froze in place. Em showed him the calm pose to take and the beast disappeared into the distance.

He let out a stream of bubbles as he sighed.

A ping on her wrist warned her that her oxygen was low, and she patted her tank and pointed back to the hull of the Nitka.

Weelar was disappointed, but he accompanied her back to the ship with slow and easy motions.

Em stepped on the hydraulic lift while Weelar boosted himself out of the water. Her hands unbuckled the tanks, and she peeled off her mask. "So, did you have fun?"

"There is so much to see." Weelar's voice was amazed.

"There is. I have been down a hundred times and still haven't seen it all." She grinned and hauled her tanks to the filter and compressor.

"Is this area pressurized?"

"Of course. If you want to go up to the deck, step on those stairs, seal the tube that will come around and walk up the spiral staircase to the deck. The hatch will open and seal behind you so that I don't drown."

He nodded and sat down. "I will wait for you."

She chuckled and worked to purge and fill her tanks again.

"You always refill them immediately?"

"Yes. If I have to return to the water, I need to be able to act immediately. Waiting to refill the tanks could cost a life." She grimaced.

"I understand. Are you going to mate with Rivvin?"

She paused. "I don't know. I think so. I am not sure what is involved."

"Genetic transfer. There is a formal ceremony that you would enact at the embassy, and during the ceremony, there is a blood exchange. We share the ceremony with the Wilders. Not all species of the Nine need to key their females to them in such a way, but most do just for the sake of tradition."

She blinked. "Wow. We just get up in front of witnesses and make a promise."

He cocked his head. "How does that stop partners from straying?"

"It doesn't."

"Then, you have an inferior system. Once a couple genetically keys to each other, they are not stimulated by anyone else."

"Ah. Well, that is nice." She twisted her lips and checked her equipment again.

"What was that fish called that you pointed out to me?"

Em smiled. "I call them sugar fish. They are sweet and have the charming tang of citric acid. I don't know what you would call them."

A clattering of the spear gun made her jump. Rivvin boosted himself out of the water, and there was a long, thin filament tied to his waist. He began to haul on it, and to Emharo's surprise, there were four huge silvery fish on the end of the line.

Weelar chortled with delight and helped Rivvin bring in the haul. The moment they were on the side of the entrance, Emharo closed the wet entry and the ramp descended again.

She began to get an idea of the strength of the Water Folk when Rivvin flipped the four fish onto the deck and he pulled a knife out of his bag to begin gutting them. Each of the silvery, hard-fleshed fish had to weigh over a hundred kilos.

He reached into the belly and pulled out something, grinning in triumph when he produced it.

Weelar was staring. "Is that what I think it is?"

"A Carring pearl. These four fish all have them inside."

Rivvin continued butchering the fish, so Emharo brought up the storage well. "What is a Carring pearl?"

"Carring was the Water Folk capitol city. If these fish have the pearls in them, they have been there."

"I don't understand. What is the significance of the pearls?"

Weelar explained, "The power of the city was generated from a combination of ambient radiation and geothermal vents. The pearls contain traces of those minerals and the energy signature, so with a little analysis, we should be able to find the lost city."

She withdrew a bottle of water. "Give me one of the pearls."

Rivvin had all four out, so all four were dumped into her hand, covered with blood. She wrinkled her nose and washed the pearls in clean water.

With them held in her hand, she opened the charts that she kept on the vessel.

A bit of concentration and a spot glowed green. She grabbed her marker and placed an X on the spot. "There. That is your lost city."

Rivvin looked over her shoulder. "It was that easy?"

She arched her eyebrow and held out the pearls. "Here. You try it."

He chuckled. "No thanks. I still have work to do."

His hands were covered with blood up to the elbow, and he returned to the fish to complete his work.

Whistling to herself, Emharo grabbed a bucket, tied it to a line and swung it overboard. As Weelar followed her gesture to the storage chest, she started washing blood off the deck.

Rivvin finished his work, and she splashed the deck at his feet before she handed him a fresh bucket to wash his arms. He rinsed his knife and wiped it carefully on his wrap before returning it to the sheath on his leg.

She put her hands on her suited hips. "So, do you want to see your lost city today?"

"Are we that close?"

"In Nitka, we are only an hour away from most places in the open ocean. Do you want to see the city?"

Weelar nodded frantically, and Rivvin inclined his head. "Please. I have a few beacons left, and it would be a coup to have found one of the ancient cities."

She didn't need to be told twice. She directed the ship, and soon, it was speeding over the waves.

CHAPTER EIGHT

"Come with me." Rivvin held her hands and whispered it in her ear.

"I can't. It is too deep, and I can't take the pressure." She patted his cheek regretfully. "Go and find your city. I will remain here."

Emharo watched as Rivvin and Weelar dove through the hole in the bottom of the ship and saw their gleaming pale skin disappear in the dimness of the water.

She curled up against the wall and waited for an hour until, finally, they returned with goofy grins on their faces.

"We set the markers. I will ask our archaeological team to file for permission to examine the site." Rivvin had something in his hand, but he skilfully avoided bringing it into her viewing area.

"Good. Are we ready to return to the lab?"

Weelar was still grinning. "Yes, but it was amazing, simply amazing. Thank you for taking us out here, I am sure that it is a once-in-a-lifetime experience."

Emharo sealed the entrance again, and they returned to the deck. She directed Nitka back home and peeled her dive suit down to her hips, leaving her dressed in the leather bodice that was her normal swimwear.

The sunlight was still bright when they arrived at the dock.

Rivvin and Weelar lifted the storage chest out of the holding slot and walked it down the ramp to the dock.

Morro and Harold were waiting for them. With the audience, Em was glad she was back in her jumpsuit and boots.

Her father smiled at the storage container. "What do you have there?"

Em shrugged. "Something that Rivvin found. It's enough for a week, even for our large party."

The Water Folk grabbed the container and brought it up to the lab.

Em watched them go, her gaze fixed on Rivvin's legs and butt far more than she was comfortable with. She shook her head and looked at the resigned expression on Morro's face.

He asked her outright. "So, you have agreed to mate with him?"

Her father was shocked. "What?"

"I have agreed to let him court me. But yes, I think that he is probably the one male who won't run screaming just because I have to find something at dawn or in the middle of the night." She shrugged.

"If that is the way it is, you might just be meant for each other. Water is a very patient thing." Morro offered her his arm, and she took it, walking back to the habitat and lab.

Harold was following, "Mating?"

"Married, Dad. Rivvin proposed, and I am seriously considering it."

"Oh. That's all right then." Her father was trying to grapple with the concept.

"Ask Mom, she has been pushing me at him since he arrived."

Morro laughed as Harold froze in amazement. "I am going to tan her backside."

"Don't be too hard on her. She finally found a guy as nuts about the ocean as I am."

Her father was still grappling with the idea when they entered the kitchen where Weelar had one length of a fish out and Rivvin was loading the rest into the freezer.

"It looks like red meat." Morro was more interested now than he had been previously.

"It is. Tastes like it too. We had some for lunch." Rivvin smiled and lifted the empty container in his arms. "I will just wash this out and put it back on the Nitka."

Em smiled at him as he passed. No matter how much time he and Weelar spent in the sun, they didn't change colour. She had asked them about that, and it was simply a matter of them being evolved for a little more radiation and a little less dryness.

She shivered as her skin complained of its coating of salt. "I am off for a shower. I will see you at dinner?"

Morro nodded. "I am eager to find out what you discovered today. It is obvious that you have done far more than simply tagged some fish."

Emharo shrugged. It was not her story to tell.

Rivvin called the embassy and spoke with Daphne. "I want to take her to mate, but I want to make it official first."

"So you want to use the mating gardens?" Daphne smiled. "Not a problem. Did you also wish to use the quarters for the Water Folk?"

"For one night, please. We will return to her private retreat for the second night."

"Understood. Does she need proper attire?"

"I don't care what she wears, as long as she says yes."

Daphne chuckled. "That is a yes then. Women need more trappings than you do. We need to feel the solemnity of the moment or it will just be another day, and you don't want that."

"You are correct. Please arrange the formal dress of the Water Folk." He grinned, knowing that Emharo would look stunning in the necklaces of pearls and shells . . . and nothing else.

"For you as well?"

"Yes. Is tomorrow too soon? We will need retrieval."

"It will be done. There will be a skimmer for you at noon."

"Thank you, Daphne. Give my best to Ambassador Leoraki." He inclined his head at the image in the small view screen.

"I shall. Congratulations."

"Thank you." Rivvin disconnected the call and sat back. It was done. Tomorrow evening, he would have a wife, now he just had to convince her that it was a good idea.

Dinner was quiet. Everyone rampaged through the fish steaks, the crisped kelp salad and the roasted tubers from the shoreline.

When dinner was over, Emharo smiled.

Morro asked Rivvin, "So, explain where you went today?"

"The Water Folk city of Carring. Emharo took us directly there. There was no delay, and Weelar and I swam down to mark the edges of the city with beacons."

"So, you went for fish and you found an ancient city? That is a pretty good day."

Rivvin smiled slowly at Emharo. "And it isn't over yet."

She was suddenly the recipient of every gaze in the room. Emharo cleared her throat. "Well, I think I will be heading to my office. It has been quite a day, and I need a solid night's sleep."

She got to her feet, cleared her plate and cup, heading swiftly into the kitchen. Once there she rushed to her room, got a change of clothing and spare towels as well as a small data pad for her notes about the day.

With the pack on her shoulder, she tried to slip out the habitat door, but

Rivvin was leaning on the exterior of the building. "Sneaking off without me?"

"I am only going to my office so I can be alone. Don't you have to deal with Weelar's hero worship or something? He is so excited to finally be a proper Water Folk." She began walking, but he paced beside her, his shirt tucked in and his trousers fading into the tops of his boots.

"Why are you running?"

He didn't mean literal running, but she understood him well enough. "Because I am not sure. I am not used to not being sure about something. You look so brilliant to me that I am not sure that my own senses aren't deceiving me. Maybe my body wants you but my mind is being lied to, or perhaps the opposite." She kept walking.

Rivvin sighed and walked with her.

"I am going to hold you tonight, and perhaps, your mind and body can achieve some clarity."

She stopped halfway through the forest of stone. "Really? All night? What if I get up and go collect something?"

"I will be with you, no matter where the search takes you."

Emharo's heart fluttered happily at his words. They entered her cave, she turned on the heat and he took a swim while she recorded her notes from the day. She was the daughter of two researchers after all.

Wrapped in a towel around his hips, Rivvin joined her on the couch and tugged her against his chest. "How did you come by the name Emharo?"

"My parents have an equal relationship. When I appeared and I was a girl, my father wanted to name me after my mother and my mother wanted to name me after my father. So, I am Em for Emaline and Haro for Harold. It could be worse. It could be Haroline."

He chuckled and ran his fingers through her hair, straightening and tugging the tangles free.

"I want you to marry me."

Em licked her lips. "I am aware of that."

"Tomorrow. A shuttle will come for us at noon, and we will be wed in the tradition of the Nine. If you want a Gaian ceremony after that, I have no objections."

"So, if there is a wedding tomorrow, there will be a wedding night tomorrow night?"

He paused. "That is the general sequence of events. The housing for the members of the Water Folk is being reserved for us."

"So you have arranged it all."

"It is only a matter of time. If I leave you, my body will call out for yours and yours will begin to pine for mine. A wedding calms us both down and allows us to focus on things that we wish to."

"Can I stay on Gaia?"

He turned her in his arms and pulled her up on his chest. "As long as the mother ship is in the sky, you can remain on Gaia with only occasional forays into space. If they leave, we will need to go with them. Can you accept that?"

She bit her lip and nodded. "If you are with me, I can."

His smile was slow and preceded a kiss that melted her bones. He was careful with the sharp teeth in his mouth and his lips had a dexterity that left her shivering.

She broke the kiss, "Yes, I will marry you tomorrow."

He stroked her cheek. "Fine, now go to sleep. I will be here when you wake."

Em snuggled against his chest and let the rhythm of his breathing take her under.

Chapter Nine

It was a full skimmer that returned to the embassy. Harold and Emaline Baker insisted in seeing their daughter off as she entered the mating garden.

Daphne whisked Emharo away as Apolan spoke to the others of her party. Rivvin came up with them in the lift, but he left her with a wink as Daphne took her down another hall.

"I foolishly asked Rivvin if he wanted you to wear Water Folk traditional garb. He said yes, so I am recommending to you that you not move around too much." Daphne entered a room with a large pool in it and lifted the costume in question.

"Oh. Wow. Okay. Well, it is tradition and only one day in my life. I can deal with this."

She stripped and tied the swath of long strands of shells and pearls around her hips. The top was made up of necklaces that went on in gradually widening circles that incidentally covered her breasts. Her back was bare, her waist was exposed and she grinned as she let her hair tumble down to cover her.

"That looks wonderful. Oh, he left this for you."

A tiara made of three Carring pearls was in Daphne's hands. She knew it must have been what he carried up from the city. He had not had time to set any of the found pearls.

With dignity and solemnity, she set the pearl tiara on her hair. It glowed the same bright blue that overlapped Rivvin every time she saw him. It was hers. Of that, she had no doubt.

She walked with Daphne to the edge of the gardens where a guard and her family were waiting.

The guard inclined his head to allow her into the garden, and the moment she was inside, Rivvin appeared from behind a tree. His hip wrap was made of shimmering fabric, and he wore a shell necklace that matched hers. "You look stunning."

"You are very pretty as well." She smiled shyly and took his hand.

"Thank you. Shall we?"

He led her through the trees until they reached a garden full of white flowers that gave off a sweet perfume.

Emharo breathed deeply, and she calmed immediately.

Rivvin withdrew a knife from the altar and handed it to her.

"What do I do with it?" She frowned at the blade.

He pulled her down so that they were both on their knees. "You cut my skin, I will bite yours. Then, we press the wounds together."

She placed the knife blade on his skin and made a small, shallow cut.

He pressed his hand to hers and deepened the cut. He then took her knife hand and lifted her wrist to his lips. A kiss to her wrist preceded the bite, but the moment he pierced her skin, he pressed her wound and his together.

"Emharo Baker, you have agreed to be mine. You are my wife, share my life and all my possessions."

"Rivvin Sequelar, you have agreed to be mine. You are my husband, share my life and all my possessions." She smiled, "Even Nitka."

He smiled, and they got to their feet. The knife was filed back in the altar stone before they slowly made their way back to those waiting for them.

Apolan waited with a spray-on bandage that would be water resistant. "Congratulations, Emharo and Rivvin Sequelar. Your quarters await."

Rivvin lifted her in his arms and walked past her family with a polite nod.

Emharo was listening to the humming in her bloodstream. Something was pressing at her mind, and she knew that in time she would make it through the mental barrier and stumble into Rivvin's thoughts. This day was simply the day the change started.

He stood her in front of the bedding. "A swim is traditional, but as you are not Water Folk yet, you would drown if we made love underwater for the first time."

She grinned and lifted the necklaces over her head to drop them beside the bed. "I am willing to pace myself and do a few things on dry land before we get on to the advanced stuff."

He grinned as she untied the skirt of shells. "I am able to adapt, as well, to something new."

"Oh good." She swayed toward him, touching the knot of his wrap, and with a few tugs, it joined her skirt on the floor. His last adornment was the necklace, and it struck the floor a moment later.

He wrapped his arms around her and pressed his lips to hers, bearing her down to the bed and confirming that he was completely at home on dry land.

She rolled, rocked and twisted with him until her body surrendered to his touch and starlight danced behind her eyes.

When their bodies were sated for the first time, Rivvin wrapped his arms around her and held her to him until their bodies woke again. The slow slide of his skin against hers was a memory she wanted to keep. The feeling was exquisite and the intimacy caused an ache in her heart.

The next day, they would return to the lab, the ship and the exploration of the Gaian oceans. Emharo didn't know how long they would remain on Gaia, but she was going to take every opportunity to see her own planet. Rivvin had his own agenda, and it intersected nicely with hers.

It was a good thing that they intersected mentally and physically. They might clash from time to time, but Rivvin seemed prepared for it. There was nothing more attractive to her than a man who saw a storm coming and simply lashed himself to the mast.

If her body changed into something that could breathe water, she might finally get the opportunity to see some of the things that had eluded her until now. She hated something out of reach when she wanted it.

Chuckling as she dozed off. She was really glad that, with Rivvin, it was no longer the case. He was hers, and she was going to test his patience at every opportunity. After all, everyone needed a hobby.

Hunting
Return of the Nine Book Six

By

Viola Grace

CHAPTER ONE

Niika looked around and waited. The grass in the meadow was ruffling lightly and the trees bent and swayed as wind moved them in rhythm.

Niika crouched down and held her breath as the hoof beats of one of Gaia's rarest creatures brought it close to her.

The beast broke free of the forest and its thudding feet brought it into the open. Niika couldn't stop the grin on her lips as it lifted its head, shook out its mane and horn and its nostrils flared.

Niika held perfectly still as the beast came toward her. Her heartbeat was slow and steady, but he sought her out with alarming accuracy.

The horn speared through the brush and stopped an inch from her chest before it eased in to touch her. She held perfectly still until the horn retreated and the lovely equine head nudged her. "Hello, love."

She felt the warmth of his mind in hers, and she laughed. It had taken her years of running through the Archives with Daphne, but she had found an obscure reference to a mythical beast. A unicorn was here on Gaia, and it made for an excellent companion.

Niika came out of cover and wrapped her arms around his neck.

He rubbed her back with his chin and snorted.

"Who's a good boy?"

He made a peculiar chortling sound and stepped back into the centre of the meadow. He bounced up and down on his hooves, waving the deadly blade of his horn around.

To Niika's surprise, another one of his kind slowly came out of the green shadows and moved to stand at his side. She was lovely, a silvery black to his blue and ivory. He rubbed his head along her neck, and Niika smiled. She sent him warm wishes, and he trotted back over to her, placing his muzzle against her palm.

His mate looked at her with shy curiosity. She came up and carefully extended her muzzle to Niika.

Moving carefully, Niika held her other palm out and let the female touch her. When the light contact was made, Niika curled her fingers and stroked the underside of the female's jaw slowly. The unicorn's lids lowered in enjoyment, and she leaned forward in silent demand.

A sound in the distance brought her head around, and she stared with the two beasts at her side. "I am sorry. It seems my survival group has woken up. I look forward to seeing you again when I am in your territory."

The male shook his long, glossy mane out and steered his female back into the cover of the trees.

With the last look at their swishing tails, she turned and walked back to the campsite. Time to take her city folk back home again.

They were scuffed, they were grubby and they were ragged, but her group of survival-training enthusiasts were alive and very glad to return to their homes.

Niika dropped them off at the outfitting station and headed for the com station to get her messages.

Her eyes widened as she heard, "Sorry you missed it, Niika, but I was sort of in a hurry."

Emharo was framed in the screen and smiling brightly. "Yes, Nik, I have gotten married to a member of the Nine. Rivvin is one of the Water Folk, and he is as crazy about the ocean as I am. Come by the habitat, and Mom and Dad will fill you in. I knew you would be gone a while and you wouldn't begrudge me this, but I want you to meet him as soon as you can get some free time. Love you, Nik."

Niika sat through the notices from her aunt and uncle, as well as a greeting from a male with a decidedly green tint.

"Greetings, Niika Baker. I am Rivvin Sequelar, and your cousin Emharo and I have become mates. Know that I will take good care of her when she needs it and get the hell out of her way when she doesn't." His smile said that he had already experienced that particular phenomenon at least once.

Niika chuckled.

"I look forward to meeting you. My wife says that you do on the land what she does in the ocean, and those are skills that are in desperate need at the moment. Ambassador Leoraki is assembling a gathering of those who wish to learn more of the wild, and he will be requesting that you lead them in their education. From what Emharo has said about you, there is no one better on all of Gaia."

She blushed and looked from side to side to see if anyone was paying attention to the praise she was getting from her cousin's new alien husband.

"Contact the ambassador or his wife when you are able, and they will have your next course ready to go. Again, I look forward to meeting you. Emharo speaks of you every day. She misses you."

Niika swallowed. She missed Em as well. It was part and parcel of the residue of the Tokkel attacks that kept her moving through the woods, learning and seeking out whatever random idea sprang through her mind. She had sought out minerals, rare plants, animals that no Gaian had imagined, and she had done it all for the sheer joy of movement and life.

After all, she had almost lost everything with that one blast to the spine.

When the folk who wanted to take her course had been forwarded to the organizer, she made the call to Daphne Leoraki. "Hiya, Daphne."

Daphne was wearing a lovely shirt embroidered with layer upon layer of vines and leaves. Her dark hair swung heavily down her back and over her shoulder. "Hiya, Niika. You look disgustingly fresh after your three weeks in the wild."

Niika shrugged. She knew how to keep herself tidy. If her student's couldn't figure out how to shower in the woods after she had explained it to them three times, they could return home stinky but alive.

"Thank you. I do try. So, I hear you have a group for me?"

"Yes, some biologists and historians. Stone and Wilders for the most part. Are you free?"

Niika cocked her head. "Not free but reasonably priced."

Daphne groaned. "That joke was old before you said it the first time. I will have the money transferred to your account immediately. I am guessing that two weeks in the wild will suit them. Will that suit you?"

Niika mentally grunted. "As long as I can have one day to shower and get a change of clothing, I should be fine. What are they looking for?"

"They will have to tell you. There are some things that even the Nine don't admit to." Daphne winked.

They finished their pleasantries, and Niika spoke to the coordinator, completing the reports on her students before getting her air-cycle out of the shed and heading for home.

The wind in her hair tasted of summer. It should be easy to find whatever the Nine needed, but first, she needed a tune-up.

Chapter Two

The moment she was in her small home, she powered up the lights and headed for the shower. Just because she could survive without a hot shower didn't mean that she didn't enjoy them.

When all her outside gear was gone and her underwear was in the hamper with everything, all that was left on her body was the Tokkel torture straps that kept her upright.

She stepped under the hot spray, breathing in the mist of the steaming water as she ran soap over every inch of her before she lathered her hair.

With the straps wet, she could twist in them, getting water under them to clean off any grime or oils. They were a prison and a memory of pain, but they were also the only way she could get around.

The bands held her upright, restricting movement but going around her spine and giving her the movement that the blast to the spine had taken.

Five years. It had been five years since she and her cousin had discovered the wreckage of the Tokkel ship and the crewmember still alive inside it. Emharo had gone for help, but the remaining thug had come out of stasis and shot her in the back before binding her in the torture harness to control her.

As she towelled off, Nik bet that the Tokkel had not had any idea his little sadistic game would cost him his life. It wasn't the first throat she had slit, but it had left her with a body to destroy before her cousin came back with reinforcements.

Ularica had taken in the harness and modified it for Nik's use. She wore it every moment of every day.

Whistling, she dried her hair and picked out clothing to take with her during her next jaunt. She was going to need a few changes of clothing and far more knives from what she had seen of the Wilders.

Tomorrow was going to be a fun day.

Four men looked at her with surprise. One was huge and silvery grey, one was smaller but of the same species, and two had the ferocious countenance of the Wilders.

She smiled brightly and said, "May I please see anything you brought with you?"

They blinked.

"I am Niika Baker, your guide and master hunter of Gaia. Please, your supplies?"

Bemused, they opened their packs, and she rifled through them as quickly as possible. "Fine. What are you seeking in the wilds of Gaia?"

One of the Wilders spoke. "I am Morro, this is Tidae, and we are biologists in search of some protein species that can be easily propagated in captivity."

She nodded. "How many people are you feeding?"

Tidae cleared his throat. "Fifteen hundred? They need an animal-based protein at least once per week. Grown protein only gets us so far, and it has a detrimental effect on our instincts."

Niika nodded, a list of species beginning to form in her mind. "Fine. I can show you a few things that may suit you. Do you have a measurement of the facility you would keep them in? I am assuming that you want them to be self-propagating."

Morro cocked his head, "Not necessarily. We can butcher and store the larger animals quite easily."

She nodded. "Very well. There are a few species I will point out not to touch, but other than that, I can find some likely herds that could use some culling. Stompers are especially easy to harvest if you don't mind dealing with huge swaths of flesh."

Morro and Tidae looked at each other and nodded. "That will be a good start. We have records from our ancestors, and I was wondering if the same species still run free here. I will show you when we camp for the night."

The taller of the two grey men stepped forward and bowed low. "Miss Baker. I am Cavos vi Whyaner of the Stone Folk, this is my companion, Trusk er Vasku. We are historians in search of one of our ancient homes. I have heard that certain Gaians have a knack for locating the homes we once called our own."

She shrugged. "Fine. Where do you want me to take you?"

They all huddled around a map of the area, and finally, Cavos circled one spot about fifty miles in circumference. "In here, I believe. What do you think?"

She closed her eyes and reached out to press her hand on top of his. His city, she was looking for his city. His hand moved with hers to the north, and when she opened her eyes, the point on the map was glowing with red ferocity. She dug her finger to the precise spot. "There. That is where we will start the search. It is rich in plains and forest animals as well as some of the more esoteric plants that are probably on your list. We have to go in by skimmer. It will take too long otherwise, and with that crevice there, we would never be able to hike it."

The Wilders looked disappointed, but Morro nodded in agreement after he and Tidae shared heated looks. It was all that Niika needed to get things going.

In ten minutes, the flight was registered, the gear was stowed and Niika was ready to give her companions the final word. "Gentlemen. We are going into the wild areas of Gaia. Only one word matters there. Mine. If you do not like to take orders, stay here. I will get you in and out alive and in one piece. This is your final chance."

The men looked at each other and filed into the skimmer, taking seats and strapping in.

Grinning, Nik jumped in and took the pilot station. "Let's get this party started."

She fired up the engines, checked the backup power cells and lifted off, taking them to the area that glowed red in her mind. There was nothing else for it, she had begun a hunt, and she had to see it through.

It was a three-hour flight that landed them right in the centre of the pulsing red zone. She set the skimmer down near a stand of trees and a fall of water from the nearby rock face. They would have what they needed close at hand, and Nik knew from experience that that water was icy cold.

Without a word, she left the skimmer and started to pull her supply packs and bedroll from the hatches. The men followed her, and when they had cleared the skimmer, she activated the seal. "That will only loosen when we are on our way out. It will keep the skimmer safe, dry and charged. There is a code to open it under duress, but it is rare that it gets used."

Cavos shrugged and looked longingly at the cliff face. "Can Trusk and I go for a climb? It has been too long since we have been on a world with gravity that matches our needs."

Morro and Tidae smiled hopefully. "Can we go for a run?"

She held up her hands. "Set up camp, and then, you can go running and climbing."

She had to stifle her amusement at the events that turned fierce warriors into little boys wanting to go out and play.

The camp was set in record time. She set up her own tent, bedroll and then she hoisted her supplies up into the trees, but she kept them on the thinnest branch that would support the weight. Kilash were tree dwellers with an intense curiosity. They would ruin anything they touched with the bacteria they carried on their little hands.

To her amusement, the Wilders and Stone Folk followed suit. They copied her placement exactly, and as they worked together on the fire pit, one of the little scavengers tiptoed down a branch and squawked as it was tipped to the ground by its own bodyweight.

Morro reached out and caught the Kilash by the scruff, holding the little shrieking creature at arm's length. "Okay, so that makes sense now."

Nik laughed. "They are notorious for digging into foodstuffs and leaving their digestive bacteria behind. It rots what it touches. Don't leave any food out, and if you do, burn it. They can only eat what they have corrupted."

The men were staring at her in horror. Morro walked to the edge of the forest and let the Kilash run back to the trees.

When he returned and they resumed work on the fire pit, Nik paused, "Welcome to Gaia."

The slow laughter around the pit made her smile. It might just be an okay trip after all.

CHAPTER THREE

This trip was pure hell. Getting the men of the Nine together for one event was like herding cats, Hakkik cats. The kind with the acid fangs and eight legs.

The Stone Folk wanted to do two things, the first was climbing the rocks and simply enjoy being outside, the second habit was Cavos's alone. He enjoyed staring at Nik no matter what she was doing. After two days of it, she confronted him.

"What are you looking at?"

"A woman as lovely as a dark sunset over a granite cliff. You have a lithe grace that I find quite attractive."

The Wilders were busy analysing a bunch of leaf samples from that morning, so they were no help in distracting Cavos. Trusk was trying to interpret the lay of the land from ancient symbols supposedly in the cliff face.

Niika sighed. "How about, I show you to your hidden city, you find what you are looking for and, then, we help the Wilders with their digestion problems."

Cavos blinked. "You know where it is?"

"Of course. I knew the day we landed, but it was a little soon to show you what you wanted to see. I needed to see how you managed in the wilds of Gaia. Frankly, you would do fine for about three months. As soon as the seasons turned, you would be history."

Cavos smiled and stepped close to her. He had been bathing in the waterfall, because she could find nothing in his scent but male and the lightest hint of dust. "History is my speciality. Please, show us what we have been missing."

Niika whistled sharply, and Morro and Tidae walked over. "You called, mistress?"

She rolled her eyes. "Yes. We are going to find the ancient Stone City today, and the day after tomorrow, we can tag some herds. Is that acceptable?"

The Wilders looked at each other and nodded. "Can we still take a run before dinner?"

She sighed. "We will see. You will need knives, rope and one meal pack."

Everybody prepared, leaving Niika to look around the campsite to check for possible dangers. The camp appeared secure, so as they walked out, she activated her favourite item designed by the Nine, the dome. It covered their meal packs, their bedding and the fire pit.

It should be safe enough if they ended up being gone longer than she anticipated. One day's rations was a test. If they couldn't feed themselves in case of danger, they could go hungry.

She settled her water and blades in place and set off to show the Stone Folk how to get into their own city.

They didn't have a problem letting her lead, but as she walked down the hall created by the base of the crevice beginning into two towering cliffs that just jutted from the landscape in a growing swell, she could feel them getting close in their eagerness to see what was ahead.

She could hear Cavos and Trusk murmuring back and forth as they recognised the environment, but she kept walking until she stood in front of the entrance to the hidden city. "It's behind there."

A tumble of rock fifteen feet high spoke to something being hidden beneath. Cavos asked, "You are sure?"

"I am. The door glows red hot, but it glows through those rocks. I can find a few keystones in there as well, if you like."

Trusk raised his dark grey brows. "Keystones?"

Niika nodded. "Keystones. Stones that you pull to bring the others down."

Cavos smiled, "Not necessary. Just a moment." He stepped into the fallen stones and disappeared.

Niika looked at the Wilders, and they simply looked resigned to the Stone Folk showing off.

The rocks shifted, so they stepped back a moment before the landslide erupted outward in a shower of stone chips.

Nik turned and looked at Trusk. He shrugged with his hands open. "Blowing rubble is best left to the high families."

She checked her arms and face for cuts, but none of the bits had broken the skin. She checked her companions and shouldered her pack once again. Cavos was standing in the now-open cavern, smiling and dusting his hands together.

He stepped aside as she moved forward. "Miss Baker, we are loyal followers."

She gave him an evil look and moved across the stone, following the burning red that pulsed and flared as she got closer to the source. "Nice trick, by the way."

Cavos shrugged. "We all have our skills. The Wilders can shift into a more deadly form of their already formidable selves, the Stone Folk can manipulate rock. It is what we are born to do in our different ways. This world shaped us, changed us just as it is changing your people."

Nik tilted her head in acknowledgement and kept walking toward the heart of the tracking pattern. "Why do you want to find your city?"

Cavos chuckled and drew even with her. "Wouldn't you?"

The laughter that came out of her did it with a rush. "I suppose I would."

The scent of water rushed at them when they turned a corner. The suddenness caught Nik by surprise. She turned back and walked through the restriction and then returned to her party. "That is rather neat."

With the turn of the corner, the light was gone. "Does anyone mind if I use a light source? We have a way to go."

Morro and Tidae shrugged in the dimness, and since Cavos and Trusk were ahead, she had to assume they didn't mind.

She removed her lamp from her pack and fired it up. The path they were on was no longer rough rock. The walls were smooth and the floor under their feet was tiled. "Wow."

Morro and Tidae looked around nervously. Morro said, "We don't like being confined like this."

"Do you have a preferred method for being confined?"

She could swear that Morro blushed. "Never mind."

Nik put her hand on his shoulder. "Don't worry. We can feel fresh air on both sides, and this is a fairly clear path with no side tunnels. We can get out. I can always find a way out."

He cocked his head and looked at the hand on his shoulder, reaching up to touch her but missing her when she pulled her hand away. "How do you find it?"

"I hunted it. I hunt what I need. When I need to locate a specific thing, I can locate it without hesitation. Right now, I need to hunt Cavos and Trusk. Those bastards have gone on without us."

He laughed, Tidae looked relieved, and together, they moved forward.

Chapter Four

C avos and Trusk had turned everything on before the rest of their party arrived. Cavos wanted to show the home of the Stone Folk to an advantage, and Trusk just wanted the light and water.

When Niika came out of the cavern entrance with Morro far too close to her, Cavos realised that he might have made a tactical error in regards to the female he wanted.

He walked toward her, watching the stilted pace she was walking with. Concern filled him, and he reached out to take her hand, helping her down the final four stairs.

The contact electrified him, just as it had the first time she touched him. "Welcome to the city of Trasidil, the home of the Stone Folk."

"Thank you." She smiled, but he could see the fatigue in her features.

Morro was looking at him, and challenge was flaring in his eyes. Cavos would deal with that later.

"Come this way. We started the water pumps and the potable water should be ready by now. If we can get the rest of the systems working, you should be able to take a hot bath before we eat."

She smiled wryly. "Who is in charge here?"

"I am. This is my home city, and the object of my studies for the last twenty years. I know every inch of this city in theory, and I look forward to proving the product of my imaginations."

Niika was exhausted. The moment that she found what she was hunting for, her mind drained her body of all energy. It was not a great effect when hunting living prey, but it usually was fine when looking for plants and medicinals.

Cavos was full of energy. He seemed more substantial here underground, as if this was what he needed to come into his own.

Nik moved carefully. Her supports were cutting into her back as they did when she moved too quickly. They were designed to pull and keep the subject contained, so she had worked hard to develop a gait that wouldn't trigger it.

Hiking through tunnels had caused a tension in her thighs and that tension was now hobbling her.

"A hot bath sounds wonderful. Where can I procure such a rare creation?"

He straightened and kissed the back of her hand. "I shall make it my first priority."

She blushed at how silly it made her sound. "Don't. We need to find a place to stay the night, first."

Trusk walked up and grinned. "I have taken care of it. One of the city halls is still habitable. It has living quarters in it."

Niika paused and looked around her, taking in the vista that expanded as far as the eye could see. The city was arranged in a wheel and spoke pattern. The centre was filled with a fountain that splashed water thirty feet into the sky.

The arch of stone above them left two hundred feet between roof and ground.

"How is all of this supported?"

Cavos offered her his arm, and she took it, ignoring the shudder that passed through his body.

He walked with her toward the city, pointing out the buttresses that had been formed in the rock above in a web so tight, nothing could fall.

She heard a noise that was very familiar coming from half a kilometre away. She turned her head and asked, "Morro, Tidae, are either of you up for a bit of hunting?"

"I haven't hunted in so long that I am afraid I have forgotten how." Morro's voice was amused.

"I teach an excellent five-minute course in catching Zaphlings. They are usually the tastiest of the easy prey." She smiled at the thought of getting the Wilders to chase down the small creatures. Tiny hooves, pudgy bodies and faster than thought, one Zaphling would feed them for two days.

There was no way she could catch one with her braces acting up, but there was no sense in having two strong predators with her if she wasn't going to use them to provide a meal.

"Why are you creaking?" Cavos's whisper brought her out of her thoughts.

"Ah, that. Well, let's just say a lady needs her secrets, and as I am one helluva lady, I need more than most." She chuckled softly.

His skin shifted for a moment, and she swore that she could see it turn to stone for an instant. "As you like."

She wished she could tell him, tell anyone, but being mobile via Tokkel tech was not something that most women on Gaia would admit to.

The Tokkel had been most curious to seek out and examine the newest inhabitants of the same world that twisted them but elevated the Nine. The Gaians—most recently of Earth—had been shocked to be under alien attack and even more perturbed when citizens went missing. Everything Tokkel was to be despised and that meant her braces were in danger.

A few days without mobility had been more than enough for her lifetime.

A fire via firestones was crackling merrily. The rocks that Trusk and Cavos had gathered were brightly glowing once they cracked them with a fire poker and exposed their interiors to oxygen.

Niika sat near the fire and extended her legs, moving slowly and stretching them back to full mobility. The men watched her curiously, but they did not ask what she was doing. Once her legs were completely under her control once again, she got to her feet and reached into her pack. "Gentlemen, it is time to learn the fine art of Zaphling hunting."

She wore her knives, held a small folded pack in her hand and led the way out to the field where the deliberate smacking of skull against skull told her that this herd was in the middle of mating season.

Perfect.

Cavos and Trusk were following, their curiosity bristling out of them.

She stopped and turned. "Gentlemen. We are about to go into battle against Zaphlings. They are fast, sturdy and exceptionally tasty. They are peculiar in that they can turn very aggressive when confronted. When I am saying aggressive, they can cause deep bites and nasty bruising."

Trusk asked, "Why don't you grow your protein?"

"You mean in a lab?"

"Yes."

"With an eye to survival, we tried a lot of local offerings and saved our tech for medical and practical applications. We are still settling in as colonists. The Tokkel didn't help matters, we lost a lot of good people."

She cleared her throat at their silence. "Now, to hunt the Zaphling, you need a chaser who is hopefully scarier than the Zaphlings are and someone with a net and a knife."

Niika turned and walked toward the edge of the city, looking out over the field that was holding court to a herd of over a hundred of the little creatures with several parts of the field divided for the males to have their competitions for their supremacy.

The men drew even with her, and they all stared out at the collection of possibilities. "So, gentlemen. Who will do what to which beast?"

Morro looked at her with a calculating gaze. "Which is the most dangerous, the males or the females?"

"Good question. The females. The males only notice two things, other males and females. The females watch out for everything else. Can you see anything else from here?"

Tidae looked and squinted at the small, pudgy creatures in the field. "They are crushing rocks with their teeth."

She chuckled. "Yes, they are. They use them for digestion just like some birds do on the surface. Their jaws can be exceptionally dangerous. Don't get bit."

Morro gave her a narrow-eyed look. "I thought you said they were easy to catch."

"Compared to most of the wildlife on Gaia, they are. Now, who wants to use the net?"

Cavos stepped forward. "I will. Do you have a spare knife?"

Blinking, she handed him one of her folding blades. "This should do it. Lift the head with your less dominant hand and slice back as hard as you can. The blood will scatter the herd. They won't be around the smell of their own wounded. Basically, cut fast or they will be gnawing on your limbs before you know it."

Morro asked, "You won't be joining us in the hunt?"

"I don't hunt with other people around. For me, the kill is solitary." She shrugged. There was no way she could manage it today. Her damned straps were acting up.

She looked around and found a wall that would allow Trusk and herself to remain on higher ground. They boosted themselves into position and watched the proceedings.

She looked at her companion and grinned. "This is going to be fun."

The Wilders straightened and made a run for the Zaphlings. The hunt was on.

CHAPTER FIVE

It took the intrepid trio three hours, and Niika's sides ached with laughter. Trusk had soon joined her in hooting with amusement as Cavos was knocked over by a knee-high doe.

When the death was accomplished and the three hunters thoroughly exhausted, Niika stepped down from her vantage point and walked to the kill site.

"Allow me. They are particular buggers when it comes to being butchered. You don't want to puncture the scent glands. It would ruin the entire carcass."

She drew her long knife and took charge of the field dressing. The men watched attentively, and when she had removed the gut but kept the more edible innards, they lifted the skinned animal to carry back to the city.

She grunted as she got to her feet and bit back a scream as the braces contracted. She forced herself to her feet, wiped the blades on her trousers and sheathed them before she limped back toward the city.

Cavos turned, and he dumped the innards into Trusk's arms. In the next moment, he was next to her, running his hands down her spine and outer thighs. "I knew I had heard that creak before."

Without another word, he lifted her and carried her with speed to the building they had set up camp in. He brought her into one of the empty rooms and kicked open the door of the bathing chamber. He ran water into the tub and quickly stripped off her outer garments.

He froze when he saw the bracing. "What the hell?"

She slowly turned and showed him the blaze of scar tissue on her spine. "It's what lets me walk. A friend reprogrammed it for me, but I suppose it is wearing out."

He ran his fingers over her scar, and she shivered. "That is a Tokkel blast."

She shivered. "It is. The braces keep me moving."

He helped her into the tub, and she grimaced at the pinking of the water from the blood on her hands. The warmth loosened the braces.

He sat and poured water over her shoulders and back. "Why does it have to be the braces?"

"We don't have tech to repair spinal damage."

Cavos sighed and sat back on his heels. "We do, but it would involve you going to the mother ship. Would you do it?"

Niika felt a surge of hope. "Are you serious? Yes, I would love to."

He nodded. "Will tomorrow be soon enough?"

She scowled and stretched her legs as much as she could. The band around her hips tightened and then relaxed as her muscles did. "I don't want to cut this excursion short. I will be fine for two weeks."

He looked at the expression on her face and shook his head. "No, you won't. If the system is failing and your damage is as complete as you say, it will leave you unable to move within forty-eight hours."

She groaned and pressed her forehead to her knees. Niika dreaded being immobile more than she did having to return the funds to the Nine.

"If you want to continue the excursion, it can be part of your rehab after the surgery."

Niika looked into his dark eyes and blinked. "We can just come back?"

"The surgery will take a day, recovery two, and then, we can return to this area and start with a guide that can move. I am sure the others will agree."

Morro spoke from the outer room. "We agree, so we will remain here tonight, and tomorrow, we return to the surface and call for a medical pickup."

Cavos grinned, reached between her feet to drain the water and filled the tub up once again. "Can you remove the rest of your clothing?"

To her surprise, she was sitting in her half suit. It supported her breasts and covered her entire front but wrapped low on her hips to leave her entire back exposed. "Fine. Turn around."

He turned and leaned against the tub as she sloshed and twisted to get the soggy clothing off. When it was off and the water had risen above her hips, she draped the half suit over the edge of the tub and watched as Cavos removed it to wash it out in the sink.

He twisted the suit to wring out the water and draped it over a towel rack.

Morro came in with her pack in hand and the most extraordinary thing happened, Cavos got to his feet and turned to stone in front of her fascinated gaze. Morro froze in his tracks, left the pack and walked out.

"Uh, what was that?"

Cavos changed back from icy marble to his normal grey, and he turned to smile. "What was what?"

"You turned to stone, and Morro just walked away without a word. It doesn't seem like him."

He smiled and turned to her with her pack. "Ancient custom."

He stroked her hair and pressed a kiss to her lips. His mouth was cool and firm, but her reaction was a wave of heat and a peculiar shimmy in her belly that was most distracting.

She was staring into his eyes as he leaned back, and considering her state of undress, his eye contact was as extraordinary as anything else. Niika licked her lips. "Was that an ancient custom?"

He grinned and stroked her cheek. "No, it was much more recent."

"Was it because I touched you when we were looking over the maps?" She had been told not to touch the Nine, but she forgot when it came to hunting a target.

"No. It started then, but it would not have bloomed if the ground hadn't been right. Speaking of ground, how is there so much light in the city? I haven't been able to find the source." He winked.

She sighed. "You know very well that there are strategic crystals angled to catch the sun and direct it down here in various tubes. It is the only way that the Zaphlings could have survived as long as they did."

"How did they get in here?"

Niika smiled. "There were great upheavals in the land before we got here. I am guessing that they made their way through a previously non-existent crack. They are very resourceful and quite small. This must have seen like heaven to them."

"And then, we came in and ruined it."

She chuckled. "Reducing their numbers is a boon. The normal size of a herd is around thirty, so this many will soon break into another herd, and then, the territory disputes will occur and they will kill each other. There is a finite amount of grazing available here."

Cavos smiled. "Do you have any questions about my people?"

"You can walk through stone, but what else can you do?"

"Well, it varies from person to person. Trusk is a carver. He can use his hands to turn ordinary blocks of stone into the most detailed statuary you could imagine. He is here to research some of his family's works."

The braces on her legs gave her a few more inches of play, and she leaned back in the hot water. "What about you specifically? You already know my secrets."

He turned off the tap and then rummaged through her bag until he found a soft cloth that he soaked in water before cleaning her face. "I can move through stone, find minerals and shatter rock if necessary. Far more force than delicacy, I am afraid."

Cavos seemed very attentive and careful of her skin as he finished cleaning the streaks of Zaphling blood from her cheek. The scent of roasting meat started to reach them, and he chuckled. "Did you need to soak more? I can bring you something to eat."

She laughed. "No. Give me a moment to wash my hair and I will be right out."

"I will help you."

Niika wanted to fight but having someone help her was far too tempting with her body still exhausted from the agony of the braces locking. She nodded and reached an arm out of the tub, next to his thigh, until she grabbed her bath pack and pulled out a swatch of dry shampoo. "Get this wet and work it through my hair. The gel will swell quickly."

With his hands on the paper-thin sheet of shampoo, she quickly untied her braid and then dunked her head to wet her hair. He worked his hands through her hair with the ease of previous practice.

"You have done this before."

He grinned. "I have four little sisters. Bath time was always hectic, but at least you are not trying to splash me."

She chuckled. "I could if you like."

Cavos snickered, "I can even braid your hair into a bow if you like."

He carefully kept the soap out of her eyes while they bantered. He eased her into the water and her hair was sluiced clear.

When her hair was clean and the water was pink again, she wrinkled her nose at how much blood must have been on her head.

He helped her to her feet, draining the tub with a flick of his wrist.

She blushed, but he seemed more interested in checking on the functioning of the braces than he was her nude body. It would have been insulting in any other circumstances.

She had to wipe off with the tiny towel she kept for that purpose but when she eased into her coveralls, relief went through her. If Cavos wasn't just flirting, she might be free of the braces. It was a possibility she had never considered from the moment Ularica had put them in place.

Cavos held her arm while they walked slowly back into the main room where the rest of their party had commenced roasting a meal without them. She grinned, "Well, I am guessing I have nothing to teach you."

Morro cocked his head, and his ferocious expression grew contemplative. "I believe you could explain to us why a person of Gaia is wearing a Tokkel torture device as the means to mobility."

Niika sat on her bedroll, and she stretched out her legs, massaging the muscles out of habit. "Well, since you already know, you may as well know the whole thing."

Chapter Six

Niika looked out the archway toward the fountain in the centre of the square. "It was a plain, ordinary day. Em and I were foraging along the coastline when we saw a strange streak of light, and being curious idiots, we ran to see what impacted the ground with enough force to shake us.

"Now, remember, we hadn't seen a Tokkel ship before. The attacks hadn't started, and this was the first alien craft that any Gaian had seen since before the colony began. I headed for the silver hulk while Em ran back to the habitat to alert her parents and call the authorities. The ship opened, and a gross, green, lumpy hulk of a man stepped forward, shouting at me in a language I did not understand. He fired and missed me by inches, so I turned to run. That is when I was struck in the back.

"Pain burned outward from the strike point, and I blacked out."

She shuddered at the memory of what happened next. "When I woke up, I was in a full-control harness. I could move my body slowly, but whenever I shifted quickly, I locked in place and fell over."

Cavos nodded. "That is the tricky bit of those harnesses. The moment you are in one, you are a slow, plodding worker for the Tokkel. It is a very effective restraint."

"It was three days with that creature shouting at me until I understood his language. Once I knew that he was a scout and he wanted my help repairing his ship, I knew that I was being faced with a choice. Live my life in that damned harness or die trying to escape. I managed to liberate a shard of steel from the inside of the ship, and slowly and carefully, I slit his throat from behind."

Cavos took her hand to encourage her to continue. "What happened next?"

"I left the ship and found my family. He had shifted us down the coastline, and their search party was on their way to find me. The first thing Em did was get me out of the harness and that is when we found out about my little problem. My legs didn't work. I had feeling but no muscle control. Ula was there to see the ship, and she immediately altered the harness into something that could be worn under my clothing and that I could live with. That was six months before the first warship attack on Gaia. We warned the government about what was coming, but the violence of the attacks still caught everyone by surprise."

The men in the room nodded, and Tidae grimaced. "And then, we arrived and the Tokkel were driven off."

Cavos tilted his head. "What happened to the ship?"

"With Ula's guidance, we gutted the AI and turned the ship into the Nitdka. Em's sea skimmer. It took months of work, but it was easier to tell folks that we salvaged a severely damaged ship. The AI was pulled apart, and Ula integrated it into her personal defences when she went off for her privacy."

Tidae cocked his head, "Who is Ula?"

"She is a designer par excellence, but she gives each piece a part of her soul, and when that item is misused, it becomes a point of pain for her. She is bleeding psychically, and with the Nine here to offer their assistance, she is no longer required to work for the defence of Gaia around the clock. There is no tech she can't unravel and piece together using only the most basic of tools." She smiled with pride.

"The Bakers are my family. They took me in after my parents died during a localized epidemic. Em and I managed to find herbs to effect a treatment, but it was too late for my parents. They died with fifty other colonists in a matter of days."

Cavos blinked. "How did you find a cure?"

"I found a treatment in a plant called Garish. Em found the cure in a very ugly fish named Eric."

Morro laughed. "The fish had a name?"

"It did when Emharo was done with it. You have met her. Am I wrong to say that she would name the sun and stars if it suited her?"

Morro wrinkled his nose. "No, if something needs to be told what it is, I am sure that your cousin is the one to do it."

"Anyway, so we diluted Eric's liver, and the enzymes released were just the thing to stop the virus in its tracks and reverse a great deal of damage." She sighed. "And then, we had a nice memorial service for the fallen hero. It didn't seem right to eat him after that."

The men laughed, but she was serious. There was still a stone marker for Eric, saviour of Gaia. Only the Bakers knew that it referred to a fish.

"So, my parents died and were buried, the Bakers legally took me in, and my name was changed for simplicity. I am their daughter as much as Em, but to her, I am and have always been the beloved cousin that was as close as a sister."

Morro asked, "What about Ularica?"

"She is the weird cousin that gets invited to everything but rarely comes."

Tidae got up and turned the meat.

Silence fell over the gathering, and Cavos reached out to caress her ankle. "I know what it's like to be in the harness. They put us in it while we are training for battle so that we know how to fight against those being held without injuring them. If we know their limits, we can take them down without injury."

Niika smiled. "How did you find it?"

He shuddered. "I fought so hard, I dislocated my right arm within hours."

Tidae muttered, "I was trapped in the foetal position for three hours before they let me loose."

Trusk said, "I panicked and fell down a set of stairs, stiff as a board."

Morro shrugged. "I got along fine until I had to walk across the training ground and go through the obstacle course. I ended up dangling from one of the climbing frames, locked in place."

Their travails made her feel like a professional dancer in comparison. "It took me a few minutes to move and a few hours to learn my limits."

She shivered, it had been so frightfully cold without her clothing and the Tokkel's hands had gotten more aggressive with time. It was that aggression that had cost him his life. In the case between death and honour, it was his death so she could keep her honour.

"You just went dark." Cavos's words came through her thoughts.

"Yes, I suppose I did." Niika focussed again. "I apologise. So, gentlemen, what did you think about the most benign prey on Gaia?"

The room burst into astonished laughter at the effort it had taken to down the small creature.

She grinned. "Gaians are very focussed on survival, no matter the species. As you know since your folk developed here as well."

The Wilders puffed up with pride, and the Stone Folk merely looked at each other ruefully.

Dinner was ready in another hour and conversation shifted from evolution to why Zaphlings had to be so elusive. It was as delicious as promised.

"So, where do the fire stones come from?" Niika leaned against the wall and sighed as she enjoyed the sensation of a full belly.

Trusk winked as he tossed the bones into the flames. "We make them. It is something that all Stone Folk are taught when they are children."

Nik laughed. "Like snowballs but not."

"Definitely not. Manipulating the properties of stone does not usually go any further unless a child has a particular focus for the art of molecular alteration." Trusk nodded toward Cavos.

"Why are your heights so different if you are the same branch of the Nine?" It was blurted out on a yawn.

Cavos blushed and looked down. "I am an aberration. My species was born to run through caves. This height is a distinct disadvantage."

Trusk grimaced. "The Giants amongst us usually try to find administrative work, but no, this galumphing idiot wants to travel the stars."

Niika laughed. "I am guessing that you have been around each other for a while."

Cavos sighed, "He's my cousin."

Nik yawned and chuckled. "Cousins. Can't stand them and can't enjoy life without them."

Trusk chortled and glared, "Define enjoy."

"They keep life interesting and help you find your way into trouble."

Trusk lifted his water cup. "Enjoy it is."

Cavos covered his eyes and shook his head with a grin on his face.

Nik could tell that there were dozens of stories behind that gesture, and she looked forward to hearing a few.

She slumped into her bedroll and yawned again. "Are you sure that you are all all right with my seeking medical intervention on this matter?"

Murmurs of agreement rang around the room, and she slipped into exhausted sleep with the feel of a hand stroking her forehead.

CHAPTER SEVEN

Nik was humiliated. Cavos carried her instead of allowing her to walk, and she had to admit that they were moving far faster than any pace she could manage.

Out in the sunlight, she felt markedly better, but instead of letting her walk, Cavos handed her off to Trusk while he caused a landslide that once more closed the entrance to the city.

Eye to eye with Trusk, she had to face his surprised grin. "You are very light, Miss Baker."

"Um. Thank you for the observation, Trusk. You can call me Nik, by the way."

Cavos grabbed her and continued to hike to the skimmer site while the Wilders ranged ahead, enjoying their run.

"Stop flirting with my cousin." Cavos whispered it in her ear.

"Um, I wasn't flirting. My name is Niika and my friends call me Nik. You are welcome to use it as well."

He grumbled. "You smiled at him."

"I smile at a lot of people. After what I told you all last night, telling him he can use my nickname is the least of my intimacies."

They reached the skimmer, and Niika scowled. "I hate cancelling a trip early. There was so much to show you."

Morro grinned. "You can show us all when you are under your own power. It will be entertaining to watch your recovery."

"Well, as long as I can provide entertainment." She dissolved the skin on the skimmer with a series of taps set to resonate and cause a dissolution of the shield into a fine dust.

She headed into the skimmer, but Cavos stopped her. He nodded to Morro, and the Wilder picked up the com unit, keying in a code.

"We need an emergency evac, Madame Leoraki. Medical emergency to the mother ship."

"Who is it?" the voice came out of the speakers.

"Niika Baker."

"Shuttle is on the way, clearances have been provided. The local shuttle will be with you in thirty minutes. Keep me posted." Daphne disconnected the line, and they were stuck waiting.

"Really? You are calling a medevac for me? I am so embarrassed." Niika hid her face in her hands.

She kept her face hidden when the shuttle arrived, but she couldn't keep her eyes closed when they left Gaia and headed for space.

The stars glowed so brightly that she almost didn't see the Nine mother ship until it was right in front of her, and then, she couldn't stare at anything else.

The medical staff seemed surprised to see her walking. They had come with a stretcher and were a little dismayed at her upright status.

Cavos whispered, "Get on the stretcher."

"No."

"Get on. Things will move faster if you do."

"No."

"Fine. I am sorry." He gently put his leg behind hers and bent his knee into the back of hers. The shift in balance caused her to collapse, and as her body went down, she screamed when it was held in place.

The medical team moved quickly and lifted her onto the stretcher, whisking her through the halls while she tried to force her body to relax.

She was stripped in moments, and the entire medical team paused in horror at the sight of the bands digging into her skin and pulling at her limbs.

A no-nonsense female physician stepped forward and said, "Haven't you seen Tokkel bindings before?"

She unclipped the harness and the braces went limp. She unclasped them from thighs, knees and ankles and helped to ease Niika to her stomach. "I apologise for the indignity, Miss, but we need to see what we are dealing with. Oh!"

"Please call me Niika, Doctor." She settled her upper body as comfortably as she could, shifting until her breasts no longer felt crushed.

Scanners were hoisted into position and warmth began to run across her back. Niika looked around, and everyone was staring at her ass as if fascinated.

"Can anyone tell me what the hell is going on?"

The doctor came around and said with all seriousness. "You have been shot with a Tokkel blaster."

"I am aware of that."

"You should not have survived it. Your body has compensated by going around the injury as much as it can. We can help you regenerate the damage, but it will take a few days given the extensive nature of the injury. Do you have plans?"

Niika laughed. "No. May I have your name?"

"I am Dr. Meevin, one of the Giants of the Stone Folk. Also, Cavos's mother."

That almost brought Niika right off the table. "What?"

Dr. Meevin extended her hand. "Meevin vor Whyaner, pleased to meet you."

"Niika Baker. Glad to be in capable hands." There was no way that Cavos could have told her about their interaction. She would be recognised only as a Gaian hunter with an accidental injury.

The doctor smiled and stroked Nik's hair. "Sleep now, we will talk when you wake up about why my son was holding you like a baby the whole way here when medical attendants were waiting to take over on Gaia."

Blushing, she heard a hiss, a coolness to her spine and then nothing.

Meevin worked on her son's preferred mate for hours, the cells hadn't been destroyed by the blast, they had been swollen until pressure on the spine had caused the lack of control. Scar tissue was the greatest problem, but the enzymes that would do the most good were not tested for Gaian use.

She was staring through the surgical scope when she felt her son enter the room. He carried the same energy that she did, but he could do so much more with it. She enjoyed being a scientist, biologist and researcher as well as a standard physician to the ills of the Nine.

"What is it, Cav?" She didn't look up but kept slowly unravelling the scar tissue from Niika's spine.

"Will she be all right, Mom?"

She paused for a second before continuing. The care and worry in his voice was far deeper than she had assumed.

"I will do my best. It will take a few more hours, and she won't be awake until tomorrow. Go, get some rest. Update the council with your findings, just leave me to do my work."

She felt his bow.

"Thank you, Mom. I will also set up some quarters for her to recuperate in. She won't be comfortable here. Your staff is far too interested in her."

"Do what you like, Cav. Now, shoo, Mama's busy."

She smiled and continued her work with enthusiasm, recognising that she was saving the mobility of her future daughter-in-law, whether the Gaian was aware of it or not.

Chapter Eight

The lack of pain made her lightheaded. Nik twisted to one side, and to her shock, her knee bent up to brace her in an old reflex that hadn't been used in years.

She giggled and wriggled her toes. She reached around and felt the plasticky skin over her scar. One more test. With great care, she slipped her feet off one side of the bed and kicked them for a moment before she stood upright.

She weaved slightly as she tried to balance against braces that weren't there. With her lower lip between her teeth, she slid one foot forward then another. Nik grinned and quickly jumped up, spinning in the air to face the other direction. She hooted with triumph, but her reflexes weren't up to snuff and she ended up face down on the bed. It was a small price to pay for mobility.

A slow applause brought her around with a jerk. Dr. Meevin was there with several pieces of fabric over one arm.

"I see you are testing my handiwork."

Niika grinned. "It is very good. I can move freely again."

"Excellent. Now, let's get you showered and dressed then back to medical for a check. I am not letting my son in until you are clothed. He is close to the edge of control as it is."

Niika blushed and didn't mention that he had already seen her naked and it didn't seem to matter.

The mysteries of the solar shower were explained to her, and a bright flash later, her hair and skin was squeaky clean.

"You have four daughters, Dr. Meevin?" Niika was tugging on the tight amethyst trousers that were the first layer of the clothing she had been brought.

"I do. Cavos is an excellent caretaker. He was wonderful while Whyander and I worked. Of course, when I came here, my husband had to remain with our daughters. I will be off rotation in another four months, and then, he will come to the mother ship while I handle the last days of their childhood."

Niika pulled on the long emerald chemise, the sapphire tunic that ran to mid-thigh and the elegant and peculiar ruby coat that was cut to the waist in front, exposing her legs but covering her arms and backside in a swirling flow of fabric that reached her ankles. Everything had gold and black embroidery on it but allowed complete freedom of movement.

Dr. Meevin was impressed. It was obvious in her gaze. "Well, he was right about the sizes, and you do look enough like one of the giant Stone Folk to pass in dim light."

"Why aren't you the same shade as Cavos?"

"The women aren't grey, dear. The men did the mining and the women, the science. The joke is that they have the stones, but we have the brains." Dr. Meevin grinned and offered her an arm.

It was easy enough to move, and when they entered the outer room, she asked about footwear and was told that it was a little advanced, but when she was better balanced, socks and boots were waiting.

Another Gaian was waiting for them outside the door, and while she had not met Signy before, Niika knew who she was looking at. "Hello, Lady Rothaway."

"Call me, Ziggy. Welcome to the mother ship of the Nine. I see you are in good hands. Good day, Dr. Meevin."

The doctor inclined her head with a smile. "Good day, Potential."

"Call me, Niika or Nik." It was most peculiar, the doctor didn't pause but kept going right past the Gaian in the lovely gown, hauling Nik along.

Nik was able to keep up with the rapid pace and that alone made her grin and skip a bit. She lengthened her stride for the first time in what felt like forever and imagined what she could do when she was able to run free.

Inside medical, she took a step toward the table, but Dr. Meevin directed her to a strange half cylinder against one wall. "Stand there and don't move. The scanner will close around you but relax. It is going to measure your progress."

"With my clothing on?"

"It works through clothing." The doctor gently pressed her into the scanner, and behind the tall woman, Ziggy gave her a thumbs up.

The cylinder closed around her, and to her surprise, it tilted horizontally before a light ran up and down her body.

Before she could work up a good case of nerves, the machine tilted once again and let her loose.

"I will need to analyse these findings. Lady Rothaway, would you care to take your planet-mate to lunch?"

Ziggy grinned. "Of course."

Cavos appeared in the doorway. "I have prior claim on her time, Lady Rothaway. If you do not mind?"

Ziggy looked from Niika to Cavos and back again. "No, of course. I understand. You probably want to compare notes about . . . something or other."

Ziggy winked. "By the way, I love the outfit. The Stone Folk certainly are snappy dressers."

Ziggy turned in a swirl of skirts and left medical.

Cavos extended his arm to Niika. "Well, Nik?"

She inclined her head in thanks to Dr. Meevin and walked to join the grey man who had eyes only for her.

"You are moving more easily." His first words were uttered when they were several dozen metres from medical.

"I am. You can increase your stride if you like."

"Would that bother you?"

"No. I really need to stretch, and a little soreness tomorrow is worth the increase in mobility. Your mother tells me that I can even upgrade to shoes if I don't fall over today." She chuckled. "Well, fall again."

He smiled, and the next words out of his mouth shocked her. "Will you be my bond mate?"

She almost fell on her face. "What?"

"Will you be my bond mate? I am drawn to you in a way that I have never been pulled toward a woman. I couldn't leave your side while we waited for you to wake, and you held my hand the entire time you were asleep until my mother pried your fingers from mine and banned me from your bedside."

She blinked. "May I think about this?"

He swallowed and nodded. "Of course."

She knew that he made her smile, knew that he was good for her and protective of her. That last one was going to be annoying once she got her full mobility back. She had avoided men since her incident and had been too young before it to really get serious about someone. Cavos was the first man in her orbit since that moment. Did she really want to throw caution to the wind and make him the only one?

Divorce amongst the Nine was not possible. It was a bond that went deeper than blood from what she had heard from Daphne. If she said yes, it would be a forever yes.

They walked to a café, which seemed odd on a star ship.

Cavos ordered for them and was looking forlorn when she said the word that sealed her fate. "Yes."

He blinked. "What?"

"Yes. I will be your bond mate. I want to live on Gaia for as long as we can, though. Is that agreeable?" She bit her lip, knowing that it was now beyond her control. Her agreement had been given.

He frowned. "Can I continue my research at the city?"

She blinked. "Of course. I will continue running my courses as well."

"I am not sure how I feel about that."

"Tough. I have to hunt, and teaching folks to see the woods the way I do is something that I love to do. More than that, I was born to do it. After a standard course with me, even the average citizen can feed and shelter themselves for weeks at a time. We might never face an attack by the Tokkel again, but it would be foolish to be dependent on agriculture when it is such a delicately balanced thing. It is better to always know how to find the means to survive when your entire world goes crazy around you."

He looked at her for a moment and nodded. "If it is important to you, it is important to me. Now, shall we formalize our agreement?"

"Like, paperwork?"

He grinned and got to his feet, lifting her from her chair and kissing her in full view of the café patrons and the startled server.

Niika wrapped her arms around his neck and held on as his skin went through a series of textures and temperatures under her touch.

When she leaned back, his eyes were glowing like the firestones in the hearth and her heart was pounding. A roar of applause came from the other patrons, and she sat back down with a thud and a silly smile.

Cavos took his seat, and he had a smug grin on his lips.

She blushed and nodded to the server who poured a cup of tea for her. She lifted the cup and inhaled the scent of herbs. "This is a Gaian tea."

"Of course. Lady Rothaway is working hard to bring fresh ingredients to the ship. With her connections in the florist industry, she knows where the farmers are that grow the plants. The medics here check the plants for uncomplimentary compounds and allow the new items to be introduced in measured amounts, carefully regulated."

She smiled and sipped at the tea. The rest of the meal passed in a daze.

When he said, "So, you would prefer to bond on Gaia?" She jerked out of her stupor.

"Oh. Yes, please. I have to ask, is this clothing standard for the Stone Folk? It is very comfortable."

Cavos smiled shyly. "I am glad you like it. Yes, the style is standard for daily wear. My sisters picked it out via long-range communication."

She winced. "I was a family project?"

He chortled. "Everyone, including my father. He was consulting with my mother on your estimated recovery. There are going to be papers written about your physiology, I am not even joking. You should never have survived the initial burst."

She sighed, "I know. The miracle of Gaia, I guess. She is making us better than we were before. Or at least very different."

"So, you are aware of the changes?"

"Of course. We are all aware, though we don't like to talk about it. This generation has begun to show marked increases in psychic anomalies in the population. We are not changing physically, our minds are altering and most are doing so along specific tasks."

He sat back. "I am sure that most of your population is not aware of it, so how are you?"

"My aunt and uncle are biologists. They are not stupid, and they ran a very quiet research project on my generation. Unusual intelligence was the most found symptom in men and women. After that, the more pronounced traits struck fifteen percent of the population. Daphne's ability to hide in plain sight is well known, and there are many more that have skills with a specific focus, like me." She smiled brightly.

He paid their bill with a swipe of his hand. "So, tell me about how it works."

She took his arm, and they walked along a winding pathway that led to a garden area. "I get a fix on my target, and it glows red in my mind. The closer I get, the hotter the colour."

"What happens when you lose your target?"

She pulled him to a halt. "What do you mean?"

Cavos looked into her eyes, and he asked softly. "What happens when you can't track your target?"

She smiled slowly and slid her hand up around the back of his neck, pulling him down to her. She whispered, "I never lose my target."

She let him go and skipped along ahead of him, enjoying the feel of the faux wind on the ship.

Chapter Nine

Nervous was not the way to describe her feelings. Panicked like one of her own prey was more like it. Niika Baker stood in the Nine embassy and watched her aunt fiddle with her hair.

Daphne was standing nearby with a sly smile on her face. "You know, we have never had so many people of the Stone Folk in residence."

"Well, his mother is here, so it stands to reason that there would be a few more than usual." Niika bit her lip, and her aunt grinned.

Her gown was burgundy and gold, a sweeping span of silk that wrapped her torso and flowed freely around her legs. One week since her surgery, and now, her knees were going weak.

Daphne suddenly grew solemn. "It's time, Niika."

Her Aunt Emaline took her arm, and they walked to the stairway that led into the ballroom.

Emharo and her husband, Rivvin, were in the group of people lining the walkway that would take her to Cavos.

Niika went through a dizzying round of hugging all her friends and family then greeting the cousins, clan reps and the mother of her bond mate.

The moment she took Cavos's hand, her nerves faded. She walked with him through to the mating gardens and followed the protocol for the Stone Folk by taking a crystal from the attendant and holding it in her palm.

She didn't remember the words they spoke as the blade came up out of the stone. She focussed on slipping the crystal into the hilt of the knife and then flicking it with her finger. She sliced his wrist with the humming crystal dagger.

He lifted her wrist to his mouth and bit down with sharp, pointed teeth that he had been careful to hide from her until now. Her blood coursed down the dagger, and she slipped it back into the registration stone.

Wound to wound, they sat for a moment before he lifted her wrist to his mouth and licked the bite closed. She followed on his wrist, the shallow cut sealed slowly but surely as she lapped at him. It was appalling to her sensibilities but actually not horrible in the execution of it.

When they were finished with that portion of the ritual, they kissed and

Niika felt heat running through her body. She broke the kiss suddenly. "Is that what you have been dealing with?"

He smiled and kissed her again. "Just wait, it gets worse as you synch to me."

"You always give me something to look forward to."

He chortled and helped her rise to her feet. "It is a very ancient custom."

"Yeah, I am not falling for that one again."

His grin was delight and endless smugness. He had her right where he wanted her.

The reception was hours of fun, but Niika missed most of it.

The harmonics of the crystal had let her cut his skin, but the rest of him was still hard as stone when they tumbled into bed and he stroked her from neck to knees until she twisted against him.

He was careful as he moved between her thighs, delicate and deliberate as he shifted inside her, and she felt like a cherished treasure as he took her to heights that her cousin had only whispered and blushed about.

Niika had been excited to be able to sit cross-legged again, but it didn't even come close to the delight of being able to wrap her legs around her bond mate.

Curled up against him, she stroked his chest slowly. "So, when do you think we can get back into the forest with Morro and Tidae?"

"I think we should take at least one more day to rest and recuperate from the stress of our families being in attendance." He lifted her hand to his lips and kissed her palm.

"Stress, hmm?"

"It is an ancient custom. Trust me."

She grinned and moved over him, sliding her body against his until she had his complete focus. "I don't think trust has anything to do with it."

He sighed as she joined their bodies. "I will do whatever it takes to get you back into your wilderness."

The phrasing was loaded with innuendo, but she didn't mind. She wanted to get her wilderness back into her as well. It had been far too long.

Two days later, they were back next to the skimmer with their original party. Niika had her hair braided tightly against her skull, and she had to admit, Cavos was very good at doing her hair.

They returned to their camp, and the shield was still in place. Fortunately, they had fresh supplies.

"All right, gentlemen. You know what to do."

This trip was putting the Wilders first. If they needed to run and hunt in their shifted shape, she was going to give them a worthy foe.

While they worked on the camp, she used her returned dexterity to climb a tree and saw off a few supple branches. The basics meant that everyone without claws was going to be carrying a spear or long blade. This was not easy prey.

Humming to herself, she wrapped a strip of fabric around the hilt of a knife to bind it to the stick. She heard a familiar sound.

"Gentlemen, we are about to be visited. If you injure this animal, I will gut you like a Zaphling."

She walked toward the sound and found the meadow where the creature was frolicking with his mate. She stood and watched, feeling Cavos come up behind her.

The beast took exception to the other male near her, and he charged. She dropped her spear and stepped forward until the animal jerked to a halt and shook his head in frustration. She was not going to let him spear her bond mate.

"What is it?"

"I don't know. They are highly migratory, but I have only seen a dozen or so in my time in the wild."

She smiled as it snuffled across her body and the horn finally settled against her heart. She remained calm and placid as it tested to make sure she was still herself. When he rested his head on her shoulder, she wrapped her arms around his neck.

The female was investigating Cavos. The male let out a snort of caution, but she simply flicked her mane and nuzzled at Cavos for a touch.

Nik looked to her mate and showed him how to stroke and scratch at the soft and silky hides.

The wind shifted, bringing the scent of Morro and Tidae to them. The horned animals jerked and thundered off, manes and tales flaring.

Nik grinned and turned to Cavos. "Welcome to my world."

He wrapped his arms around her and pressed a kiss to her forehead. "That was amazing. Now, let's see how well Morro and Tidae can run. Take us to their prey."

Nik laughed, "I have just the thing."

Trusk, Cavos and Nik sat up in the trees and watched as the Wilders dodged and jumped over the stampeding beasts that didn't want to be prey.

Trusk eventually asked Nik, "You are the hunter, won't you step in?"

"Just a little bit more. They haven't learned their lesson yet."

"Mate. I think Morro is getting tired. Please step in."

She grinned. "I don't think they are going to thank me, but all right. You two stay safe. I don't want to explain an injury to Dr. Meevin."

She clambered down the tree, gripped the spear she had stowed at the base and ran to help the Wilder's bring down the ten-foot tall, woolly beast that they were trying to corner.

It took three rolls under charging animals to get close. The horns and the speed were a problem, so she cheated. She killed the beast with a spear to the eye. She made a coughing noise that gave them a wide area to work with and repeated it until the herd made its way to the next meadow.

Morro's features were still all predator. He formed words with difficulty. "Thank you."

"Don't thank me. The kill may be mine, but the carcass is yours. Don't let the wool touch the meat or you will spoil it. I am going to coax my husband out of that tree now."

She turned and wandered away, leaving the spear in the animal and her two Wilders with their knives and basic knowledge of butchering. She heard the sounds of a carcass being dragged, and she smiled. It appeared that Wilders were either born with the intelligence of how to process an animal, or they actually listened when they were being lectured.

Once the animal was taken care of, they sent the signal for pickup. That animal would feed two hundred Wilder in need of actual meat.

Sitting next to Cavos with the fire burning, she looked at the two Wilders. "Have you had enough?"

Trusk shook his head as the other two sat thoughtfully. "Not smart enough to call a halt."

Cavos stroked her hair slowly as they waited.

"We need more. The fish are fine for a while, but they are not enough for us. If we don't have the meat, we lose the ability to shift or trigger our ruts. It neuters us." Tidae whispered the last.

"Fine, then, you just have to decide, do you want to go bigger or meaner?"

Cavos dragged her into their tent and told the Wilders, "You have until morning to decide. I will try to gain her assistance from the outset this time."

Nik was scowling at her bond mate when she heard Morro say, "He is a selfless man, taking one for the team."

Cavos held her tightly as she tried to clamber out and kick Morro's ass.

He was laughing silently. "Two weeks ago, you wouldn't have been able to flail around like that."

He pressed soft kisses to her neck and started to undo her coveralls.

"Two weeks ago, I wouldn't have been in a tent with you. How are we going to manage this with them close by?"

Trusk's helpful voice said, "Don't worry, we can't hear a thing."

Cavos's shoulders were shaking as he pressed his forehead to her shoulder. "Perhaps it has to wait."

Niika grinned. "Oh, no. If they want to listen, let's give them a concert that will send them running."

"Oh, I do love a challenge. Ancient custom?"

"New tradition."

He kissed her and bore her back to the bedding. "I may be a historian, but I can adapt."

She laughed as her clothing was peeled away and her new flexibility was challenged by the close confines of the tent. She had always loved a challenge.

Designing
Return of the Nine Book Seven

By

Viola Grace

Chapter One

The heap of leather and metal on the table was drawing a lot of speculation as to how a primitive with limited resources managed to repurpose an instrument of torture.

"I cannot understand how the Gaian understood the tech, let alone reprogrammed it." The head engineer of the Nine warship scowled and prodded the leather. It contracted immediately.

"She has a talent for it, much as the other men and women who have been coming to our attention. I wouldn't put anything past the Gaians at this point. They are surprising us at every turn, Father." Deniir laughed.

"I want to talk to the engineer who created this. This is an amazing work of design and practicality."

"That will be difficult, Father. She has retired from active use of her talent and has withdrawn to the cliffs. She sees no one." Deniir frowned. "She has even cut herself off from her friends."

His father shifted his shoulders restlessly. "How do you know that?"

"I asked. Cavos's mate is a friend of the designer. She is the one who used to wear the harness. Her spinal cord had been damaged, and yet, this woman rigged the straps to keep her friend upright and mobile for years before it failed."

"Extremely impressive. For a primitive to take apart and reassemble Tokkel technology is a feat that deserves to be investigated. I would like to interview her."

Deniir frowned. "She will not leave her home. Even her friends do not have permission to visit."

"Then, you will have to convince her that she needs to take a tour of our facilities. I believe that the opportunity will entice her. She can have full run of a design station and access to all our tech. That has to be tempting, even if she is in retirement."

Deniir looked at his father. "You can't be serious."

"I am very serious. A mind like this needs to be encouraged, not allowed to hide in the darkness. Bring her into the light."

He straightened and made a formal bow. "Yes, Master Engineer Darthuun. I will bring this woman into the light, whether she wishes to be here or not."

"Are you sure this is her home?" Deniir turned to ask the woman who had escorted him up the mountain.

Niika smiled. "It is where she lives. This is as far as I will take you. Whether you succeed or fail, you do it on your own."

He frowned. "You don't visit her?"

"Of course I do. The third day after the second moon is full. We have a schedule but that isn't suitable for your timeline, and she can see us from here, so you had better stop looming over me." Niika grinned at him and crossed her arms over her chest.

Deniir snorted and turned to Niika's mate. "Cavos, can't you do something?"

He grinned. "I am doing something. I am letting you take my mate away from our restoration of the underground Stone Folk city. We have a life to begin, Deniir, and while I respect your mission, it is yours and not mine."

Deniir stared up at the small door set into the side of the mountain, and he nodded. "Thank you for your assistance. I will take it from here."

He shifted his cloak around him and made his way up the narrow path that led to the door in the stone. To his shock, he caught the gleam of small monitoring cameras as he progressed toward the entrance.

He stepped on the doormat laid out and knocked on the door in the cliff face. He heard rustling inside and the top half of the door swung open, and a woman with pale skin and crimson hair faced him. "What do you want?"

"Greetings, Ularica. My name is Deniir, and I am an engineer of the People of the Light on the Nine mother ship."

She stared at him impassively and blinked slowly.

"Uh, well, you are invited to the mother ship in an effort to get you to tour the engineering department."

She nodded. "Not interested. Please leave."

To his surprise, she shut the upper half of the door, and he could hear her footsteps receding inside.

"Damn."

He heard a noise that was familiar. Birds. He followed a narrow path around the corner of the stone wall until the path ended. Sighing with curiosity, he removed his cloak and fluffed out his wings.

He flexed them a few times and then launched himself into the darkness of the space between mountains. His wing beats were heavy, but it eased as he worked out into the light and the warmer air lifted him until he was facing an entire flock of absolutely huge raptors.

The giant birds watched him warily as he settled on a thick jutting branch. He looked at the birds carefully, and he spotted two of them wearing what appeared to be saddles. The way the woman had been heading to the back of her home, she had something distracting on her mind, and there was nothing more distracting than flying. He simply had to wait, and perching in the tree was second nature.

She would come out to ride one of her birds, and he would make his pitch in the air.

Ula felt a little guilty about closing the door on the man from the Nine, but she was so tired of folks wanting to use her talent for military purposes that it was a reflex she now regretted.

She sighed and quickly braided her hair. She knew just the thing to clear her head, and the flock was right outside.

A quick change into riding gear and she was ready to go for one of her personal pleasures and fly through the Gaian sky.

The rocs were nice birds and large enough to carry a human without difficulty, but they were impossible to domesticate. She didn't have any issue with domestication; she rode them wild.

Ula clicked her tongue rapidly, and one of the birds screeched in response. Outside her balcony was a rock suitable for a landing site, and her favourite bird came at her call.

"Good afternoon, Bertrum." She clicked her tongue again, and he settled onto the perch she had built for him. "Ready for some exercise?"

Bert settled and let her mount. She slid her feet into the stirrups and latched her flying belt into the saddle. Bertrum and his mate Eleth wore her saddles constantly. They were the only rocs that didn't fight her every time. Ula suspected that the two birds actually thought of the harnesses as some kind of mating bands. They certainly clung together and preened when they were wearing them.

Once she was in place, she made a low chuffing noise and Bert took off. It was time to get the only freedom she had anymore; it was time to ride the wind.

CHAPTER TWO

Her eyes teared until she pulled her goggles into place. Bert was in fine form today. He wheeled, darted and spiralled around the cliffs of her home until she could do nothing but hang on for dear life.

Once he had gotten used to her weight, Bert began to climb.

She clung to him as he headed straight for the clouds. As the roaring in her ears eased, she heard a strange noise. There were heavy wing beats nearby, and they didn't belong to a roc.

She turned her head and had to blink several times behind her goggles. There was a flying man gaining on them, and he bore a startling resemblance to the Nine representative who had been at her door.

She rocked back in her stirrups, and Bert slowed his forward progress. She shouted. "What the hell?"

"I would like to speak with you, and I am willing to do whatever it takes to make that meeting happen." He flew next to them and smiled brightly at her as he kept pace.

"You have wings."

"I do. Now, shall we continue this conversation on the ground or do you want me to continue to pace you?"

She was so startled, she gave Bert the signal to land. He spiralled down, and she dismounted on a rocky strut jutting from the canyon below. Bert shuffled and took off, leaving her alone with the winged rep.

Ula put her hands on her leather-clad hips and looked up at the lean man looking down at her. "So? Talk."

"I would like you to come to the mother ship and take a look at our research and development department. I believe that you have skills that we can learn from and a way of viewing technology that is fresh and new."

She looked him up and down, and her mind tried to work out the means by which he flew. "Why does the Nine want to speak to me?"

"Because of the repurposing of the Tokkel torture straps. If you could teach our men to think a little more outside the standard, we might just be able to have a higher crash-survival rate." He blinked, and he exhibited a second set of eyelids. Under the standard lids, he had a clear inner lid that was probably designed for flight.

Ula throttled down her curiosity. It tended to get her into trouble. She did not want to be curious about this man. Nor did she want to wonder how someone who looked so dense could fly.

"I don't want to go to the mother ship."

"Please. We have many engineers and researchers who have not yet been able to learn your language. The translators on the ship would enable them to learn how to change the way they look at items in order to think outside common parameters."

She gave him a sceptical look. "You have to be kidding me."

"No. From what your friends and the administrators of the colony have told us, you have a knack for creating anything they need out of scavenged tech. We would like you to share that knack with us so that we can evolve past our narrow views of our own technology. We are in danger of becoming locked in a ship that needs to evolve, and we are unable to help her. Our minds do not work that way."

Ula paced to the edge of the stone and looked down into the canyon. She thought about the concept of trying to teach others how her mind worked, and it was amusing and intriguing. No one had wanted to learn from her before. They simply wanted the results of her work, not the process that had created it.

"What do I get out of it if I agree to head up to the mother ship?" She turned to face him and his wings were extended, sheltering her from the wind. It was sweet.

"I am authorized to offer you patents on anything you create, followed by bonuses for their practicality. You will have full run of our research and development department and all supplies and tech they can provide."

Ula felt a stirring of excitement. "Wait, you mean I will be able to see lists of tech and requisition what I want to play with? No one will complain?"

"They will be honoured to assist your efforts. I have not heard one person complain about the end result of your work."

She laughed. "That is politic. They complain because I won't do more. I have created self-thawing sidewalks, improved healing facilities with upgraded machines, and they still want more. I refuse to work in weaponry. Is that clear?"

He nodded. "It is clear. No weapons. So, you will come?"

She let out a shrill whistle, and Bert returned to her side. She clucked to him as she hauled herself into the saddle. "I will come with you for no more than seven days. At the end of that time, I wish to be returned here to my home.

Is that clear?"

Deniir nodded. "Yes, of course. I can have it drawn up in a contract if you like."

"It probably wouldn't hurt. I will meet you back at my home, and we can hash out the details."

She doubled checked her goggles and gently squeezed Bert with her heels. He waddled to the edge of the cliff and dropped straight down, opening his wings on the way to catch himself and begin the climb. Ularica used her control straps to steer him home, and then, she hopped off her mount and went inside to give him his treat. The treat being citrus was shocking to some people, but they didn't watch the rocs. The rocs flew through primarily desolate areas. They almost became intoxicated with the appearance of a large juicy fruit. Bert opened his mouth when she approached with it, and he quickly flew off.

"Where is he going?" Deniir settled next to her on the stone path that led out of the rocs' canyon and into her home.

"To give it to Eleth, his mate. I think she is going to nest soon, and I hope they do it nearby. I do love to watch the little ones."

He nodded.

"Are your people born with wings or do you develop them later in life?" She almost clapped her hand over her mouth but the question was out.

"The buds are there, but the wings only develop in late adolescence. It is our last stage of development."

"Ah. Interesting." Her mind was whirling, and she wanted to see him fly again so that she could design a pair of wings for herself. Inwardly, she winced. Any new stimuli and she couldn't turn her talent off. The urge to create was overwhelming.

He tucked his wings tight to his back and they folded to press against his body until they no longer resembled wings and instead appeared to be a fanciful cloak thrown over his shoulders.

Ula scowled as she realised that her curiosity was going to back her into a corner again. This time, she wasn't going to be able to hide in her mountain home. Once she was on that star ship, she was going to be examined, interviewed and put through her paces.

There was no hiding anymore. It was time to face the very men that parts of her government wanted her to destroy. She hoped that telepathy wasn't common, because she was going to be looking at them and wondering if they were aware how close they were to death at the hands of the Gaian primitives.

"Give me a few minutes to pack a bag."

He inclined his head. "Take your time. I am in no hurry."

Her tension was probably confusing him but that was for the best. The day that she had come up with a way to destroy the mother ship of the Nine was the day she destroyed all her research and climbed the mountain, never to return to the cities of her world. They didn't need the power she could bring them. They would grow slowly and the world would evolve them in its own time. She didn't need to turn them into murdering bastards. If they wanted to turn destructive, they could do it without her help.

She was getting out and up.

CHAPTER THREE

Daphne was elegantly welcoming, as befitted the wife of the ambassador. Ula greeted her formally, and the moment they were inside the embassy, she was treated to a hug that made her squeak.

"I am glad to see you too, Daph. Now, put me down." Ula kicked her heels.

Daphne set her on the floor. "It has been over a year."

"I know. I am sorry, but they have been watching for me."

Daphne scowled. "Not here they won't. My husband would kick them into next week."

"Do you have a pot of tea handy?"

Daphne laughed and led her into the main floor parlour where a tea set was waiting for them.

"You are going up to the ship?" Daphne poured, and Ula busied herself loading the teacups.

"Apparently. I think it might be good for me. I have been too insular, even for me. A week on their ship will give me a new perspective, and they might get something out of it as well."

Daphne nodded and sipped at her tea. "I have no doubt about that. While no one from the Nine Corp of Engineers has come down before, I think they are about to get a rather serious education."

Ula smiled slowly and sipped at her tea. "That is why I am going."

Deniir was a competent pilot, but being inside the ship, Ula saw at least four items she would change for convenience based on what she knew of the Nine races and their physical needs.

Her pilot spoke to her. "How does your talent work?"

"You want to know now?"

"Well, I wanted to make conversation, and it is a subject of interest."

"Ah. Well, I look at things and see what can be done to make them perfect. If they are already sound, I can see all the components that make up their form and disassemble them in my mind, identifying the components individually for their optimum versatility."

"And you can use those components."

"Of course. Even if I only have primitive tools, I can still take most things apart. They simply part in the precise weak points that I identify. It just takes practice."

"How did you alter the torture harness?"

"Trial and error, combined with terror that a friend would be paralyzed for life if I didn't succeed." She shrugged. The redesigning process was a bit of a blur. The wound in Niika's back was never far from her mind, and she had just acted. No thought required.

"You can create on instinct?"

"I don't create. I never create. I just redesign using components at hand." She shrugged. Her mind was running through her inventory and coming up with components to create a set of wings. There was no stopping it; she was going to build them. She had no idea if she would ever have the nerve to try and use them.

She opened the door to her home, and he came in, gasping in shock. Ula smiled and kept moving. "I will just pack a bag. You can dig around and play with whatever you like."

She heard a few of her machines click and twist as he examined them.

Shaking her head and thinking about boys and toys, she grabbed a bag and shoved in a few days' worth of clothing. She usually wore leathers to work. It cut down on fire from sparks when she welded. No one wanted to run around the house while on fire.

She looked around and shrugged, returning to Deniir before he found her fire extinguisher.

She paused when a shout and a hiss preceded the white cloud of vapour that tumbled down the hall toward her. "Breathe through your mouth for a moment. The taste will fade."

When she turned the corner, his gold hair was sticking up straight, his face betrayed his shock, and the expression on that face was priceless.

He closed his mouth, and it took him a few attempts to speak. "What in the name of the first feathers was that?"

His mouth sounded dry, so she moved to the side of her workspace and poured him a glass of water out of her storage canister. "Drink this."

He shuddered and swallowed rapidly, obviously running his tongue around the edges of his mouth.

She stifled her grin. "That is the fire-suppression system. It is an herbal extract that Emharo found for me in some underwater plant life. I powder it and then put it under pressure in a canister."

He blinked. "So I see. What was the cloud of gas?"

"It absorbs all heat in the area, including the heat from open sources. Fortunately, it does not take heat from anything biological. I don't know how it works, but it does." She shrugged. "I just design and build things, I don't always know how they work."

He blinked. "That doesn't seem right."

Ula snorted. "Welcome to my world. Are you ready to leave?"

He carefully put down the canister and nodded. "Yes, please. I am terrified of how you get rid of household pests."

She chuckled as they exited through the front door, and she armed her defensive systems. No one was going to get any of her projects without blowing the entire house to hell and back. There was nothing safer than a pile of radioactive matter blasting up through the floor to dissolve the floor if the right code wasn't entered.

"Will your workshop be secure?"

She laughed. "I think so. It has the best lock I could design."

"In that case, I believe we should be on our way."

He offered her his arm, and she inclined her head. "Thank you, but contact is not necessary. I have heard that your kind is sensitive to it, and I don't want to take any chances."

Deniir looked a little put out, but she merely smiled and walked down the narrow path that led away from her home. She heard a sharp chirp from behind her and turned.

Deniir had folded his cuff back and was typing rapidly with two fingers. "There. We should be seeing the pickup in a few minutes."

"You have shuttle clearance for the interior?"

"I do. The engineers have been providing your people with any number of handy devices. They are appreciative."

She snorted. "Just watch it. They can turn on you before you know it."

Ula rubbed the back of her neck and looked at the sky. A tiny speck appeared, and as they continued to walk down the path to the plateau, it grew larger in the sky until she was being pummelled by the blasts of air that it gave off in its effort to land.

Deniir stood between her and the landing shuttle and opened his wings, creating a windbreak.

She spit out a few bits of grit. "Thank you."

"It is a hazard on loose soil like this. How is it that you live in a dormant volcano?"

"Oh, it was the hardest place to get to; so after a while, the politicians stopped sending parties up here to negotiate with me." She kept her eyes closed and waited until the jets of air stopped trying to knock her over.

"Please come with me. We are about to leave for the mother ship." He lowered and snugged down his wings again, covering them with his cloak.

She nodded and dusted her features as she headed to the ship. Her leathers creaked slightly as she walked up the steps, and a voice spoke in peculiar, liquid tones.

Deniir responded and then translated. "Our pilot is Lenur of the Water People, and he has apologised for the landing. He was not expecting the sediment."

"Tell him it is fine. If I couldn't handle dirt, I wouldn't have gone into my current line of work."

The pilot spoke rapidly again, and there was no mistaking the amusement.

"He says thank you for your graciousness, pretty lady; now, take a seat before takeoff breaks your nose."

Blinking, she followed Deniir's lead. When they were settled in seats and strapped in, the ship rumbled under them, and Ula felt the peculiarity of takeoff.

Her hands gripped the arms of her chair, and she occupied her mind by looking around the cabin for materials and design flaws.

She found seven design flaws and thirty-two pieces that she could remove and use in her workshop. By the time she finished calculating where to place the items she had located, they were on their way to the mother ship through empty space.

Ula could see Gaia beneath her, and she had to admit, it was a beautiful planet.

"How are you taking to spaceflight?"

She jumped at Deniir's voice as his breath heated her cheek. He was peering out the window beside her.

She studiously pointed her face toward the window and kept it there. "I think I am adjusting fine. I have found any number of things to occupy my attention."

"Like what?"

"I have identified seven improvements in this space that would make it more efficient and comfortable." She chuckled.

"Can you make me a list?"

She blinked. "Are you serious?"

"Of course. The Nine are always seeking means by which we can change and improve. We would welcome a few new designs."

"That is refreshing. Can I choose what changes to include?"

"Of course. It is your design." He smiled and directed her to look away from Gaia toward the huge ship surrounded by tiny buzzing shuttles. "Welcome to the mother ship of the Nine."

She looked forward, and her talent kicked in. There were enough tiny changes to be made to keep her designing for a lifetime.

CHAPTER FOUR

"You have guest quarters assigned to you. Would you care to see them first?" Deniir watched her carefully as she disembarked from the shuttle.

"Yes, please. I can drop my bag and wash my face and centre myself. It should only take three minutes or so." She smiled hopefully.

"Of course. This way." Deniir bowed slightly and gestured for her to accompany him.

They walked through the halls, and several men bowed as they passed. Deniir inclined his head but didn't stop to talk.

She asked, "You have a rank here?"

"I am a master engineer, second only to my father, Darthuun. You will meet him when we go to the research and development department."

"I am guessing that you have a rank beyond that."

He grinned and shrugged. "The ranks of my people do not matter here. That is not how our hierarchy works."

She registered what he had said. "You work with your father?"

"Yes. It is not always easy, but I enjoy it. He is an excellent engineer."

She sighed. "You are very lucky."

They passed a couple, and she blinked. "Is she a tree?"

"One of the Forest Folk, yes. Like the ambassador on Gaia."

"I haven't actually met Daphne's husband. I haven't seen any of the Nine either. This is all quite interesting, but please, tell me if I am staring."

"You are doing very well so far." He chuckled.

A man with fluttering Fairy wings was coming toward them, and as he passed, he drifted in close to Ula.

Deniir moved so swiftly, she only heard the snap of his wings as he flared them, flicking the other man away from her before she could even shift her weight.

"Back off."

The Fairy held up his hands and stayed back.

Deniir waited, with the man pinned to the wall by his wingtip. When he received some signal that Ula couldn't see, he released the other man and snapped his wings together behind his back. He didn't flatten them but left them raised and the arches framed his head on either side.

As they started to move again, she asked, "What was that?"

"There are far more men than women on board. You are a new female and therefore worth trying to claim. The women of Gaia are prized mates here." He smiled slightly.

"I see. What was his species?"

"The People of the Air. They are generally harmless unless they are in a thwarted bond."

"How does that work?"

"Well, I will have the instruction manual for dealing with the Nine forwarded to your quarters." He smiled, "Your planet-mate, Ziggy, is the Potential of Gaia, and she has created a species-by-species information sheet for any of your kind on the mother ship."

"That was thoughtful of her."

Of course, Ula had heard of Ziggy and her ensconcement on the mother ship. While she didn't let her friends visit, she did communicate via com system. She knew who had married what; she simply had no images of the species that her friends were now sleeping with.

"It is. Apparently, our etiquette is a little hard to master."

Ula snorted. Gaians were fairly tactile, and being told not to make skin-to-skin contact was awkward for them. Having the members of the Nine bond to them without contact was even more bizarre, but there was nothing to do about the pheromones. Matches were made on the chemical plane, and there was little that would deter a determined member of the Nine.

"Yes, sure. You could say that."

They headed to a rail that ran into the wall, and at his guidance, she stood on the platform. A small pod came along, and he gestured for her to precede him.

Ula settled in the pod, and he tightened his wings again to fit in next to her. With quick motions, he entered something into the pod's computer, and the next moment, they were off.

"I have just programmed the path to the VIP quarters where you will be housed for the duration of your stay. This pod will take us to the nearest station, and we will walk from there."

"Sounds fine."

The rest of the trip consisted of Deniir being curiously tense and Ula staring out the window as the interior of the ship whizzed past.

The pod glided to a halt, and Deniir got to his feet, waiting for her to join him.

She stepped out with her bag still slung over her shoulder. The feel of the ship had gone from port to residential neighbourhood.

She walked with him past two guards at the side of a corridor with strange markings over the archway. Deniir identified himself and introduced her then led her into the hall, to the quarters set aside for her.

Ula stepped into the rooms cautiously. The entryway was large, echoing and opening into a larger communal dining and living room. It was larger than anything she had seen in her life.

"How is it that there is so much space allocated to one person?"

"Well, these are my quarters. Your room is this way."

She blinked rapidly. "I beg your pardon?"

"As you will be working exclusively with the engineers, it behooves us to keep you safe. Nothing is safer than these quarters." He walked with her to the wall. "This room is my father's, the next room is mine, the third room is yours."

"You live with your parent?"

"We do. We learn from our gender parent. My sisters remained with my mother to learn civic engineering and politics."

"When do you leave your gender parent?"

"When we form a family of our own. Many mates remain together, but my father wanted to leave on the mother ship, so I went with him as a matter of tradition." Deniir cocked his head. "Do you not have a relationship with your parents?"

She swallowed and shook her head. "They were lost in the first Tokkel raids."

"I am sorry for your loss."

"Well, that loss triggered my talent, so it isn't all bad." She tried not to be maudlin, but she missed them and the families of her friends were salt in the wound. She loved them, but it hurt to be with them.

"This is your room. You may come and go as you please, but it would be better if you waited for one of us to accompany you. We do not wish you to run afoul of any of the Nine males on the hunt for a mate."

She nodded tersely. "Please get me that information sheet. I want to know what I am dealing with."

She opened the door and quickly did what she had to do. She figured out how to use the en suite and scrubbed the grit from her features, quickly putting down and then binding up the red hair that she had been given courtesy of her mother's genes.

When she was ready, she left her room and nodded to Deniir. "Okay, we can go now."

He nodded. "Your data station has the list and descriptions of the species of the Nine as well as a list of the subspecies that are emerging."

"Good. Now, take me to your engineers." It wasn't the historical *take me to your leader,* but she supposed it would have to do.

Chapter Five

Research and development on the mother ship of the Nine was a wonderland of half-finished inventions that left Ula's mouth watering. She wanted to dive in and finish everything.

"Master Engineer Darthuun, this is Ularica Forniel, Master Designer of Gaia." Deniir smiled as he made the introductions.

Ula winced. "We don't actually use titles like that."

Darthuun looked at her with a calculating smile, his golden eyes were measuring her. "Are you the one who repurposed the torture straps?"

"I am."

"Then, you are a Master Designer and that is how you will be addressed during your stay on the mother ship. Has Deniir taken you and shown you your quarters?"

"He has. They are very suitable. I only need a place to sleep after a day's hard work. With no sun to tell me what time it is, I am depending on you and Deniir to tell me when to stop and sleep. Is that acceptable?"

Deniir nodded. "I will maintain a schedule for you."

Darthuun looked between them. "Deniir, take her on a tour and find out where she would like to start while she is here."

Deniir winked. "Yes, Father."

He jerked his head and she pattered after him, ready for her tour of the wonderful works that were coming together on all the workstations.

"You have no interest in weaponry, do you?"

She shook her head. "That is not an area I have any interest in."

"Right. We will show you the healing units and move on from there then."

She grinned and rubbed her hands together. It was time to play on a scale she had never imagined.

The man working with the healing units smiled. "Welcome, Master Designer. I am Engineer Trull."

She kept her hands at her sides and inclined her head. "Pleased to meet you, Trull. What are you working on?"

"A portable tissue regenerator that can tell the difference between muscle and veins. So far, I am not having a lot of success."

"May I have a look?" Ula was fighting the urge to go up on her toes to look over the man's shoulder. Trull had all the charm of a block of granite, so Ula was guessing that stone had something to do with his people.

Deniir cleared his throat. "We will complete our tour first, and then, you are welcome to choose any project you wish to work on and whatever you need will be brought to your workstation."

She perked up, "I have a workstation?"

"As you mentioned, it is not really common for the sexes to mix within the ship. We have prepared a station where you can communicate with the engineers and still remain free of any . . . interference." He twisted his lips.

Engineer Trull nodded. "Sound thinking, Master Deniir."

Deniir continued on their tour. They saw propulsion units, survival kits, emergency limb replacement as well as food-service equipment and prep units. There was literally something for every mood, and Ula couldn't wait to get started.

Her stomach growled and Deniir grinned. "Thank goodness. I was beginning to suspect that you didn't eat. You seem indefatigable."

She snorted. "No, just very excited at the prospect of working on something without having to scrounge for parts. Where can we eat?"

"My father is making dinner for you. He wishes to speak with you at his leisure, and since you are staying with us, it will make for an entertaining evening."

Ula sighed and curled her itching fingers into fists. "Wonderful. Can I get a notepad and a pen or something to start making notes?"

"Of course. Would you like to change for dinner?"

They were walking out of the research and development centre and back in the wide hallway.

She blushed. "Um, all my clothing is like this. I don't live in a place where dressing for dinner is required."

He blinked and inclined his head. "Of course. We will make a quick stop before going home then."

"Why?"

"So we can obtain a gown for you."

"I don't have any currency."

His lips twitched. "Actually, you do. We opened an account for you for the reworking of the torture harness. The modifications you made are going into some of those portable splints that we viewed earlier. They are all based on your designs, and there are already orders for the splints and braces on all of our Nine resident worlds."

"So, I have an account?"

"You have a patent that is worth quite a lot. The pre-orders are being divided between you and the current team off shooting your work. You each get five percent of the pre-orders. It is more than enough for some new clothing, but as it is our silly tradition that requires it, my father and I will pay for your formal clothing. You are welcome to pay for as much casual clothing as you like."

Ula was stunned. Back on Gaia, she had been paid with nothing more than the satisfaction she had been helping people. Here, she had earned money just for helping a friend in need, years earlier. The mother ship was truly a different place.

The dress shop was peculiar. She stood on a platform and a beam of light took her measurements. After that, racks of clothing in her size eased out and she noted that they all had a similar vein of style. The backs were all designed for wings.

A shadow eased forward. "Greetings, lady."

"Um, hello."

"I am sensing that the formal gowns of the People of the Light are not to your liking."

"Well, I don't have wings, so . . ."

"I can seal the backs easily. Will that help?" The shadow dipped and was obviously bowing.

"It will be helpful, thank you. I will take this one and this one." She pointed to one in white and one emerald green. Both colours looked amazing with her hair and were not too heavily jewelled.

"I will make the alterations and be back in a moment."

She smiled and inclined her head. "I was wondering if you had anything more practical?"

"Like what you are wearing?"

"Yeah, a bodysuit where nothing will get in the way."

The shadow turned to the back with the gowns and returned with a glittering deep amethyst bodysuit, complete with a hard sole for the foot. "How is this?"

"A little girly, but I will take it."

"Wonderful, lady. I will package it with the others."

Deniir came over and asked her, "Have you made your choices?"

"I have. The proprietor is making some slight alterations. I am not a huge fan of having my back exposed when there is no reason for it."

Deniir blushed. "No, I suppose not."

The shadow appeared with a parcel held forward. "Here you are, lady. Thank you for your business."

Deniir moved forward and extended a small object to the shadow. A slight click and the shadow retracted.

"Have a good evening." He disappeared into the back of the shop, and the clothing in Ula's size followed him.

Ula blinked and looked down at the parcel. "Oh, I owe you for a bodysuit."

"I am sure you will have plenty of opportunity to pay me back. I will get you a credit chip tomorrow so you can access your accounts."

"Is that what you just paid with?"

He nodded. "We don't use hard currency unless we are on the surface of our own worlds. Here on the ship, we use electronic funds."

It made sense, but it was beyond what she was used to on Gaia.

They returned to the VIP area and Deniir's quarters.

The scent of cooking food made Ula's mouth water. Darthuun was in the kitchen with an apron tied around his waist and his wings tightly folded to his back.

"Good evening, Master Designer."

"Please, call me Ula, Master Engineer."

"Ula, call me Darthuun. Feel free to refresh yourself before dinner."

Ula looked at Deniir and gave him a knowing look. "I suspected you would say something like that. I will be out in a moment."

She took her bundle to her assigned room and headed for the en suite lav.

A quick light shower and some hair brushing later, she was ready to try on one of the dresses.

The white dress was her choice for the evening, but it didn't go with her hair being down. Sighing, she twisted her hair up into two buns, one on either side of her head. It exposed her neck and gave her better presentation.

With the dress hiding her bare feet, she tiptoed out into the common area where she was treated to the sight of two men in the kitchen and a platter of small bite-sized items on the table in the conversation area.

"Is there anything that I can do?" She offered it even though she had no clue what was going on in that kitchen. Utensils that she had never seen before were being flipped around casually.

The two men turned and looked at her before Darthuun quickly turned back to the meal. "No, Ula. Please have a seat and a snack. Deniir will bring you something to drink. Dinner will be ready in twenty minutes."

She went to the comfortable seating area, and she took a position that would allow her to watch the goings on in the kitchen. Two men with wings were making her dinner and one of them was pouring her a drink. She was going to wake up anytime now. *What a pity.*

Chapter Six

Sitting and enjoying the appetizers while the food was under a heater nearby was peculiar. Generally, Ula ate as soon as her food was hot.

"So, what do you think of our little facility?" Darthuun munched at one of the vegetable and cheesy appetizers.

"It looks well organized, and I can hardly wait to play with some of the designs that I came up with today."

Deniir blinked. "Damn. I forgot. Just a moment."

He disappeared into his quarters and emerged with a flat screen. He slid a stylus out of the side and settled next to her on the backless couch she was sitting on.

He ran through a quick tutorial, and when she started to make notes, he nodded with approval. "You catch on quickly."

"Well, I am reading this in Gaian, so it makes it easier." She bent her head and made a few more notes.

When Darthuun's laughter reached her, she looked up and blinked.

"I don't understand. What was funny?"

Deniir's cheeks took on a darker colour. "Nothing. My father is simply very old and rather insane."

She looked back to the data pad and flicked through until she saw what she was looking for. *A Gaian Guide to the Nine.*

She flicked past the other members until she found the mating habits of the People of the Light.

Her hands tightened on the data pad, and she heard it protest her grip. "I see. So, I am not reading this in Gaian. I am reading it in Nine Common."

Darthuun was still amused. "Apparently. I have been speaking our tongue to you since you arrived this evening. My son seems to have invaded your mind."

"My speech centre, certainly. I did wonder why all the engineers were so easy to understand when Deniir had made it clear that they hadn't learned Gaian yet."

"It is understandable. I didn't know, nor did he, that a bonding could happen with casual contact."

Ula frowned. "We haven't had any contact. Not even a handshake."

Darthuun blinked. "Really?"

Deniir nodded. "Really. Ula made it very clear that she was aware of the dangers of contact with our kind, and we maintained a circumspect distance."

Darthuun frowned. "That is unusual, but her ability to use your linguistic skills is proof that there is a bond."

"But, the bond will be broken when I return home, correct?" Ula's voice was firm. She wasn't leaving room for anyone to disagree.

Darthuun shrugged. "I do not know. I have never heard of a spontaneous link in the last five generations."

Deniir rubbed the back of his neck. "This is going to require some research."

Ula frowned. "Should I stay somewhere else?"

Both men said, "No!"

She jerked back at their vehemence. "Um, okay."

Deniir spoke more calmly. "I mean, it would be awkward for you to be in the home of a mated couple, and that is the only safe place for you right now."

Ula was about to say something, but Darthuun got to his feet. "Dinner is ready. You have to let it rest or all the juice runs out when you cut into it."

Ula shrugged and rose to her feet, lifting the hem of her gown as she crossed to the dining table.

Deniir held her chair out, and she settled carefully on the narrow-backed seat. When Deniir took a seat to one side of her and Darthuun took the other side, she had the feeling that she was the guest of honour.

Dinner passed as each food was described and a small portion was put on her plate. She used the eating prongs in the method that Deniir showed her, and soon, she was making inroads into the food that Darthuun had so carefully prepared.

"So, Ula. How long have you been a designer of the useful and fascinating?"

She blinked. "Since the Tokkel raids. When the first scout landed, a friend of mine was injured and that was when my mind sort of split and the images started to appear."

Darthuun blinked. "Not before then?"

"There were a few small creations before then but nothing on a truly useful scale."

Deniir spoke quietly, "You mentioned that your parents had passed on."

Ula focussed on her meal. "They were taken in one of the first Tokkel ships, along with twenty others that we can pinpoint. They are presumed dead."

The two men with her paused. Deniir asked, "Didn't any of your people go looking for them?"

She snorted. "We don't have space technology yet. There was no way for us to find them, and by then, the other attacks started and they were simply casualties of the Tokkel."

Deniir winced. "Of course."

Silence fell and Ula took pity on them. "Don't fret about it. It isn't something that most people know. Even on Gaia, everyone forgets the first few to disappear."

"Do you think that they could still be alive?" Darthuun's tone was soothing.

"I doubt it, but anything is possible. If there were a way to find them, I would be on it immediately." She blinked. "Do you have gene trackers?"

Deniir blinked. "Only for short distances."

She lifted the data pad and scribbled more notes for the morning before she tucked it back under her chair. "I apologise, but I wanted to make a note to look into the gene trackers."

Deniir nodded with a smile. "As long as it doesn't involve fire suppression, I will help where I can."

She snorted. "I don't think fire suppression will be needed, but there may be some propulsion required."

He chuckled and inclined his head. "May I add that you look lovely this evening. That gown suits you."

"Thank you. The ways of buying clothing amongst the Nine are peculiar, but I am sure I will adapt. Dinner is wonderful by the way."

Darthuun blushed and his feathers fluffed up. "Thank you. Your compliment is well received."

She sipped some of her beverage and nibbled on a few more morsels from her plate. It was a good meal, but then, any meal she didn't have to make for herself counted in the plus column.

She asked Deniir, "How is it that your wing can be used as a weapon? It looks so soft."

Darthuun looked at his son, "Yes, how are they used as weapons?"

"Well, there are tendon struts that stiffen when we need to defend our . . . friends or family. We can spike an opponent to the wall, using the tip of the wing as a stabbing weapon and the flexibility inherent in the rest of the wing makes it a multi-directional weapon."

"Ah, that would explain it." She smiled, and she placed her eating prongs carefully on the edge of the plate. A yawn was inside her, trying to get out. She blinked furiously trying to stay awake.

Deniir suddenly noticed. "You are tired. I am so sorry. I am a horrible host. Please, get some rest."

"Is it all right? I mean, I could help with dishes."

"Go and rest. Tomorrow, we intend to work you until you fall asleep at your workstation." He winked at her and inclined his head.

She rose to her feet. "Thank you for a lovely meal and interesting conversation, Darthuun, Deniir. I am going to do some homework and then get some rest."

Ula slipped past them and headed for her room with the data pad in her hand. She had some research on the bonding of the People of the Light to do. Finding out that mates shared a mind across distances was something that scared her. No wonder Darthuun was so calm at leaving his wife. They were still inseparable.

Ula rubbed her forehead. She didn't feel different, but then, she hadn't felt first contact with Deniir either.

She shook her head and made notes on a gene tracker coupled with a Tokkel tracer. If she could find the parts, she might be able to locate the retreating Tokkel who might still have some Gaians on board. It had been years, but there was still a chance that there were marks in space that would allow the lost to be found. It was so thin a chance as to be ephemeral, but she had to take it.

Ula was going to make a tracking beacon, and if there were any of her people out in space, she would know. She would finally know.

CHAPTER SEVEN

The purple bodysuit fit her faithfully, and Deniir's wings were up and out as they walked to the R and D department.

"Is the suit too much?" She was getting more than what she would consider normal attention.

Deniir cleared his throat. "No. You look amazing. It is just very . . . fitted."

"Well, I normally wear leather, but I get the feeling that it would mark me as a bit of a barbarian up here." She chortled.

After breakfast with Darthuun, they had begun their commute while the master engineer did the dishes.

"I like your tool belt." Deniir grinned.

Her belt was wrought with woven strips of various leathers and metals. She considered it her emergency designing supply. Her basic tools rode on her hips and rocked as she took every step.

"Thanks. It was a gift from my friends before I moved." She tapped it with her fingers.

"Why do you live so far from your people?"

She rubbed the back of her neck. "I had a disagreement with the administration about the direction of my creations, so I simply removed myself from their influence."

"I sense there is a story behind that."

She shuddered. "Not one you want to hear."

He nodded. "Accepted. I reserve the right to ask again."

"Fair enough." She smiled and entered the R and D section of the mother ship with a sense of anticipation.

Today, she was going to play with big toys, and she couldn't wait.

Four hours later, Deniir appeared at her side.

"Ula, what have you figured out for that portable healer?"

"It's done. On the edge of the table there. It now generates a beam that works on the clotting principal. It identifies the proteins in the tissue by doing a calibration analysis of stable tissue and then the beam can be used to encourage the generation of healed tissue." She flapped her hand at the unit.

"Already? Trull has been working on that for two years." Deniir picked it up an examined it.

"Well, that is why you asked me here, right?"

She felt a touch on her shoulder, and she turned, blinking up at him. His features were calm and sober. "I brought you here to see how your mind worked, to see if you could inspire the engineers working here. I didn't bring you here to drain your brain."

"You are touching me."

He nodded. "You need to be touched. I am getting the feeling that contact is a thing you left behind when you moved to your aerie."

His wings shielded their conversation from the other engineers, and his hand moved from her shoulder to cup her neck.

She could feel the warmth of his fingers, and her heart stuttered in her chest. "It was my choice. My people or my self-respect. I chose me, I always choose me."

"There doesn't have to be a choice between doing what you love and being with someone. You can have socialization and job satisfaction." His thumb skated along her jawline.

Ula stared up at him, and she was completely hypnotized by the warm, seductive scent of Deniir with the blend of a wild storm. It made her want to cuddle close for safety, and she guessed that it was a genetic ploy to have a female do just that.

"How did the planet do that?" She asked him softly.

"Do what?" He was leaning toward her.

"Key my species to respond to yours."

"No one knows, but I am not complaining."

His lips made contact with hers, and she felt an electric jolt of energy and a sparking of ideas that she had never even thought of involving technology that she hadn't heard of. Thoughts that were not her own.

Her eyes widened in surprise, but Deniir's hand tightened on her neck, keeping her lips pressed to his. Her mind organized the new information as it streamed into her thoughts, and she could only imagine that the same was happening to him.

She heard a throat clearing, and Deniir continued their kiss for another minute before leisurely lifting his head, a dazed look in his eyes. He smiled softly and caressed her cheek. "Hello."

Ula blinked. "Hello. Learning to fly looked like fun."

He grinned and grimaced a moment later. "And I understand your reasoning for your life of solitude. We will deal with that another day."

The sound of Darthuun clearing his throat was repeated. "My son, as much as I enjoy the thought of you finding a partner, the pheromone cloud you two are producing is distracting the other engineers."

Ula blushed. "Sorry, Darthuun."

"My apologies, Father."

The master engineer was standing with his arms crossed over his chest, his wings flared out to frame him. He wore the same type of clothing that Deniir wore. A sleeveless shirt slit up the back to allow for the wings' free movement and tight trousers that tucked into knee-high boots.

His sandy hair was caressed by silvery strands, which hinted at the changes that Deniir would eventually undergo.

"Ula has already made great strides on the portable healing unit."

Darthuun looked sceptical. "How great?"

Ula smirked, "It is finished."

It was hard to be smug while she was leaning against Deniir, but the moment she realised it was her own body shifting toward his on its own, she stepped back until she was leaning against her workstation.

Darthuun looked sceptical. "Really?"

Ula smirked and leaned over, grabbing the unit from where Deniir had set it down. Out of the way but within reach.

She grabbed a blade from her belt, and wincing, she placed her hand on the table and plunged the knife through her left hand, between the bones. The searing agony distracted her, and she heard Deniir shout and Darthuun gasp.

Through gritted teeth, she hissed, "Stand back. I have to do this."

He stood back but it was reluctantly.

Her hand throbbed, but she picked up the new portable healer. She calibrated it against her forearm, and the moment it turned green, she pulled the knife out of her flesh, pressing the healing unit to the back of her hand.

The unit's indicator light turned blue and the pain stopped. It was telling her nerves to calm down while it used the clotting and repair factors of her body to do their work in the most efficient way possible.

Once the blue light turned white, she rotated her hand to heal the interior of her palm.

When the light turned purple, the healing was done.

She raised her hand to Darthuun and flexed her palm. "I trust you will believe me now?"

He bowed low, his wings fully extended. "My apologies that my doubt caused you pain, Master Designer."

"Testing a design on my own body is only what anyone should ask of themselves if they expect others to trust their lives to it."

Deniir looked at her as if she was the most precious thing in the world, and Darthuun bowed lower.

"Please get up, Darthuun." She returned to her workstation and smiled at Deniir as she started back on the tracking pod that she was working on.

The master engineer stood up again and folded his wings in. "We thank you for your help. Are the schematics in the system?"

"They are. I took images of the unit as I built it." She sealed the casing with a few snaps, and the small rocket was complete. She would need to build more, and one per day would increase her chances of finding any traces of those first few Gaians.

"If you are done with that project, it is time for the mid-day meal." Deniir smiled. "Would you care to join me?"

She looked across her workstation at the pieces in progress but acknowledged that her mind would be clearer if she had something to eat. "I would enjoy that."

Ula extended her hand to him, and he took it, bringing her bloody knuckles to his lips. Meeting his gaze over her hand, she smiled. It was an interesting way to start a relationship, but how much of a future could they have, separated by space and culture?

As if performing a magic trick, he reached into his shirt and removed a small object while their server poured their drinks. She was sticking to fruit juices and plain tea. She didn't want to take chances on getting intoxicated.

"This is your debit chit. You can use it to buy anything on the mother ship, and you can use any terminal to check your balance." He held it between two fingers and extended it to her.

She examined it, and it was a simple piece of recording media. A small chip that could easily be concealed within clothing was sitting in her palm. She lifted it and tucked it into her work belt. That would keep it safe until she could make a wristband that would keep it in place.

She smiled brightly and was startled when a man appeared at her elbow. It was Engineer Trull. He bowed low. "Thank you for your genius. I could never have shifted the design in that direction."

"Thank Gaia for the inspiration. My poor brain does nothing that the planet didn't put there. I am merely a tool of her design."

"As are we all. Well, thank you for coming to the ship to share her wisdom then. That was under your control, and it is appreciated."

She grinned, "For that, you are welcome."

He was going to reach for her hand but a wing stopped him, flicking out with the sudden aim of a weapon. Deniir raised an eyebrow at Trull, and the other man excused himself and left.

Ula took her cup and sipped from it. "That was rude. How long are you going to keep doing it?"

He shrugged. "Until I have a mate of my own, it seems." He gave her an innocent smile.

She focussed on the menu and made a selection. "Focus on finding a match for your lunch. Leave your mate to the future."

"I am an engineer, I make my own future." He winked and gave his focus to the menu.

CHAPTER EIGHT

The next two days went by in a blur of flirting and stolen kisses. When she was able to think straight, she knew that there was only one thing to do. She had to talk to his mother.

Ula made the arrangements with Darthuun, and he left her alone in his office while she waited nervously for the connection to be made to the Light home world.

A woman finally filled the screen, her midnight hair showed streaks of white and silver. "Greetings, child."

"Hello, Maurikan. I am Ularica of Gaia, and I want to ask you something."

The woman's clear features smiled, "So my husband has said. What do you wish to know?"

"Do all of the People of the Light separate when they have children? Darthuun has no answer for me."

Maurikan grimaced. "I did not marry him for his tact. No, our choice was so that Deniir could get his position on the mother ship. There was no other way for Deniir to leave home as we always travel with family until we are mated, and he had to leave. There was nothing for him here."

"No woman with big wings begging to be his?" She grinned.

She laughed and then sobered. "Not one that made his heart beat faster. When you can't find your mate at home, it is time to take to the stars."

"Oh. I see."

"No, I don't think you do. You must understand that the Nine do not find their mates via casual contact. Our very souls cry out to us when we meet the one we are destined to be with. In the case of the Light, our minds reach out first and determine if we are like-minded. Once that is out of the way, our bodies follow suit. When Darthuun asked me to let him travel with Deniir to the stars, I said yes, because we were of the same mind. Our daughters grow and flourish in his absence, and it hurts him, but he is doing it for our son, which enriches us both."

"So, if Deniir gets married, Darthuun can go home?"

Maurikan nodded. "Yes, Deniir will have his new family to start. So, if you

253

say yes, there will be more than two hearts involved."

Ula blushed, "What do you mean, if I say yes? He hasn't asked me anything."

"Really? Close your eyes and listen for a moment to what your soul is hearing. Listen to the question that you have been avoiding." Deniir's mother widened her snow-white wings and raised them high until they framed her completely in the screen.

Ula closed her eyes and heard the question she had avoided. *Will you be mine?*

It echoed in every corner of her thoughts, and she couldn't believe that she had missed it.

Blushing, she opened her eyes. "I didn't hear it."

Maurikan smiled. "I know. I ignored Darthuun for two months before I gave in."

"Does it bother you that I don't have wings?" She blurted it out.

"No. I have known that he was going to find a wingless woman for his mate. It was a logical direction. Now, while I have enjoyed this conversation, Darthuun is waiting restlessly outside the door and talking to both of you is giving me a bit of a brain ache."

"Well, it was nice meeting you."

"The same here, also your grasp of our language is quite impressive. Your bond is quite strong."

Ula snorted. "So I have been told. Have a good day, Maurikan."

Maurikan inclined her head and disconnected the call.

Ula straightened and headed back to her workstation. She opened the cabinet she had ordered and checked on her private project. The wings were almost complete, she just needed two more components, and when she checked her inbox, they were waiting for her. The energy cell was amazing and could power more than her simple construction.

The wings were her first truly personal project in years, and she wasn't sure that she would get the help she needed to test it.

"Excuse me, are you Ularica?"

Ula turned her head and smiled at the woman that she knew by reputation only. "Signy?"

"Call me Ziggy. I got your message, and I was surprised that they have managed to sneak another Gaian on board." She came forward and embraced Ula. "Belated welcome to the ship."

Ula returned the hug. "Thank you. Now, will you help me with my project?"

"Right to the point, huh? Well, if you don't want to use one of the People of the Light as backup, I suppose I can ask Tonos. He can probably manage a catch if he has to. Well, if Tiera lets him."

Ula smiled. "Do you want to see them?"

"Of course. Would you like to come for dinner?" Ziggy looked hopeful.

"If I survive, I would love to as long as Deniir is also invited."

"I will have Rothaway extend the invitation. Give me a moment to make the arrangements and I will have Tonos meet us at the central hub."

"I will finish the wings. My com unit is available to you." With her heart humming, she put in the final components before she slipped the wings on her back. The straps held them snugly to her body, and she moved into an open space to do the first extension tests.

The wings flared at her movements, and they flapped twice before tucking up and out of the way.

A wry voice said, "I hope you aren't thinking of flying without me."

She blinked. "Ah, Deniir. Yeah, I was going to take these for a maiden flight with someone else for backup."

He was immediately in front of her, bristling with jealousy. "Who?"

"A friend of Ziggy's. Tonos, I think she said. He is the husband of another Gaian."

Air slowly left him. "Oh. The Prince of the Air. Of course. He's a good choice, but I am going to be there anyway. Wait, where am I going to be?"

"We are going to the central hub. It's the least gravity and the longest fall. If I can even get these to stick out enough to glide, that is definitely something."

He nodded. "Sensible. You can have Tonos there as backup, but I am going to be there as his backup. You are not plummeting into the unknown with a piece of flapping metal at your back if I am not there."

Ziggy returned and smiled. "All set. He can meet us there now if you like."

Ula shifted with her wings on her back. They were surprisingly light, but that was the point. These were not for serious flight; they were purely recreational.

Deniir disappeared and came back with one of his cloaks. "No sense gathering more attention than is necessary."

He settled it over her shoulders and gave her a quick kiss. She could feel his question hammering at her, but now was not the time. If she didn't splat in the arboretum, it would be time to answer him.

Ziggy stood next to her friend Tiera and held her hand. Tonos was grinning and flexing his Fairy wings.

"I will head out and keep out of your way as you launch. I will be ready when you are." His tone was calm and encouraging.

Deniir removed her cloak and said, "When you first jump, you want to scoop the air. Once you have slowed, use the wings to flap for height and control your descent."

She nodded and touched the head-based controls as well as the emergency devices on her harness. The harness controls were a last resort.

The walkway that they stood on was half a kilometre from the *floor* of the central hub. If she couldn't figure it out, she would know soon enough.

Ula nodded to Tonos, and he flitted up and over the safety railing.

Deniir lifted her chin. "I can't move as fast as Tonos can, but I will be there before anything bad can happen, all right?"

She nodded and breathed in. "All right. Now, shoo. I need to get into the air before I lose my nerve."

He kissed her again before climbing to the railing and falling backward. His wings opened with ease, and huge sweeps kept him airborne twenty metres away.

The ladies gave her thumbs up, and it was now or never. Before anyone could stop her, including herself, Ula climbed the railing, extended her wings and jumped.

The wings beat slowly, and it was fifty metres before she got the rhythm. Tonos was on one side of her and Deniir the other as she changed direction and began to scoop her way through the air current being pushed up from the vents far below.

She climbed up and up, past Ziggy and Tiera and toward the observation bubble crafted in the centre of the ship. Deniir kept pace with her, beat by beat. Tonos zipped around and switched from side to side far more rapidly than she could.

The wings were a success, though she would definitely advise users to get some ground practice before jumping into the air and hoping for the best.

She heard Deniir call out. "Time to land, Ula!"

She nodded, and together, they started a slow spiral descent, controlled and careful. It took five minutes for her to touch down in the gardens, and by the time Deniir was next to her, a crowd was applauding wildly.

He put his arm around her and kissed her in full view of all the watching men and women. A gasp of surprise was the first sound, but soon, the applause returned.

"We have been asked to dinner by Councillor Rothaway and Ziggy. I think we should get ready." Deniir kept his arm around her as they made their way through the crowd, his wings out and curled around her protectively.

She was heady with triumph as they made their way back to the VIP quarters, and once inside, she unbuckled her wings and casually said, "My answer is yes, by the way."

Before he could respond, she dove into her quarters and locked the door a moment before a thud marked Deniir's moment of impact.

Dinner was going to be entertaining.

Chapter Nine

Ula tried to stay calm, but next to her, Deniir was humming with tension. He wanted to be alone with her, and there was no doubt about it.

Rothaway had lovely manners and very sharp teeth. Ziggy dealt with him as if he wasn't almost twice her size and could snap her in half, and he treated her as if she was a delicate flower he was afraid of crushing.

"So, you really built wings that enabled you to launch and fly immediately?" Rothaway leaned back in his chair and shook his head.

"Apparently. I got the idea the first time I saw Deniir, and it has been humming around in my thoughts since." Ula sipped her wine.

Ziggy smiled, "Your grasp of the Wilder language is fairly exact."

Ula looked at Deniir. "It is his fault. His languages are embedded in my mind, and apparently, he knows Wilder."

Deniir grinned.

"So, when are you two going to formalize it?" Ziggy nibbled at a vegetable stalk.

Deniir turned his glass between thumb and forefinger. "After dinner. She agreed this afternoon after she survived her flight attempt."

Ula looked at him. "After dinner?"

He shrugged. "It is either that or I go to medical again for a suppressor shot."

She cocked her head, and Ziggy filled her in.

"When a male of the Nine is—thwarted—in love, he needs to get a shot or go a little feral. I have never seen one of the People of the Light go feral, but I am guessing that it can be a little violent. I know Tonos was."

"Feral? What constitutes feral in the Light?"

Deniir took her hand in his and brought it to his lips. "Sharper teeth, our light glows through our skin and our feathers become coated with a light sedative."

Rothaway snorted. "They also give off a sedating pheromone that knocks out all males in the area, giving them full access to the female of their choice. The light they emit blinds pursuers for half an hour, and they fly away with the female, hopefully gaining her agreement at some point."

"What if she doesn't agree?"

Deniir answered, "If his mind is linked with hers and he has gone feral and she rejects him, he goes insane and crashes into a large body of water."

Ula flinched. "So, finding a match is important to you."

He kissed her hand again. "It is everything once we find a compatible female."

Rothaway changed the conversation to the designs that Ula had improved on and Deniir proudly listed them. Ula blinked as the list went on and on. She had been busy, but it had felt so much like playing that it had zipped past in a joyful blur.

Ziggy whistled softly. "Impressive, Ula."

"Thank you. It has been fun. I just have one question."

The table at large turned to her as she looked to Deniir. "What happens next?"

He blinked and blushed.

Ziggy laughed and filled in. "She means where will you two live? Here or on Gaia?"

He frowned. "I thought here would be more conducive to your creativity."

She smiled. "Good. I like it here, but I need to have my workshop moved up here. I don't want any of my work left for the Gaian government."

He nodded. "We can send a crew down—"

"No! I have to go down. I have booby-trapped the hell out of the place. If I am not there, the blast will be devastating and the volcano goes live."

Rothaway grinned. "Thorough."

"And I want to say goodbye to Emharo and Niika. I don't have many friends down there, but they are two of the best." She smiled. "Aside from that, I am done with my home. There is nothing there to keep me."

Deniir's hand tightened on hers. "In a few days, we will return to the surface. In the meantime, I will have a guard placed at all entry points to your home, just in case."

"Good. Safety first. Well, safety when you can't get away without it."

He smiled, "Good motto. I will try and work it into our family crest."

They all laughed together, and when Deniir's tension couldn't be ignored anymore, their group trouped off to the gardens to find the special copse that was open only to mating couples.

Ziggy hugged her for luck and gave her a quick whispered rundown of the procedure. Ula was not fond of the blood element, but it was integral to the Nine, so she was up for it.

Deniir took her hand, and together, they entered the sacred space to join their blood and their lives. Their minds and bodies would come later.

Ula knelt with the knife in her hand as Deniir bit her wrist; she sliced his own skin and their blood mingled on the blade, dripping down her hand to mix with his.

"I, Deniir of the House of Arkithan, son of Maurikan and Darthuun, do hereby pledge my life, body, mind and soul to you." To her surprise, he started to glow with a golden tint.

She blinked. "I, Ularica Forniel, daughter of Ulana and Ricard, do hereby pledge my life, body, mind and soul to you."

His light grew and he kissed her, the blade between them. Her wrist throbbed, and she felt warmth crawling up her skin to her elbow, her shoulder, spreading through her body.

Light started to creep through her; hers was white hot, his was a bright gold. Together, they rose to their feet, and he walked her to the stone where he held her hand as she slide the blade into the receptacle where their bloodlines would be registered as bonded.

"Hello, my bride." He was beautiful, glowing with all the energy that she could feel in his thoughts but never quite understand.

"Hello, my groom. Well, are we going to stay here all day?" She blinked up at him as her light continued to spread.

He lifted her wrist to his lips, and she jolted in surprise as he licked the wound closed. She shivered as the touch of his tongue resonated in parts of her that had remained dormant until this point.

When he lifted his wrist to her lips, she could see that the cut was already healing, but she stuck her tongue out daintily and licked away the visible traces of blood. Her mouth felt lit up from the inside as if she had just consumed energy, which she supposed she had.

He pulled his hand away from her, and she could feel his body vibrating. Without another word, he lifted her in his arms and he headed back down the path, out of the mating garden.

Ziggy, Rothaway and Darthuun were waiting, but they flinched back as Deniir passed them. With huge sweeps of his wings, he lifted off with her weight in his arms, and a moment later, they were going down the halls with all the decorum of a loose meteor.

She could see the shadows that were cast in their wake, but her focus was on the winged man carrying her home.

He didn't put her down until they were in his quarters and the door was locked.

She smiled up at him, her arms around his neck and her body pressed to his. "How do we turn the light off?"

"You will control it . . . after a while." He nibbled at her lips, worked down her neck and he released her gown with a few deft moves.

She shivered at the cool of the air, but he wrapped his wings around her with that strangely comforting flexibility. Ula found and released the closures of his shirt, but she was afraid to pull in case it was hooked on his wings.

As his hands skimmed over her, she focussed on the heat that her body was generating. When he tipped her to the bed and tossed her shoes aside, his own clothing was not far behind.

Deniir entered her mind as he entered her body, his wings protected her on all sides as he moved with her, his light and hers blinded them both when they reached climax and his thoughts tangled inexorably with hers.

He shifted some of his weight off her but remained covering her. He kissed her, "Hello, mate."

She smiled and returned the kiss. "Hello, mate. So, how long for the glow to fade?"

He chuckled. "Give it a week. You will have it throttled back by then."

Ula sighed. "I don't have a week. I have to get my stuff to safety."

"Then, we will go down to Gaia with you glowing like the stars. I don't see a problem."

She covered her face and tried to imagine explaining herself to her friends. Mind you, they were mated to members of the Nine themselves, so they had probably seen stranger.

Niika looked her over. "Well, you will save on power bills, and you can work until midnight or beyond without any problem."

Ula crossed her arms and looked at Emharo. She beckoned for an insult.

"Nothing here. I think you could be a boon for either Niika's cavern work or my underwater investigation. Where do we plug you in?" Emharo chortled.

Three shuttles had landed to take her stuff up to the mother ship. A steady stream of men carried objects that were understood only by Ula.

"You two aren't upset that I am leaving?"

Niika put her hand on Ula's. "You were not happy here and we are no longer at war. If we need your help, I know you will give it, and if I just want to visit, I am sure my other half would be happy to run around in space once again. I am having him do most of the hunting, and it is wearing on him."

Ula chortled. "I have seen what you hunt. He is lucky he is still alive. So, does your guy do anything physically weird?"

Niika gave her an innocent look. "Like in bed?"

"No, like glowing."

"Oh, that, yeah. He turns to living stone when I am threatened. Emharo's breathes underwater, so he is weird from the get go. How is it flying?"

"You mean with him carrying me or with my mechanical wings?"

That led to a chat with the girls about the wings, and it was a good thing she had brought them with her, because they didn't believe her.

With her wings in place, she got Deniir's attention and she pointed up. He nodded. He would be with her in a moment.

"I have to take the harnesses off my rocs. I will be right back."

She set the wings to flapping, and with a few steps and a jump, she was airborne and climbing.

Bertrum and Eleth greeted her with surprise as she set the wings for a laborious hover that was helped along by the updraft. With some effort, she landed near them and she stroked Bertrum. "I don't know when I am going to be back, so I am taking these straps off. I know you like them, but if you got hung up on something, I would never forgive myself."

She unbuckled the harness and slid it from him before she moved to Eleth. Eleth didn't want to part with her pretties, but she eventually settled and let Ula slide the harness free.

"You miss them already."

She looked up, and Deniir was perched high on the rocky cliff above her. "I do."

He held his hand out. "Come on, you can ride me all you like. You can even use those straps on me."

She laughed, and it was a good thing that her wings were not dependant on her ability to speak, because she laughed all the way to the shuttle, her hands filled with leather and her mind filled with light.

The stars were waiting.

Seeing
Return of the Nine Book Eight

By

Viola Grace

Chapter One

Vida walked through the memorial garden and touched some of the carefully cultivated flowers. Five and a half years since the Tokkel invasion and she still was frustrated by the dead end that her investigations led to.

Every spare moment, she turned her mind to the stars and looked for those who had been lost. It was just too large a span to search.

"Ms. Senior, we have an investigation we would like your assistance with."

The voice jarred her out of her remembrance.

"Of course, Detective Morser." She nodded toward the head of the colony's police service. She blinked rapidly to clear the tears of frustration that always welled in the garden.

"I am sorry to have intruded, but a woman has gone missing."

Vida straightened her shoulders and pulled her mind back to the here and now. "What does she look like?"

"Same as the others, brown hair, brown eyes. It has been six years. I thought that this ended when the Tokkel came." He muttered it as they walked out of the gardens.

What he meant was that everyone in law enforcement had hoped that the killer had been one of those murdered by the attacking aliens. Apparently, that was not the case.

"Do you remember how to do this?" Detective Morser spoke low as they settled in his car.

"Yes, do you remember that I have to be where she was last seen? I can't go to where the trail starts; I have to track her from earlier in the day. If I can't see her before it happened, I won't be able to find her."

"Yes, Ms. Senior."

He had tried to trick her the first two times, and it had resulted in the deaths of the two women. The third had been found in time, but it had been the day of the attack. Vina didn't even know if the woman had survived the Tokkel after the other monster had taken her.

Now, he was back again.

The car rolled to a halt near the market place. She got out and looked around, getting the rhythm of the people in the area.

"Winara Elwin was last seen here."

"How long ago?"

"Forty-five minutes."

"Picture please." Vida pulled the length of gauze from her belt.

An image of a smiling woman was held out by the detective. Winara liked to smile, it showed in her picture and that was another thing she had in common with the other women.

Vida stared at the image, closed her eyes and tied them shut. She turned her head and watched as Winara went shopping.

Being able to navigate with her inner eye was a peculiar skill. Her parents had both been functionally blind after a chemical spill in their research lab, so navigating in the dark had seemed normal to Vida. She had no idea that other people could not see clearly in the dark until she was a teen, and she didn't know that she did it with her eyes closed until she finished school.

Binding her eyes helped her move around in daylight and *see* the psychic traces left behind by the living beings on Gaia. She had to see the woman in her normal daily activities and lock on to her. If she panicked, as she would if she were being abducted, the animal side of her nature would preclude getting a solid fix on her.

Vida moved swiftly through the market, tracing the path that the victim had taken until she found the alley where the abduction had taken place. She felt the panic, the pain that Winara had experienced.

Without a word, she picked up her speed, running blindfolded down the alley and onto the street where the victim had been shoved into a vehicle.

She sprinted six blocks, glad that she made running part of her daily exercise. The detective and others were on skimmers behind her.

Winara had been dragged out of the vehicle and into the building. Her energy was pulsing hotly inside. A dark shadow appeared next to her, and Vida hit the ground with a bolt in her shoulder.

She ripped the gauze off her eyes and crawled out of the line of fire as the city law enforcement gassed the interior of the small house. The darkness that was laid over her vision disappeared. He had killed himself.

The officers rushed inside, and Detective Morser came out with Winara in his arms. She had puffy eyes and tears from the gas, but she was alive with only minor scrapes and bruises.

Vida struggled to sit up, and she pressed her gauze blindfold to her shoulder. "Officer, if you could get me a med kit?"

He stared at her and swayed as if he didn't know what to do. Fortunately, Morser came back and ordered a second medical unit to attend the scene while he grabbed one of the kits from an official vehicle.

"Well, Ms. Senior, the bolt went right through you. You are bleeding on both sides."

She snorted. "That is what it feels like. Why are your officers freaked out?"

"You ran six blocks blindfolded and led us to a serial killer without so much as an interview."

"You know that it is what I do."

He sighed and applied pressure on her wound. "I know that and they know that, but even with the Nine in orbit, it seems a little spooky."

She straightened and winced. "That is it! Orbit. I need to get up there."

"You aren't going anywhere. This wound needs work." He paused. "Thank you, by the way."

"I am only sorry that I didn't find him sooner. Now that I know what his darkness looked like, I could have tracked him anywhere." She hissed as he shifted his hands.

"Stay still, Ms. Senior. You are bleeding excessively."

The medics arrived and bustled her into the second vehicle. The victim in the first vehicle looked at her curiously, but her medics closed the door and drove off.

"What happened, miss?" The older medic removed the gauze from her shoulder and looked at the wound.

She sat and let them tend her while the vehicle swayed on the way to the hospital.

With a small smile, she said, "I was finally in the wrong spot at the right time."

Chapter Two

With her bandages in place and a borrowed shirt covering the blood on hers, Vida headed for the Embassy of the Nine.

The guards on either side of the gate stared at her as she passed them. She guessed the not a lot of bloody Gaian women hiked through the gates. She heard them calling up to the main building as she trudged past.

Daphne came out to greet her. "Vida, good lord. What happened?"

"I figured it out. I finally figured it out. I have a chance at finding them, but I need to get up there." She staggered and clung to Daphne when she was close enough.

They walked slowly into the building where Daphne let out a shrill whistle.

A woman with ice blue skin came forward. "Yes, madam?"

"I need some grafting patches and a clean dress, please, Tynyan."

"Yes, madam. Right away."

The woman glided away, and Daphne coaxed Vida into the lift. Vida was impatient. She wanted to get up, to get on her way to finding those who were lost, but her vision blurred.

"Relax, Vida. I have you."

With a woman she knew she could count as a friend, she relaxed. In a quiet room, her clothing was removed, her wounds were cleaned and whatever a grafting patch was, it kicked the ass of stitches. Pale, shining gel showed where the bolt had entered but the ugly threads were gone.

The dress was loose, but it belted snugly at the waist, providing shape.

"You know I am not a fan of dresses."

Daphne smiled, "I am afraid that it is all I wear most days. Now, let's settle you and you can tell me what the hell happened."

With the help of the housekeeper, Daphne got Vida to her feet and into a comfortable chair in the sitting room.

She was still drowsy from the drugs they had given her at the hospital, but Vida stared into Daphne's eyes. "I figured out how to do it."

"Do what, Vida?"

"To find those who were stolen and never retrieved. I have been trying to see the trail for the last six years, and I have failed. I have been looking at it from the wrong angle. I need to get onto the mother ship and get into one of the shuttle pathways. If I can see the trail and the Nine are agreeable, we can get someone to go looking for them." Vida swayed.

"How were you injured, Vida?"

"Oh, I was shot with a bolt gun by a serial killer." She smiled. "I saw her and I found her."

The housekeeper was standing by; she said, "The news reports did mention a murderer with a surviving victim. No mention was made of this woman, though."

Daphne snorted. "They never mention Vida. She and I were in primary and secondary school together. She could find me no matter where I hid. She could always see me, even if her eyes were closed."

Vida leaned back and closed her eyes. "Can you make arrangements for me to visit the mother ship? I need to be up there. I need to see."

The images of the two women in the room nodded to each other as if they thought she was asleep. Vida relaxed in the chair as they tiptoed from the room.

She was where she needed to be. The embassy was the best bet to get to the mother ship. Daphne also knew who she was and what her talent was. If anyone could plead her case, it would be the ambassador's wife.

For now, she would rest and heal. Everything else would happen as it was meant to.

Hours later, she saw Daphne come in with a man whose body was outlined in deep green. Their connection was obvious.

"Are you sure she can do what you say she can do?"

Vida sighed. "If that is a whisper, you need to work on your covert voices. Your Gaian speech is excellent, Ambassador."

She saw his body jerk in surprise.

He moved around the room in silence, and she smiled, "If you are going to jump out that window, you might want to open it first."

"You really can see through your eyelids."

She blinked slowly, adjusting to the dimness in the room. "Sort of. I can see the energy of living creatures and track them back by the trail they have left behind. I can see it. I have always been able to see it. I have always been able to spot Daphne as well."

Daphne turned on a light. "The better Vida knows you, the faster she can find you."

Vida stretched slowly, not wanting to tear the patches on her shoulder. "In your case, Ambassador, I used your connection to Daphne."

He smiled and sat nearby. "I am pleased to meet you, Vida Senior. Call me Apolan."

"Apolan then. Call me Vida. Has Daphne explained what I am after?"

"The Tokkel ship with your people on it. Some of the first ones to be taken just as we arrived."

"I am not looking for the ship. I am looking for my parents." She sat up and gave him a serious look, only slightly marred by her flinch.

He scowled. "Surely, if you find one, you find the other."

"I really doubt that they will still be on a ship." She scowled. "If I can find their path, I can find them."

Daphne cleared her throat. "You might need someone a little more aggressive for the retrieval mission."

"If I can find the path, I will call Ianka. They are her parents, too."

"Right. Ula has been working on a probe. This might just be the missing piece of the puzzle."

Vida smiled. "Is that where she went? I have been missing the sight of her in the sky."

Apolan frowned, "You were shot."

She shrugged with her good shoulder. "I got in the way of a bolt gun. It won. I can't really see inanimate objects in someone's hand unless they always use them."

"What use have you put your talent to?" Apolan smiled politely.

Daphne grinned, "She rescues miners, finds lost children and tracks down the elderly who have wandered off."

"Day or night?"

Daphne snickered and waved for Vida to explain.

"I do my best seeing when my eyes are bound during daylight. At night, it is fine, but during the day, the multiple images cause me to lose focus."

"Bound?"

"Yeah, I keep a swath of fabric to tie my eyes shut. It helps me see nothing but the traces left behind by people."

"What about the buildings?"

"Well, I have noticed that living beings tend to walk around buildings and through doorways. If you are following a trail, you step where they stepped."

He nodded. "How does this talent of yours work in a confined environment?"

She sighed and rubbed the back of her neck. "It doesn't. I will have to send my senses out and find the path that my parents were taken down. Once we have a trajectory, I will see if I can get help in approaching their destination."

"You wish the Nine to help you in jetting yourself across the stars in search of a Tokkel ship with folk who may be dead by now?" He spoke slowly and clearly as if working it through his thoughts.

Vida got to her feet. "I would know if they were dead. I can feel my sister, half a world away from me. My family is bound into my mind and senses."

She crossed to the open part of the room and began to pace. Daphne quietly got to her feet, drew the curtain and turned off the light.

Apolan's gasp was harsh.

"Daphne has told me that my being upset is striking. Normally, I am completely neutral, but when I get like this..." She held up her hands and stared at the swirling glow of light and dark energy.

Daphne turned the lights on again, and Vida concentrated on balancing her mind. It was a delicate operation. The hole in her life left by her parents was something she felt every day. The burning ache of her twin half a world away was something else.

Ianka had a talent for the physical while Vida worked on the psychic level. They had argued all of their life, and their parents had let them do it, knowing better than to get between their stubborn brood. Their house was perpetually dark. None of them needed light to navigate in their home, but Ianka had craved daylight, fresh air and the stimulation of others... until the Tokkel attacks.

Their parents were at the lab on the day it was raided. No one knew what was happening, and Vida could only stare skyward. Ianka had shaken her into alertness, and they had begun to seek out those who had been pinned under rubble, while avoiding the Tokkel troops on the ground.

Vida created a mental template for the Tokkel and used it to hide those around her while Ianka rounded up survivors and brought them back to their dark home. Vida kept watch for six days until her body and mind were at the shattering point, and then, the Nine fought the Tokkel off in the skies above.

Vida had spent every spare moment on the ruins of the lab where the best and brightest of Gaia had been taken without a whisper of warning. Other ships had taken Gaians from surrounding areas, but the scientists had been first to disappear, and they had been the only ones that had never been traced. No bodies, no wreckage, no sign that they had ever existed, except for the families left behind.

She could feel the power crackling along her skin, but it was still within normal ranges. She didn't need to discharge a bolt quite yet.

Daphne nodded, "What happened yesterday, Vida?"

"I was attending to my morning errands when Detective Morser found me and told me that the murderer we had been tracking before the attacks had surfaced again. This time, he didn't play games. He took me to where she had been before she was taken and I was able to follow the path. The officers pulled up with all fanfare, and he came to the window before I could alter my vision to normal. The bolt knocked me to the ground and the officers were able to rescue the proposed victim before she had been more than kidnapped."

She carefully touched her wound with her fingers. "Those grafts worked really well."

Apolan got to his feet, looked at his wife and nodded before returning his gaze to Vida. "The shuttle will be here at noon tomorrow. Be ready to travel."

"Thank you, Ambassador." She smiled and bobbed a quick curtsy. With steady steps, she walked to the window, opened it and exhaled. The light was dimming and the pent-up energy of her frustration came out in a mist of power that floated out and over the gardens below.

Daphne came up beside her and rubbed her good shoulder. "I am glad that you are fine, Vida."

Vida turned and leaned her forehead against Daphne's shoulder while she bawled. She was the farthest from fine that she had ever been.

Chapter Three

Vida was sitting quietly in the boots and modest dress that Daphne had given her. The shuttle pilot wasn't the chatty sort. He simply engaged the engines and lifted off.

She wanted to bite her nails, but instead, she folded her hands in her lap and concentrated on breathing. In, out.

The pressure of the acceleration shoved her back in her seat. Breathing took up her entire world until they released from the atmosphere. The mother ship glowed in the sky.

Vida watched as the shuttle she was in approached a minute port in the metal hull. It was amazing to think that she was heading toward the largest collection of aliens that the Gaians could ever have imagined, and they had a greater right to the planet than the current colonists.

They had landed eons earlier and evolved their own distinct adaptations to the world until they had travelled out into the universe to split up and become distinct societies from one parent species.

Knowing and learning all she could about the Nine was her hobby. Vida had known deep inside that they would be the key to her quest. Now, she was about to test that theory.

The shuttle glided into position and lined up with a series of lights inside the ship. It cruised inside, and she stared out the thick plexi window at the hundreds of fighter ships parked in bay after bay of the inner workings of the giant vessel.

The moment that the vehicle settled, she could see a walkway extending along the side a moment before she heard the thunk of contact. Her harness released itself, and she took that as a hint to get to her feet.

Her legs wobbled and her body didn't feel quite right. Vida used the seat backs for support as she walked toward the door she had used to enter. It hissed and popped open before she reached it, and a familiar face poked around the corner.

"Vida!"

Vida grinned and ran to her, bumping in to the cushions and careening into Ziggy's arms.

Her friend had changed, Ziggy had added more power to her already considerable energy, but her innate signature was unmistakable.

In the time after the Tokkel attacks, Ziggy had become a friend. Ianka had enjoyed the scent of flowers as a break from the blood and smell of fear, and anything that kept her sister happy had made her happy.

Eventually, Vida's obsession with looking for their parents had driven Ianka to seek silence on the far side of Gaia. She had requested, and been granted, one of the sled-like transports, and every six months, she returned with samples of faraway lands.

"Ouch, Vida. That is quite the download."

She quickly broke their hug. "Sorry, Ziggy. This trip has gotten me all wound up."

Ziggy smiled and linked arms with her. "It is fine. So, it has been a while since you saw her?"

They walked down the walkway and into the ship.

Vida was glad that she was using her eyes and not her other senses. There were people everywhere, and they all looked fascinatingly strange.

She prodded Ziggy, "I know that there are supposed to be nine races, but this looks like considerably more."

"Ah, just like with the Gaians, there are variations in size and function. Each race has its own hierarchy. Light, dark, air, water, forest, rock, beasts and, of course, then there are the two that you will be dealing with." Ziggy wrinkled her nose. "They are harder to describe."

"How so?"

"Well, we have the Fury and the Balance. The Fury look like ancient Earth demons and the Balance ... well they look like pieces of starscapes come to life. You don't run into them that often. They don't mix well with the other races. Well, they do, but the other races get uncomfortable."

"Why will I be dealing with them?"

Ziggy rubbed the back of her neck. "For what Apolan described and knowing what I do about your talents, a power boost seemed a safe bet. The Balance are nothing but power."

"And the Fury?"

"They are some of the best pilots and most aggressive fighters. Their auras make them hard to look at, so most folk just look right past them as if sensing evil and not wanting to tempt it."

"Are they evil?"

"I have spoken with their magistrate on this matter. He seems polite and well spoken."

They paced up to a pod on a rail platform. Ziggy tucked her inside and sat next to her.

"Where are we going?"

"To the medical bay. According to the news reports, you ended up with a bolt through the shoulder, though the news didn't name you . . . as always." Ziggy sighed heavily.

"When do I meet your husband?"

"Once you have been healed. Rothaway is always eager to meet new Gaians, especially ones that I consider to be friends. Once you have been up here for a while, you will appreciate Gaians just as much as I do." Ziggy smiled.

"I only want to remain here long enough to find the trail and follow it."

"We will see what the doctor thinks. She's a lot of fun once you get to know her but a little hard to get used to. She is one of the people of the Rock, but one of the taller ones. We would call her a giant."

Once they arrived in medical, Vida had to admit that Ziggy wasn't kidding; the doctor was indeed extremely tall.

"Stand in the scanner, miss. We don't want any infection to set in, so I need to get a check of your general health."

Vida winced and stepped into the scanner, knowing what was going to be found.

"Madam Potential, please leave the room. I need to have a talk with your friend."

Vida sighed. "Anything you want to tell me, you are welcome to do in front of Ziggy."

The doctor read the scans and focussed them on several points. "Your bones are not strong. You have broken over a dozen individual bones in your lifetime and several of them have been broken more than once. I am amazed that the trip up here didn't crush you. It is like you are made of pressed paper instead of calcium."

Ziggy scowled. "So you are telling me she is not fit for space travel."

"Good lord, I wouldn't allow her back to the surface without weeks of treatment to build up the levels across her body. How could this happen? Don't your people have regulations about supplements?"

Vida stepped out of the scanner. "They do, but my body does not absorb and reuse the calcium like it should. I was the feeble twin."

Dr. Meevin cocked her head. "Identical twin?"

"No, fraternal. She is stronger, faster and generally in better shape than I am."

"Too bad, I could have cultured a treatment from her system if she was amenable. Ah well, I will treat the torn tissue and you can be on your way. I will design a calcium treatment, and you will be here tomorrow morning to start it."

Vida blinked. "I will?"

Ziggy nodded. "You will. How did you break so many bones?"

"Well, I run around blindfolded a lot. Sometimes, I miscalculate my trajectory." She shrugged. It was a side effect of looking for missing children in the woods. She banged into things quite often if she was moving at speed.

The doctor pointed to a medical bed, and Vida hopped up onto it without comment. Dr. Meevin loomed over her and shot several hyposprays into the tissue around the wound.

"Whoever gave you first aid knew what they were doing."

Vida smiled. "Daphne, the ambassador's wife."

Dr. Meevin grinned. "She is taking to our ways. Good. It saved your arm. There are traces of an infection here that could have easily turned septic, but the traces of the strong antibiotics in your system have them on the run."

"She was very thorough."

The doctor grunted and squeezed lightly at Vida's arms and legs. "Any problem moving?"

"No. A slight ache in my right wrist, but it has been broken three times."

The focus shifted to her wrist, and the doctor hummed to herself before disappearing into the outer office. She came back brandishing another hypogun, and before Vida could brace herself, she was jabbed in the arm and that limb felt like it was being dipped in fire.

Vida writhed on the table, and Ziggy wisely kept back. This was knowledge she didn't need.

When the first wave of agony faded, Vida was covered in sweat. She sat up with a dazed expression. "You could have warned me."

Dr. Meevin winced. "Sorry, you may experience some slight discomfort. It is an enzyme that the Balance have been working on to restore harmony in the body. I didn't know what it would do to a Gaian."

"That was the worst of it, right? It was just my arm, right?"

The doctor winced. "I think so. You may want to contact Researcher Lerinian. He designed it."

Ziggy helped Vida off the table. "I will bring her in tomorrow morning. We will consult with the researcher."

Vida hobbled out of medical feeling far worse than she had entering it. They hopped back onto a pod and were whisked through several distinct neighbourhoods before arriving at a series of structures all lined with heavy plexi to allow for a full view of the stars.

"Oh wow. The Balance, I presume?"

"Yeah, they have battle shields that cover those views during a fight. All the different races have their own environments. It was part of the initial agreement to get this ship together."

Unlike the area near the shuttle bays, there were no people randomly milling around. Occasionally, a cloaked figure would pass through the open area near the rail, but they didn't stop or even look over.

"Come on, Vida. The labs are over here."

Vida closed her eyes and sighed. This area of the ship was the kind of spot she could get around on her own. Every path was clearly marked by the slow paces of dozens of the robed figures. Their energy was all slightly different, but it vibrated and swirled with a slow and steady roil of light against dark. Whatever the Balance was, it was powerful.

Pain began to tighten on her arm, and it spread through her chest. She tried to hide it, but Ziggy had her ways of knowing these things. "Come on, Lerinian's lab is this way."

They walked past the occasional silent robed figure until they were in a wheel of large bubbles filled with lab tables and equipment. Ziggy looked into one and scowled. "Damn. I thought he would be here."

Another crippling wave of pain went through her. "Can you call him?"

A robed figure approached. "May I help you, Potential?"

The voice was low, even and soothing. It rang like a deep soft bell to Vida's fried senses.

"Yes, I am looking for Lerinian. Is he around?"

"He is doing a locked meditation. May I assist you in some way?"

Vida's tense muscles were the only thing holding her up. Her teeth were clenched and the pain was spreading.

"Dr. Meevin administered a treatment that Lerinian had been working on to my friend here, and she is having a rather extreme reaction to the meds."

"Ah, the regeneration project. There are other contributors with the research, including myself. If you will come with me, I will run a diagnostic."

Ziggy turned to follow him and Vida moved more slowly. Her entire body was going into rigor.

The member of the Balance opened the door to his lab, and when his hooded gaze turned toward her, she heard his bell-like tone curse. He quickly grabbed her and brought her into the lab. The medical bed was firm under her, but her body couldn't appreciate it.

"Easy, Lady. I will counteract the treatment. It was never tested for use on Gaians."

Vida muttered through clenched teeth. "I guessed as much."

Ziggy was wringing her hands. "What can I do?"

The man said, "Call the Gaian, Ularica. She has a compression suit that she has been working on. It will help with the pain."

Ziggy went to the com unit and made a call. Vida's body twisted while the member of the Balance took a blood sample and analysed it.

His head turned toward her. "My name is S'rin, by the way. It will make me seem less off putting."

She wanted to say that if he could help with the pain, she would accept the devil, but nothing came out.

She was locked in place, and she clenched her eyes so she could see what was going on around her. Her inner panic eased when Ziggy's energy pattern calmed.

S'rin was always calm. He really was as advertised, balance.

Chapter Four

The hypo came too late. Her entire body was on fire and the hypo didn't do a thing. Once again, breathing was an issue.

When Ula came through the door, she almost sobbed with relief. At least something was happening.

"I thought you were bringing a suit?" Ziggy was wringing her hands again.

Ula's aura perked brighter. "I did."

"Help me get the dress off her. This suit needs to go onto bare skin."

Vida would have blushed if she could. They cut the dress and boots from her using everything at their disposal.

Once she was bare, Ula pressed a small unit to her chest. Bands flew out in a spider web of metal.

The moment that pressure was on her skin, her body sighed in relief. She whispered, "It's working." She slumped onto the med bed with relief. "That was not fun."

S'rin said, "You can open your eyes now."

Ula laughed, "She doesn't have to. She can see better through closed eyes than most people can with their pupils focussed."

Vida wiggled her fingers, and even they were encased in metal. The pressure on her limbs had eased the pain. With effort, she pushed herself into a sitting position.

Ula was looking at the suit critically. "I think I can make some adjustments to the design. Is it helping?"

"Oh yeah. S'rin, whatever you gave me didn't do anything. My entire body was already in the grip of whatever this was." Vida looked at him and gave him a weak smile. "Thanks for trying."

"The compound I used will slowly reduce the effects of the treatment, but I am fairly sure that it has been effective in removing some of the scarred bone. If you will allow me to do a few scans, I will be able to determine its effectiveness. Do not blame Dr. Meevin, she was told it was safe." He dropped the hood of his cloak back, and his peculiar features were finally exposed.

"Oh." Ula and Vida both spoke as one.

Ziggy was the only one not surprised, she just watched her friends stare at the previously unseen species.

"I am breaking Nine protocols by letting you see me, but I felt that since a careless thought of my race put you in this position, you should at least get an idea of why we think the way we do."

She looked at the man whose energy was literally swirling under his skin, and she nodded. "Don't take this wrong, but you look better with my eyes closed. Your energy has free rein there."

His lips parted and a surprised laugh escaped him. "You are the first person to have ever given me that particular compliment."

"I am glad you recognised it for what it was. Now, let me guess. The original injection was supposed to be used on members of the Nine who had been injured away from the ship and who had healed a little crooked."

S'rin raised his hood again. "Many of ours get injured away from bases or regular medical attention. This was an attempt to repair bone and remove the original damage."

"Do your scans and find out if it worked. Just a question, though, why does the pressure of the suit help?"

Ula winced. "I can field that. It reduces the blood flow to your skin and the nerve ends don't get the same reaction that they would if they were given everything you need. The suit will only work for about sixteen hours, so I had better get back to the drawing board before your body starves for oxygen."

Vida blinked. "Okay, great. Good to see you, too, Ula."

Her friend nodded and waved, "I will greet you properly tomorrow. Tonight is for working."

Ziggy and Vida both waved at her and said cheerfully in unison, "Bye, Ula. Have fun."

Ula was out the door of the bubble in a moment.

S'rin's gloved hand pressed Vida back to lie on the bed. "Allow me my scans, please. I don't have the same equipment as Meevin, so I will need you supine for this."

Vida figured the supine meant lying down, so she relaxed with the suit giving her the occasional squeeze.

With her eyes closed, she could see that there was a rhythmic pulsing to S'rin's energy signature. She knew that pulse. He was singing a song in his head as he worked. It somehow made him a little more human than his shifting marbled skin and pointed ears. The braided hair and silver beads was a nice touch. Surprisingly, they kept themselves apart, possibly by the energy of their owner. There was no clash or swing as he moved. The beads tumbled soundlessly on their braids against the straight dark silk of his hair.

She played the image of his physical appearance over and over as he ran scan after scan. It was a bit of a shock, but as she thought about it, it suited him. She wondered if his skin was as cold to the touch as it looked. Well, the light swirling in him looked both cold and hot at the same time, as did the dark. She wondered which would win if she was touching his cheek. A moment later, she wondered if she was tall enough to *reach* his cheek. He was pretty tall.

Vida winced when she realised she was obsessing over him. *Why him? Why a man that was wearing so much fabric he could be hiding nine legs under the robe?*

She stifled a groan and wished for a moment that the world went dark when she closed her eyes. If she could blank her mind and her sight, life might occasionally get easier.

"Are you in pain? I heard you groan."

Vida snorted. "No. Do you have the scans you need?"

"I do. They will occupy my evening most pleasantly. I will discuss them with Lerinian when he returns."

Vida sat up again and dangled her legs over the edge of the bed. Her limbs tingled and she wiggled her toes. Even her toes were individually wrapped in metal.

She blinked and reset her vision to deal with the living world. "Too bad we have to leave. I find the peace here soothing."

Ziggy chuckled. "We can come back for a visit, but the Balance are not very chatty."

S'rin bowed. "We are interested in our research and the songs of the stars. Nothing else registers on our minds."

Ziggy gave a stage whisper. "There are no girl members of the Balance. They find their mates in the other species and the boys are always the same as their fathers."

It seemed rude to be discussing it with S'rin right there, but she asked, "What about the little girls?"

"There are none. The Balance have never been able to breed females. Our elders posit that it is because females already have balance within, they don't need it without."

Vida chuckled. "That is an enlightened view."

He laughed. "That is why the Balance never varies in its population. We do not thrive, but neither do we dwindle. We are the same in number now as we were when our people left Underhill."

Underhill was the Nine name for the world that the colonists had called Gaia.

Vida remembered her genetics lessons. "Since you always breed out, there is no degradation in the line, and if your power controls the genes, it wouldn't fade either."

"You seem to have a grasp on it."

Vida chuckled. "My parents are scientists. Biology and basic genetics was my nursery school class."

Ziggy laughed, "It is true. She has a scientific mind that can rival that of Ula's, but hers is aimed a little more toward the motivational sciences."

S'rin reached out his hand to help her back to her feet. She resented the lack of tactile feedback, but she accepted the help. Once she was standing flatfooted on the lab floor, she looked up and up into the cowl of S'rin. Yup. He was very, very tall. Seven foot easily.

She smiled brightly into the confines of his hood, and she swore she could see a flash of light.

Ziggy spoke to S'rin. "I am taking her to Meevin again tomorrow. If Lerinian can meet us there at midmorning, that would be great. He can take charge of the situation. Thanks for helping out."

"It was my pleasure. I am eager for our little project to find a use. I will pass this information along to Researcher Lerinian. I am sure he will be there."

"I second Ziggy's thanks. I know I was unable to articulate it when we arrived, but I am deeply relieved that you were here to consult." She extended her hand to him, and he seemed surprised by the gesture. Instead of shaking her hand, he raised it to his lips.

She really wished she could feel it, but Ziggy pulled her out of the lab before she could figure out how to get the suit to retract.

The Balance zone was soon to be a thing of the past, which was a pity; Vida enjoyed the clear pathways.

CHAPTER FIVE

Vida had seen images of creatures like Rothaway in the Gaian monster books. He had thick, wavy hair, pointed ears, wide shoulders and his fingers looked as if claws could appear at any moment. His doting on Ziggy made his appearance a little less aggressive.

"So, Vida, that is a striking robe you are wearing."

She ate another morsel of food that Ziggy gave her a nod for and inclined her head. "It is Ziggy's. I am afraid that the gown I came with suffered an accident."

Rothaway filled her wineglass and chuckled. "So I gathered. Feel free to requisition anything you need on Ziggy's account. She doesn't use nearly enough of her income as it is."

Ziggy made a face. "That is because you buy me stuff all the time. I don't have a chance to go shopping."

"If you shopped, you would not choose Wilder clothing."

Ziggy sighed, "That is the point."

Vida felt that she had stumbled into a domestic issue. "Um, if you would like, I can just head to my room."

Rothaway looked over at her. "Don't worry about it. We bicker about her clothing all the time. She has to dress according to her station. She is the first representative of your species and eyes are on her every time she leaves our quarters."

Vida winced. "That must be stressful, Zig."

Ziggy shrugged. "It will be worse when the baby shows up."

Rothaway sat back and grinned. "We have no idea what it is going to be. Dr. Meevin is beside herself. The geneticists are waiting eagerly, but we have forbidden testing until the child has arrived. Aside from the other Gaians living on the mother ship, you are the first to know about the pregnancy. It shows that she has great trust in you."

Vida nodded. "I already saw the addition, but I didn't want to mention it. Some folks react badly to having things seen that are not in their consciousness yet."

281

Rothaway blinked and rubbed the back of his neck. "That explains your lack of shock."

She shrugged. "When you can see the way I do, very few things in a living body can shock you."

"So, you are in search of one of the lost ships?"

Vida leaned forward. "What do you know about them?"

"Before we arrived, no more than four and no less than two Tokkel ships escaped with samples of Gaian citizens and scientists. We had assumed that the Gaians had been killed, but Ziggy tells me that you think that is not the case."

"They are alive. I am linked to my family. I know where my sister is and what her mood is, and I can feel my parents going about their tasks somewhere. I just need help in finding them."

Rothaway nodded and placed his hand on the table, palm up. Ziggy took it and smiled at Vida.

"We can provide you with a probe, but we need coordinates. Are you going to be able to follow? I am guessing that you are having medical issues."

Vida rubbed the metal over her forearm. "I have always been a little brittle. It never crossed my mind that it would be an impediment to me doing whatever I wanted."

Ziggy chuckled. "Where I concealed my talent, Vida and Ianka have always worn theirs out for everyone to see. They worked tirelessly during and after the attacks. They found the living and sought the dead. They don't flinch."

"Your sibling also has this sight?"

Vida wrinkled her nose again. "Ianka is a tracker. She can find someone by traces left in the physical world. She uses scent, sight and touch predominantly. Possibly similar to your senses."

"You and your sister don't reside together?"

Ziggy turned her head to one side and squeezed Rothaway's hand, but the question was out.

"No. She does not approve with my constant search for our parents. I have spent too much time staring into the empty sky, searching for traces, for the path that would lead me to them. The path from Gaia goes to orbit and then stops short. Our planet's rotation has spun us away from that point in space that we had occupied during the attacks. I don't know where to start looking, but I know I am not going to stop until I regain that signal." Vida rubbed at her forehead with metal-clad fingers.

Ziggy got up, kissed Rothaway's forehead and smiled. "I will be right back, she's exhausted."

The moment that Vida heard Ziggy's words, she acknowledged that she was right. It had been over twenty-seven hours since she had slept, and her wound had taken a lot out of her. She still wasn't quite right.

"It was nice meeting you, Rothaway."

"I look forward to many more meals together while you are here, Vida. Enjoy your rest. I am sure that Ziggy will have you up on your feet at first rising."

Vida got up and nodded farewell. She and Ziggy walked the short distance to the VIP quarters that had been commandeered for her. The robe swung loose and was covered in delicate dark rainbows. It was rather girly for Vida, but bodysuits were not usually worn on the ship with nothing over them or, at least, not by women. The female-to-male ratio in the Nine in general was incredibly small. Families had a lot of children because they had to, to maintain population levels, but not all members of the Nine found mates amongst their own kinds. Ziggy and Rothaway were perfect examples.

"Are you feeling all right, Vida?"

"I am as good as I can be. Let's see if I can sleep in this can and I will give you a breakdown of my night in the morning or first rising. However you tell time on a space craft."

"Then, I wish you good night."

"Oh, Ziggy? Congratulations. You will make an annoying but loving mother."

Ziggy raised a brow. "Annoying?"

"You will know everything your kid is up to. Trust me. That will be annoying." Vida retreated into her room, and when the door closed and locked, she found her bed.

She waited for the urge to use the bathroom but nothing happened. Either the suit took care of it for her or she was going to be in the sprint for her life the moment it came off. As she settled in and let fatigue take over, she could hardly wait to find out which one it was.

In her dreams, she called for Ianka. She couldn't continue her journey, but if she could convince Ianka that she had found her parents, she knew her sister would continue the quest.

She called and called for her sister, yelling through forests, across oceans of water and sand. Finally, she heard a reply.

The chime woke her. Vida got to her feet with a groan and opened the door.

Ziggy was wearing another lovely gown that made her pretty, elegant and casually formal. If casual and formal could exist in the same place, it was on Ziggy.

"Come on. Dr. Meevin is waiting and she sounded a little freaked out. Apparently, the researcher has arrived."

"What about breakfast?"

"After you get out of that suit. We have no idea how you are going to feel once you have been freed from it, and you are at the edge of the dangerous zone."

Vida scowled. "Fine. Lead on."

They walked back to medical; the borrowed open robe flowed around her and belied her mood with its cheerful colours. Mornings were not her favourite time. Everyone's auras were scrambled in the mornings. Too much of the dream state overlapped the waking body.

There was a crowd outside the medical bay, but it wasn't the procedure that drew the attention. There were *two* researchers from the Balance waiting for them with a nervous Meevin while Ula was fiddling with a length of fabric on a hangar.

Vida smiled as she entered the room. "Just for the record, I am not getting naked with an audience. Ula, if you could get this suit off me that would be great."

Dr. Meevin opened a panel at the back of the room and unfolded it. "Here. This should allow you privacy. There is a med robe folded up for the rest of the exam before Ula fits you with the second suit."

"Where is the lav in case I need it?"

"Over to the left behind that panel."

"Thank you." She smiled brightly, and Ula accompanied her behind the privacy screen.

"How are you feeling?"

"A little rough. My body aches like I am coming down with an illness. Can you get the suit off?"

"Yes, but I warn you that the pain could return, so if you do need the lav, do what you have to do quickly. I can have you wrapped up again in under a minute."

"Thanks. Are you enjoying yourself?" Vida raised her eyebrows as Ula put her hand on the flat control panel in the centre of the suit.

"I am. This has been the first real-world test of this survival suit. It is designed to act as an emergency exoskeleton in case of injury. It won't heal you, but it will keep you intact and process all of your body's excretions for a limited amount of time. I am working on the timeline, but this is definitely proof of concept."

Ula pressed a few of the buttons and the suit began to retract into the handheld size it had started off as.

As the external support disappeared, Vida grabbed for the shelf holding the robe. It held her while the suit crawled away from her skin and back into the pod. She thudded to the floor with a splat sound.

Since the robe had become clutched in her hands, she wrapped it around her while Ula tried to pull her to her feet.

"Tell people who are wearing the suit to remove it while they are seated or lying down. Having someone cut your strings is disconcerting."

With her body partially covered, she got to her feet and finished arranging the robe.

"Sorry, Vida, I had no idea that it would drop you like that."

"You said it yourself, exoskeleton. My muscles thought they had the day off. Oops, I will need that lav after all."

She walked as quickly as she could around the corner and toward the lav in the medical lab. Relief was not a strong enough word. She had begun to feel that her eyes were swimming the moment that the suit came off.

After she was no longer feeling pressure, she hung up the robe and recalled the instructions for using the solar unit. The shower was in the small cubicle, and she stood in position for a moment while the blast of light scrubbed her clean. Even clenched eyes didn't manage to stop the bright after-flares on her vision.

She put the robe back on and felt a little more like herself when she exited. At least she was clean and no longer smelled like the inside of a can. That metallic tang had been driving her nuts.

The crowd that was waiting for her was a little surprising. Two members of the Balance were standing side by side, but S'rin's aura glowed.

Vida paused, "Dr. Meevin, Researcher S'rin, Researcher Lerinian? I was under the impression that there would only be one member of the Balance here today."

The stranger bowed. "S'rin insisted on accompanying me here today."

Dr. Meevin looked impressed with the turnout. "Step into the scanner please, Vida."

As she had the day before, she stepped into the scanner and waited. Her skin was tingling, and there was an ache in her limbs that was a shadow of the day before.

S'rin and Lerinian were in quiet conversation as the data began to spill onto the screen.

Dr. Meevin was making notes with Ula on the readouts, and Ziggy sat on the medical bed across the way making faces at Vida to keep her entertained.

It was almost as if Ziggy knew how odd it felt to be examined like a bug. Come to think of it, being the first Gaian to live on the mother ship of the Nine, she might just know exactly how this went.

The machine beeped, chimed and pinged the occasional alarm. Apparently, whatever had gone into her body the day before had created an issue.

When the machine had worked out all the details it needed, Dr. Meevin released her from the unit and asked her to have a seat on the medical bed that Ziggy surrendered.

The collection of the Nine gathered at one side of the room, murmuring and comparing notes. Eventually, they called Ula over.

Ziggy smiled, "Don't worry. I can read those reports. You are fine. I mean, you still aren't in shape to travel, but your bones have completely reset and all ridges caused by breaks and remodeling have been removed."

"Oh goody, so I am good as new?" Vida wiggled her toes.

"Well, something is up. I can't recognise all the energy patterns of the Nine on a readout, but I am guessing that yours has shifted since yesterday. You know what that means."

Vida did indeed. She literally wasn't the same person she had been the night before.

Chapter Six

Ula made a few final adjustments to the blue and white fabric before she shook it out. "Here, try this on."

Everyone in the room had an eye on Vida, so she grabbed the suit and returned behind the screen. The robe was off in a moment and she stepped into the legs, working the soft skin up and around her. It was a change from the metal suit, like water was to rock. The blue and white fabric hugged and supported her, but most of all, it felt like comfort.

She fluffed out her short hair and poked her head around the screen. "Nobody laugh."

The room was very solemn as she came around, and Ula came up, tugging slightly until the fit was perfect. "Excellent. It has been wired to channel your sight and amplify your perceptions. I know enough about your ability to make a guess at the means by which you operate. Your eyes are your focus, so the power needs to flow through there."

Dr. Meevin used a hand scanner and nodded. "It is helping to balance your body temperature. Good. How are you feeling?"

"My bones ache a little."

"They were resurfaced and are still in the process of being reinforced. It will be an extensive remodel. Your body has taken to the injection that you received yesterday. It has decided to rebuild you using the DNA as a template."

Ziggy cleared her throat. "The DNA of what?"

"Whom, really." Lerinian bowed slightly. "S'rin designed the bone builder, but it was set for members of the Nine. We used my DNA as a starting point, but in your body, it has become something else."

Vida narrowed her eyes at the cloaked figure. "What has it become?"

S'rin answered her. "Something new. We don't know what it is, but it is making changes to you that normally do not happen outside of a bonding, and yet, there is no identifiable DNA left in your system. You have taken it apart."

"So, am I Balance, Gaian, something in between?"

S'rin chuckled. "Yes."

Vida sighed. "Right, well. Can we stop it?"

Lerinian and Meevin shook their heads. "No."

"Fine. It is happening without my willing it, so do we just wait and see?"

S'rin spoke up, "You will come to my lab once a day, and we will go over your alterations. Dr. Meevin has agreed to have a standing scanner sent to my work area."

Lerinian cleared his throat. "We are still working out the details. However, on to the other portion of your reason for being here, I have volunteered to assist your search."

S'rin made a strange noise before murmuring, "As have I."

Ziggy took Vida's hand, and the strangest thing happened. An upload of the mating habits of the Nine bloomed in Vida's skull.

It could be summed up in one thought. The noise S'rin made wasn't good, but hostilities amongst the Balance were not common.

Ula smiled, "I am going to have a bunch of suits made up for you while you go through this change and until you finish your search."

"Good. Where can I get a robe so I don't feel like I am flashing my butt to all and sundry?"

Ziggy laughed. "I will take you and get you fitted out. Are you up to some shopping?"

Vida realised that Ziggy had basically told everyone that the meeting was over. Even Ula grinned and waved as she headed out of the room.

The doctor remained in conversation with the two members of the Balance while Ziggy and Vida headed to the door.

"What is going on between the researchers? Oh. I got your message. It hurt like hell though." Vida rubbed her forehead.

"Sorry about that. Downloading information is harder than acquiring it. I thought you might want to know that what I saw, I interpreted as those guys facing down and trying to wrestle for contact with you."

"It seemed very polite."

"Well, they are the Balance. They do everything a little differently." Ziggy grinned.

"I am certainly getting that idea. Now, shopping?"

"I think I owe you breakfast first. I know just the place."

At the mention of food, her stomach roared. "Good. I think we have ten minutes before my stomach goes critical."

"We can be there in five."

Vida had no idea what she had eaten, but her stomach didn't care. It was happily going to work on her meal.

"Where are we going to shop? Come to think of it, I should have gotten a robe before I stuffed myself."

"Not an issue. You aren't shopping for anything form fitting." Ziggy smiled at the server and swiped her chit across the payment screen.

"Thank you, Potential. Have a good day." The young man flicked his wings and bowed.

Vida got to her feet with a groan and followed Ziggy across the walkway.

The shop was peculiar and Ziggy was speaking with a shadow.

"The Potential tells me that you need a robe to go with that amazing suit."

Vida extended her arms slightly. "Something a little more subdued if possible."

"Black then?"

"You tell me. I just want this covered up."

The shadow moved around her and hemmed and hawed. Suddenly, he retracted and disappeared behind the counter.

Vida asked her friend. "Is this normal?"

"It is part of his process. He has analysed your hair, eye and clothing colour. I briefed him on your physical activities, so this is going to be interesting."

It took three minutes until a rack with several long robes was brought out. The shadow lifted one off the rack and settled it on her shoulders. "How is that?"

Vida walked to the mirror and turned from side to side. From the hip down, the robe was sliced to allow for full movement of her legs. She could run in this.

"I like it." She smiled and the shadow slipped it off her shoulders, producing the next one that included a belt that changed it from robe to coat. It would be fine on Gaia, but it seemed a little silly to wear a coat on the ship.

"Nah. A little too much."

"Right. How about this?"

They went through twelve robe styles, which amazed Vida. She didn't realise that there were twelve robe styles.

In the end, she picked three with hoods and two without. She wore one of the hooded robes out of the shop. Ziggy paid for it all with a swipe of her chit and had everything sent to the delivery slot in Vida's rooms.

Ziggy steered her toward a shop that specialized in footwear when her wristband got a call.

Vida continued looking at boots with the shopkeeper while Ziggy was on the call. The moment she finished, she came over and grabbed Vida by the arm.

"Please excuse us. There is a matter we need to witness. We will return as soon as we can." Ziggy fired the statement over her shoulder as she hauled Vida to the transport pods.

"What is going on?"

"There is a challenge taking place in the atrium, and I am hoping that we haven't missed it." Ziggy scowled as their pod whisked them along the rail.

"What kind of a challenge?"

"That is just it. No one has any kind of idea. The Balance don't normally settle their matters in public, and there haven't been any face-offs of this nature since the ship left their home worlds."

The pod slowed to a halt and they got out. Ziggy lifted her skirts and scooted down the steps toward an archway that contained a green space.

The way Ziggy spoke of it, Vida expected a huge crowd, but less than twenty people were standing near the open, grassy meadow in the centre of the park.

Two members of the Balance were facing each other twenty feet apart, and what surprised Vida was that she had met both of them.

She caught up to Ziggy who was next to her husband. Rothaway held his wife's hand as the strange and silent battle was waged.

Vida slipped to the front of the small crowd and closed her eyes. She had a front-row view of the actual battle that none of the others could truly appreciate.

Dark and light energy were lashing back and forth across the distance between the two men, each was trying to upset the balance in the other. It was strange, but each contact of power was absorbed and intensified by the victim. The two men were lashing each other into a fury of power and light.

It was a stunning display, and finally, Lerinian allowed his power to drain back to normal levels.

S'rin stood motionless and mastered the energy from the fight. He didn't dispense with it; he wore it and balanced it.

Lerinian bowed low, surrendering the field.

Ziggy came up next to her, "Who won?"

"S'rin. He managed to hold more power and maintain the balance while he did it. I think that was the point." Vida shrugged. "Do you know what it was about?"

S'rin turned his face toward her, and he approached her slowly as if carrying a wobbly burden. When he was five feet from her, he stopped and bowed.

She bowed slightly in return. It seemed the thing to do. "Congratulations on your success, S'rin."

"Thank you, Lady Vida. I have won the right to assist you in your investigations and pursue you socially if you are amenable."

"Pursue me? Am I running away?" She opened her eyes and blinked at the duality of his energy over the calm, dark robes of his daily garb.

She could hear amusement when he said, "No, I don't think you are the type to run from danger."

"Are you dangerous?"

"To you? Never. Would you care to accompany me to the Balance area where we can look into the best means by which to use your talent?"

She looked back at Ziggy, and her friend waved her on with a smile. "I know where to find you. There is a tracker in your suit."

"Then, S'rin, my afternoon is all yours." She stepped toward him, and he offered her his arm.

With a sense of destiny, she wrapped her hand around the fabric that covered him. He shivered and her body heated. There was something between them, and it went deeper than a shared fashion sense.

CHAPTER SEVEN

"I did not think you would be so agreeable to joining me." S'rin's voice was bemused.

They had made it through the pod in silence, and when they reached the Balance segment of the ship, he had begun to speak.

"Why not? I can see you, and I find you wonderful to look at on both planes. I cannot say that about many men of my acquaintance."

"You burn brightly as well. I find your urge to run into danger in complete harmony with your compulsion to help those around you. It is an odd balance, but a balance nonetheless."

Vida laughed. "And balance is your primary point of attraction?"

"Each race has their own points of interest. Balance just happens to be ours."

"What happened with you and Lerinian?"

"He wanted to help you with your search. I could not allow him to blend his energies with yours. It would be an intimacy that would bind you whether you knew it or not."

"Ah, and you are willing to bind yourself to me?"

"In a heartbeat. You are the brightest star I have ever seen, and you simply walked into my lab by chance. That has to be the design of the stars."

She cleared her throat and fought her blush. "Where will we run our first test?"

They had crossed the Balance spaces and were walking along the outer edge of the ship. He pointed to a platform that was raised and separated from the walkway by a small metal barrier.

He opened a gate with a small catch and closed it behind them. "I believe that this will work if you stand in front of me and I place my arms around you."

"I can see why you thought Lerinian and I would get too close. It is a rather intimate position without adding in the mental connection."

She knew she was babbling but staring out into space was making her a little dizzy. She swayed and his arms came around her, offering her support

292

and an anchor to the world where gravity still held sway.

"Open your senses and look at the world beneath you and the endless space stretching in front of you. I will keep you safe."

He held her tight and breathed slowly until her breathing matched his.

Vida leaned back against his chest and closed her eyes, letting her vision soar. She could see traces flying from the planet to the mother ship, but beyond the mother ship, there was nothing.

"There isn't anything." Depression gripped her.

"We are going around Gaia every few hours. Keep looking and you will see something. I will keep you supported. You need not fear."

She could feel his energy wrapping around her, and the balance of hot and cold, calm and passion, almost made her dizzy. It also made her feel more powerful, and she extended her vision far beyond her normal range.

He was right, the world was turning under them or they were spinning over it. Either way, the five-and-a-half-year-old traces left by the Tokkel soon became visible. She could follow their paths from space to the ground.

Anticipation burned in her as she caught a trail leaving the planet and entering space. It broke up, and she howled, the connection broken.

S'rin stroked her hair and murmured in her ear. "We will find the path again. We just need a different vantage point."

She was sobbing at having come so close and having it taken away from her the moment that the ship left the atmosphere. "Why can't I see them?"

He stroked her hair again and smoothed it away from her face. "Because you aren't looking in the right spot. We will work this out. I have a few ideas as to how to find them. Will you work with me?"

She swallowed and looked into his strange glowing eyes. "I will."

"Will you have dinner with me?"

Vida smiled. "I will."

Dinner with a member of the Balance was apparently not something that most women did. The servers fell over themselves to bring the food out and they never had the same one two times in a row.

Vida leaned toward S'rin. "I think this is a little odd."

"We normally eat our meals in the Balance section of the ship, and courtship is done in the same manner. We separate the women from their communities to see if they can accept our ways."

"You didn't think that it was necessary with me?" She laughed and sipped at the strange cool-hot wine that had been served with dinner.

"You are one of the most accepting women I have ever met and the most determined to have your own way at the same time. The balance is incredible."

"What will you think if I solve my problem by finding my parents and I have to surrender my quest?"

She could hear the smile in his voice.

"You will find another quest to drive you. You cannot remain still."

Vida cocked her head. "You actually are getting satisfaction from that thought."

"Yes, I am. You have a difference from the women more often chosen by our community, and yet, you fit in perfectly."

"Do I?"

S'rin took her hand. "Your aura calms when you enter the Balance area. Your mind clears and you smile a little. You already want to be there. With us, with me."

Vida sighed and placed her hand over his. "I do. I fight every day to keep myself calm, to keep my sight clear. In that one place, it comes to me effortlessly. I haven't felt anything like that since before the Tokkel attacks."

"You can feel that every day if you agree to be mine for life."

She blinked. "Just like that?"

"There is surety in my mind, just as there is in yours." He kept his hand on hers.

"How is it done?"

"We go to the gardens and exchange blood for blood. We can return to your quarters for the night and make the announcement tomorrow, but we will have to bond on the same day that we mate for the first time."

She blinked and pulled her hands back. "Too fast. Ask me again tomorrow. I am still getting over having my bones overhauled."

He reclaimed one hand and pressed a kiss to her fingers. "I will accept that and I will ask you again tomorrow."

Ziggy escorted her to the Balance section the following morning and left her alone with S'rin.

He ran a detailed exam on her with the scanner that Meevin had brought in. Her transformation was still underway, but she was getting stronger.

Once the exam was over, she found a chair and pulled it over. She stood on it, flipped the hood of his robes back and kissed him, just to try it on for size.

His arms snapped around her and held her tight to him until he was ready to release her.

When she had finished her exploration and her head was spinning with energy that wasn't all hers, she lifted her lips from his. He slowly opened his embrace and she braced herself on his shoulders as she stepped to the floor.

"That is going to be hard on your neck, S'rin." She smiled. He was a foot and a half taller than she was. It was going to be an adjustment for him.

"I believe that the mating ceremony will let you meet me halfway."

It took her a moment to absorb what he meant. "You are kidding."

"No. Most Balance brides gain height as a side effect of the bonding process."

She blinked. "I just got clothing that fits me. I don't know that I will be amenable to throwing that all away."

He stared at her in astonishment. "You would throw away a proper match because of clothing?"

Vida looked at him with narrow eyes. "Do you know how hard it has been for me to keep myself fed and clothed over the last six years? Clothing that is new and that fits is definitely a consideration."

He sighed. "I will set you up with an account so that you can replace the clothing as needed. Now, would you like to hear my idea on how to see your family?"

She blinked. "Fine, but we are going to revisit the clothing thing. I don't take. I earn my own keep."

He grinned and flipped his hood up. "I expected nothing less. Now, come with me. We are heading to the projector."

He explained his theory as they walked through the Balance section until they reached a theatre.

He led her to the centre of a huge room where a cushion was waiting on the floor. "Sit on the cushion and get comfortable. We are going to be there a while."

She followed his direction and sat with her legs loosely crossed. He sat behind her and once again wrapped around her. He poured energy into her until her skin was tingling.

"Now, think of your parents and hold their image in your mind."

Vida pulled her memory of her parents' energy patterns in toward her and held them tight.

"Good. Now, extend your mind toward them, keeping your mind focussed."

"Should I close my eyes?"

"Not yet." He made a small gesture and the theatre above them filled with stars.

"Vida, keep your eyes open and look through those stars. Try to see what they face when they look up through the night sky."

She shivered and followed his low instructions, trying to fasten more firmly to her parents, hundreds of worlds away. Her parents were blind but they had a feeling for space that she hoped would kick in.

Vida actually felt a flicker on the other end. "I have a connection!"

"Excellent. Hold it and remain calm. Find an image of the night sky through their eyes. Find it and hold it."

She looked through her father's eyes and saw the signature of a red star, a blue planet with orbital rings, and a series of moons. Vida relayed them all to S'rin, and he relayed them to the man running the projector.

"Now, close your eyes and look. Tell us what does and doesn't match."

He kept her power level high, but she could feel her father fading. She sealed the memory in her mind and said, "I have to let him go. He is tired."

"Fair enough. Look and tell us what you see."

She looked through closed eyes and shook her head. "Not that one. The rings are whiter."

"More moons."

"Redder sun." The feeling on her face needed more energy.

Nineteen different combinations were found, and finally, she opened her eyes and senses. "That is it. That is the one."

S'rin helped her to her feet, and she was able to line herself up until she had the same view that her father did. "That moon shouldn't be there. I can't see it through my father's vision."

S'rin smiled and expanded the view of the moon. It was green, lush and heavily armed with bases and turrets visible from space. "Your parents are on this moon. That is why you couldn't see it. They are standing on it."

She smiled and took a few steps before she collapsed.

Dr. Meevin shook her head, looming over Vida with a curious look. "You unmated morons. I am shocked how you Gaians fight the bonding. You should have locked in the moment you met."

Vida sat up and groaned. "What the hell?"

S'rin was next to her in an instant. "You fainted. Your system was in shock."

Meevin flicked her hand at him. "If you were accurate when you said she had sent her mind across the stars, I have no doubt that she was in shock. She was lucky that her brain wasn't scrambled."

"She is sturdier than that, and I was backing her up."

"And yet, you aren't linked, so it was not a perfect seal. Idiots."

Vida rubbed her head and swung her legs off the medical bed. "You have an excellent grasp of the Gaian language, Doctor."

"It has been growing by leaps and bounds since your compatriots have begun arriving. No one gets into odd medical scrapes like a Gaian."

"We have a talent for it."

Meevin laughed. "That is what you all say. Now, you are fine, you need to eat and get some sugar in you. Your system is out of balance, oddly enough."

"I will see that she gets what she needs, Doctor." S'rin helped her off the table and held her against him for a moment.

"See that you do. I have never seen a Gaian with mating weakness before, but I suppose there is a first time for everything."

Vida made a face and said, "Thank you, Dr. Meevin."

S'rin walked out with his arm around her, hauling her along.

"We are going to lunch?"

He made an odd sound. "No, we are going to the mating gardens. Then, we are going to lunch."

"What?"

"In a woman of the Nine, your little fainting spell is considered a sign that a true mate has been found. The bonding is carried out immediately before your body goes into full revolt."

"But I am not a lady of the Nine, so what is going on?"

"We don't know, but if a bonding can solve it, we will not wait. Will you bond with me?"

She snorted. "Yes, S'rin. I will."

Over lunch, Vida tried to recall the details, but all she knew was that he had bitten her, she had sliced him and their mingled blood was placed into a stone that registered their union.

There had been some vows about sharing everything, but all she remembered was the glow of his soul as he looked at her with his entire being. It had been like being bathed in adoration.

She was hungry enough to devour her meal, but she didn't remember it either. They were eating in the Balance section of the ship and the meals were carefully prepared and designed to please the eye. All she saw was S'rin.

After the meal, he took her to his quarters and they rivaled Ziggy's for space. He disrobed and removed the black and white suit that he wore underneath. His skin had the same swirling light all over.

Vida shucked her clothes off and folded them neatly before turning to S'rin and taking his hand. He led her into the bedroom and kept the lights off.

Together, they struck a balance, and when it was over, they did it again.

EPILOGUE

She slapped dust off her clothing and headed for the gates. Two guards tried to bar her way, but a short glare from her and they backed off.

She entered the building and waited while the eager receptionist ran to get the ambassador.

Daphne was at his side, and she smiled warily. "Hello."

She nodded curtly and turned to the ambassador. "Ambassador Apolan, I am Ianka Senior and I believe my sister needs to discuss something with me. I need to get to the mother ship."

TRACKING
RETURN OF THE NINE BOOK NINE

BY

VIOLA GRACE

Chapter One

Ianka felt Vida's call. Instead of the normal obsession that her sibling was broadcasting, pain had begun to radiate and her life had been in danger.

Ianka had struck camp and headed back to what little civilisation Gaia could offer. Her sister was no longer on their world, but Ianka knew where to find her.

She filled her pack and looked skyward. The new star in the sky contained her sister and she was going to get to her as quickly as she could. There was something very wrong and Vida needed her. She would find out why when she arrived. She had some walking to do.

With plains and hills between her and the city, she had better get started on the hike.

She set her senses to track Vida and was on her way.

Five days later, she was stomping up the drive toward the Embassy of the Nine. Vida was no longer in danger, but she wanted Ianka. The call of her sister vibrated through Ianka with every step.

She must have looked savage as she walked toward the gates. The guards took one look at her and released the gate to allow her entrance to the grounds. She nodded and kept plodding on.

Daphne ran out of the building and came to a surprised halt. A greenish man was behind her, and he put a protective arm around her.

Ianka nodded to Daphne and turned toward her husband. "Ambassador Apolan, I am Ianka Senior, and I believe my sister needs to discuss something with me. I need to get to the mother ship."

He nodded. "Of course. I will make the arrangements, but first, I believe we will offer you the hospitality of a bath and a change of clothing."

Amusement tinged her smile. "I will gratefully accept."

Relief flickered across his features and Daphne laughed. "Come this way, Ianka."

She followed the ambassador's wife, her one-time friend. She hadn't seen Daphne since before the Tokkel attack.

Ianka had cut all ties with the Gaian colony when her sister Vida insisted on her obsession with finding their parents. There was no way to find them, and it had been impossible to get that through her sister's head.

Now, the pull to her sister had grown strong again and there was a certainty in what Ianka was doing. Vida needed her to do something and Vida was in the mother ship, so that is where she would go.

When Daphne showed her to the guestroom, she sighed in admiration. Years of being on her own and wearing leather that she had tanned herself meant that she was a little more attuned to the scents of nature and her own aroma has ceased to be an issue. Being clean was a luxury, and it was something that she looked forward to.

Daphne hesitated in the doorway. "Do you need help?"

A little embarrassed, Ianka cleared her throat. "Is there any chance you could find me something to wear? I don't think that these clothes are fit for company."

Daphne smiled. "I will put them on the bed while you are in the shower. Drop your clothing on the floor and they will be cleaned."

"Thanks. I apologise for the grime, but it has been a while since I have seen plumbing."

Ianka headed for the bathroom, dropping her pack inside. She closed the bathroom door and heard Daphne close the outer door. Ianka peeled off her fitted boots, undoing the laces with pride. They were her favourite creations. Her trousers hadn't turned out quite right. Scraping the skins had been awkward. The top had been made to wrap in place and it slid softly from her shoulders to lie in a sad heap on the floor. Her breast wrap was more difficult, but when she was only dressed in her skin, she flexed her fingers and toes in anticipation.

The plumbing had more options than she was used to, but once she had the water the right temperature, she stepped in and shuddered in delight.

It took her quite a while to get her hair scrubbed to her satisfaction, but once it was clean, she attacked the rest of her body with enthusiasm. She normally soaked in a creek next to her small hut, but she hadn't had time to stop for amenities while she was hiking.

The hot water was so welcome that it swept the tears away for the years she had spent hiding from the reality that she and her sister were all that was left, and no matter what she said, her sister would not listen.

They had been close until the attack. Her sister saw psychic traces while Ianka saw everything else, and neither of them could stop their parents from being taken.

Rescuing and gathering survivors, hiding from the incursions, had been the first step in atoning for their inability to find their parents. Vida had seen the path that they took, and it reached skyward before it ceased entirely.

She had stared at that trail through eyes closed tight until Ianka couldn't stand it anymore and left the guilt of her inability to save their parents behind. Now, she was back in the thick of it.

Once she had sat on the floor and scrubbed at the bottoms of her feet, she carefully stood upright. Sighing with regret, she turned off the shower and wrapped herself in a thick towel, putting another around her hair. A little digging around turned up a hairbrush, and she crept out into the bedroom to sit on the bed and work at the mess that her scalp had become.

There was a dress and shoes sitting on the bed, and she reached out to touch them. Dresses had never been her favourite, but she was looking forward to this one. First, though, she had to tackle the neglect she had enforced on her once-pretty golden locks.

It took her an hour and her arms had started to ache, but she finally had her hair hanging straight and clean. Her fingers moved awkwardly but got her hair into a loose braid held by strands of hair scavenged from her brush. Once her hair was settled, she slipped into the dress. It was tight across the bust, but it fit everywhere else. She slipped into the shoes and got to her feet. With a nervous air, she headed for the mirror in the bathroom.

A lump formed in her throat as she saw the old her for the first time since she had left. It was time to become herself again, and in the process, she needed to figure out who that really was.

Through their connection, she could feel Vida and the calm satisfaction that now marked her once-frantic mind. Vida had found her balance, so now, it was Ianka's turn to search and find her true self. She could track any living being anywhere, but she couldn't find herself. The irony was not lost on her.

With straightened shoulders, she headed out to find Daphne. Her track was clear, and after two sets of stairs, a hallway and three offices, Ianka cleared her throat. "Hello again, Daphne."

Daphne had been sitting in close conversation with her husband and she turned in surprise. "Eek!"

Ianka smiled at the childhood name. "I suppose. Ambassador, it is good to finally meet you. Travellers have given me briefings on your presence on the surface. It has been interesting to hear versions of your description from a dozen mouths. If I may say, they all got it wrong."

He stood up and stepped toward her but stopped a few feet away.

Daphne must have seen her confusion, because she said, "The Nine don't shake hands. Their mating senses link with contact, so it is a habit not to touch the opposite sex if they are not mates to begin with."

It left the question of how they finally got around to making contact, but Ianka simply inclined her head in formal greeting.

"I am pleased to meet you. Your sister is a whirlwind, but you are a force of nature yourself. Your parents must be very proud."

She jolted. "My parents were taken in the first raids."

He nodded. "So Vida mentioned. According to the report she sent in, there is every reason to believe that she has found them."

Ianka swayed in shock and Daphne jumped to her side, leading her to a chair. A glass of water was pressed into her hand and she gulped at it blindly. "They are alive?"

Daphne knelt in front of her and smiled. "They are alive, and she finally found them. She said she had contacted you but not how."

"So, you knew I was coming."

Apolan nodded in his position behind his wife. "We knew but we had no idea when you would arrive. The shuttle is landing this evening, and you will leave at dawn after a solid night's sleep with your cleaned clothing. You will be as fit as we can make you before you meet your sister again."

His kind smile set her at ease and she set the glass down.

"I shall repay your hospitality." She inclined her head.

Daphne smiled. "There is nothing to repay. You are family, more or less. Just go and do what you need to do and do it knowing that we are cheering you on. Whatever you find, at least you went looking."

Ianka smiled and tears welled in her eyes again. "In that case, can I request a meal? I didn't stop to hunt on the way and I am a little peckish."

They both laughed and suddenly everything was completely normal. It was strange to be in the middle of normal, but she was up to it.

Chapter Two

The next morning, Daphne brought in another dress; this time, it had a little more room in the bustline, but it was still rather tight.

The housekeeper triumphantly produced her pack and everything was in clean and new condition. She certainly knew her job.

"Thank you, miss."

The woman ducked her head, smiled and retreated.

Daphne smiled. "She is a woman of few words and your look on arrival scared the hell out of her."

Ianka chuckled. "It has been a few years since I have seen a mirror. The few folk I have run into haven't bothered commenting. They were too busy thanking me for fishing them out of the wilderness."

"Is that what you have been doing?"

"I have been tracking animals, finding Gaians and building my own little retreat away from the city. It is primitive but it is mine."

"I have heard of a wild thing in the North Country, but I hadn't realised it was you." Daphne wrinkled her nose in amusement.

Ianka laughed. "They told me that there were rumours of a creature rescuing hikers and botanists in that area. It took them a while to realise that they were in her clutches."

They went downstairs for breakfast, and the pilot who would be taking her was sitting at one end of the table with Apolan at the other. It seemed that there were only two remaining seats on either side.

Ianka faced Daphne across the table. "Your housekeeper did a wonderful job on the leathers. They are as clean as could be. They will be a delight to wear now."

"She does enjoy natural fibres, and skins are just some of them. The pants seem an odd fit."

Ianka laughed as she followed Apolan's lead and started helping herself to breakfast. "They were rather urgent. My original clothing had shredded away by that point. Dressing myself became rather important. Unfortunately, I didn't have a pattern to work from."

Daphne laughed. "So, you improvised."

"Yup. The shirt was easier. I used the shreds of my last blouse to make the pattern and it fits like a dream. The bra bands were hit and miss."

"How did you cure the leather?"

Ianka smiled. "Lua pods. They dissolved the hair and the oil softened the skin. They are easy to use if you wrap your hands. Soak the skin in water the moment you have the result you want."

"Nice. Your boots are lovely."

She beamed. "Thank you."

The pilot, who was so deep red he was nearly black, chuckled and spoke in careful Gaian. "It figures. Put two women together no matter their species and they will talk about shoes."

Ianka looked squarely at him and he grinned, showing deadly teeth. She stated in clipped tones. "It was not a conversation that you chose to enter in its infancy so critiquing it shows bad manners."

He blinked and leaned back slightly. "You are correct. I am unfamiliar with the object in question and therefore my comment was unwarranted. I apologise."

She inclined her head. "Apology accepted."

Daphne and Apolan were looking at each other with amusement. Apolan cleared his throat. "How long were you living on your own in the wild, Ianka?"

"I saw four winters out there, but I am not focussed on the exact dates. I lived in the moment." She shrugged.

The pilot cleared his throat. "You lived here on Underhill without companions or shelter for four years?"

She shrugged. "Yes. I found a few hunting parties and helped them back to the city, but I did not return myself."

"You fed and sheltered yourself for four years?" He raised his brows.

"Yes. Is there a reference to this in the Nine languages? You seem confused." She worked on her meal with good appetite. It had been a while since she had consumed fruit out of season. She had missed the greenhouses of the city. Dried fruit just wasn't the same.

Apolan chuckled. "Our females are not really trained for self-sufficiency. There are so few that we tend to take great care of them. Dorum was simply surprised that you had survived on your own."

She swallowed and sipped some water. "I can track my own food, and after a while, I got used to killing for defence and meals. Once I reached that point, not much bothered me."

Dorum nodded. "Yes, once you have your first kill under your belt, it is like a rock down a hill. Not much will stop you, though you may be redirected."

Ianka inclined her head. "Now you have it. So, when do we leave?"

He grinned. "As soon as the meal is done. The ship has been checked and is ready for takeoff."

"Good. I need to find out what she wants. She has become most insistent." Ianka rubbed her forehead. She knew what Daphne had told her, but she wanted to hear it from Vida.

Dorum was looking at her curiously. "You can sense your sister?"

Ianka frowned. "Now and then. Right now is one of those moments."

Daphne smiled. "They have always had their link. Before the Tokkel, they were one of the best tracking teams that had ever been seen, not that folks knew who they were. They did their best work without anyone knowing. Ianka even delivered meat to those who had suffered a death or illness and were unable to work."

She sat up. "How do you know that?"

"I saw you. I was hiding and you brought it all the way out to my cottage on several occasions before you left. I truly appreciated it."

"Where were you?"

Daphne chuckled. "I was hiding."

"Oh." Ianka blushed. She had forgotten that Daphne had her own set of skills when she chose to use them.

The rest of the meal was completed in silence.

Ianka's belly was full but not uncomfortable when she placed her cutlery carefully across the edge of her plate.

She felt a touch on her shoulder and the housekeeper pointed toward the corner where her bag was sitting and gleaming with a solid cleaning.

"Thank you for the care you took." She spoke softly.

She wasn't sure if the woman spoke Gaian or not, but she blushed a soft grey and smiled shyly.

Daphne grinned as the woman left. "I think she is smitten with you. No other woman could have scattered the guards with a look, like you did."

"It was my smell, not my face that scattered them." She sat with her hands in her lap.

"I beg to differ. You looked deadly coming through the gates." Apolan smiled.

They rose from the table and Ianka took the hint. She grabbed her pack, checked for her knives and followed Pilot Dorum to the tarmac a fair distance from the embassy.

Daphne came with her.

"Thank you, Daphne. That shower was wonderful."

Daphne laughed. "The mother ship has solar showers, so think fondly of this one."

"Right. Limited water on the ship." Ianka braced herself for what was about to be her first space flight.

She gave Daphne a brisk hug and waved to Apolan before following Dorum into the ship.

He carefully took her pack from her and settled it in a storage container, locking it closed. "We don't want anything coming loose. This is a quick and bumpy trip."

She nodded and swallowed quickly. "It will be my first."

He showed her to the front of the shuttle and he demonstrated how to buckle into one of the dozen seats, all without touching her. She snapped the harness into place and he nodded with satisfaction. "Right. We shall be on our way."

Ianka swallowed again and curled her hands on the armrests. The shuttle started to move and then they were tilting upward. She felt the tugging as the engines pushed against the atmosphere.

She closed her eyes at the pressure and held tight until there was a switch in the drag downward. It went from overwhelming to steady and even in a few moments. From that moment until they entered the huge vessel of the mother ship, she concentrated on her breathing and not crushing the armrests in her grip.

A curl of excitement ran through her and she sat up as much as she could. Vida was seeing her arrive. They would be together again and the pain of the separation would finally ease.

CHAPTER THREE

Ianka looked at her sister from the walkway that led away from the ship bays. Vida was clenching her hands together and a large dark figure was behind her, his hands on her shoulders

Ianka tried not to run to the door that separated them, but she got there in seconds and waiting for the panel to slide open took an eternity.

Face to face with her sister, she had no words. She hugged Vida carefully, and to her surprise, her twin had grown several inches taller.

Vida chuckled. "I will have to explain the height, Eek, but that can wait for later. I am so happy that you have come."

Ianka parted from her sister and tears were running down both their cheeks.

They stared into each other's eyes for a moment before laughter began and another hug ensued.

The man with Vida cleared his throat. "Ladies, I believe we should take the reunion to an area where we are not blocking traffic."

Ianka turned and gave the men behind her a blank stare. They shifted and moved around her, edging around their little group.

Sighing, she turned back to her sister. "Your mate is right. Is there somewhere else we can make spectacles of ourselves?"

Vida linked arms between them and started hauling them along. "Ianka, this is S'rin of the Balance. His people are a little unusual, even for the Nine, but we get along. S'rin, this is my twin, Ianka Senior. Her skills are as physical as mine are not." She chuckled.

Ianka nodded to him around her sister's increased height. He nodded in return.

"It is an honour to meet you, Ianka."

"And you as well, S'rin."

Vida dragged them to a series of pods and explained the inner ship transport system to her sister. Ianka smiled at this new world that her sister was so keen on. It was good to see her excited about something that wasn't her habit of staring at the stars.

Twins always knew that one day their worlds would part, but Ianka had never imagined it would be literally.

"We live in the area used by the Balance. It is the quietest section of the ship, so it will be easy to talk, and the food is peculiarly attractive." Vida smiled.

It had been two hours since her meal at the embassy, but if Vida wanted to eat while they spoke, Ianka would jam in whatever would fit.

They settled in the pod, and without any delay, they were whisking through the ship and Ianka took in everything around her.

Seated across from her sister and S'rin, Ianka looked into his hood and smiled, "So, are those stars everywhere or just on your face?"

He jumped a little and looked at her more closely. "You can see through the shadows?"

Vida said proudly, "She can see through fog, run faster than local predators and find anything that has left a trail. Your little hood trick is no match for her sight."

He chuckled and lowered his hood, exposing the stars that floated under his skin with the occasional streaking meteor.

Ianka could only imagine what his skin looked like under his robes, but it didn't stir her at all. He was Vida's and that was the end of it.

Ianka drank tea while they ate and nibbled at bits that her sister recommended from the platter of designs crafted from food. It was almost too pretty to eat.

Vida winced a few times during the meal. S'rin stopped and held her hand while she breathed through whatever spasm she was having.

"What is going on?" Ianka wanted to know. Vida was wearing a tight bodysuit, but it seemed to be nearly structural in places.

Vida sighed. "I had a break in my arm that was treated here, but they haven't calibrated the treatment for Gaians yet, so there were side effects. My normally brittle frame is being reinforced on the molecular level and my bonding to S'rin is increasing my height. There are definitely twinges as the change progresses."

S'rin continued to hold her hand. "She is unfit for spaceflight. I am afraid that there was no option but to contact you in an effort to rescue your parents."

Ianka let that sink in for a moment and sipped her tea. "Rescue?"

Vida smiled and leaned forward. "They are alive, I have found the description of the star that they are nearest to, and I was inside Dad's head. He and Mother are both alive and well. Well, not well, but they are alive and together. With S'rin's help, I was able to see through his eyes. Things were blurry, but we found the likeliest location."

Ianka remained silent and leaned back, sipping at her tea for a moment. When she set the elegant little cup down in the saucer, she looked at her sister and smiled. "When do I leave?"

Vida nearly upended the table as she cried out happily and flung herself into Ianka's arms.

S'rin rescued the table and got to his feet. He waited until Vida was finished with her hugs before holding her chair for her and helping her seat herself.

S'rin turned toward Ianka. "You will need a round of medical scans and some ship suits. We will assign you to a pilot and he will take you to the location. The ideal outcome will be for you to find all the Gaians who were taken, but if you do not, bring home your family."

"If Vida can see them, I can track them. Find someone to get me to that world and I will bring them home, just make sure that the ship is big enough."

She knew every member of the missing by scent. Despite her frustration at her sister's obsession, she had gone to every private residence and memorized the scent of all the missing. Her frustration had been at her own inability to track her family through space. She was being offered a chance to change that, and so now, she was going to do everything she could to make the most of this opportunity.

If they were on that world or moon or station, she was bringing them home.

After dinner, it apparently was time to get her kitted out. There was no hesitation and no time to waste. A rack came out with a series of suits hanging from it. The shadow plucked several selections and S'rin nodded. "She will take them all and boots as well."

Ianka watched as S'rin swiped a small chit. "You shouldn't pay for me."

"Dearest sister, it is an honour and a privilege." He bowed low.

She blinked as the shadow handed her a suit. She could see the man inside the swirling darkness and he was smiling. "There is a change room off to the left there. If you would care to put this on, you can be a little more comfortable."

She blushed. "Thank you."

With a nod from Vida, she headed to the change room and slipped the dress off with relief. Tight clothing was not really her forte. She liked it to hug her but not restrict her and the dress was highly restricting when she moved her arms.

She tugged on the bodysuit and it formed to her, leaving her feeling covered but free. Her bust was incredibly grateful. She got support and was uncompressed. It was a nice feeling. She smoothed the closures together and exited the change room with her dress over her arm.

S'rin coughed and Vida elbowed him. "We are not identical twins, stop staring."

Vida held out a robe. "Here, this might stop the gawking while you are on the mother ship."

Grinning, she tossed the dress to S'rin and turned her back to Vida so she could slip it in place. Once the sleeveless robe was on her shoulders, her more noticeable assets were camouflaged. She twirled. "Better?"

S'rin had her dress over his arm. "No, but it will be better for morale. You have a striking figure."

Vida wrinkled her nose. "She really does. I have always envied it."

Ianka grinned. "And I have always envied you your perky nose."

S'rin chuckled. "And I will be the envy of every man on the ship but only if we can get out of here so that I can show you off."

The amusement seemed out of his character, but Vida moved close to him, and it was obvious that the joy was coming from her and out of him.

Their little trio left the shop and headed for the medical centre.

They had to wait for half an hour but Dr. Meevin beckoned them into her office to wait. Ianka's presence was causing a bit of a stir. Members of the Nine were popping by medical just to get a look at her.

"Why am I such a draw?" Ianka was looking at her sister with suspicion.

Vida chuckled. "Every Gaian woman that they have seen has found a mate in the population of the ship. They are just trying to increase their chances."

Ianka snorted. "They would run the other way if they had seen me enter the embassy. I was a little on the wild side."

"The Wilders might have taken a shot." Vida laughed and took a chair.

"Not if I was upwind, I had been walking for five days." She wrinkled her nose.

S'rin blinked. "Where had you been living?"

"In the wild. No Gaians, no politics, no having to face the wreckage of where our parents disappeared. It was cowardly but I just couldn't take it anymore."

Vida sighed. "It wasn't cowardice, it was survival. I was constantly looking for the path that only I could see and you were stuck trying to track something that wasn't there. You needed to be active and I forgot about that. We both went mad in our separate ways."

It was said. They had both gone mad. Ianka walked over and took her sister's hand. Vida had already found her balance. Ianka was going to have to work for hers.

Chapter Four

The medical exam was a surprise to S'rin and Dr. Meevin. Most of Ianka's strange talent resided in her body itself. She had more receptors in her nerve endings and sensory apparatus than any Gaian examined so far.

Vida chuckled. "And for me, my mind is lit up like a holiday in the square. Sections spark all at once. S'rin loves me for my mind."

He wrapped his arm around her and kissed the top of her head. "And your body, dearest, don't forget that."

Dr. Meevin rolled her eyes. "Right. That is enough of that. You are the fittest woman I have ever had the pleasure of examining, Ianka Senior. While I am curious to have your speed and strength tested, it is unnecessary to my declaring you fit for spaceflight and hand-to-hand combat if it comes down to it."

The doctor had taken the dress, wrapped it up and forwarded it through a tube system. It would be at Vida's quarters when they returned there.

"I don't have any experience in fighting other bi-pedals. I stick to hunting and killing what I need to eat."

Dr. Meevin blinked. "Right. Well, that would explain a few things."

Ianka laughed. "It would?"

"Your body is more carnivorous than omnivorous. You need more protein than vegetation. It isn't a common adaptation and must be difficult to deal with."

Ianka shrugged. "I will need to get serious about it in a day or two."

Meevin nodded. "Right. I will make a note for your rations so that you are in fighting form when you arrive."

"Thank you. It will be a relief because I get a little upset when my meals are messed with."

"Noted."

Dr. Meevin took a final tissue sample and smiled. "There. All done. You can continue on to your next appointment."

Ianka rubbed at her wrist and looked at Vida and S'rin. "Next appointment?"

Vida wrinkled her nose. "We had an itinerary prepared the moment that we

313

knew you were on the way. You are going to meet with Ziggy and her husband, Councillor Rothaway."

"Why?"

"Because he is on the council and can authorize anyone who cares to join your expedition." Vida beamed.

"You think others will want to join?" She was a little surprised.

"Of course. You might not be going to battle, but you are engaging in something exciting. The mother ship has a batch of warriors waiting for action. They are a little restless and in need of a target."

"Fine. Shall we get going?" Ianka had no idea how this was going to turn out, but she was definitely sympathising with folk who wanted to take action. She favoured that tactic herself.

Ziggy was exactly as she remembered, with the slight addition of moderately pointed teeth and a predator-like gaze. Her husband was a predator without a doubt.

He met Ianka's open gaze with a smile and the respectful inclination of his head. "It is always pleasant to meet one of Signy's people."

Ziggy took her hands and squeezed them. Ianka carefully squeezed back. "It is good to see you again, Eek."

"It is good to be back with people, though the increasing amount of them is getting a little distressing. Is there somewhere on board I can run?"

"Of course. We will have to clear a track for you, but it should be fine."

"Clear a track?"

"Yeah, female sweat can have an unsettling effect on unmated males of the Nine."

Ianka sighed. "I don't want to be any trouble. Isn't there a women's gym somewhere?"

"I am afraid not. The women of the Nine don't work out much, so we are stuck with the men's facilities. The women go for tea and long walks in the central green space."

Ianka made a face and Ziggy laughed.

"Right. We will make the arrangements once Rothaway figures out the scale of this endeavour. We know you want to get in and out with your parents, but we need to send Ula's probe in to send us telemetry."

"How long will that take?"

"Two days before we get a signal back. She has already altered it to fit with Vida's information."

To Ianka's surprise, they had drifted away from those gathered and were standing off by themselves.

Ziggy's face grew serious. "I have a question to ask. Would you agree to get the common language of the Nine directly into your mind? I have heard that it hurts, but I have only done it once before, so I can't say that it will happen again."

"Pain fades. If it will ease working with the Nine, I will do it."

Before she could say anything else, Ziggy's hand shot out and grabbed hers tight. Fire flowed up her arm and exploded in her brain.

Ianka stiffened but held back the scream that wanted to erupt. She breathed through her nose as her language centre was overloaded and as suddenly as it started, it was over.

Ziggy released her hand and looked at her. "Was it horrible?"

"It was definitely painful, but I can feel the words in my mind."

S'rin drifted closer. "They are coming out of your mouth. You are speaking Nine Common. Well done."

"Thank you, brother." Ianka blinked as the formal response came from her lips. "That will take some getting used to."

Ziggy blinked. "Right. He is your brother or brother-in-law."

She laughed and flicked her long hair over her shoulder. "I think the members of the Nine will be lining up for you. They don't have multiple births."

Ianka covered her eyes. "Oh, dear stars."

Ziggy patted her shoulder. "There, there. I am sure there will be a bare minimum of flexing involved. These men preen like firebirds if you give them the opportunity."

S'rin was grinning in the depths of his hood. He had raised it the moment that they left the relative safety of the Balance section of the ship. The Balance seemed to be odd even by the standards of the Nine.

Rothaway called them all to a boardroom where they sat and discussed the needs of the mission. Ularica chipped in from her workshop on board the ship via a com link.

When they had the basics discussed, screens descended from the ceiling and the races of the Nine were formally invited into the venture.

Dorum sat as head of the Fury and Ianka smiled and waved politely at the one face she recognised. To her amusement, he waved back.

Ziggy and Vida looked at her with surprise, and she merely smiled back with a smug smirk.

Dorum led the charge. "I will be sending my son, Derion and fifty of our best. The Fury are honoured to be able to participate in this mission."

Rothaway smiled and said, "And very smart in thinking that if they rescue the Gaians, the feeling of relief and thanks might spill into the ability to meet some of the young ladies of the family of those rescued."

Ianka blinked. "I had not thought of that. If they come with and not only work with a Gaian but rescue survivors, there may indeed be a bond formed between our two peoples once again."

Her words brought on a sudden surge of participation and five hundred warriors in twenty ships were volunteered in short order, each race of the Nine worked to one-up the one before it.

The men would need four days to properly equip and arm their ships for the event, and by then, the probe would have done its job.

By the end of the meeting, Ianka had a few days to kill.

Vida and S'rin arranged guest quarters for her and forwarded her new clothing and her pack.

With the basic language of the Nine in her mind, Ianka was able to read histories and watch documentaries on the variety of races that had all split from the single source.

She occupied her time by doing push-ups and running in place. Her body wasn't used to relaxing and inaction was not in her forte.

The chime from the communication unit was a relief. She stood in front of it and pressed the flashing key. "Yes?"

"Hello, Ianka. I have arranged some time around the track for you. You can run as much as you like. Dorum is sending you an escort who should be arriving momentarily."

"Um, why is Dorum sending an escort?"

"Because you will be flying out with his son, Derion, and it would be a good idea to get to know him before that happens. Oh, and because you can't run around the ship on your own and I am occupied."

Ianka gave her a narrow-eyed look. "When will he arrive?"

"He is on his way. Your language skills are improving by the way, you are speaking clear Nine Common."

"Well, I figured that I had it, I may as well use it."

Ziggy chuckled and inclined her head before disconnecting the call.

Ianka snorted then jumped as there was a chime from the door. "That was quick."

She checked to make sure that her suit was properly sealed before she palmed the panel to open the door.

Resignation was stamped on the features of the stranger in front of her. "Good evening, Miss Senior. I am Derion and I am here to take you to the exercise centre of the Fury holdings."

Ianka nodded. "Thank you. I am unused to inaction."

"This way, please."

He waved her on and she followed his lead. They walked out of the VIP quarters, past the guards and down a long hallway.

He didn't seem chatty and she wasn't going to attract attention. She kept her mouth shut until he opened a blank door and led her into a huge gymnasium. Tracks, bars, weights, fight rings, they were all in place and all completely empty.

"I hope this wasn't too much trouble."

He looked at her with surprise. "The Fury do not sleep. Being deprived of the option to exercise will not be well received, even if my father ordered it."

She nodded. "I will try to be quick."

Without another word, she sprinted toward the track, and once on it, she began to run at an easy lope. When she warmed up, she started to run, and with the speed blowing air past her cheeks, she finally felt her centre stabilizing around this new place.

She only had to keep herself contained for four days and they would be on their way.

Chapter Five

She ran until she felt the full-body rush of adrenaline in every cell. Once she was done with the track, she headed to the weights and quickly learned how to set them. She slid onto the bench and set to work.

"How are you lifting that?" Derion stood just in the corner of her vision.

She grunted and kept pressing, focussing on the weight and the steady burn of her muscles.

After a few minutes, she felt pleasantly tired and set the bar back in the holders over her head. She sat up and looked around. "Is there some way to clean the machines off?"

He nodded and pointed to the sidewall where a towel dispenser and a container sat.

"Thank you." She sprayed the bars with the antibacterial spray and carefully wiped off all traces of her grip before she did the same on the bed of the machine.

She returned the container back to where she had picked it up and then she sprayed the cloth and rubbed the container down as well. "Where can I dispose of this towel so it won't cause any issues?"

Derion walked over and pointed out a small chute. "It will immediately be in a cleansing solution so no worries. You are good at removing traces of yourself."

She wrinkled her nose and shrugged. "It was practice. You can't hunt if you leave your scent everywhere you go."

"My father mentioned that you were expert at surviving. I thought he was simply trying to make an introduction by piquing my interest."

Ianka snorted. "No. He was impressed when I explained to Apolan and Daphne how I had survived the last few years. I didn't have a chance to tell him that I had a lot of practice. There is nothing extraordinary of the practicing of an existing skill."

"I believe he was amazed that you had gained that skill to begin with. Even if your tracking ability is as extraordinary as he says, it has still taken willpower to hone it. That is worth admiring." Derion was speaking directly to her, his red-on-black gaze was looking into her eyes and the sincerity was on his blood-red features.

She blushed and rubbed the back of her sweaty neck. "Um, thank you for the observation. Can you show me back to my quarters? I think I need a shower to take care of the rest of this."

He inclined his head and smiled. "I can and I will also send the message that the others can resume use of the facility."

"Thank you. If the facility can be spared for about an hour per day on the ship, that would be great. I only need the track and the weights so it doesn't take that long."

Derion nodded. "Right. I shall pass that on to my father."

They left the gym and Ianka was feeling much better. Her body was humming with energy and earned fatigue. She couldn't sleep if she didn't exercise, so she should be able to rest well that evening.

There was a tension on the way back that wasn't out on the way there. She chuckled. "If you are this talkative now, I can only imagine how chatty you will be on the trip to find the survivors."

To her surprise, a small smile that flitted over his lips. "I am lost in thought. I thought you were something else and I have begun to see that my supposition was mistaken."

"Were you reading reports on my sister?" Ianka smiled. It happened frequently on Gaia that folk had met Vida and assumed that Ianka was just as frail. It seemed that the physical strength had gone to one twin and the mental capabilities to the other. Ianka was always happier when she could act and not think.

"I may have heard rumours about her being physically frail before she arrived. You seem a little more . . . fit."

Ianka wanted to howl with amusement. "Again. Thank you for that observation."

He looked like he wanted to say something else, but a cluster of Fury members approached them and something extraordinary happened the moment one of them looked at her. Derion got bigger.

He didn't just shift his arms and legs, he went from six and a half feet tall to nearly eight feet with a corresponding increase in width as he snarled at the men looking her over.

Two of the men responded in kind, and while she stood there, there was a clash of fists and skin in the hall as they fought. There were claws, teeth flashed and bodies thudded to the ground. Ianka stayed out of the way, smart enough to know males in rut when she saw them. The other two males of the Fury

stepped back and watched from the other side of the fight.

Security rushed to the scene and waited while the men sorted themselves out. One of the officers gestured for her to ease out of the potential damage area, but she shook her head. Instinct told her that if she moved, Derion would switch his focus and that might not be a good thing.

He sent one of his opponents skidding across the floor and the other one shifted and knelt at his feet, head down. It was a very formal pose, and Derion paused, stood straight and then cuffed the other male lightly on the side of the head.

They both shrank back to normal size and Ianka blinked. Their clothing had remained intact the entire time. The tailors of the Fury knew their stuff.

Security moved in and spoke to all concerned. Ianka was surprised to be questioned.

"How long have you been in a relationship with Attack Master Derion?"

She blinked. "We are not in a relationship. We haven't had any physical contact whatsoever. All I know is those guys started looking me over and then poof, Derion got taller."

"Did you touch him at all?" The officer had wings that flicked in agitation.

"No. I was warned against it. Is he in trouble?" She looked around to find him.

Derion was calm and he was speaking quietly with another officer.

"Yes and no. He will be taken to medical and a check will be made on his blood to see if he has triggered any mating reactions. If he was just being protective of you, he will be released immediately. If there was another reason, he will be treated."

"Okay. Good. As long as he is released before we are due to leave. I don't want anything to interfere with launch."

The officer's eyes widened. "Oh, you are *that* Gaian."

She could feel her forehead wrinkling. "What do you mean?"

"All of our councillors have asked for participation in the action you are heading up. There are more volunteers than spaces on the ships, though if this fight gets out, that number might double."

She asked the officer, "Why are you all so eager to fight?"

"We come from active and aggressive races. This is the first opportunity to go into action and we are all eager for the chance."

The officers across the hall were trying to get Derion to accompany them, but he was shaking his head.

"I was charged with watching out for her, and I will see her safely to her quarters before I go to medical." He crossed his arms over his chest and had an immovable stance.

The officers looked at each other but the one speaking to her raised his hand. "I will go with them and escort Master Derion to medical."

Derion looked at him and nodded. "Acceptable, shall we go?"

Ianka nodded. "Lead on."

The men gathered in the hall parted, and Derion and Ianka walked at a leisurely pace through the halls with the officer that had spoken to her. She could feel his gaze on them and there was approval at her back. It was nearly palpable.

At her quarters, she thanked Derion for his escort and smiled wistfully. "I guess that I will have to find somewhere else to exercise."

He chuckled. "Why? The Fury fight often. With the gym closed, it just made it harder to find a place to let it out. If I had run into them an hour later, the result would have been the same, but it would have been in the facility."

"Seriously? I wasn't the cause?"

He rocked his head a little. "You were and you weren't. Their interest was growing and you are under my charge. I had to stop two of them from escalating into interest in you and the others would be distracted."

"It certainly was distracting." She grinned.

He smiled. "Good. I was worried you would be frightened."

"Nope, just a little surprised. You have a very good tailor."

It took him a moment before he laughed and he grinned at her. "Have a good evening, Miss Senior. Welcome to the mother ship."

She slipped into her quarters and closed the door as the officer took Derion back down the hall. It had certainly been an interesting evening, but she needed a shower and then she needed some sleep.

The probe was on its way and it would start broadcasting as soon as it got close to the target area that Vida had found. Ianka hated waiting, but perhaps she could find someone to show her how to fly a ship. How long could that take?

Chapter Six

The next morning, she ran the request for flight instruction past Ziggy, and an hour later Derion was at her door smiling slightly.

"I am here to give you instruction in the pilot's seat."

She blinked. "Just like that?"

"Sure. I was pronounced clean by medical so there is no danger that I will go into mate madness. Would you like to get a morning meal?"

She wrinkled her nose. "Please. I wasn't able to work out the dispenser. It baffled me."

He chuckled. "Come with me."

She followed him, wearing another of the stylish bodysuits and the long robe over it. She felt more centred today. It was strange but she felt at home.

The walk to the restaurant was quick and the servers were attentive as she picked a few items that Vida had recommended on the first day and entered them into the ordering unit.

When their server returned, he set her selections down in front of her as well as a large pot of tea.

Derion poured her cup of tea before his own and sat back to enjoy his own meal.

"So, your check in medical was fine?"

He inclined his head. "I was found to be within my rights as your assigned escort. Things can escalate quickly here, so my actions were deemed appropriate."

She smiled and nodded. "Good." She sipped at the tea and got on with her breakfast.

"Were you worried?"

"Well, your father has assigned you to me during the mission, so I was concerned that you would be detained." She used the eating utensils with growing confidence to increase the speed of her consumption.

He chuckled. "I am sure they would have found you another partner and pilot for the event."

"I have a hard time dealing with strangers, and spending a few days in a shuttle with someone I haven't met is a tricky prospect."

"You seemed fine when we met."

"I was told you were arriving, I have met your parent, so your scent is familiar, and by the time I finished my workout, I was used to you."

He paused and raised a brow. "You identify folk by scent?"

She wrinkled her nose. "Yes. The air got acrid when those other guys entered the hall yesterday and grew worse when they started eyeing me."

Amazement covered Derion's features. "You have surprised me yet again. Strength and enhanced senses. Congratulations."

"Thank you again for the observation." She finished her meal and sipped at her tea. "Why did you agree to act as my escort on the ship?"

He chuckled. "The Fury have a strict hierarchy. We are a military unit. We may fight amongst ourselves during off times, but we are deadly serious about following orders from our commanders."

"Ah. Right. So, do you have much family aside from your father?"

He smiled and his blood-red features softened. "My mother and younger brother are still at home on Neecrad."

Ianka sympathised. "Is it hard to be away from them?"

He inclined his head. "Duty called and we answered, but yes, we do miss them."

Silence fell between them for a moment and she nodded. "I can understand that."

After their meal, he took her to a training centre where she was seated behind the controls, and he took the position next to her, explaining the controls and walking her through the preflight checks. By the end of the afternoon, she was hungry, her arms ached and she had managed to power up the simulator.

Vida and S'rin came to take her to dinner and Derion smiled. "Same time tomorrow, Miss Senior?"

She nodded. "I am going to get the hang of this before we leave. I promise."

He nodded. "I have no doubt."

It was routine by the day that they were ready to launch. Derion greeted her in the morning and they had breakfast together while discussing the information found by the probe.

The afternoon was spent on the simulator and Ianka had managed to take off, fly and engage in battle manoeuvres, as well as landing. She wasn't graceful but she could get them where they were going.

The evening meals were spent with Vida, Ziggy and any other Gaians who had time. Late in the night, she answered the knock on her door and went out with Derion again for her exercise.

The day of the launch, she had her bag with her when the knock on her door told her it was time.

The flight time would be twelve hours. The larger ships had more power than the probe and could travel far faster.

She opened the door to see Vida and S'rin. "Morning, Veed."

Vida smiled weakly. "Would you like some breakfast?"

Ianka chuckled. "Please. Never miss an offered meal. That is my motto."

Vida laughed. "It always was."

They linked arms and went for breakfast before the rest of the day shift had stirred into action.

It had less the feeling of a last meal and more of a holiday gathering. There was hope as they discussed the mission and Vida kept tearing up.

When she was escorted to the shuttle bay, S'rin stopped her with a glance and he bowed deeply. "Come home safely, sister."

She bowed in return. "Take care of her and do not let her get too excited until we return. I expect a tense family dinner when we get back here. You will get to meet our parents, and though they are not talented in the same way Vida and I are, they can see things you could never imagine."

She smiled softly in remembrance of her functionally blind parents and their vision that went far beyond the physical.

Vida lunged at her and squeezed her tight. "Take care of yourself. I want to see all my family together, not in pieces. I am going to see everything you do, so take care or I will kick the tar out of you when you get home."

"Yes, Veed. I promise I will take care." She whispered it in her sister's ear and she heard Vida sob. "Vida you did the hard work; now, let me do my part."

Vida leaned back and swiped at the tears in her eyes, moving back against S'rin.

Before she could start snivelling on her own, Ianka turned and headed for the walkway that extended into the ship she would be ensconced in. Derion stood aside as she entered, and once inside, she nodded to the guard on her left.

"To the right and down the hall until you see a staircase. Go up the staircase and then turn left."

She nodded. He had briefed her the night before. As commander, he was the last one into the ship, because the moment he was in place, they would leave. She needed to be strapped in before he sat down or she could tip over.

Ianka kept on track with his directions, and after ten minutes, she was sitting in the cockpit on a jump seat with her bag stowed in a locked shelf behind her. She needed the contents of the bag for the mission and wanted to keep them close.

Two other members of the Fury were on the command deck and they linked to the probe that Ula had sent out and used that for telemetry. The moment that Derion was strapped in, they started the engines and the ship began to move.

Ianka was fascinated by the flight. It was so different from lifting off from a world. There was no pressure, no discomfort, only a slight indication of motion before all exterior signals ceased.

Humming to herself, she followed the motions of the crew and unbuckled her launch harness. She unlatched the storage box and removed her bag, fishing out the tablet with the information programs that she wanted to watch. She had twelve hours to kill and she was finding the history of the Nine fascinating.

Derion smiled and got to his feet. "Miss Senior, this is Uradik and Morwil. They will be at your disposal if you require anything. Medical is ready if you want to take a nap."

She smiled. "I am fine. I can stay awake and alert for a few days if needed. I don't need to use the bed in medical. Will this documentary disturb any of you?"

Uradik and Morwil shook their heads. Derion shrugged. "It will be fine. What are you watching?"

She flicked her fingers across the screen. "The origins of the Balance, since Vida is married to one."

She set the volume down as low as she could and still hear it and settled in to watch the documentary. She might be able to make her way to the People of the Air if she kept her focus. With her blood singing in an urge to action, focus was all that kept her from screaming with tension.

Chapter Seven

One meal and a gearing up later, Ianka was ready to land on the moon base.

The moon had the same profile as Gaia and the base was heavily fortified. The other nine ships were going to distract the Tokkel by engaging in direct confrontation while Derion's ship skulked in through firefight and let their contingent onto the base.

From the moment they left the ship, Ianka would lead the way.

Uradik kept looking at her as they staged for the attack.

She raised her eyebrows. "Yes?"

"You are wearing weapons?"

"Yup. My kind don't get taller with claws when confronted. I have to pack my own knives." She may have overdone it, but wearing knives strapped to her calves and thighs was a comfort with her long blade riding in a leather harness down her back.

Morwil looked nervously at Derion. "We just think that your weaponry shows lack of faith in your mate."

Derion sighed. "I have told you, she is not my mate, she is my charge."

Ianka chuckled. "Even if he was my mate, I would not expect him to jump in front of me when danger rises. I will be leading the charge into the base, in search of the scents I am looking for. I will be in front, so having someone ahead of me distracting my senses is not a good idea."

Everyone in the room nodded, and Derion turned to check the position of the other ships. With a quick barked command, the ships mobilized and took up their attack formations.

Things were underway. Ianka pulled on the gloves and pulled up the hood for just this moment before heading out of the command deck and down to the cargo area where the rest of the Fury were waiting to land and surge into the base.

She grabbed a bar and held tight as the ship rocked as it entered the atmosphere. The warriors in the hold with her looked at her with curiosity, but she gave them the blank repelling stare that she had perfected, and they nodded and looked away.

Ianka had no idea what they saw when they looked into her features, but if they turned away in respect, that was good enough for her.

The ship pitched and rolled as gravity took hold, and they avoided the firefight that was now becoming audible with the atmosphere to carry the sound waves.

Derion arrived and his men snapped to a rocking attention. "Are you ready, Miss Senior?"

"Yes. Is the medic?"

"Yes. Dr. Meevin pulled a lot of strings to come along on this mission. She is ready and waiting to see what older Gaians look like."

Ianka laughed and shifted her footing as the ship twisted again. "Just like me only wrinkled with greyer hair."

The ship jolted, heaved and then set down with a thud.

Ianka and Derion moved to the door, and she pulled her thigh blades. The doors to the ship opened and they headed toward the base at a run.

North Senior asked, "What can you see, Maklin?"

"There are ships coming and one has landed, disgorging a lot of aliens with dark skin. Wait, there is a Gaian with them. A woman."

North smiled, wishing that he could see his daughter's approach. "What is she carrying?"

"Two huge knives, blonde hair, and an expression that reminds me of Beeda's. Do you know her?"

North knew it was his Ianka. No other Gaian woman would have the guts to charge along next to aliens on a strange world. Well, guts or insanity. It was hard to tell with Eek. "It is my daughter, Ianka. Pass the word to cooperate with the aliens. They have finally found us and we are going home. Vida promised."

The male researchers and females were housed separately, but the small com devices that Maklin Dorning had cobbled together let them speak at night when they felt the separation most keenly.

North sat back and listened to Maklin speaking urgently to all the Gaian researchers who had been brought to this base. The order to cooperate with the new aliens was urgent as the Tokkel began to mill in the halls. They didn't know what was going on either, and it was just a matter of time before they decided to kill the researchers and abandon the base.

North hoped that Ianka's senses were still keen. She was racing the clock.

Ianka sprinted through the halls, a sense of urgency swamping her. Derion was at her side and growing bigger with every attack. Her knives dripped with Tokkel blood, and she paused at crossed corridors to make sure she was heading in the right direction.

The barricade of Tokkel was a hint that she was in the right place.

She turned to Derion, "Down that hall."

He nodded and let out a hunting roar that shook the halls. Members of the Fury, ready for battle, appeared around them, and as one deadly red tide, they surged forward.

Ianka dove through the heaving bodies, sliding along the ground until she was in front of a cell door. Her sense of smell told her she had reached her goal.

There was probably a key or a pass code or something, but she grabbed the bars and hauled with a strength she rarely accessed. The door tore off in her hands and she tossed it aside.

There were two women huddling together on the bed and one was belovedly familiar. "Mom?"

Beeda Senior got to her feet and made a beeline for her daughter. "Eek. Oh for the love of cellular degradation, I have missed you."

Ianka hugged her mother but kept her blades ready. "Where is Dad?"

"The other side of the compound. They saw you coming with an army of aliens and warned us to cooperate."

The other woman got to her feet and smiled. "It has been a long time, Ianka. You are looking well."

Ianka grinned. "Thank you. Please keep my mom from tripping on anyone. I have to set the others free."

Dr. Wells nodded. "Over there on the wall. A palm print from one of the guards will do the trick to open them all."

Ianka nodded and headed back to the battle, finding a body and hacking off one of the hands.

She spoke to her mother and Dr. Wells. "The men at the end of the hall are members of a friendly species referred to as the Nine. They are also hostile to the Tokkel, so this is the best of both worlds for them. They won't hurt you, but don't touch them. They link chemically and even shaking hands can be foreplay if you are compatible."

She slapped the hand against the pad and the doors slid open. Women cautiously crept into the hall whose entrance was being cleared by huge red creatures.

"They are the Fury, one of the species of the Nine. I need you to get onto the ship and to safety with a few of them guarding you while we head off to rescue Dad." She was speaking to her mother but the other women nodded.

"Dr. Wells, take care of my mom. The ground will be a little slippery."

Derion had been listening to her and he gave a few hand signals to his men, sending six of them with the thirty women.

Sighing in relief that her mother was out and on her way to freedom, she headed out to find her father.

She had kept the hand of the deceased Tokkel, and she used it to open all the men's cells. One hundred twenty men appeared in the hall, but there was only one face she cared about.

"Dad!" She ran to the familiar figure, and he embraced her when she was in front of him.

He laughed and tears came from his eyes. "I felt Veed in my head last week. I knew you wouldn't be far behind."

"Come on, Dad. We have ships and we are all going home!"

One of the scientists snorted. "We are trading one set of aliens for another."

She walked up to him and stared until he backed away. "What do you think happened after you were taken? Let's cut the polite speech. We were blasted back to first gen colonization with our technology. We couldn't fight and the Tokkel kept coming until the Nine arrived. They have a ship in orbit and have assisted us with medical treatments, rebuilding and protected us. The Gaia that you left is gone."

"So, they have taken over?"

She chuckled. "No, they have not, though they have more of a right to it than we do. They evolved on that planet just as our race is evolving with every generation. Their people called it Underhill and they have cities that have been lost to time, but as we gain the ability to travel longer distances, we have been finding them."

Murmurs began and she lifted her hand. "You are all going to be on different ships, each run by a different species, but they are all members of the Nine. Nine distinct races, shaped by the very same world shaping us. Be polite. Not all of them speak Gaian yet."

The men nodded and most were obviously weary and just wanted to return home.

None of them were a match for the warriors that had accompanied Ianka, so she was satisfied in that at least.

She kept her arm around her father's waist. "Come on, Dad. Mom is waiting."

His shoulders flexed in relief. "You did go to her first?"

"We did."

The stream of scientists was confined between banks of the Fury, but Derion and two others waited for her. He was still in his battle form, and she blinked at the enormity of the transformation.

He was huge. Much larger than he had appeared in the ship. Now, she knew that that first ruckus had been for discipline. This form was all about destruction.

"Father, this is Attack Master Derion of the Fury. Derion, this is my father, North Senior."

In a low rumble, Derion answered, "It is an honour to meet you; your daughters are extraordinary."

North smiled. "Beeda and I have always been proud of our girls. It is an honour to meet you as well. Ianka's tone has informed me that she is more than a casual acquaintance."

She was going to slap herself in the face and cover her eyes but she was still carrying the Tokkel hand. With a wet thud, she dropped it and sighed. "Enough of that, let's get back to the ship."

North patted the hand she had around his waist and smiled. "Derion and I can discuss it later. I am sure that the flight will be long enough for one conversation."

Ianka winced. "I don't know if you want to do that. Why not just enjoy cuddling with Mom for the twelve hours back to the mother ship. From there, you will be medically checked out and you can return to Gaia right away."

They started walking with Derion in front and two members of the Fury behind them.

"*We* can return to Gaia? Where will you be?"

She cleared her throat when Derion looked over his shoulder at her with a grin.

"I will be visiting with Vida. She has married a member of the Balance and seems quite happy about it. He boosted her signal so that she was able to reach you."

North nodded and then scowled. "How much time has passed?"

"It has been six years."

He stiffened. "That is unexpected."

"How long did you think it was?"

"Six months. This base is brand new. They opened it up to use us as weapons researchers. Until six months ago, I believe we were in cold sleep."

Ianka's mind felt eased. They didn't know how long they had been gone. They hadn't counted on a rescue that never came because the Gaians didn't have spacecraft.

They exited the base and were on their way to the ship when a Tokkel body sat up and took aim at their party. Moving on instinct, she threw one of her knives at him and it struck him between the eyes, knocking him back.

Derion was staring at her in shock and she shrugged. "What?"

Chapter Eight

Derion was staring and a strange tingling was moving through her body. Suddenly, her arm around her father's waist went limp. She looked down and there was a large smoking burn on the left side of her torso.

The guards behind her grabbed her father and hauled him into the ship while Derion carefully lifted her, sprinting into the ship and directly to medical.

Dr. Meevin cut her suit free and started working on her during takeoff. Ianka was strapped down so that she wouldn't hit the floor.

"I am sorry you have to be awake, but we need to keep you alert to test for the progression of the nerve damage."

Ianka gritted her teeth as the area was cleaned of scorched flesh and a numbness crept up her left arm.

She mentally kicked herself for not being a second faster with her throw. She knew what damage a Tokkel blaster could do. Numbness was the least of her worries.

Dr. Meevin worked on her for hours while others who had been injured were treated and released. Finally, she couldn't do any more. Frustration was written on her features.

"I am sorry. I can't seem to stop the damage. I don't have the right treatments for a Gaian."

With half her face paralyzed, she smiled weakly. "S'okay. You tried. I tried. Vida has my parents again. It will all be good."

Dr. Meevin drew a privacy screen around her and said, "We will be on the mother ship in a few hours. Perhaps we can figure something out there."

With her moving right hand, Ianka gave her a thumbs up. She had done what she set out to do.

Her cubicle was dark and quiet, but she heard someone moving. A hulking figure took a blood sample, and she heard a small hiss. She dozed, thinking that one of the medics had come in to do some checks.

The figure returned, and this time, the hypo was pressed to her wound. The hiss preceded the warm input of the injector and was withdrawn in complete silence.

Her eyes had both been taken over by the paralysis, so all she could make out was a dark figure that stroked her hair back and she could see the hand touch her cheek, even though she couldn't feel it.

Fire burned through her limbs and she started to thrash her arms and legs. The monitors went berserk, and Dr. Meevin knocked the screen down as she came in to check on the seizure.

Ianka was still strapped to the bed but only for a moment as she was transferred to a gliding gurney and escorted out of the ship with a mask giving her an inhalation of sedative with every motion of her lungs.

Dr. Meevin began to run tests the moment that she was back in her regular facility. When the results curled upward on the monitors, she stared at them without comprehension.

The paralysis was reversing. That much Ianka could feel for herself. She could see clearly now that her eyes could focus and her face was once again under her control. "What is it, Doc?"

"Did you mate while you were lying strapped down and paralyzed?" Dr. Meevin turned to her with raised eyebrows.

She shifted as much as she was able. "Not that I recall. I had a peculiar hallucination but there wasn't any mating involved."

Vida came in with their parents behind her. "Not that kind of mating, Eek. Did you swap blood with anyone?"

"Someone came in the night to take a blood sample, and an hour later, I was given a shot. Does that count?"

Meevin frowned. "It could."

North came to Ianka's side and carefully found her hand. "It was Derion. He asked us if we would give you up to save your life. I didn't understand so he explained."

Beeda came up as well, wearing a fetching gown in black and red. "Every parent with a daughter will lose her, but I would rather have you in orbit than underground, Eek."

"So, that was it? We swap blood and I heal?"

Meevin shrugged. "Members of the Nine are not damaged the same way by the Tokkel blasts. We are merely burned, not paralyzed, and the Fury aren't damaged at all, so he gave you his immunity."

"What were all those guys in medical?"

"Those were cuts. Easy fixes." Meevin patted her knee. "I will register the mating since you two didn't make it to the garden for the formal recording. Your blood samples are already in. He just needs to finalise it."

Vida took her hand. "You did it, Eek. You got them home."

Surrounded by her family, she blinked back tears.

North must have sensed her mood, because he piped in, "Ularica has an idea for an artificial sight mechanism. She is looking for volunteers, and you know how your mother and I enjoy that sort of thing, and the chemists have asked us to come in and contribute to their work. We might not be leaving for the surface right away. After all, everything we love is up here."

Beeda came around and kissed her on the forehead, while to her surprise, S'rin squeezed her blanketed toes.

Vida smiled. "Now that you are linked to Derion, you are safe to touch."

A deep voice spoke from the doorway. "Miss Senior, what have you done to my son?"

Dorum was standing there and scowling.

Ianka struggled to sit up and something flickered in his eyes. "What is wrong with Derion?"

"He is suffering. His body is on fire. What did you do to him?"

"He took some of my blood and then gave me his a while later. If he is having a problem, bring him into medical." She scowled.

Dorum tensed. "He won't come."

"Tell him I ordered it. He will love that."

"He won't listen." It was obvious that Dorum was worried.

"Right." Ianka sat up, wrapped the bed sheet around her and hopped to the floor with Vida's help. She tucked the sheet into place and minced up to Dorum. "Take me to him."

"You aren't dressed."

"My clothes are in the shuttle. Do you want to keep delaying?"

He shook his head and offered her his arm. She took it and kept hold of the sheet as they slowly walked to the pods, and from there, they were whisked to the area occupied by the Fury.

She continued to mince along in bare feet and he was radiating a protective aura. When they got to the living quarters, he brought her to the door and pounded on it. From the other side, she heard a thud. "Go away, Father."

Ianka scowled. "Don't talk to your father like that, Derion. Open up the damned door."

The door opened and an astonished Derion stepped back as she shuffled in.

Ianka turned and closed the door in Dorum's face saying, "We will call you if we need you."

"You should be in medical." He was sweaty and pale.

"So should you. You look worse than I do." She reached out and touched his forehead, surprised when he leaned into her hand.

His skin cooled the moment that she touched him. "That was easy."

He gave her an apologetic look through his black and red eyes. "I am sorry that I did not have time to court you properly."

She sat on his lap and looped her arms around his neck. "I am sorry that I got shot."

She didn't have a lot of experience with kissing, but she gave it a try. He wrapped his arms around her for a moment before pulling her tightly against him.

The sheet hit the floor at some point, but by then, it didn't matter. She was firmly involved in getting to know her mate.

Vida disconnected her viewing when clothing began to fly. "Okay, she is definitely staying on the mother ship. He has quite the grip on her and it looks like they are going to be negotiating terms all evening."

Beeda laughed at her daughter. "It is about time. If it has really been six years since the attacks, I am surprised that you didn't seek out husbands before this."

Vida explained about the limited amount of Gaian men, the evolution of talents beyond that of the Senior family, and then, she had to get into the details of what the girls had gone through after their parents had disappeared.

North and Beeda held hands while they heard the story, and tears slowly made it down their faces.

S'rin held Vida's hand and explained the involvement of the Nine and the delight in the discovery of an evolutionary change that complimented the one their ancestors had engaged in generations earlier. The Gaians were the tenth race and they were only too happy to help them become all they could be.

"So, would you have come after me if I returned to Gaia?" She leaned her chin on her hands and met his gaze with a smile.

He chuckled and shifted under her. "I would follow wherever you led, at a respectful distance. I have seen you in action, and a woman who can tear a door off hinges is a woman to be courted carefully."

She stroked her fingers on his chest. "Wise. Very wise. So, what alterations can I expect as the wife of a Fury?"

He grinned. "Well, you will gain a few inches in height."

"Yay. It was bugging me that Vida got taller."

"Do not worry about it. The transformative power of the Fury is also within you if you tap into it. Give it a few weeks but it might emerge. We can practice." He ran his hands up her back and smiled.

"Practice what?"

He chuckled and rolled her under him. The rest was self-explanatory.

About the Author

Viola Grace (aka Zenina Masters) is a Canadian sci-fi/paranormal romance writer with ambitions to keep writing for the rest of her life. She specializes in short stories because the thrill of discovery, of all those firsts, is what keeps her writing.

An artist who enjoys a story that catches you up, whirls you around and sets you down with a smile on your face is all she endeavours to be. She prefers to leave the drama to those who are better suited to it, she always goes for the cheap laugh.

More Books by Viola Grace

CPSIA information can be obtained at www.ICGtesting.com
Printed in the USA
LVOW04s1521180515

438914LV00019B/1086/P